Drawing as deep a b................ manage, Sammie opened her mouth to let loose with a scream. The sound had no sooner left her throat when the arm anchored around her middle tightened, cutting her cry into a mere wheeze.

"Don't scream," he whispered against her ear. "I won't harm ye."

Unconvinced, she opened her mouth again, but his lips pressed against her ear stopped her.

"I don't want to stuff my handkerchief in your mouth, but I will if I must."

Sammie reluctantly swallowed the scream trembling on her lips. Although she was not one to panic, she couldn't stop the alarm quivering through her. "I demand that you stop this horse and release me. Immediately."

"Soon, lass."

"You've made a mistake. My family cannot pay a ransom."

"'Tis not a ransom I'm after." He leaned closer, his warm breath sending a shiver down her spine. "Fear not, Miss Briggeham. You're saved. . . ."

The
Bride Thief

Jacquie D'Alessandro

A Dell Book

Published by
Dell Publishing
a division of
Random House, Inc.
1540 Broadway
New York, New York 10036

ISBN: 0-440-23712-2

Printed in the United States of America
Published simultaneously in Canada

April 2002

10 9 8 7 6 5 4 3 2 1

OPM

Acknowledgments

I would like to take this opportunity to thank the following people for their invaluable help and support:

My critique partners, Donna Fejes, Susan Goggins, and Carina Rock, for their weekly keep-me-on-track sessions.

My agent, Damaris Rowland, for her faith and wisdom.

Beekeepers Angus Stokes, Dave Cushman, Jacob Kahn, Chris Slade, Albert Knight, and Brenda McLean for the wealth of information they provided.

My mom and dad, Kay and Jim Johnson, for a lifetime of love, support, and lots of cheerleading.

My in-laws, Lea and Art D'Alessandro, for the priceless gift of their son, and lots of cheerleading.

My sister, Kathy Guse, for all the good times and lots of cheerleading.

Marcia Hopkins, for all the therapeutic shopping adventures.

Martha Kirkland, my best research source, for being so generous with her time and knowledge.

I would also like to thank the wonderful people at Bantam/Dell, most especially Theresa Zoro, Marietta Anastassatos, and cover artist David Gatti.

A very special thank you to Wendy Etherington and Jenni Grizzle, and a cyber hug from Princess Shoes to Don Vito, Filbert, Jilly/Jan, Happy Jack, the Virgin, Slick, Dimwiddie, Kaffeine, and Brocodile. Thanks also to Steve, Michelle and Lindsey Grossman, Jeannie and Ken Pierannunzi, the members of Georgia Romance Writers, the terrific ladies on my tennis team (even though you guys voted me in as captain when I went to the bathroom!), and all my friends and neighbors who have shown such incredible support.

And finally, thank you to all the wonderful readers who have taken the time to write or e-mail me. I love hearing from you!

Chapter 1

Kent, 1820

Samantha Briggeham turned from the opened window where the cool night breeze drifted into the drawing room, and faced her beloved but clearly addle-brained father. "I cannot believe you're suggesting this, Papa. Why would you think I'd consider marrying Major Wilshire? I barely know him."

"Pshaw. He's been a family friend for years," Charles Briggeham said, crossing the drawing room to join her near the window.

"Yes, but most of those years have been spent in the Army," she pointed out, striving to keep her voice calm and suppress a shudder. She couldn't imagine any woman entertaining romantic thoughts of the dour Major Wilshire. Heavens, the man sported a puckered frown that made him look as if he'd just tasted a lemon. She strongly suspected this conversation was the result of Mama's well-intentioned, but unwelcome matchmaking machinations.

Papa stroked his chin. "You're nearly six and twenty, Sammie. 'Tis time you married."

Sammie fought a strong urge to look heavenward. Papa was the dearest, sweetest man alive, but in spite of having a wife and four daughters, he was as thick as a plank when it came to understanding females—especially her.

"Papa, I'm well beyond marriageable age. I'm perfectly content as I am."

"Nonsense. All girls wish to marry. Your mother told me so."

His words confirmed her suspicion that Mama was at the root of this mess. "Not *all* girls, Papa." The shudder she could no longer suppress edged down her spine at the thought of being leg-shackled to any of the men with whom she was acquainted. They were either tiresome dolts, or they simply stared at her with a mixture of pity, confusion, and in several cases, downright horror when she dared discuss mathematical equations or scientific matters with them. Most of them regarded her as "eccentric Sammie," a *nom de plume* she philosophically accepted as she knew she *was* eccentric—at least in the eyes of her peers.

"Of course all girls wish to marry," Papa said again, jerking her attention back to the matter at hand. "Look at your sisters."

"I *have* looked at them. Every day of my life. I love them dearly, but Papa, you know I'm nothing like them. They're beautiful and sweet and feminine—perfectly suited to be wives. For the past decade we've all but tripped upon their constant stream of suitors. But just because Lucille, Hermione, and Emily are now all married doesn't mean *I* must marry."

"Don't you wish to have a family of your own, my dear?"

A long pause filled the air, and Samantha ignored the twinge of longing that tugged her insides. She'd buried such unrealistic fantasies long ago. "Papa, we both know that I am not the sort of woman to attract a man to marriage. Not in appearance *or* temperament. And besides, I'm much too old—"

"Nonsense. You're prettier than you think, Sammie. And there's nothing wrong with a woman being intelligent—so long as you don't let anyone know." He shot her a pointed look. "Luckily, Major Wilshire finds neither your advanced age nor your keen intellect overly offputting."

Sammie pursed her lips. "How incredibly kind of him."

Her sarcasm floated over Papa's head. Stroking his chin, he continued, "Indeed. In fact, the Major prefers a mature bride. Of course, helping Hubert with his experiments, gathering insects and toads and all that, will have to stop. Quite undignified for a married lady to be crawling about in the dirt, you know. Your brother will simply have to carry on without your assistance."

This situation had gone quite far enough. Sammie cleared her throat and pushed her spectacles higher on her nose. "Papa. I love working with Hubert in his laboratory and have no intention of stopping, especially now as my own experiments are showing promise of a breakthrough. And I am perfectly happy at the prospect of being a doting aunt to my future nieces and nephews. I have no desire to become Major Wilshire's wife, and frankly, I'm stunned that you would even suggest such a thing."

"Major Wilshire is a fine man."

"Yes, he is. He is also old enough to be my father."

"He is only three and forty—"

"Provided he had children when he was quite young," she continued smoothly, as if her father hadn't spoken. "But more importantly, I don't love him, and *he* does not love *me*."

"Perhaps not, but he certainly holds you in some affection."

"Certainly not enough to *marry* me."

"On the contrary, he quite readily agreed to the match."

A heavy silence filled the air as the significance of his words settled upon her. "What do you mean, he agreed to the match?" she asked, when she finally located her voice. "Papa, please tell me you haven't already discussed this with Major Wilshire."

"Well, of course I have. Everything is settled. The Major couldn't be happier. Nor your mother and I. Congratulations, my dear. You're officially betrothed."

"Betrothed!" Samantha's explosive reply rang through the air like a pistol shot. She squeezed her eyes shut and forced herself to draw deep, calming breaths. Mama had tried unsuccessfully in the past to find suitors for her, but had finally abandoned the effort in favor of focusing her attention on her three younger daughters—all beauties of the first water.

But ever since Emily's wedding three months ago, Mama's matchmaking eye had once again focused on her one remaining unmarried daughter—a turn of events Sammie should have anticipated, but hadn't. Clearly Mama had not given up such ridiculous hopes. Still, she'd shrugged off Mama's efforts, knowing full well that there wasn't a man amongst her acquaintances who would consider marrying a plain, bespectacled, outspoken, socially inept, firmly on-the-shelf bookworm.

Except, apparently, Major Wilshire, whom Sammie could only conclude had taken leave of his senses.

Papa fitted his monocle over his left eye and peered at her. "I must say, Sammie, you don't look quite as ecstatic as your mother assured me you would be." He looked truly perplexed.

"I have no desire to marry Major Wilshire, Papa." She cleared her throat, then added very clearly, "And *I will not do so.*"

"Pshaw. Of course you will. Everything is already arranged, my dear."

"Arranged?"

"Why, yes. The banns will appear this Sunday. The wedding will take place next month."

"Next month! Papa, this is madness. I cannot—"

"Now don't worry, Samantha." He reached out and patted her hand. "I'm sure you'll be happy once you and the Major get to know each other a bit better." His voice dropped to a conspiratorial level. "He's planning to call on you later this week to present you with a betrothal ring. A sapphire, I believe."

"I do not want a betrothal ring—"

"Of course you do. All girls do. Your mother told me so. Now, it's terribly late and I'm exhausted. All this marriage arranging is quite wearying, and I wish to retire. Your dear mother harangued me for hours, and I'm quite incapable of talking any more. We'll discuss the plans further tomorrow."

"There are no plans to discuss, Papa. I will not marry him."

"Of course you will. Good night, my dear."

"I will not marry him!" Samantha shouted to his retreating back as he closed the door behind him. An exasperated *oohh!* escaped her, and she massaged her temples, where a thumping headache was rapidly forming.

What had brought on this madness? And how on earth could she fix this tangle?

Hellfires scorched her cheeks when she imagined what Mama must have said to convince Major Wilshire he wanted to marry her. She knew all too well how determined her mother could be when she'd made up her mind about something. One often left Cordelia Briggeham's company with the sensation of having been smacked in the head with a cast-iron skillet.

Yes, Mama's good intentions were unfortunately not always tempered with tact, but Sammie couldn't help but admire—occasionally in a horrified way—how her mother could outmaneuver anyone. She had no doubt that if Mama had been allowed to serve in the Army, Napoleon would have met his Waterloo years earlier than he had.

Twisting her fingers together, she paced the floor, her footsteps muffled by the thick Axminster rug. What on earth was she going to do? The thought of spending the rest of her life with Major Wilshire, listening to him recount his every military maneuver in excruciating detail, sent a shiver akin to panic shuddering through her. And he would certainly demand that she cease her scientific work—something she most certainly would *not* do.

Surely she could bring Papa around. But the finality in his voice when he'd said *everything is already arranged,* echoed through her mind. She could usually bend Papa around to her way of thinking, but there was no swaying him once Mama embedded an idea in his head. And her marrying Major Wilshire was clearly embedded in his head.

Humiliation burned her cheeks. God in heaven, this was just like her coming-out eight years ago. She'd begged not to endure the pomp of it all—the parties where she knew people whispered about her behind their hands, pitying her because she possessed none of the beauty or grace of her younger sisters. The frilly dresses that made her feel conspicuous and awkward. Yet Mama had insisted, and Papa had fallen meekly into line. So with her head held high, she'd endured the whispering and the pitying glances that were made away from Mama's sharp eyes and ears, and buried her hurt behind countless false smiles.

She pressed her hands to her churning stomach, recalling how Mama had arranged Hermione's marriage with a tactical brilliance that would have rendered Wellington breathless. True, Hermie was happy, but the poor dear had barely known Reginald when they'd wed. She just as easily could be miserable, although Sammie couldn't imagine sweet-natured Hermie being anything but content. And Reginald worshipped the ground his beautiful wife's petite slippers tread upon.

Sammie could not imagine Major Wilshire so much as noticing whether she even wore slippers unless he could somehow relate them to military strategy.

Flopping down on the chintz-covered settee, she huffed out a frustrated breath. If she refused to honor the arrangements Papa made, her family would suffer from the ensuing gossip and scandal. She couldn't disgrace them. But neither could she marry Major Wilshire.

Heaving a tired sigh, she rose and closed the window. After extinguishing the candles burning on the mantel, she left the room, closing the door behind her.

Dear God, what was she going to do?

In the flowerbed, Arthur Timstone heard the window click shut and drew his first deep breath since he'd heard the voices above him. He slowly rose from a crouch, his knees creaking in protest, then stifled a yelp when his backside found the rose hedges.

Glaring at the offending bush, he muttered, "I'm too bloody old fer this sneakin' about in the bushes in the middle o' the night. Unseemly, that's wot it is."

Stubble it. A man approaching his fiftieth year shouldn't be gallivanting about after midnight like a randy lad. Ah, but that's what love did to a bloke, made him act like a slow-witted, puppy-eyed fool.

If anyone had suggested that he'd take one look at the new cook at the Briggeham house and fall instantly in love, Arthur would have called them daft, then laughed himself into a seizure. But fall instantly in love he had. And because of it, he'd just spent the last half hour trapped beneath the Briggeham's drawing-room window, afraid to move lest Miz Sammie or her pa should hear him, and trying his best not to long for his warm bed an hour's ride away. If he'd left Sarah's quarters only a few minutes earlier . . . ah, but that would have been impossible.

Leaning back against the house's rough stone exterior, he paused to rub his stiff joints before dashing across the darkened lawn where he'd tethered Viking at the edge of the woods. Poor Miz Sammie. Clearly she didn't want to marry Major Wilshire, and Arthur didn't blame her for one moment. While the Major wasn't a bad sort, his nonstop talk of the War and his important role in it, could bore the feathers from a chicken. Why, he'd drive Miz Sammie straight to Bedlam. And salt of the earth Miz Sammie was. Always a kind word and a smile for him, always asking after his mother and brother in Brighton.

Emerging from the bushes, Arthur set off across the lawn at a brisk trot. Determination stiffened his spine. Something had to be done to help poor Miz Sammie.

Arthur knew only one man who could help her . . . the mysterious man whose name hovered on everyone's lips from London to Cornwall. The man eagerly sought after by the magistrate for his daring exploits.

The notorious, legendary Bride Thief.

Through the window of his private study, Eric Landsdowne, Earl of Wesley, watched Arthur Timstone cross the terrace lawns on his way back to the stables.

The stableman's words rang in his ears. *'Tis a terrible situation, my lord. Poor Miz Sammie wants not a thing to do with that stuffy Major Wilshire, but her pa's insistin'. Bein' forced to marry this way, why, it'll just break Miz Sammie's heart, and a kinder heart I've yet to meet.*

Eric had sat behind his desk listening to his faithful servant, neither one acknowledging by so much as a flicker of an eyelash why Arthur would bring this news to him, but both knowing exactly why. The secret they shared bound them together tighter than a vise, although they rarely discussed it during the day when the servants were awake, for fear of being inadvertently overheard.

Such a mistake could cost Eric his life.

But simply knowing that Arthur shared his secret, that he wasn't completely alone in the dangerous life he'd chosen, afforded Eric a strong measure of comfort. He loved Arthur like a father; indeed, the servant had spent more time with him during his formative years than his own father ever had.

Now, watching Arthur striding across the perfectly manicured lawns, the early-morning sun glinting on his graying hair, Eric noted the man's slight limp, and his heart pinched. Arthur was no longer a young man, and although he never complained, Eric knew his aging joints were often stiff and painful. He'd offered him a well-appointed bedchamber in the manor house, but the servant had refused. Tears had glistened in Arthur's pale blue eyes at the generous offer, but he chose to remain in his rooms above the stables, close to the horses he loved and cared for.

A smile tugged at Eric's lips, for he knew Arthur had also refused his offer so as not to risk sneaking into the main house in the middle of the night after returning from seeing his lady love. Even though there were no secrets between them, they rarely discussed their respective love lives. Arthur would be mortified if he suspected Eric knew of his late-night trysts, but Eric was happy for the man.

Perhaps that wasn't a limp at all, but rather a spring in his step, Eric mused to himself.

Shifting his gaze, he looked toward the woods in the distance, his thoughts returning to the matter at hand.

He shared only a casual acquaintance with the Briggehams,

as he did with most of the families in the area. He spent most of his time in London, keeping in close contact with his solicitor and man of affairs, spending only several weeks during the summer here at Wesley Manor. During those few short weeks every year, he expertly dodged the matchmaking eyes of the village mamas, one of the most notable of whom was Mrs. Cordelia Briggeham. Of course Mrs. Briggeham would know, along with every other mother in Tunbridge Wells, his long-standing aversion to marriage, although they were not privy to *all* his reasons. Unfortunately, that aversion only served as a challenge to the intrepid daughter-ridden matchmakers.

He had to admit that the three youngest Briggeham daughters were rare beauties. One of them, he couldn't recall which, had recently married Baron Whitestead. He had only a vague recollection of Samantha. Frowning, he tried to remember what she looked like, but could only conjure up a shadowy image of chestnut hair and thick spectacles. He knew via the gossip mill that she was considered an eccentric bluestocking and sadly lacked feminine appeal, a fact rendered all the more glaring by the extreme beauty of her sisters.

In contrast, he had no trouble calling to mind Major Wilshire—a large, blustery, arrogant man with a ramrod stiff military bearing. Eric found him tolerable only in small doses. As far as Eric knew, the Major never smiled, and laughter was out of the question. He sported thick, graying side whiskers, a quizzing glass, and tended to bark out orders in a booming voice as if he still commanded a battlefield.

Still, the Major was intelligent and reportedly not unkind. Why didn't Miss Briggeham wish to marry him? She was well beyond the first blush of youth, and if she were as dowdy as he'd heard, she couldn't possibly attract many suitors. Arthur had reported that she'd claimed not to love the man. A snort escaped Eric's lips, and he shook his head.

He'd be hard-pressed to name even one marriage among his acquaintances that had been based on love. Certainly not his parents' marriage, and God knows not Margaret's. . . .

Turning from the window, he strode across the Axminster rug to his desk. Reaching across the mahogany surface, he picked up the miniature of his sister. She'd had it painted for him just before he entered the Army. "Keep it with you, Eric," Margaret had said, her encouraging smile not masking the deep concern in her dark eyes. "That way I'll be with you. Keeping you safe."

A lump tightened his throat. Her lovely face had accompanied him to places he chose to forget. She'd been the one spot of beauty in an existence of ugliness. Yes, she had kept him safe. Yet he had failed to keep her safe in return.

He stared at her image resting in his palm, and a vivid memory rose in his mind's eye. The day she'd been born. His father's disgust with his wife for presenting him with a girl. His exhausted mother's sadness. Creeping into the nursery that night, staring at the tiny, cooing bundle. "It doesn't matter that Father doesn't like you," he'd whispered, his five-year-old heart filled with resolve. "He doesn't like me either. *I'll* watch over you." She'd wrapped her minuscule fist around his finger and that, quite simply, had been that.

A myriad of images flashed through his mind. Teaching Margaret to ride. Helping her rescue a bird with a broken wing. Patching up the scrapes she'd sustained when she fell from a tree limb, so their father wouldn't scold her. Escaping to the quiet of the forest to evade the constant strain and arguing in the house. Teaching her to fish, then rarely ever catching more fish than she. Acting out Shakespeare's plays. Watching her grow from an impish child into a beautiful young woman had filled him with deep pride. *We were all we had in this unhappy family, weren't we, Margaret? We made it bearable for each other. What would I have done without you?*

But he had failed her.

His fingers closed around the miniature. Like Samantha Briggeham, Margaret had been forced to wed, a fact Eric hadn't forgiven his father for, even when he lay on his deathbed. He had bargained innocent, beautiful Margaret away like a piece of jewelry to elderly Viscount Darvin, who wanted an heir. Rumors of Darvin's debauchery had circulated through the *ton* for years, but he had possessed the attributes Eric's father had sought when making the match—money and several unentailed estates. In spite of his own substantial holdings, Marcus Landsdowne had greedily wanted more. He'd thought nothing of Margaret's feelings, and the marriage had devastated her. Eric had been fighting on the Peninsula at the time and had been unaware of her situation.

He'd been too late to rescue Margaret.

But he'd vowed upon his return to help others like her, and bring attention to their plight. How many poor young women were forced into unwanted marriages each year? He shuddered to consider the number. He'd tried to convince Margaret to leave Darvin, promising he'd help her, but she'd refused to dishonor her marriage vows, and he had reluctantly honored her decision.

Since first donning his costume five years ago, he'd helped more than a dozen young women escape. And by doing it with such dash and drama, rather than by quiet financial means, he'd succeeded in bringing the problem to national attention.

He'd accomplished his goal, perhaps *too* well. Several months ago a reporter for *The Times* had dubbed him the Bride Thief, and now it seemed as if everyone in England hankered for information about him—most especially the magistrate who was determined to unmask the Bride Thief and put an end to what he called "the kidnappings."

A substantial reward was offered for his capture, igniting interest in his activities even further. Arthur had recently reported a rumor that several irate fathers of "stolen" brides had banded together with the common goal of capturing the Bride Thief. Eric rubbed his fingers over his throat. The magistrate, not to mention the fathers, wouldn't be satisfied until the Thief hanged for his crimes.

But Eric had no intention of dying.

Still, the search for the Bride Thief's identity had now escalated to the point that each time Eric donned his costume he risked his life. But knowing he would free another poor woman from the untenable fate that had robbed Margaret of her happiness made the risk worth the possible price. And helped ease his guilt over failing to aid Margaret.

He would not allow the heartache and despair that ruled his sister's life to destroy Miss Samantha Briggeham.

He would free her.

Samantha sat in the family coach, staring out the window at the fading light. Bright orange and purple streaks fanned across the sky, marking the beginning of twilight, her favorite time of day.

Adjusting her spectacles, she breathed deeply and tried to calm her jittery stomach. When she arrived home, she faced speaking with Mama and Papa—not a welcome prospect as she suspected they would not be pleased by the errand on which she'd just been.

Looking out the window, she observed a tiny flash of color in the waning light. Heavens, could that have been a firefly? If so, Hubert would be ecstatic. He'd been trying to breed the rare insects for months—both in the woods and in his laboratory—from larva he'd had shipped from the colonies. Could his experiments be bearing fruit?

She quickly signaled Cyril to stop the coach, and pulled a small bag from her reticule. Her inner voice told her she was only delaying the inevitable argument with her parents, but she had to capture the insects for Hubert if they'd hatched. His fourteen-year-old mind was fascinated by the soft intermittent light the bugs exuded.

Exiting the coach, she inhaled the cool evening air. The heavy scent of damp earth and decaying leaves tickled her nostrils, and she sneezed, sending her spectacles sliding downward until they halted on the upturned end of her nose. She pushed the glasses back into place with a practiced gesture and scanned the area, searching for the fireflies while Cyril settled back on his perch atop the coach to wait. He was well used to these unplanned stops in the woods.

Sammie walked down the path toward where she'd seen the glow. Warmth spread through her as she imagined Hubert's thin, serious face wreathed in smiles should she return with such a treasure. She loved the boy with all her heart—his brilliant, sharp mind and his tall, gangly frame with large, awkward feet he hadn't yet grown into.

Yes, she and Hubert were cut from the same cloth. They wore similar spectacles and possessed the same blue eyes and thick, unruly chestnut hair. They both enjoyed swimming, fishing, and searching the forest for flora and fauna specimens—activities that had more than once driven Mama to the vapors. In fact, Samantha and Hubert's secret name for Mama was Cricket because she emitted a series of high-pitched chirps just before she "fainted"—always artistically—onto one of the many settees scattered strategically about the Briggeham home.

Mama will most definitely chirp when she discovers where I've just been. And what I've done.

Tiny flashes of yellow light caught her eye and her heart jumped with excitement. It was indeed fireflies! Several hovered near the ground at the base of an oak a short distance away.

"No running off now, Miz Sammie," Cyril called as she moved toward the oak. " 'Tis gittin' dark and me eyes ain't what they used to be."

"Don't worry, Cyril. There's still plenty of light and I'll not go farther than this." Dropping to her knees, she gently captured the rare insect in her hand and placed it in her pouch.

She'd just slipped another in the bag when a sound coming from the dense forest caught her attention. A horse's faint whinny? Lifting her head, she listened for several seconds but heard nothing more than the rustling of leaves from the breeze.

"Did you hear something, Cyril?"

Cyril shook his head. "Nay, but then, me ears ain't what they used to be."

With a shrug, Sammie returned her attention to her task. Clearly she'd been mistaken.

After all, who would be riding on her family's property? And with darkness swiftly approaching?

Sitting astride Champion, he silently observed her through the trees. Pale streaks of moonlight glimmered down, and his heart clenched as he noted her posture.

Bloody hell, the distraught chit was praying. On her knees, bent at the waist so far her nose was nearly skimming the ground. Anger and frustration heated his blood. Damn it, he would save her from such misery.

Champion shifted beneath him and let out a soft whinny. Placing a comforting hand on the beast's sleek neck to quiet him, he watched Miss Briggeham. She clearly heard the sound, for she looked up. A shaft of waning light glinted off her spectacles as she glanced around. Then with what appeared to be a shrug, she lowered her head and resumed her prayers.

He'd followed her through the woods, waiting while she was inside Major Wilshire's home, wondering why she'd visited him. Clearly their time together hadn't gone well, for now she was kneeling on the ground, praying in the woods as darkness approached. Pity tugged at his heart.

He glanced at her coachman and noted the man was dozing in his perch. Excellent. The time had come.

With quiet concentration, he slipped on his tight-fitting black mask, adjusting it until he knew his entire head was covered, except for his eyes and mouth. He tugged the material to settle two small openings over his nostrils. His long black cloak draped on the saddle behind him, and snug black leather gloves encased his hands. His black shirt, breeches, and boots rendered him all but invisible in the growing darkness.

His gaze settled on the distressed girl kneeling at the base of the oak tree.

Never fear, Miss Samantha Briggeham. Freedom awaits you.

Chapter 2

It happened as quickly as a lightning flash.

Kneeling, gently cupping a firefly in her hand, Sammie lifted her head at the rustling in the nearby bushes. Without further warning, a black horse emerged from the trees, vaulting over a low hedge. Her heart nearly stalled with surprise, then fear flooded her as she realized the horse was headed straight for her.

Springing to her feet, she stepped hastily backward. She caught the shadowy glimpse of a rider who clearly didn't see her as he veered in her direction. She opened her mouth to shout a warning, but before she could issue so much as a peep, a strong arm scooped her off the ground.

Her breath left her body in a loud *whoosh* and pain shot up her backside as she was deposited sideways on the saddle with a bone-jarring thud. Her glasses flew from her nose, and her bag of insects fell from her fingers. What appeared to be a bouquet of flowers sailed past her. Cyril's distressed voice cried out, "Miz Sammie!"

The strong arm tightened around her like a vise, pinning her sideways to a large muscular frame as the horse raced into the woods. "Do not worry," a deep velvety whisper flavored with a faint Scottish brogue sounded in her ear. "Ye are perfectly safe."

Speechless with shock, Sammie tried to move her arms, but her captor held them trapped to her sides with his own. Turning her head, she found herself staring at a black mask. Fear snaked down her spine and clogged her throat. What manner of madman was this? A highwayman? But if so, why had he taken her instead of simply demanding money?

Realization slapped her. Dear God, was she being *kidnapped*? She shook her head to clear it. Logic labeled the idea utterly preposterous, but the fact that she was speeding through the night in the iron-clad grasp of a masked man certainly indicated an abduction. Why on earth would someone kidnap *her*? While her family was financially comfortable, they were not wealthy enough to pay an exorbitant ransom. Had he made a mistake and abducted the wrong woman? She didn't know, but she had to get away from him.

Drawing as deep a breath as she could manage, Sammie opened her mouth to let loose with a scream. The sound had no sooner left her throat when the arm anchored around her middle tightened, cutting her cry into a mere wheeze.

"Don't scream," he whispered against her ear. "I won't harm ye."

Unconvinced, she opened her mouth again, but his lips pressed against her ear stopped her.

"I don't want to stuff my handkerchief in your mouth, but I will if I must."

Sammie reluctantly swallowed the scream trembling on her lips. Although she was not one to panic, she couldn't stop the alarm quivering through her. "I demand that you stop this horse and release me. Immediately."

"Soon, lass."

"You've made a mistake. My family cannot pay a ransom."

" 'Tis not a ransom I'm after." He leaned closer, his warm breath sending a shiver down her spine. "Fear not, Miss Briggeham. You're saved."

Cold dread filled her. He knew her name. Clearly this was not a case of mistaken identity. But who was he? *You're saved.* Saved? What on earth was he talking about? God in heaven, he really must be insane.

"How do you—?"

"Quiet, please," he whispered. "We'll talk after we arrive at the cottage."

Cottage? A fresh wave of fear rolled over her, but she forced herself to concentrate. Inhaling as deep as his binding arm would allow, she logically and quickly weighed her options. Obviously he couldn't be reasoned with, persuaded to release her. Did he mean to harm her? Anger edged some of her fear aside, and she pressed her lips together. If he had it in his mind to hurt her or force himself upon her, he'd have a devil of a fight on his hands.

Escape. That's what she had to do. But how? The horse was running at full gallop. She attempted to wriggle a bit, but his muscular arm only tightened around her, pinching her ribs and expelling the air from her constricted lungs. Even if she managed to throw herself from the saddle— which judging by his strength would be impossible—the fall would no doubt kill her. At the very least injure her gravely. And then she'd be at his mercy.

She pushed that disturbing thought aside with a resounding shove.

Who on earth was he? She peered up at his masked face. Black material covered his entire head. There was a slit for his mouth, two small holes for his nostrils, and narrow oblong cutouts for his eyes. She squinted, trying to determine their color, but could not.

Apprehension prickled her skin as she noted the power in his frame. Even through the layers of their clothing, there was no mistaking his hard muscles. His chest, pressed into her side, possessed all the flexibility of a brick wall. And the thighs cradling her felt like stone. He held her as if she were a doll in his grasp. There was no way she could physically overpower him.

Unless she found a weapon and struck him over the head with it. A wave of grim satisfaction washed over her at the thought of rendering the brigand unconscious.

Unfortunately she'd have to wait until they reached whatever destination he had in mind. But then she would escape him, either by outwitting him or coshing him.

In the meanwhile, she forced herself to focus on her surroundings. They were traveling deep through the woods, but without her glasses, any landmarks she might have recognized were mere blurs. Glimmering shafts of moonlight filtered through the trees, but still the path was shrouded in darkness. Sammie wondered that he could even see, between the darkness and his mask.

They traveled for nearly an hour, and try as she might, she could not determine where they were. His grip on her never relaxed, and she forced herself not to think about the strength of the masculine body pressed against her. Her backside felt bruised, and her arms tingled from lack of circulation caused by his tight hold on her.

Finally he slowed their pace to a trot. Clearly they were approaching the cottage he'd mentioned, but without her spectacles, she couldn't see it in the darkness. She had no idea where they were and she wondered if he'd purposely ridden in circles to confuse her. Still, by the time he slowed the mount, she'd planned her strategy. It was simple, straightforward, and logical: get off the horse, find an object to cosh him with, commence coshing, get back on the horse, then find her way home.

He pulled back on the reins, and the horse halted. Squinting, Sammie discerned the outline of a cottage. Still holding her, her captor dismounted and set her on her feet. Frustration suffused her when her watery knees threatened to buckle. If he hadn't retained his grasp on her upper arms, she would have slithered to the ground. How was she to attack the libertine if she couldn't even stand? Gritting her teeth, she locked her knees and prayed for the quick return of feeling in her numb limbs.

"Damnation, did I hurt ye, lass?" His husky whisper held a note of concern that surprised her. Before she could answer, he swept her up in his arms and carried her toward the cottage. "Shouldn't have held ye so snug, but I couldn't have ye falling. Let's get ye inside and take a look at ye."

Sammie silently swore that if he tried to take a look at her, she'd poke his eyes out. She wanted to pummel him with her fists, but to her infinite disgust, her arms possessed all the strength of porridge. However, tingles pulsed up her limbs, prickling her skin, a sure indication that feeling would soon return.

Perhaps it was best if he thought her weak and defenseless. That would surely lower his guard. Then she could find something inside the cottage to use as a weapon—a nice sharp knife or fire poker—and escape this fiend.

He opened the cottage door and entered, pushing it closed behind them with his foot. A low fire burned in the grate, casting the small room with a pale golden glow. Sammie looked around and her heart sank.

The room was empty. No furniture, no rugs, and nothing resembling a weapon.

His boots clicked against the wood floor as he crossed to the fireplace. Her gaze ran over the mantel, hoping to spy a candlestick, but like the rest of the room, the mantel was bare. Hope leapt through her when her blurry vision locked on what looked like a set of brass fireplace tools propped against the wall on the opposite side of the fireplace. Too far for her to reach, but she'd figure out some way to grab one. All she needed to do was bide her time.

Her captor knelt, lowering her to the floor near the fire with a gentleness that surprised her. The instant he released her, she scooted backwards until her back hit the wall.

"Stay away from me," she ordered, proud that her voice didn't quaver. "Don't touch me."

He went completely still. Sammie stared at him, wishing mightily for her spectacles so she could see him more clearly. Although she could barely make out his eyes between the slits in his mask, she felt the weight of his steady stare.

"You've nothing to fear from me, Miss Briggeham. I wish only to help ye—"

"Help me? By kidnapping me? By holding me against my will?"

"Not against your will." Bowing his head, he said in a husky rasp, "Rejoice, lass. 'Tis the Bride Thief, come to rescue ye."

Eric watched Miss Briggeham through the slits in his mask and waited for relief and joy to replace the apprehension shadowing her eyes.

Miss Briggeham regarded him with a blank stare. "Bride Thief? Rescue?"

Poor woman. She was clearly dumbstruck with gratitude. "Why, yes. I'm here to help ye start a new life . . . a life of freedom. I know ye've no wish to marry Major Wilshire."

Her eyes widened. "What do you know of Major Wilshire?"

"I know he is your betrothed, and that ye are being forced to marry him."

Her expression immediately changed, and unmistakable annoyance streaked across her face. "I've had quite enough of people telling me I am engaged." Straightening her spine, she pointed her finger at him, punctuating each word. "Major Wilshire is *not* my betrothed, and I am *not* going to marry him."

Eric froze, unease creeping down his spine. Not her betrothed? Damn it all, had he taken the wrong woman? Is that why she wasn't leaping about with joy that he'd rescued her?

His gaze slid over her, taking in her disheveled appearance. Her bonnet hung from her neck by its ribbons. Dark hair surrounded her face in wild disarray, several strands sticking straight upward in a way that reminded him of devil's horns—not a happy comparison under the circumstances. Her eyes appeared huge in her face—a plain, pale face that currently bore an expression of clear displeasure. Definitely not a look he was accustomed to seeing on the faces of the women he rescued.

"Are ye not Samantha Briggeham?" he asked.

She glared at him and squeezed her lips together.

Damn stubborn woman. He leaned closer to her and ignored the twinge of guilt when her eyes flickered with fright. "Answer the question. Are ye Samantha Briggeham?"

She nodded stiffly. "I am."

Confusion assailed him. He had the right woman. Bloody hell, had Arthur's information been incorrect? If so, Eric had made a terrible error. Forcing himself to remain calm, he studied her carefully. "I understood your father had arranged for ye to marry the Major."

She watched him through wary eyes. "Indeed he had, but as I'd never heard of a more unappealing, not to mention idiotic, plan in my entire life, I *un*arranged what my well-meaning but ill-advised father arranged."

Eric's unease tripled. "I beg your pardon?"

"I visited Major Wilshire this evening and explained that, while I hold him in high esteem, I have no wish to marry him."

"And he agreed?"

She averted her gaze, and a crimson blush stole over her cheeks. "Er, yes. Eventually."

Eric's hands fisted in his gloves at her clearly embarrassed reaction. Damn it, had the Major attempted to take liberties with her? "Eventually?"

She squinted up at him for several seconds, then shrugged. "Not that it's any of your concern, but even after explaining in the politest of ways that I didn't want to marry him, I'm afraid the Major was still rather . . . insistent."

By God, the reprobate clearly *had* touched her. Feeling totally out of his element, Eric raised his hands to rake his fingers through his hair, only to encounter his masked head.

She cleared her throat. "Fortunately for me, however, no sooner had the Major finished his long-winded 'you-most-certainly-will-marry-me, the-arrangements-have-already-been-made' speech, then Isadore appeared. He quite saved the day."

A breath he hadn't even realized he held, escaped Eric. "Isadore? He's your coachman?"

"No. Cyril is my coachman. Isadore is my toad."

Eric knew that if his mask wasn't so tight, his jaw would have dropped. "Your *toad* saved the day?"

"Yes. Isadore likes to nestle in my reticule and accompany me on coach rides. I'd quite forgotten about him until he hopped out and landed right on one of the Major's highly polished Hessians. Heavens, never have I witnessed such a fuss. Anyone would have thought he'd been stripped of his rank the way he carried on. Amazing how a man who claims such acts of military bravery could harbor such fear and aversion to a toad." She shook her head. "Of course, seeing as he objected so strenuously to Isadore, I thought it best to warn him about Cuthbert and Warfinkle."

Bemused, Eric asked, "More toads?"

"No. A mouse and a garden snake. Both perfectly harmless, but Major Wilshire turned quite pale, especially when I hinted that I housed them in my bedchamber."

Half-amused, half-horrified, Eric asked, "Do you?"

There was no mistaking the sheepishness in the myopic glance she sent him. "No, but then I only *hinted* that I did. Surely I cannot be held accountable for any incorrect assumptions the Major may make, do you not agree?"

"Indeed. What happened next?"

"Well, as I chased Isadore about the room, in a fashion the Major later described as 'appalling and unladylike,' I deemed it only fair to share with him some of my other hobbies."

"Such as?"

"Singing. I raised my voice in what *I* thought was a particularly well-done rendition of 'Barbara Allen,' but I'm afraid the Major found my voice less than adequate. I believe 'dreadful' is the word he muttered under his breath. He appeared quite alarmed when I informed him that I sing every day, for *at least* several hours.

"And he grew even more alarmed when I told him about my plans to convert his drawing room into a laboratory. Really, he raised an incredible fuss, even after I assured him that the few times my experiments had resulted in fires, the flames had been doused *very* quickly and with almost no damage at all."

Bloody hell, the chit was a menace. But undeniably clever. "Dare I wonder what came next?"

"Isadore, who was proving quite impossible to catch, saw fit to jump onto the Major's lap. Goodness, I never would have suspected the Major possessed such . . . agility.

By the time I captured Isadore and restored him to my reticule, then coaxed the Major down from the pianoforte, the gentleman was quite willing to concede that we would not suit." Her expression turned fierce. "I was returning from his house, intent upon telling my parents of the dissolution of my betrothal, when you so rudely absconded with me. Perhaps now *you* would care to explain *your*self?"

Momentarily robbed of speech, Eric's mind raced with the unholy mess he'd landed himself in. He rose to his feet and stared down at her. Unmistakable apprehension flickered in her eyes, and she scooted farther into the corner, an action that annoyed him further.

"Stop looking at me as if I'm a bloody murderer about to hack ye to pieces," he uttered in a husky growl. "I told ye, I won't hurt ye. I was trying to *help* ye. I'm the man they call the Bride Thief."

"So you've said, and in a tone that suggests I should know you, but I'm afraid I don't."

Eric stared at her, completely nonplussed. Surely he'd misheard her. "Ye've never heard of the Bride Thief?"

"I'm afraid not, but apparently you must be he." She looked him up and down twice, and his skin actually heated under her scathing stare. "I cannot say I'm pleased to make your acquaintance."

"Saints above, lass. Don't ye ever read a newspaper?"

"Certainly. I read all the articles pertaining to nature and scientific matters."

"And the Society pages?"

"I do not waste my time reading such drivel." Her distasteful expression clearly stated that she found him sadly lacking if his name could be found only in the Society columns.

Sheer disbelief rendered him speechless. He opened his mouth to speak, but no words came forth. How could she not know about the Bride Thief? Did the chit dwell in a dungeon? Not a day went by when the Bride Thief wasn't discussed in London's clubs, at Almack's, in country pubs, and written about in every publication in the kingdom.

Yet Miss Samantha Briggeham had never heard of him.

Well, bloody hell.

If he wasn't so confounded by the realization, he would have laughed at the absurdity of the situation—and at his own conceit. Clearly he wasn't quite as notorious as he'd believed.

His amusement quickly vanished, however, when he realized the gravity of his error. Miss Briggeham was not being forced into marriage. He'd nabbed a woman who did not need his assistance. And now the Bride Thief would have to do something he'd never done before.

Return a woman he'd rescued.

A woman who was squinting toward the fire poker with a gleam in her eye that indicated she'd like to see it wrapped around his neck. He squeezed his eyes shut for a brief moment and silently cursed his rotten luck.

Damn it all, sometimes being England's Most Notorious Man was a bloody pain in the arse.

Chapter 3

"What do you mean you're not marrying my daughter?"

Cordelia Briggeham stood in her drawing room and stared at Major Wilshire in her most imperious manner, somehow resisting the urge to beat the arrogant soldier with her lace fan.

The Major stood ramrod stiff next to the fireplace and looked down his long nose at Cordelia. "As I stated, Miss Briggeham and I mutually agreed earlier this evening that a marriage between us is inadvisable. I was certain she'd have told you by now."

"She's told me no such thing."

The color drained from the Major's florid face. "Egad, surely the chit doesn't claim we're still betrothed?"

Cordelia was certain she detected a shudder run through the Major's large frame. Then he glanced down at his Hessians and wrinkled his nose. Such odd behavior. Perhaps the man was daft.

"My daughter has made no claims of *any* kind, Major. I've not seen her nor spoken to her since dinner." She turned to her husband, who sat in his favorite wing chair in the corner. "Charles, have you spoken to Samantha this evening?"

When silence greeted her question, Cordelia pursed her lips and for the second time in minutes considered coshing a man. Men. They were going to be the very death of her. "Charles!"

Charles Briggeham's head snapped up as if she'd jabbed him with a stick. His glazed eyes clearly indicated he'd been dozing. "Yes, Cordelia?"

"Has Samantha discussed her betrothal with you this evening?"

"There is no longer a betrothal. . . ." Major Wilshire's voice trailed off when Cordelia shot him her most glacial glare.

"Haven't seen Sammie since dinner," Charles said. He turned to the Major. "Excellent pot roast, Major. You should have—"

"What have you to say about the Major's outrageous claim, Charles?" Cordelia cut in.

Charles blinked rapidly. "Claim?"

"That he and Samantha are no longer engaged?"

"Rubbish. I heard nothing of the sort." Charles turned toward the Major with a frown. "What's this about? All the arrangements are in place."

"Yes, well, that was before Miss Briggeham paid me a visit this evening."

"She did no such thing," Cordelia stated, praying she was correct. Lord, what sort of mess had Sammie conjured up now?

"She most certainly did. Told me she didn't think we made a good match. After some, er, discussion, I agreed with her assessment of the situation and took appropriate action." The Major cleared his throat. "To put it bluntly, the wedding is off."

Cordelia eyed the sofa and decided it was too far away for her to properly swoon. Damnation.

No wedding? Lud, this presented a ticklish mess. Not only might there be a scandal depending on what Sammie had done to dissuade the Major, but Cordelia could just hear that odious Lydia Nordfield once she got wind of this debacle. *Why Cordelia,* Lydia would say, batting her eyes like a cow in a hailstorm, *how* tragic *that Sammie's no longer betrothed. Viscount Carsdale has shown an interest in my Daphne, you know. And Daphne is so very lovely. It seems like I'll have all my daughters married before you do!*

Cordelia squeezed her eyes shut to banish the horrible scenario. Sammie was worth ten of that vapid Daphne, and Cordelia's blood all but boiled at the injustice of it all. Daphne, whose sole talents lay in swishing a fan and giggling, would capture a viscount simply because she possessed an attractive face. While Sammie would remain on-the-shelf, forcing Cordelia to listen to Lydia harp about it for the next twenty years. Oh, it was simply not to be borne!

She'd arranged for Sammie to marry a perfectly respectable gentleman—and now Major Wilshire thought he was going to ruin all her plans? *Humph. We shall see about that.*

Tightening her jaw, Cordelia inched closer to the sofa in case she needed to employ it, then turned her attention back to the Major. "How can a man who calls himself honorable disgrace my daughter in such a way?"

Charles rose and tugged on his waistcoat. "Indeed, Major. This is most irregular. I demand an explanation."

"I've already explained, Briggeham. There will be no wedding." He fixed a steely stare on Cordelia. "You, madam, led me astray when describing your daughter."

"I did no such thing," Cordelia said with her most elegant sniff. "I informed you how intelligent Samantha is, and you well knew she wasn't fresh from the schoolroom."

"You neglected to mention her fondness for slimy toads and other assorted vermin, her predilection for crawling about on the floor, her frightening lack of musical talent, and her habit of setting up laboratories and starting fires."

Cordelia made a beeline for the sofa. Emitting two breathy, chirp-like *oohs*, she dropped down in a graceful swoon. "What a dreadful thing to say! Charles, my hartshorn!"

Waiting for the hartshorn, Cordelia's mind raced. Ye gods, the Major must have met Isadore, Cuthbert, and Warfinkle. Of all the rotten luck! *Oh, Sammie, why couldn't you have simply brought along a book?* And what was this about crawling about on the floor? Of course, she'd known the lack of musical talent and the laboratory situations could prove troublesome, but whatever did he mean about starting fires? Great heavens above, what outrageous tales had Sammie told the man?

Heaving a sigh, she wondered what was taking Charles so long with the hartshorn. There was much to be done to remedy this debacle—she couldn't lay about on the sofa all night.

"Here you are, my dear." Charles waved the hartshorn under her nostrils with an enthusiasm that brought tears to her eyes.

Pushing herself upright, Cordelia thrust his hand away. "That's quite enough, Charles. The idea was to revive me, not put me in the grave." Settling her features into her most forbidding frown, she glared at the Major. "Now see here, Major. You cannot—"

The study door burst open and a wild-eyed Cyril rushed into the room. "Missus Briggeham! Mr. Briggeham! 'Tis the most awful thing wot's 'appened."

"Good God, man, I can see that," Charles said, taking in

the coachman's disheveled appearance. "Your cravat's completely unraveled and you're sporting grass stains on your breeches. And are those *twigs* in your hair? Why, you're completely undone. Whatever has happened to put you in such a state?"

Cyril attempted to catch his breath, then mopped his forehead with the back of his hand. "It's Miz Sammie, sir." He swallowed hard, his Adam's apple bobbing. "She's . . . gone."

"Gone?" Charles asked with a puzzled frown. "You mean from the house?"

"Yes, sir. On returning from her visit to the Major—"

"Ooh! Ooh! It's true, then," Cordelia chirped, swooning back onto the sofa. "My baby! She's ruined!"

"No, Missus Briggeham. She's kidnapped," Cyril intoned, bowing his head.

Cordelia jumped to her feet. "*Kidnapped?* Oh, you're daft. Why would you think such a ridiculous thing? Who on earth would kidnap Sammie? And why?"

For an answer, Cyril held out a bouquet of flowers.

Cordelia fought the urge to roll her eyes. "That's very sweet, Cyril, but this is not the time for posies."

"No, Missus Briggeham. This 'ere's wot the kidnapper gave me. Tossed it to me, 'e did, right after he plucked Miz Sammie up like a weed from where she were gatherin' insects for Master Hubert, and raced off with 'er on a big black 'orse." He handed her the flowers. "There's a note attached."

Cordelia stared at the bouquet, rendered utterly speechless for the first time in her memory.

Charles pulled the note from the flowers, then broke the wax seal. Scanning the contents, the color drained from his face, and Cordelia wondered if she'd need to apply the hartshorn to *him*.

Somehow she managed to remain standing on her watery legs. "What does it say, Charles? Has she truly been kidnapped? Is there a ransom demand?"

Looking at her over the top of the ivory vellum, Charles regarded her with stricken eyes. "She has indeed been stolen, Cordelia."

For the first time in her life, Cordelia's knees folded without a thought to where she would land. Luckily she plopped onto the sofa. "Dear God, Charles. What fiend has taken our Sammie? How much money does he want?"

"None. Read it for yourself."

Cordelia took the note from his shaking fingers and held it away from her like a snake. The words she read staggered her.

> *Dear Mr. and Mrs. Briggeham,*
> *I write this note for the purpose of allaying your*
> *fears for your daughter Samantha. Rest assured she*
> *is perfectly safe and no harm shall come to her at my*
> *hands. I've simply given Samantha the opportunity*
> *for freedom, for a life of her own, without the*
> *prospect of having to marry a man she doesn't wish*
> *to wed. I hope you will find it in your hearts to wish*
> *her the happiness she deserves.*
> *The Bride Thief*

Cordelia's gaze fixed on the signature, her thoughts in turmoil.

The Bride Thief.

The most notorious, sought-after man in England had absconded with her baby.

"Dear God, Charles. We must call the magistrate."

Lightning flashed, followed by a clap of thunder that rattled the cottage windows. Seconds later rain splattered against

the roof. Eric smothered an oath. The last thing he needed
was a storm to delay his and Miss Briggeham's departure
from the cabin.

Reaching down his hand, he whispered in his Bride
Thief voice, "Please allow me to assist ye to your feet."

She cast his hand a baleful glare. "I can manage on my
own, thank you." Keeping a wary eye on him, she rose to
her feet.

He studied her as she brushed dust from her plain gown,
then hastily adjusted her bonnet, shoving several tangled
curls beneath the material. She was petite, the top of her
head rising no higher than his cravat. The little he could see
of her disheveled hair under the bonnet appeared thick and
glossy. With the room illuminated by only the low-glowing
fire, it was impossible to distinguish her exact eye color,
but they were pale—blue, he'd guess—and very large in
comparison to her small features. Except her lips, which,
like her eyes, seemed too big for her face. While she could
not be described as beautiful, he found her face, with those
too-large eyes and too-full lips, intriguing.

His gaze wandered down her form and his brows rose
beneath his mask. Quite the curvaceous piece, this Miss
Briggeham. Even her dowdy gown could not hide the generous swell of her breasts. His gaze dipped lower, and he
wondered if her hips matched the ripeness of her bosom.

The thought slapped him like a pail of cold water in the
face. *Bloody hell, man, get hold of yourself. You've got to
get the chit home without getting hanged for your trouble.*

Snapping his gaze back to her face, he saw she regarded
him with clear suspicion. "I demand to know what you plan
to do with me."

He had to admire her show of bravery. The only thing
that ruined it was the rapid rise and fall of her chest. "Fear
not, lass. I shall return ye home to the bosom of your
family."

A bit of the wariness left her eyes. "Excellent. I'd like to leave immediately, if you don't mind. I've no doubt my family is concerned."

Eric glanced toward the window. "'Tis raining. We'll wait a few minutes to see if it passes."

"I'd prefer to leave now."

"As would I, but I want to get ye home in one piece." To ease the tension in her stance, he added, "I'll strike a bargain with ye. We'll stay here for another quarter hour. If the rain hasn't let up by then, we'll leave regardless."

"How do I know you're telling the truth?"

"You've my word of honor, lass."

An unladylike snort escaped her. "Coming from a man named 'Thief,' I'm not certain that's a comfort."

"Ah, but surely you've heard there is honor even amongst thieves, Miss Briggeham." Bending his knees, he settled himself on the floor, scooting back until he leaned against the wall. "Come sit by me and we'll have a chat," he invited in his husky brogue, patting the space next to him. "I promise not to bite. As long as we're stuck here for a wee bit, we might as well be comfortable."

When she hesitated, he rose, then walked to the opposite side of the fireplace. Pulling the fire poker from the brass stand, he held it out to her. "Here. Take this if it will make ye feel safer."

She squinted first at the poker, then at him. "Why would you give me a weapon?"

"As a show of faith and trust, lass. I took ye by mistake and it's back to your home I'll bring ye. In all honesty, have I hurt ye in any way?"

"No. But you frightened me half to death."

"I'm truly sorry."

"I also lost my spectacles during the fray, and dropped my pouch."

"Again, I offer my sincerest apologies." He indicated the

poker with a nod. "Take it. I give ye permission to cosh me should I attempt to harm ye."

Sammie ignored the hint of amusement lacing his voice and snatched the poker from his outstretched hands. Stepping hastily back, she gripped the warm brass tightly, ready to render him senseless if he didn't keep his word. Instead of pouncing on her, however, he merely lowered his tall frame to the floor, propped his back against the wall, and watched her.

Sammie held the poker and pondered what to do next. Rain slashed against the windows and she had to admit that attempting to make their way through the woods in the rainy darkness was not a wise idea.

But how could she possibly consider trusting him? True, he'd given her the poker, but he no doubt believed he could disarm her should she attack him. Drawing a deep breath, she forced her thoughts to align in logical order.

The Bride Thief. She searched her memory and realized that she might have heard mention of such a person, but as she almost always turned a deaf ear to the gossip that her sisters and Mama delighted in, she couldn't be certain. Still, now that she thought upon it, the name did sound vaguely familiar.

Surely her best course of action was to engage him in conversation. Perhaps she could glean some information that would help her decide if he could be trusted—or clues that would assist the authorities.

Still gripping the poker, she sat on the floor on the opposite side of the empty room, then squinted at the blurry black blob that was her abductor. Keeping her tone light, she asked, "Tell me, Mr., ah, Thief, have you stolen many reluctant brides?"

A deep chuckle emanated from the black blob. "Aye, 'tis a blow to my pride, to be sure, that ye've truly never heard of me. I've helped more than a dozen brides, lass. Unfortunate women, each one on the brink of being forced to marry against her will."

"If you don't mind me asking, how exactly do you 'help' them?"

"I provide them with passage to the Continent or to America, and with enough funds to establish them in their new life."

"That must be quite costly."

She fancied that he shrugged. "I've enough funds."

"I see. Do you steal those as well?"

Again he chuckled. "Suspicious sort, aren't ye? No, lass, I've no need to rob anyone of their baubles or gold sovereigns. The money I give is my own."

Sammie couldn't hide her surprise. Heavens, what manner of man *was* he? After taking a moment to assimilate his words, she nodded slowly. "I believe I'm beginning to understand. You're rather like Robin Hood, only instead of robbing jewels, you steal brides. And instead of giving monetary spoils to the poor, you offer the gift of freedom."

"I never thought of it quite like that, but yes."

Realization dawned and Sammie's breath puffed out. "And you were prepared to offer that gift of freedom to me . . . to save me from marrying Major Wilshire."

"Indeed I was. But clearly you're a lass of strong convictions and took care of the problem on your own." He muttered something that sounded suspiciously like *if only I'd known I'd have saved myself a bloody lot of trouble,* but she couldn't be sure. "Tell me, lass, why did ye not wish to marry the Major?"

Heavens, a full explanation could take hours. Clearing her throat, she said, "We've little in common and would not suit at all. But in truth, I've no desire to marry *anyone.* I'm very content in my life, and spinsterhood affords me the freedom to pursue my scientific interests. I fear most men, the Major included, would attempt to thwart my studies."

She waved her hand in a dismissive gesture. "But enough about me. Please tell me more about this absconding with the brides. You may regard it as helping, but surely the families of these women view your actions as kidnapping."

"Aye, that they do."

"And I imagine the magistrate would like to find you."

"Indeed, he'd like to see me with a noose decorating my neck."

Sammie leaned forward, fascinated in spite of herself. "Then why do you do this? What can you possibly gain from placing yourself in such danger?"

Silence met her question for the space of several heartbeats. Then his husky rasp floated across the room, his tone harsher than before. "Someone I loved was forced to marry a man she loathed. I failed to save her. So I try to help others like her. A woman should have the right to choose not to marry a man she finds distasteful." He paused, then added so softly she had to strain her ears to hear, "My gain is the gratitude shining from the women's eyes. Each one loosens, just a bit, the knot of guilt that binds me for not being able to help the one I loved."

"Oh, my," Sammie said, expelling a long, pent-up breath. "How incredibly . . . noble. And romantic. To risk your life, and for so worthy a cause." A shiver that had nothing to do with fear trembled down her back. "Heaven knows I'd have been grateful for your help, had I in fact needed it."

"Yet ye *didn't* need my assistance, which places me in the awkward position of having to return ye."

"Yes, I suppose it does." Sammie stared across the room at him, her heart slapping against her ribs so loudly she wondered if he could hear it. Oh, how she wished she could see him better, for here was a man who clearly embodied all the qualities of her secret fantasies—all the dreams burrowed deep in her plain, socially inept, bookwormish soul.

He was big, and strong, and she just knew his mask hid a fascinating face—one filled with purpose and character. He was dashing, brave, swashbuckling, and noble.

He was a *hero*.

It was as if he'd materialized from her imagination and stepped from the pages of her personal journal, the only place she dared reveal her innermost, secret desires. Desires sparked by impossible dreams that a man such as this would ever find a woman such as her worthy of his attention, would sweep her off her feet and bring her to magical places.

A heartfelt sigh escaped her—the sort of dreamy, useless, impractical feminine sigh she rarely indulged in. She had to know more . . . about him and this exciting, danger-fraught life he led. Setting the poker on the wooden floor, she rose, crossed the room, then sat next to him.

She stared at his mask and their gazes met through the narrow slits. A tingle washed over her, and she wished she could discern the color of his eyes. All she could tell in the muted firelight was that they were dark. And fathomless.

"Are you ever afraid?" she asked, trying not to sound too breathless.

"Aye, lass. Every time I don this costume." He leaned closer to her and her breath stalled. "I've no desire to die, especially not at the hands of the hangman."

He smelled wonderful. Like leather and horses and . . . adventure. "Do you carry a weapon?" she asked.

"A knife in my boot. Nothing more. I cannot abide the feel of a pistol in my hand."

She fancied pain flashed in his eyes, but she couldn't be certain. "Tell me, where would you have sent me?" she asked. "America or the Continent?"

"Where would ye have wanted to go, lass?"

"Oh," she breathed, her eyes drifting shut at mere thought of choosing. Longing rushed through her like a raging river, forcing a crack in the dam behind which she hid her innermost desires. "There are so many places I yearn to see."

"If ye could travel anywhere, where would ye go?"

"Italy. No, Greece. No, Austria." Opening her eyes, she laughed. "I believe it is fortunate I do not require your services, sir, for I'd not be able to decide where you should send me."

His gaze seemed to bore into hers, and her laughter trailed off. The weight of his intense stare chilled and heated her at the same time. "Is something amiss?" she asked.

"Ye should do that more often, Miss Briggeham."

"What? Be horribly indecisive?"

"No. Laugh as ye just did. It . . . transforms ye."

She wasn't certain that he meant his words as a compliment, but still, delivered in that velvety rasp, they enveloped her like a coating of warm honey.

"Tell me," he whispered, "if ye had to choose just one place, where would it be?"

For some odd reason, her heart beat in slow, hard thumps. "Italy," she whispered back. "I've always dreamed of seeing Rome, Florence, Venice, Naples . . . and every city in between. To explore the ruins of Pompeii, trek through the Colosseum, visit the Uffizi, view the works of Bernini and Michaelangelo, swim in the warm waters of the Adriatic . . ." her voice trailed off into a vaporous sigh.

"Explore?" he repeated. "Trek? *Swim*?"

Heat scorched her cheeks and embarrassed confusion washed through her as she realized that with her unguarded words, she'd inadvertently told this stranger things she'd only ever shared with Hubert.

Humiliation prickled her skin. Was he laughing at her? She squinted at him, trying to see his eyes, fearing the certain derision she'd read there. But to her surprise, his

steady gaze revealed no amusement. Only a deep intensity
that oddly unsettled her and rippled flutters through her.

Anxious to break the uncomfortable silence, she remarked, "I assume no one knows your true identity."

He hesitated for a moment, then said, " 'Twould cost me
my life if anyone knew."

"Yes, I suppose it would." A rush of sympathy washed
through her. " 'Tis a lonely life you've chosen, sir, in pursuit of your noble cause."

He nodded slowly, as if considering her words. "Yes, it
is. But it's a small price to pay."

"Oh, but it's not. I . . . I'm often lonely myself. I know
the emptiness that can accompany it."

"Surely ye have friends."

"A few." A humorless sound escaped her. "Actually, a
very few. But I have my family. My younger brother and
I are particularly close. Still, sometimes, it would be
nice . . ."

"Yes?"

She shrugged, feeling suddenly self-conscious. "To have
someone else besides a young boy who understands you."
She studied her wrinkled gown for several seconds, then
raised her gaze to his. "I hope some day you'll find someone or something to ease your guilt and loneliness, sir."

He studied her for several seconds, then, slowly reaching out, he ran a single gloved fingertip gently down her
cheek. "As do I, lass."

Sammie's breath caught at the brief touch that whispered over her skin like a soft breeze. Unable to move, she
simply stared at him, confused by the unprecedented
warmth pulsing through her. Before she could examine the
feeling more closely, he rose to his feet in one fluid motion
and held his hand down to her. "Come. The rain has
stopped. 'Tis time I brought ye home."

Home? Sammie stared at his outstretched hand and

mentally shook herself from her dreamlike stupor. Yes, of course. Home. Where she belonged. Where her family—

Good heavens, her family! They must be frantic with worry. Surely Cyril had reported her disappearance by now. Her stomach churned with guilt when she realized that she'd been so caught up with her masked abductor, she'd forgotten how concerned Mama, Papa, and Hubert must be.

"Yes," she said, placing her hand in his and allowing him to assist her to her feet. "I must go home." She *wanted* to go home. So why did this hollow feeling of regret wash through her?

Without another word, they left the cabin. He gave her a hand up, then swung into the saddle behind her, cradling her between his hard thighs. One muscular arm held her close against his chest. Warmth from his body seeped into her, but in spite of that heat, a legion of chills skittered down her spine.

"Don't worry, lass. I won't let ye fall."

Before Sammie could assure him she wasn't worried, they were off, speeding through the forest. This time, instead of fear, nothing but exhilaration raced through her. Closing her eyes, she savored every sensation: the wind whipping over her face, the scent of moist earth, the rustle of leaves. She imagined she was a beautiful princess, held by her handsome prince as they dashed across the kingdom on their way to some exotic locale. Silly, foolish imaginings. But she knew these moments with this masked hero were precious, and she would never live them again.

All too soon he pulled on the reins and halted the horse. She opened her eyes and squinted. She could make out pinpricks of light in the distance, reminding her of the fireflies she'd caught earlier.

"Briggeham Manor lies just beyond these trees," he

whispered. "I fear an alarm has been raised by your absence."

"How do you know?"

"Listen."

She strained her ears and heard the low murmur of voices. "Who is that?"

"Judging by the number of lanterns held aloft and the crowd gathered on the lawn, I'd say half the town is present."

"Oh, dear. Just leave me here and I'll walk to the house. I wouldn't want you to risk capture."

He paused for a moment, and she sensed him scanning the area. "It doesn't appear as if anyone is brandishing a weapon," he said against her ear. "I shall therefore bring ye to your family. I do not want ye to walk into a hole or fall in the darkness. I will, however, say good-bye here, as I will regrettably need to execute a hasty exit."

"Thank you, sir."

"No need for thanks. 'Twas my duty to bring ye home, lass."

"Not for that, although I do appreciate it." Staring up at him, a lump of emotion clogged her throat. Forcing a smile, she said, "I thank you for this incredible evening that I shall never forget. This has been a grand adventure." She lowered her gaze. "I've always wanted one, you see."

Placing his gloved fingers under her chin, he raised her face. "Well, then, Miss Briggeham, I am glad I was able to provide ye with your grand adventure."

"I wish you Godspeed with your endeavors, sir. It's a noble and heroic thing you do."

She sensed that he smiled beneath his mask. "Thank ye, lass. And I hope ye get to explore all those places ye dream of some day. I hope all your dreams come true."

With that, he urged his mount into a gallop. They

emerged from the fringe of trees and raced across the grass. Sammie squinted against the rush of air, her heart pounding as they drew closer to the crowd.

He pulled on the reins and the horse halted not ten feet from the crowd. A chorus of audible gasps, followed by a hum of whispers reached Sammie's ears. He lowered her to the ground then turned to the group gaping at them.

"I return Miss Briggeham with my apologies." He jerked the reins and his magnificent stallion reared up on its hind legs, pawing the air. Sammie, along with everyone else, stared, mouths agape at the awesome spectacle of the masked rider silhouetted against the glow of a dozen lanterns. She looked toward her father and watched his monocle fall to the ground.

The instant its hooves touched the ground, the horse galloped away, the Thief's long black cape flapping behind. Within ten seconds the darkness swallowed them.

"Samantha!" Her father's voice, rough with worry, broke the stupefied silence.

"Papa!" She ran to him and he wrapped her in his arms, so tight she could barely draw a breath.

"Sammie, my dear sweet girl." She felt him swallow and blow out a long breath. "Thank God." Loosening his grip, he held her at arm's length and ran his anxious gaze over her. "Are you all right?"

"I'm fine."

Lowering his voice, he asked, "Did he hurt you?"

"No. In fact, he was very kind."

He gave her a searching look, then, apparently satisfied she was unharmed, he nodded. Glancing toward the woods, he remarked, "I suppose there's no point in going after him. It's too dark and he has too much of a head start. Besides, all that matters is that you're home. And safe." He reached into his waistcoat pocket. "Here are your spectacles, my dear. Cyril found them in the woods."

Grateful, Sammie slipped them on her nose. The crowd pushed in, expressing their happiness over her safe return, while casting wide-eyed glances toward the forest. Cyril mopped his tears with a huge hanky and squeezed her until she thought her eyes would pop.

"I 'ope I never get another scare like that again, Miz Sammie," he said, giving his nose a hearty blow. "Took ten years off me life, it did. And me 'eart ain't what it used to be."

Hubert engulfed her in a mighty hug, his bony arms crushing her to his narrow chest, the metal frame of his spectacles biting into her cheek. "I say, Sammie, you gave us all quite the fright."

She kissed his cheek and tousled his unruly hair. "I'm sorry, darling. I—"

The front doors of Briggeham Manor flew open. "My baby! Where's my baby?" Cordelia Briggeham rushed down the steps and pushed her way through the crowd. She launched herself at Sammie with such force, she nearly propelled them both to the ground. Only Papa's restraining hand kept them upright.

Enveloping Sammie in a bone-jarring, floral-scented hug, Mama moaned, "Oh, my poor, poor child." Thrusting Sammie back a step, she peered into her face. "Are you hurt?"

"No, Mama. I'm fine."

"Thank heavens." She emitted a single chirp and raised her hand to her brow.

Papa stepped forward and whispered in a furious undertone, "Do not even consider swooning here, Mrs. Briggeham, as I swear I'll leave you where you fall. I've had quite enough of your hysterics for one evening."

Mama couldn't have looked more shocked if Papa had claimed to be King George himself. Taking advantage of her temporary speechlessness, Papa raised his voice and said to the crowd, "As you can all see, Samantha is fine. Thank you all for coming, but now if you'll excuse us, we wish to get our daughter into a warm bed."

Calling out good wishes, the neighbors departed for their homes, and the servants returned to their quarters. As they climbed the stone steps leading to the front door, a man on horseback rode up.

"Mr. Briggeham?" he called out.

Papa halted. "Yes?"

"My name is Adam Straton. I'm the magistrate. I understand your daughter was kidnapped by the Bride Thief."

"Indeed she was, sir. But I am happy to report that she has been returned to us, unharmed." He indicated Sammie with a nod of his head.

The magistrate studied Sammie with keen interest. "That is happy news, sir. I've never known the brigand to return one of his victims. You are fortunate."

Sammie bristled at the man's words, but before she could open her mouth to protest, he continued, "I'd like very much to speak to you about your abduction, Miss Briggeham . . . if you're feeling up to it."

"Certainly, Mr. Straton." She relished the opportunity to disabuse him of his misconceptions. Brigand, indeed!

"Why don't you show Mr. Straton to the drawing room, Charles," Mama suggested in a voice that brooked no argument. "Samantha and I will join you in a moment. I'd like a private word with her."

"Very well," Papa agreed. "This way, Mr. Straton." They entered the house, closing the door behind them.

The instant they were alone, Mama turned to her. "The truth now, dearheart. Did that man hurt you? In . . . any way?"

"No, Mama. He was a perfect gentleman, and very kind. And very apologetic for absconding with me in the first place."

"As well he should be, although I must say that I lay the blame for this *entire* episode at Major Wilshire's feet. He's a horrid, horrid man, darling, and I *refuse* to allow you to marry him."

Sammie tried to speak, but Mama rushed on. "Now don't try to talk me out of this, Samantha. My mind, and your father's as well, is quite made up. You will not, under *any* circumstances, wed that cad Major Wilshire. Do you understand?"

Totally at sea, but knowing better than to argue, especially when she wasn't *going* to wed the Major, Sammie said, "Er, yes, Mama. I understand."

"Excellent. Now I have one more question before we go inside." Mama leaned closer and lowered her voice. "I've read all about this Bride Thief in *The Times*. They say he wears all black like a highwayman, and a full-head mask as well. Is that true?"

"Indeed it is."

A delicate shiver shook Mama's shoulders. "They also say he is strong and ruthless."

"He's very strong. But not ruthless." An involuntary sigh escaped her. "He's gentle and thoughtful and noble."

"But a thief."

Sammie shook her head. "He does not steal money, Mama. He has plenty of his own. He wants only to help women who are being forced into unwanted marriages to be free to start new lives, because someone he loved was forced to marry a man she loathed."

Mama heaved out a long breath. "As noble as that sounds, darling, the fact remains that you spent several hours in a man's company. Unchaperoned. We must face the fact that you could suffer social ruin."

Sammie didn't know what to say, as she hadn't considered such an outcome to her adventure. While she didn't particularly care how others viewed her, she had no desire to foist scandal upon her family. Heavens, this could indeed present a problem.

She looked at Mama, and dread slithered down her spine at the grim speculation in her eyes. Sammie knew that expression all too well. It was Mama's infamous "there-must-be-a-way-to-turn-this-debacle-to-my-advantage" gleam that invariably preceded her most outrageous schemes. She could almost hear the thoughts whirling through her mother's pretty head.

"You must join your father and Mr. Straton, Sammie. I'll be along in a moment. I need to collect myself."

"Shall I fetch your hartshorn?"

"No, I'm quite all right." She cradled Sammie's cheek in her warm palm. "I simply need a bit more air to gather my wits. You go, and I'll be in shortly."

Sammie kissed her mother's soft cheek, then entered the house, praying that whatever plan Mama might hatch would prove less disastrous than the Major Wilshire scheme.

Alone on the stone steps, Cordelia paced rapidly and prayed for inspiration. How on earth she was going to keep this botched kidnapping from turning into a scandal that could ruin the family, she didn't know. How could she possibly shed a positive light on these events? Her daughter abducted by the most notorious man in England? In his company, unchaperoned, for several hours? Ye gods, her head ached just thinking about it. And the thought of Lydia's reaction sent a chilled shiver through her. What on earth was a mother to do?

Staring off into the distance, where the moonlight caressed the fringe of trees marking the edge of the forest, she wondered about the man who had stolen Sammie.

She pursed her lips. According to Sammie he was gentle, thoughtful, and noble. And possessed plenty of money.

Perhaps he was a kidnapper—but he was clearly a *decent* kidnapper. And wealthy. Hmmm.

She couldn't help but wonder if he was married.

Chapter 4

From the *London Times*:

The Notorious Bride Thief has struck again, absconding with a young woman from the village of Tunbridge Wells in the county of Kent. This time, however, the Thief actually *returned* the young lady after realizing he'd kidnapped her in error. The woman, who was thankfully unharmed during her ordeal, showed great fortitude when questioned by the authorities. She was unable to provide a description of the Thief, as he wore his full head mask, but she did reveal that his voice was low-pitched and raspy, and that he is a superior horseman.

In related news, a group of fathers of previous kidnap victims have banded together, dubbing themselves the Bride Thief Posse. They have upped the price of the reward for the Thief's capture to an incredible five thousand pounds! Every man in England will be in pursuit of such a fortune, and no stone will be left unturned to bring the Bride Thief to justice.

* * *

"There you are, Lord Wesley!"

Lydia Nordfield's high-pitched voice scraped over Eric's eardrums, and he forced himself not to wince. Cursing the night shadows that obviously hadn't concealed him as well as he'd thought, he emerged from the darkened corner of the terrace and made his way across the stone surface toward his hostess. He couldn't help but marvel at Mrs. Nordfield's extraordinary eyesight, although he suspected that not even the most daunting circumstances, such as utter darkness, could prevent her from spotting a member of the nobility.

He stopped in front of her, making a formal bow. "You were looking for me, Mrs. Nordfield?"

"Yes, my lord. We barely spoke when you arrived."

"Ah, you need not fear I took offense. I understand the demands of hosting an elegant soiree such as this." He waved his hand in an arc, encompassing her manor home and the perfectly manicured gardens. "You've outdone yourself."

She all but preened like a peacock—a resemblance made all the more pronounced by the colorful feathers fanning from her turban. "After our conversation last week, I simply *had* to host a soiree for Miss Briggeham." She leaned closer to him, her feathers brushing his sleeve. "As you suggested, Miss Briggeham's botched abduction is the most titillating *on dit* we've heard in years, especially after the article in *The Times*."

"Indeed, madam. By hostessing this soiree in her honor, you are the toast of Tunbridge Wells."

Even the shadowy light could not disguise the avarice that flashed in her eyes. "Yes, just as you'd predicted. And while other parties have been thrown for Miss Briggeham, no one else was able to lure *you* to their homes. Of course, no other hostess has a daughter as lovely as my Daphne.

She slipped her gloved hand through his elbow, her fingers clenching his arm like steel talons. "And, naturally, ensuring that poor Samantha's kidnapping was thrown into a positive light is the *least* I can do for her. After all, her mother and I have been the *best* of friends for years."

She heaved a melodramatic sigh, then continued, "I do hope the gel enjoys her popularity, as it will, naturally, be only fleeting."

Eric cocked a brow. "Fleeting? What makes you say that?"

"After the bloom of interest in Samantha's adventure fades, she'll go back to being what she's always been, the poor dear."

"And what is that?"

She leaned closer still, her voice dropping to a conspiratorial tone. "'Tis no secret, my lord, that the gel is . . . unusual. Why, she collects *toads* and *insects* in the forest! 'Twas shocking enough when she was a child, but it is behavior nothing short of *unseemly* for a woman of her advanced age. And rather than at least *trying* to learn to play the pianoforte and dance steps, she spends her time with her *odd* brother in his *odd* shed, where they perform scientific experiments that can only be described as . . ."

"Odd?" he suggested, unable to keep an edge from his tone.

"Exactly! And while I'm not one to gossip, I recently heard that Samantha *swims* in the lake on their property!" A shudder wriggled through her body. "Of course I would *never* say a word against her, but I cannot imagine what poor Cordelia must suffer because of her daughter's . . . predilections."

An image of Miss Briggeham frolicking in the lake flashed in his mind, her gown clinging to her soft feminine curves. Or did she perhaps shuck her gown and wear only a chemise . . . or less? Heat rippled through him at the provocative thought. "Perhaps her mother finds Miss Briggeham's . . . predilections endearing. And interesting."

"Nonsense, although Cordelia *does* try to make everyone think she does." Leaning back, she beamed a sharptoothed smile at him. "Thank goodness my Daphne is a *perfect* lady. Such a *delightful* young woman. So accomplished musically, and her singing voice rivals the angels. And a talented artist as well. You must tour the gallery while you're here."

"It would be my pleasure."

Her fingers tightened on his arm. "And you *won't* forget your promise to dance with Daphne."

"I am a man of my word," Eric said, knowing full well his indication that he would dance with her daughter was half the reason Mrs. Nordfield had hosted this party.

"Excellent." She cast her gaze toward the French windows, then cocked her head to the side. "It sounds as if the musicians are starting a quadrille. I shall help you locate Daphne—"

"You go ahead," Eric interrupted, offering her his most charming smile. "I wish to enjoy a cigar before returning to the festivities, and I wouldn't dream of keeping you from your other guests any longer."

Clearly torn by the pull of her hostess duties, she slid her hand from his arm with obvious reluctance. "Yes, I suppose I *must* return." She narrowed her eyes at him. "I shall tell Daphne to expect your invitation to dance, my lord."

"I pray she will consent to do me the honor, madam."

Muttering something that sounded suspiciously like *she'd crawl through flames for the opportunity,* Mrs. Nordfield dipped her head and curtsied, then crossed the stone terrace to re-enter the house.

The instant she disappeared through the French windows, Eric stepped back into the shadows, brushing away the wrinkles his hostess's clinging fingers had wrought upon his jacket. Although he was well used to dealing with marriage-minded mamas like Lydia Nordfield, for some reason he found her manner particularly annoying. Her condescending comments regarding Miss Briggeham had grated on his nerves.

But the irritation was worth the price. As he'd known she would when he'd called upon her last week, Mrs. Nordfield had spread the positive light he'd purposely cast upon Miss Briggeham's abduction faster than fire-burned paper, his cause aided by the article that had appeared in *The Times* just that morning. After exclaiming over Miss Briggeham's bravery, he had informed Mrs. Nordfield that while he'd received numerous invitations to parties hosted in Miss Briggeham's honor—invitations he'd sadly been unable to accept due to prior engagements—he'd been surprised to note that *she*, the foremost hostess in the area, had yet to invite him to a party. He would certainly clear his engagements to attend her soiree—and be granted the honor of dancing with her one remaining unmarried daughter.

He'd received an invitation to her gathering two days later.

The ever-vigilant Arthur Timstone had already reported that rather than being shunned or immersed in scandal after her abduction, Miss Briggeham was the toast of the village. Still, Eric knew that Mrs. Nordfield's stamp of approval was necessary to ensure that Miss Briggeham didn't suffer socially from her encounter with the Bride Thief—an encounter he'd been unable to erase from his mind.

Once he'd realized that Miss Briggeham had provided the authorities with little new information regarding the Bride Thief, Eric had assumed he'd forget all about her.

He'd assumed incorrectly.

Her words, uttered in that wistful tone, had embedded themselves in his mind. *This has been a grand adventure. . . . I've always wanted one, you see.* He could well imagine a young woman such as Miss Briggeham—an on-the-shelf-spinster bluestocking who'd spent her entire life in Tunbridge Wells—yearning for adventure.

I'm often lonely myself. Her poignant statement had touched him deep inside. He sensed a kindred spirit in her, and God knew he understood loneliness. The isolation brought on by the secret life he led sometimes threatened to strangle him. Even when he was surrounded by people, he still felt alone.

Training his gaze on the house, he noted that all the French windows leading into the crowded ballroom stood open to capture the cool evening breezes. In the garden, crickets chirped a nocturnal chorus, competing with the strains of violin music, the hum of conversation, and the tinkling of crystal glasses drifting toward him from the house. Sweet scents floated from the rose trellis, surrounding him in a cape of flowery fragrance.

The soiree was in full swing. But where was Miss Briggeham? Remaining hidden in the shadows, he craned his neck, searching the crowded room. When he finally caught sight of her, his heart performed an odd leap.

Yes, indeed, his machinations had clearly succeeded, for it certainly appeared that Miss Briggeham was faring well, just as Arthur had reported. She currently stood in the midst of half a dozen ladies, who surrounded her in a way that reminded him of vultures circling carrion. Two gentlemen joined the throng, each jostling the other to hand Miss Briggeham a glass of pale yellow punch.

Positioning himself more comfortably against the rough stone exterior, he extracted his gold cigar case from his waistcoat, then withdrew a cheroot. After lighting it, he inhaled the fragrant smoke and observed the woman he'd been unable to dismiss from his thoughts.

Her chestnut hair was arranged in a simple chignon at her nape. Although her pale blue muslin gown was modest, it couldn't completely hide her feminine curves. She stood straight, her head held high, but even with perfect posture she remained petite in stature.

Another gentleman bearing punch joined the group surrounding her, and Eric marveled that she could stand to drink one more glassful. His gaze fastened on her lips, which spread in a smile of thanks to the newcomer. Even at a distance there was no mistaking the beguiling fullness of her mouth. The newcomer made her a bow, eyeing her with an expression of unmistakable interest. Annoyance pulled down Eric's brows, an inexplicable reaction that irked him further.

He observed her for a quarter hour. Gentlemen and ladies alike buzzed around her like bees to a hive. At first he thought she was enjoying herself, but after several minutes' observation, he realized that her smile seemed forced. And it appeared she was gritting her teeth. Curious reactions, surely.

But even more unusual were the unmistakable twinges of sadness he detected shadowing her eyes. Clearly she tried to hide her unhappiness, but by watching her closely, he was sure he wasn't mistaken. The instant she believed her audience wasn't looking, her smile vanished, her shoulders slumped, and she gazed toward the windows leading outdoors with unmistakable longing.

Guilt, along with sympathy, tugged at his heart. Why was she unhappy? Was her encounter with the Bride Thief somehow responsible?

With a brisk nod and tight smile, she extricated herself from the group surrounding her, making her way around the perimeter of the room. A tall, fair-haired gentleman Eric recognized as Viscount Carsdale waylaid her, quite close to the French windows near where he stood. While he couldn't hear their conversation, he clearly saw Carsdale lift her gloved hand to his lips for a kiss that lingered far longer than proper, while the bastard treated himself to a prolonged leer down Miss Briggeham's bodice.

Bloody hell. Outrage pumped through Eric. Was Carsdale treating her with so little respect because of her encounter with the Bride Thief? Was this the source of her unhappiness? Were other men treating her the same way? Damn it, perhaps her reputation *had* suffered. He recalled the feel of her enticing curves pressed against him, and his jaw tightened. He wouldn't allow anyone to disrespect her—especially as a result of the situation he'd unwittingly thrust her into.

Tossing his half-smoked cheroot on the ground, he extinguished the glowing tip beneath his heel, intent upon rescuing Miss Briggeham from that bastard Carsdale. The instant he entered the room from the terrace, however, Lydia Nordfield plastered herself to his side.

"I see you've finished your cigar, my lord," she cooed, commandeering his arm in her steely grip.

He offered her a polite bow, while deciding the best way to shake her off. Miss Briggeham, however, managed to escape from Carsdale on her own, so he spent a few more moments with his hostess. Accepting a glass of champagne, he responded to her banal chatter, all the while keeping one eye trained on the petite, chestnut-haired woman making her way across the room. Two gentlemen he recognized as Misters Babcock and Whitmore—both sons of local wealthy men—intercepted her. Eric's fingers tightened around his champagne flute when Babcock kissed her hand.

He was about to stride across the room, when Miss Briggeham pointed out the French windows toward the terrace. The instant Misters Babcock and Whitmore turned to look outside, she dashed across the parquet floor and secreted herself behind a copse of palms. Eric bit back a smile and nodded absently at whatever Mrs. Nordfield was saying. Hmmm . . . Those palms looked very similar to the ones he kept in his conservatory—a coincidence that definitely warranted further investigation.

Sammie pushed her spectacles higher on her nose and cautiously peered through the dense foliage provided by Mrs. Nordfield's potted palms and ferns.

Good heavens, there they were—Alfred Babcock and Henry Whitmore. They remained near the French windows, confusion stamped on their faces as they clearly wondered where she'd nipped off to.

Sammie heaved a sigh. Never in her life had she encountered two more tiresome individuals. Worse, it was nearly impossible to maintain a serious countenance in their company, as Mister Babcock's excessive, bristly facial hair lent him an unfortunate resemblance to a hedgehog, while Mister Whitmore's black hair, close-set eyes, and beak-like nose put Sammie firmly in mind of a crow. She'd listened to them extol the methods of tying the perfect cravat until she'd wanted to strangle them with their own neckwear. In desperation she'd pointed toward the darkened garden and exclaimed, "Look! A herd of deer!" The instant they turned their heads, she'd sprinted toward sanctuary as if pursued by a pack of rabid dogs. She was safe for now . . . but how long could she hope to remain undiscovered?

"La, Sammie, whatever are you doing hiding amongst Mrs. Nordfield's plants? Are you all right?"

Sammie barely stifled a groan. Clearly not as long as she'd hoped. She turned to face Hermione. Her beautiful sister, whose eyes filled with gentle concern, flapped open her delicate lace fan and joined her behind the palm fronds.

"I'm fine, but please keep your voice down," Sammie implored, peeking through the leaves.

"Sorry," Hermione whispered. "Who are you avoiding? Mama?"

"Not at this particular moment, but that is an excellent suggestion. Right now I'm trying to escape the dandies standing by the French windows."

Hermione craned her neck. "Misters Babcock and Whitmore? They seem like perfectly nice gentlemen to me."

"They're lovely, if you like cabbage-headed nincompoops."

"Oh dear. Have they been unkind to you?"

Hermione looked ready to do battle in her defense, and a rush of gratitude warmed Sammie. Forcing a smile, she said, "No. Even worse. They both wish to *dance* with me."

Hermione's fierce expression relaxed. "Which is why you've taken up residence behind the palm trees."

"Exactly."

"What are you two doing back here?" The loud whisper close to her ear nearly startled Sammie out of her skin. Turning, she watched her sister Emily jostle herself into position next to Hermione.

"You're always involved in the most unusual pursuits, Sammie," Emily said, adjusting her cream-colored muslin gown, her green eyes alight with interest. "Upon whom are we spying?"

Before Sammie could reply, Hermione reported in a loud whisper, "She's not spying. She's hiding from Misters Babcock and Whitmore."

An inelegant snort completely at odds with her ethereal beauty escaped Emily. "The Hedgehog and the Beady-eyed Crow? Wise decision, Sammie. Those two could bore the paint from the walls."

"Precisely," Sammie agreed in an undertone. "Which is why both of you must return to the party. Someone is bound to notice the *three* of us standing back here. In fact—"

"Whatever are the three of you doing there behind the palms?"

Lucille's high-pitched voice all but echoed off the wall-paper. Reaching out, Sammie grabbed her sister's gloved hand and unceremoniously yanked her behind the foliage, setting the leaves in motion.

"Please keep your voice down, Lucille," Sammie begged. Good heavens, her quest for peace was turning into a complete debacle. A very *crowded* debacle. She knew her sisters meant well, but the potted plants barely provided enough hiding space for two people. Four was simply out of the question.

Pressing tighter into the corner, Sammie barely suppressed a gasp when Hermione's heel pressed down on her toe. "You must all leave," she said in a desperate whisper. "Shoo!" She waved her arms at her siblings as best she could manage in the tight quarters.

"Stop elbowing me, Lucille," Emily said in a heated undertone, ignoring Sammie's plea.

"Then stop bumping me with your hips," Lucille shot back. "And keep your ostrich feathers to yourself," she added, flicking the plume adorning Emily's headband.

"Who is nudging my back?" Hermione asked, trying to look behind her. "I was here first—"

"Actually, *I* was here first," Sammie muttered, yanking her abused toes from under Hermione's heel.

While her three siblings argued about who was jabbing whom, Sammie separated the palm fronds and peered across the room, praying no one noticed the activity occurring behind the palms.

Her prayers were in vain.

Misters Babcock and Whitmore, among others, were casting curious glances toward the copse of potted trees. But worse, Mama was approaching the foliage, eyeing the quivering leaves with clear suspicion.

"Mama is coming this way," Sammie said, flapping her hands at her trio of sisters. "If she finds me, she'll parade me all around the room again and I'll be a candidate for Bedlam. Please, help me!"

The mention of their mother immediately silenced her sisters, then set them into action. Hermione laid a comforting hand on Sammie's shoulder and whispered brusquely, "Lucille, you take Mama on the right, Emily, the left. I'll bring up the rear."

Employing the military-like flanking procedure they'd used for years to divert their mother's attention, Hermione, Lucille, and Emily emerged from behind the palms in a rainbow-hued flurry of muslin, feathers, and ribbons. Peeking through the leaves, Sammie watched them intercept Mama and adroitly turn her around. Mama glanced over her shoulder toward the trees and frowned.

"Have you girls seen Sammie?" Mama's question drifted over the music. Sammie shrank back against the wall, willing herself to become invisible.

"Why, I believe she's by the punch bowl," Lucille said, leading Mama away. They disappeared through the crowd, and Sammie blew out a long breath.

You are nothing but a coward, her conscience scolded. Sammie balked at the description, but she couldn't deny its truth. She hadn't resorted to hiding behind the shrubbery at a party in years, but drastic action had been necessary. And while she couldn't spend the remainder of the interminable evening hiding, she desperately needed a moment to herself before rejoining Mrs. Nordfield's soiree. Her temples throbbed with the effort of remaining pleasant while everyone stared at her, whispered about her, and asked her ceaseless questions. Heavens above, she'd never expected that the end result of her mistaken abduction would be . . . *this*.

While she was grateful that no breath of scandal had touched her family as a result of her late-night encounter with England's Most Sought-After Man, no one, not even Mama, had predicted that Sammie would become the Most

Sought-After Female in the village. No longer was she "Poor, Odd, Sammie." No, now she was regarded as "Witty, Fascinating Sammie Who'd Conversed with the Bride Thief."

Surely her newfound popularity should have pleased her. Flowers arrived daily from gentlemen who only a fortnight ago had avoided her. Female callers stopped by every afternoon or sent invitations to tea.

Yes, everyone who had previously slighted her—whether to her face or behind her back—now professed to be her friend. Everyone clamored for details about her adventure with the Bride Thief. In spite of the fact that she was an abysmal dancer, gentlemen wished to partner her for the quadrille and the waltz. The ladies of the village now sought her counsel—but on ludicrous subjects such as fashion and jewelry. Even her own family, with the exception of Hubert, lavished praise upon her, as if she were a clever pet who'd performed a remarkable trick.

No, she couldn't enjoy this surge of popularity because in her soul, in the deeply buried part of her that had always secretly longed for acceptance, she knew that the interest in her was only superficial. None of her new "friends" were interested in *her*. They only wished to question her about the Bride Thief. She knew full well that once their curiosity was satisfied, their interest would quickly wane. And somehow, even though she tried not to let it, that hurt worse than the twitters she'd learned to ignore over the years.

Yet she'd tolerated the constant stream of callers, not willing to diminish her sisters' and Mama's utter delight with her newfound popularity. Smiling until her face ached, she endured countless hours sitting in the drawing room, sipping enough tea to float a frigate, answering countless questions, all the while wishing she were with Hubert, poring over their scientific journals, assisting him in his Chamber of Experiments, and furthering her own experimental studies.

When she wasn't trapped in the drawing room, she stood for endless hours before the seamstress, being fitted for frilly gowns that made her feel conspicuous and awkward. Yet she'd gone along with Mama's plans, refusing to mar her mother's happiness at her popularity, and reluctant to tempt the fates that miraculously hadn't immersed her family in scandal.

Even more vexing than the nonstop visitors, however, were the constant rounds of fetes, soirees, and musicales. Although she loved music, she normally attended few such functions. She'd grown weary of trying to mold herself into a graceful, witty conversationalist, and enduring indifference—or even worse, pitiful expressions that clearly said, *Oh, isn't it a shame that poor Samantha isn't more like her beautiful sisters.*

She'd philosophically accepted her physical and social shortcomings long ago, knowing her family loved her in spite of them. Still, social functions made her feel uncomfortable and inept. Yet over the past fortnight she'd attended literally dozens, her smile permanently affixed to her lips, unwilling to disappoint Mama. Her patience, however, had reached its limit. How long could this intolerable situation continue? When would these people grow tired of her and leave her alone? *Soon, dear God, please make it soon.* Thankfully this soiree was the last one scheduled for a while—at least that she knew of. She could only hope Mama wasn't hoarding another stack of invitations somewhere.

She heaved a heartfelt sigh. As much as she wished to remain hidden, she knew the time had come to return to the party. But she vowed to avoid Misters Babcock and Whitmore. And to depart the festivities as soon as possible.

Bracing herself with a fortifying breath, she turned.

And found herself staring at a perfectly knotted, snowy white cravat.

Startled, she stepped back, her legs bumping the huge urns containing the palms and ferns. Thank goodness the porcelain urns were so tall, else she would have tumbled backward and fallen ignominiously into the plants. Tilting back her head, she looked upward. Her gaze met questioning dark brown eyes.

Sammie drew a deep breath and tried to curb her impatience. Lord above, it was utterly impossible to find a private moment. Couldn't this blasted man find some other corner to escape to? Her gaze wandered over this latest intruder upon her solitude. His black, formal evening attire, accentuated by a silver brocade waistcoat and blinding white shirt, fit his tall, broad-shouldered frame perfectly. His face was arresting rather than handsome, as if an artist had hewn his features with bold, broad strokes to create high cheekbones, a square jaw, perfectly straight nose, and a firm yet well-shaped mouth. Her sisters and Mama would no doubt think him very attractive.

She thought him a cursed pest and fervently wished he would take his leave of her sanctuary.

"Forgive me for startling you, Miss Briggeham," the gentleman said in a deep voice. "After I observed that trio of ladies departing from behind the trees here, I assumed the spot was empty."

Sammie barely managed to suppress a groan. He knew her name. Just like everyone else at this soiree, he no doubt wished to question her regarding the Bride Thief. At best, he'd merely lure her into mind-numbing conversation, then somehow lead the discussion to the topic on everyone's lips. At worse, he'd question her *and* ask her to dance.

Striving to be polite, even as she inched away from him, she asked, "Have we met, sir?"

He stared at her for several seconds before replying, and Sammie's skin heated under his intense regard.

"Yes, we have, however it was a number of years ago."

He made her a formal bow. "I am the Earl of Wesley. At your service."

Pushing her spectacles higher on her nose, Sammie peered at him, then frowned. "Forgive me, my lord, for not recognizing you. I thought you were much . . . older."

"That would have been my father. He died five years ago."

Heat rushed into Sammie's cheeks at her *faux pas*. No doubt every other person present knew the earl's father had died years ago. Except her. Just another reason she inwardly cringed at these social gatherings. She never knew the proper things to say. "I'm sorry. I didn't mean—"

"Quite all right," he said, waving his hand in a dismissive fashion. He quirked one brow at her, mischief lurking in his dark eyes. "Tell me, Miss Briggeham, what brings you to seek refuge behind the foliage?"

Pesky gentlemen such as yourself. She quirked a brow right back at him. "I might ask the same of you, my lord."

He smiled, displaying white, even teeth. "I'll tell you if you tell me."

Sensing his amusement, and relieved that he'd chosen to overlook her *faux pas*, she said, "Two gentlemen were pestering me to dance."

"Indeed? Which gentlemen?"

"Misters Babcock and Whitmore." She peeked through the ferns and noted the gentlemen in question still stood near the French windows.

He moved closer to her and looked through the camouflaging leaves. Sammie inhaled, filling her head with a combination of sandalwood and—she sniffed again—an intriguing scent she could only describe as *clean*. She pointed to the duo by the windows.

"Ah, yes, I am acquainted with them," Lord Wesley said, "although only in passing. I'm afraid I do not attend many local social gatherings."

"Consider yourself fortunate," Sammie muttered, releasing the leaves. "If you'll excuse me, Lord Wesley—"

"Of course, Miss Briggeham. However, you might wish to remain for another moment." He separated several leaves higher than Sammie could reach and peered through the opening. "It appears Misters Babcock and Whitmore are looking for someone. If you show yourself now . . ."

His voice trailed off and Sammie suppressed a shudder. While she had no great urge to talk to Lord Wesley, he appeared, for the moment at least, to be the lesser of two evils.

"Thank you for the warning, my lord. Under the circumstances, I believe I'll remain here for a few more minutes." Straightening to her full height, she realized he was quite tall. The top of her head barely reached his shoulder. She wished she possessed such useful height. How convenient to be able to reach high shelves in the Chamber without the aid of a ladder.

As it appeared he wasn't going to leave her alone, she reminded him, "You never did say what brings you behind the foliage, my lord."

"Mrs. Nordfield was chasing me down with the accuracy of a seasoned hunter, and with what I can only describe as a 'matchmaking gleam' in her eye. This was the most expedient place to duck out of sight for a moment."

Sammie nodded in sympathy. She could well imagine Lydia Nordfield tracking after the eligible Lord Wesley like a hound after a fox. And that "matchmaking gleam" was familiar to Sammie as well, much to her dismay. It was the same look Mama had been casting in her direction with renewed determination over the past two weeks. The mere thought sent an uneasy chill down her spine.

Her gaze ran down his tall, muscular body. "Don't fret, Lord Wesley. No doubt you can outrun Mrs. Nordfield. You appear to be quite a healthy specimen."

"Er, thank you."

Peeking through the ferns once more, Sammie observed with dismay that Mama was conversing with Misters Babcock and Whitmore. At that instant the trio turned toward the copse of potted plants, and Mama's eyes narrowed. Gasping, Sammie hastily stepped back, as if the ferns had caught fire.

"I'm afraid I must be going, Lord Wesley," she said, performing an awkward curtsy. "I fear my mother has detected my presence. Good evening to you."

He made her a bow. "And to you, Miss Briggeham."

She scooted from behind the palms. Keeping her head bent low and eyes downcast, she prayed no one would observe her. Before she'd taken a half-dozen steps, Mama pounced upon her like a cat after a ball of string.

"Samantha! There you are, darling. I've looked for you everywhere. Misters Babcock and Whitmore wish to *dance* with us! Isn't that wonderful?"

Sammie looked over Mama's shoulder at the two hovering dandies and forced herself to smile, although she suspected she merely bared her teeth. "Wonderful doesn't begin to describe my feelings, Mama."

Mama beamed. "Excellent! The quartet is about to begin a quadrille."

"Actually," Sammie said, trying to keep the impatience from her voice, "I don't want to—"

"Miss a single note," Mama finished with a laugh and a warning glare. "Come along, Samantha."

Somehow managing to suppress a groan, Sammie cast a quick longing glance toward the sanctuary of the potted trees. She recognized that admonishing look in Mama's eye. The only way she could hope to escape the quadrille would be if Mrs. Nordfield's floor obligingly opened up and swallowed her. She stared at the wooden floor, praying for a miracle, willing the parquet to yawn open before her, but her prayers went unanswered. Stiffening her spine, Sammie braced herself to allow Misters Babcock and Whitmore to lead her to the dance floor, vowing that this was the last soiree she would ever attend.

"I'm afraid Miss Briggeham promised the upcoming quadrille to me," came Lord Wesley's deep voice behind them.

Sammie, Mama, and the dandies turned around in unison. Sammie watched Mama's eyes widen at the sight of the earl.

"Lord Wesley," said Mama, dropping into a low, graceful curtsy. "What a lovely surprise to see you here." Mama straightened and flashed him her most beatific smile, while adroitly elbowing Misters Babcock and Whitmore aside. "And how divine that you wish to dance with Samantha."

"Yes, divine," Sammie echoed without a lick of enthusiasm.

Amusement flashed in Lord Wesley's brown eyes. "Perhaps, Miss Briggeham, you'd prefer to accompany me on a tour of the gallery? I understand Mrs. Nordfield and her daughters are talented artists." He turned to Mama. "You're welcome to accompany us, Mrs. Briggeham, if you wish."

Mama's face lit up like a candle. "How kind you are, my lord. I would be delighted—"

"I say"—broke in Mr. Babcock, peering through his quizzing glass and thus resembling a one-eyed hedgehog—"If Miss Briggeham isn't going to dance the quadrille with Wesley, I think she should—"

A series of chirping sounds emitted from Mama's lips. "Heavens," she breathed, clutching Mr. Babcock's arm. "I feel quite faint. Mr. Babcock, will you and Mr. Whitmore please escort me to my husband?"

"Are you all right, Mama?" Sammie asked, knowing from experience that the question was expected of her. She also knew, however, that Mama would never "faint" without a settee nearby.

"I'm fine, darling. I simply need to rest for a moment. So much excitement, you know."

"Allow me to assist you, Mrs. Briggeham," Lord Wesley said, offering his hand. Mama waved aside his concern. "I'll be fine, thanks to the kind assistance of Misters Babcock and Whitmore. You two go tour the gallery. There's no need for me to chaperone. I can see from here that there are at least a dozen guests enjoying the paintings." Seizing Misters Babcock and Whitmore each firmly by an arm, Mama led them away, emitting several more chirps.

Sammie observed Lord Wesley from the corner of her eye and fought to hide a smile at the half-dazed, half-amused expression he fixed upon Mama's departing back.

"Your mother is very efficient at social . . ." his voice trailed off as he clearly struggled to find the proper word.

"Manipulation?" she suggested.

He turned to her, his lips twitching. "I was going to say strategy." Extending his elbow, he offered his arm. "Shall we tour the gallery?"

Sammie hesitated. "I appreciate you rescuing me, my lord. However, it is not necessary for you to continue the ruse."

"What ruse is that, Miss Briggeham?"

"The 'I'll escort you to the gallery so you aren't forced to dance with those nincom—I mean, gentlemen'—ruse. I'm most grateful, but—"

"You're quite welcome. However, it was no ruse. I very much would like the honor of your company."

She looked up at him, searching for the telltale signs of calculated speculation she'd grown accustomed to over the past weeks. To her surprise, however, she only saw what appeared to be warm courtesy. Still, he no doubt only wished to escort her to question her about the Bride Thief, a prospect that filled her with resignation. Deciding to get the inevitable over with as quickly as possible, she queried, "Why do you wish for my company?"

He leaned forward in a conspiratorial way. She breathed in, enjoying his clean scent even as she dreaded his answer. "I promised Mrs. Nordfield I would view her paintings, and I believe she wishes me to do so with her unmarried daughter. You would be doing me a service to accompany me." He leaned back. "Besides, I understand the paintings are . . . unusual, and I'd welcome your opinion."

"I'm afraid my knowledge of art is limited, my lord."

"With all due respect to our hostess, I fear 'art' is most likely not what we shall be observing, Miss Briggeham."

Laughter bubbled in Sammie's throat. At least this man was amusing. And after the way he'd rescued her from the horrors of the quadrille, she supposed she owed him a boon. Relaxing a bit for the first time in hours, she inclined her head and curved her gloved hand around his extended elbow. "You've piqued my interest, Lord Wesley. I'd be delighted to view the gallery with you."

Chapter 5

Eric walked slowly toward the long gallery, very much aware of the small, gloved hand resting lightly against his sleeve. Very much aware of the petite woman strolling next to him.

You've piqued my interest, Lord Wesley.

As you've piqued mine, Miss Briggeham.

The touch of her dainty hand radiated heated tingles up and down his arm. He wasn't sure why she evoked such a reaction in him, but there was no denying that she did.

They paused in front of the first canvas. From the corner of his eyes, he watched her study the painting for nearly a minute, angling her head first right, then left.

"It's very . . . interesting," she finally offered.

Eric stared at the hodgepodge of dark colors. "It's appallingly awful," he whispered.

A noise that sounded suspiciously like a giggle erupted from her throat, and she hastily coughed. She looked up at him, and he was struck by her eyes . . . keenly intelligent eyes that appeared magnified behind the thick lenses of her spectacles. They reminded him of aquamarines—brilliant, shining, and sparkling clear.

He studied her upturned face carefully. A smattering of pale freckles paraded across her small nose. His gaze drifted to her mouth and his attention was captured by one lone freckle dotting her pale skin near the corner of her upper lip . . . her sinfully plump upper lip that along with its equally full mate appeared too large for her heart-shaped face. Her thick, chestnut hair was pulled into a chignon, with artful curls framing her face. Several shiny strands had worked free of their pins, lending her a slightly disheveled air. A sudden urge to sift his fingers through those disarrayed curls washed over him, and his brow tugged downward in a frown.

She leaned a bit closer to him. "You're the art expert among us, my lord. What does this painting depict?"

He inhaled and a tantalizing whiff of honey tickled his senses, along with the faint scent of . . . freshly dug dirt? He suppressed a smile. The woman called a toad, a mouse, and a garden snake pets, and her "perfume" revealed she'd spent time digging in the mud before attending Mrs. Nordfield's party, yet that elusive trace of honey smelled good enough to eat. What an . . . intriguing combination.

Forcing his attention back to the god-awful painting, he said in a serious tone, "This is a barn during a particularly fierce rainstorm." He pointed to a shapeless brown blob. "Here you can see a horse dashing back to its stall." He looked down at her. "Do you not agree?"

She offered him a smile, and his breath caught as it had at the cottage. Her smile transformed her, lighting her features with an endearing hint of deviltry and mischief. "Hmmm," she said, tapping her chin with her fingertips. "I think it more likely that this is a painting of the bottom of a lake."

"Indeed? What would a horse be doing at the bottom of the lake?"

"But that blob isn't a horse at all, my lord. It is a large, openmouthed fish."

"Oh! I see you're admiring my portrait of dear Aunt Libby," Lydia Nordfield said, joining them at the picture. Her sharp eyes took note of Miss Briggeham's hand resting on his arm.

"A wonderful rendition," he murmured, schooling his features into a suitably serious expression. "Indeed, when Miss Briggeham and I have completed our tour of the gallery, I look forward to discussing your talents with you, Mrs. Nordfield."

Mrs. Nordfield snapped open her fan, waving it with a vigor that set her carefully arranged rows of sausage curls in motion. "Why, thank you, my lord. Of course, I'm delighted to accompany you—"

"I wouldn't dream of monopolizing your time," Eric said. "I shall seek you out once I've formed my impressions of your collection."

"I look forward to it, my lord," Mrs. Nordfield replied in a tone that made it clear that nothing short of death would keep her from discussing her art with him. She excused herself with clear reluctance.

"Heavens, whatever will you say to her?" Miss Briggeham asked in an undertone. "You compared dear Aunt Libby to a horse!"

"At least I didn't compare her to an openmouthed fish," he teased, and was rewarded with a becoming peach blush. "In truth, I most likely won't need to say anything, as Mrs. Nordfield will no doubt carry the conversation."

She nodded slowly, her expression turning serious. "You're quite right. I see that you share my mother's talent for—"

"Manipulation?" he broke in with a smile.

"No!" Her cheeks bloomed brighter. "I meant social gatherings. Polite conversation. Idle chitchat."

"I'm afraid it's inevitable given how many functions I've attended."

They strolled toward the next painting. "I suppose you're very popular."

He raised his brows. "I receive a great many invitations, if that's what you mean. But then, it appears you do as well."

A humorless laugh escaped her. "Yes, I'm afraid so. At least lately."

"You sound . . . disappointed?"

"I fear that in spite of my sisters' kindhearted attempts to teach me, I'm a horrible dancer. And as I'm sure you've discerned, I'm not an accomplished conversationalist on idle matters."

"On the contrary, Miss Briggeham, you've yet to bore me."

There was no mistaking the surprise that widened her eyes. They paused in front of the next painting and he forced himself to look at it. After careful consideration of the unrecognizable swirls, he ventured, "I'm at a loss. What do you think?"

"Perhaps this is dear Aunt Libby's vegetable garden?"

He turned toward her. "Or perhaps her husband?"

She laughed, her face again lighting up with that smile he could only describe as enchanting. After several seconds, however, her merriment faded. She opened her mouth, then closed it, a frown creasing her brow. Finally, she said, "I'm no good at pretending, my lord. If you wish to know about my encounter with . . . him, I prefer you simply ask and be done with it, rather than wasting your time escorting me about the room for half an hour to gently lead up to your queries."

"Him?"

"The Bride Thief." She slipped her hand from his arm, and he immediately missed its warmth. "I'm well aware that my mistaken abduction is the only reason everyone is seeking my company."

"Surely you do not believe that your popularity is based solely on your encounter with that Thief person."

"On the contrary, I'm positive it is. And a more vexing situation I've never encountered."

She started walking again, and he fell in step beside her, resisting the urge to recapture her hand and curve it through his arm. His heart pinched at her words, and his gaze quickly swept over the guests strolling the gallery. What was wrong with these people? Could they not see that Miss Briggeham was amusing and intelligent? But of course, her intellect would work against her. She was not flirtatious or frivolous, and he could well imagine that she would therefore not garner an abundance of male attention.

"I would have thought most young women would enjoy being the center of attention," he remarked, as they paused at another hideous painting.

"I fear I am not most young women." She huffed out a sigh. "Before my encounter with the Bride Thief, I enjoyed attending the occasional soiree. I'd settle myself amongst the matrons and chaperones, watch my sisters and mother dance, and visit with one of my dearest friends, Miss Waynesboro-Paxton."

"I don't believe I know her."

"She lives at the west boundary of the village. Unfortunately she was unable to attend this evening due to her health. Her eyesight is failing and she also suffers severe bouts of joint pain, the poor dear."

They walked toward the next painting, and she continued in an exasperated tone, "*Now*, however, there's a party to attend nearly every evening. In spite of the fact that I constantly trod on their toes, gentlemen insist on asking me to dance." She indicated her muslin gown with impatient hands. "I look ridiculous in these frilly clothes. I know nothing of fashion, yet ladies now solicit my opinion on the subject. Gentlemen approach me to discuss the weather. Lord Carsdale engaged me in conversation about the latest *rainfall* for nearly a *quarter hour*. And all of it is merely polite chatter to lead up to their questions regarding my abduction."

He barely managed to suppress the need to inform her that while Carsdale had discoursed on the weather, he'd also been leering down her bodice. His own gaze dipped and his lips tightened at the sight of her generous curves. Damn, no wonder Carsdale hadn't been able to take his eyes off her. "Did Lord Carsdale inquire about the Bride Thief?"

"*Everyone* has inquired."

"And what do you say?"

"The truth. That he was kind to me, especially after he realized his error. And that he only wants to help the women he steals."

"And how do people respond to that?"

"The men ask about his horse and whether or not he carried any weapons. And those two nincom—I mean, Misters Babcock and Whitmore—wished to know the details of how the gentleman tied his cravat."

Suppressing a smile, he asked, "And the ladies?"

"They heave sighs and ask such silly questions as 'was he handsome?' or 'was he strong?' or 'what color were his eyes?' "

"I see. And what do you tell them?"

"That his mask completely hid his features. And that he was very strong. He scooped me off the ground as if I weighed no more than a sack of flour."

You barely do, my dear. "How do you answer about his eyes?"

"I tell them it was too dark to tell. But his eyes were intense. And glowing with intelligence. And commitment to his cause."

"It sounds as if the brigand made quite an impression on you."

She halted, then turned to face him squarely, blue fire igniting her eyes. "He is *not* a brigand, Lord Wesley. He is a man committed to helping women in need, in spite of the risk to himself. He has nothing to gain and everything to lose by his unselfish actions. Dare I be so bold as to say that if more people were like him, the world would be a much better place, indeed."

Indignation, like her smile, did wonderful things to Miss Briggeham. Becoming color flushed her cheeks, and her chest rose and fell with her deep, rapid breaths. Her magnified eyes burned like blue braziers, filling him with the urge to slip her spectacles from her nose to observe that fire without any obstacles.

"In fact," she continued in a heated whisper, "I would dearly love to help the man in his noble cause."

Pleasure that she believed his cause noble filled him, but the feeling was quickly replaced by foreboding. Help the man? Bloody hell, what was she thinking? Whatever it was, he needed to discourage her. Immediately.

Forcing his voice to remain even, he asked, "How could you possibly help him?"

"I don't know. But if there was something I could do, I pledge I would."

"Don't be ridiculous, Miss Briggeham," he said more sharply than he'd meant to. "The man and his outrageous escapades are dangerous. It is preposterous for you to consider involving yourself with him."

The frigid look she leveled at him clearly indicated that he'd said the wrong thing and that their earlier companionability was severed. All vestiges of warmth disappeared from her eyes, and an acute sense of loss washed over him. "I'm only thinking of your welfare," he said.

"Do not concern yourself, my lord." Her frosty tone

matched the chill in her gaze. "I am quite capable of looking after myself. And allow me to congratulate you. Your
method of questioning me was much more clever than
most." She performed an awkward curtsy. "I bid you good
evening."

He stood, rooted to the spot, watching her hurry by several wandering couples on her way from the gallery. He
could not recall ever having been so summarily dismissed.
And if he had, it certainly wasn't by a woman. And he certainly couldn't remember anyone, save his father, looking
at him with such disdain. Clearly, in her opinion, he was no
better—albeit more clever—than all the other people who
had sought her company solely to glean information about
the Bride Thief, a fact that filled his chest with an odd, hollow ache.

Her pledge to help the Bride Thief echoed through his
mind, and his hands fisted at his sides. Bloody hell, she
couldn't possibly be contemplating trying to find the Bride
Thief and offer him her assistance. . . . Could she? While
he didn't fear that any efforts on her part to locate the Thief
would prove successful, he did worry that she might do
something that could prove potentially dangerous to herself. He well knew the dangers involved in what he did.

He raked his hands through his hair and blew out a frustrated breath in an attempt to calm the unease coursing
through him. On the bright side, Miss Briggeham had
clearly not suffered any social repercussions as a result of
his kidnapping blunder. Indeed, she was experiencing her
first taste of popularity—which, although she may not like
it, was certainly preferable to being ostracized.

Yes, all had worked out well for Miss Briggeham, and
he'd been fully prepared to cease worrying about her . . .
until she'd voiced her ridiculous pledge. He gave himself a
mental shake. What could she possibly do? *Nothing.* She
was simply making a statement, the way many women did.

Only instead of declaring that she'd dearly love to own a twenty-carat diamond, Miss Briggeham wished to help the Bride Thief. They were just words spoken in the heat of the moment. They meant nothing.

Precisely. Now he could stop thinking about her. About her huge aqua eyes that reflected a fascinating combination of intelligence, innocence, seriousness, mischief, and vulnerability. The fact that those eyes had last looked at him with chilled disdain instead of warmth unsettled him in a way he could not name . . . but he could forget that.

Just as he could forget those incredible lips, along with her curvaceous figure, both more suited to a practiced courtesan than a country miss.

Exiting the gallery, he caught sight of her heading toward the foyer, her mother at her heels.

Still, perhaps he should see Miss Briggeham one more time. Just to ascertain that she'd meant nothing by her comment. Yes, that was an excellent idea. He'd make a point to call on her within the next week.

Maybe even tomorrow.

Chapter 6

The morning after Mrs. Nordfield's soiree, Sammie sat at her escritoire, leafing through the ivory pages of her private journal—the place where all her secret fantasies lived. She paused at an entry dated three months earlier.

He was the most beautiful man I'd ever beheld, yet his beauty had little to do with his handsome features and manly physique. There was a kindness in his eyes, and a generosity in his spirit that attracted me—that and the fact that he overlooked faults that others did not. Indeed, he claimed it was those traits that others viewed as odd that so endeared me to him. He gazed at me as if I were the most beautiful woman he'd ever seen. Love shone from his eyes, warming me, but something else filled his gaze . . . a dark longing that sent heat rippling down my spine.

He gently touched my face, and his hands trembled, as did mine. Slowly he lowered his head until his mouth hovered just above mine.

"You're everything I've always wanted," he

*whispered against my lips, his breath beating softly
against my skin. Surely he could hear my heart
pounding, for it was about to burst from my chest.*

*His mouth brushed softly across mine, and my
pulse soared as if on wings. He then gathered me in
his strong arms, tucking my head beneath his chin.
"I love you, Samantha. I want us to travel the
world and share exciting adventures together."*

*I breathed in his wonderful scent and nodded my
agreement. I'd found the man of my heart.*

Sammie heaved a deep sigh, then gently closed her journal. Had she really been that naïve only three short months ago? Of course, three months ago, nary a gentleman had been interested in her. Now, however, she realized how silly and utterly unrealistic her fantasies were.

Based on what she'd observed so far, a man such as the one she'd created on the pages of her journal simply did not exist. While properly polite, at least to her face, none of the gentlemen now bestowing attention on her appealed to her. None wished to discuss meaningful topics, and there was no mistaking the glazed look in their eyes when she attempted to do so. And even while they brought her punch and conversed with her, it seemed as if they looked through her—until they brought the conversation around to the Bride Thief. Then their attention focused on her like a specimen under a microscope.

But none of them were interested in *her*. In what she thought or felt. None appeared to share her zest for adventure, or her thirst for knowledge. If they did, they clearly didn't choose to discuss such topics with her. Her mind had always told her as much, but in the deepest recesses of her heart, she'd always cherished a kernel of hope. . . .

Only on these vellum pages did she dare reveal her secret longings. Foolish, silly dreams that would never come true, but still, she couldn't stop them from invading her mind. And her heart. So rather than fight her yearnings, she recorded them, pouring out all her unfulfilled dreams of love and adventure, re-reading them on those long lonely nights when sleep eluded her.

Her sisters and Mama would be stunned if they knew that her logical, practical thoughts wandered in such a manner, and she was careful not to let them know. She couldn't bear to see their beautiful faces filled with well-intentioned but unwanted pity, knowing that "poor Sammie" would never live out any of her cherished dreams. Or find a man who embodied all her feminine imaginings . . . a man who loved adventure. Nature. Animals. Science.

Her.

Yes, growing up with three gorgeous sisters, she knew the futility of her longings. Gentlemen admired beauty above all else. And if a woman was not blessed with a lovely face, she at least had to possess feminine talents such as conversation, fashion sense, musical and dancing ability, and a pleasant singing voice.

No, there wasn't a man alive who would overlook all her resounding flaws. But he existed in her mind, and in her journal, and she would continue to write about him there. And dream . . .

With lingering thoughts of adventure wandering through her brain, an image of the Bride Thief flashed through her mind, bringing with it a warm tingle. Now *he* was a man who could inspire daydreams of adventure. For the first time in her life, she avidly read the Society pages in *The Times*, looking for word of him. The fact that a group of men had formed the Bride Thief Posse was most disturbing, and with a veritable fortune now being offered for his capture, the danger the Bride Thief faced increased significantly. Had he rescued any more women? Was he safe? She'd prayed for his safety every night before retiring, asking the Lord to watch over him.

She'd carefully worded her replies to the probing questions everyone from the magistrate to the neighbors had asked her, partly because she did not wish to say anything that could endanger the Thief, but also because her heart simply couldn't share all the wonderful, enthralling details of their short time together.

The Bride Thief. Yes, there was no denying he embodied many of the qualities her fantasy gentleman possessed. She would never forget the brief time she'd spent with him, the thrilling exhilaration of dashing through the dark forest with a man who seemed more mythical than real.

Yet he was flesh and blood, and impossible questions nudged at her. What was he like under the mask? Where did he live? Her imagination conjured up a hidden fortress, and she nearly laughed aloud at her fanciful thoughts. Of course she'd never know, but she *did* know he was a man to admire . . . a man of strong convictions and moral fiber. Certainly not the *brigand* so many people wished to cast him as. People such as Lord Wesley.

Her brows collapsed into a frown. For reasons she could not explain, her thoughts had circled back to the irritating man a dozen times since their meeting last evening. She'd easily dismissed all the fops she'd encountered. . . . Why hadn't she forgotten him?

Perhaps because he'd discussed topics other than fashion and the weather with her. Or the fact that he'd made her laugh. Perhaps because she'd actually enjoyed his company before their awkward parting. Before he'd proven himself to be no different than any of her other false admirers.

But no matter. She would most likely not find herself in Lord Wesley's company again. After all, except for last evening, she hadn't seen him in years. Even though her family enjoyed prominence in Tunbridge Wells, the earl's social world orbited far above hers. She knew from Mama that the earl spent most of his time in London. No doubt pursuing all manner of debauchery, as the nobility was wont to do.

Yet, while so many others gazed upon her with speculation and shrewd glances, there had initially been something in Lord Wesley's eyes—an unexpected warmth, a surprising kindness—that had put her at ease. And had attracted her.

She drew in a sharp breath. Attracted? Heavens, no! She most certainly was *not* attracted to that man! Of course any woman would find him physically . . . pleasing, but a handsome face meant nothing. Not when one was arrogant and presumptuous and claimed her desire to help a noble man was "preposterous."

No, indeed, she didn't find him the least bit attractive. The only reason she hadn't dismissed him from her mind was because he had managed to anger her . . . and recalling their parting angered her still. Yes, that was all there was to it.

Satisfied, she carefully tied her journal closed with a strip of satin ribbon, then slid the well-worn leather book into the hidden compartment she'd fashioned in her escritoire.

Rising, she wandered to her bedchamber window. The late-afternoon sun gleamed, casting a swatch of bright warmth across the colorful braided throw rug.

Pushing aside the dark green velvet drapery, she opened the window, then leaned on the sill to gaze upon the grounds. Flowery scent wafted up from Mama's roses, which bloomed in a wild profusion of reds and pinks. No one in the village had finer roses than Cordelia Briggeham, and Sammie loved to wander the paths meandering through Mama's garden, breathing in the glorious, heady scent.

The tap of footsteps on the terrace caught her attention.

Looking down, she saw Hubert crossing the flagstones with his gangly stride, nearly staggering under the weight of a large box.

"What do you have there, Hubert?" she called.

Hubert stopped and peered upward, his face breaking into a wide grin at the sight of her. A lock of chestnut hair fell across his forehead, lending him a childlike air at odds with his sixteen years.

"Hallo!" he called. "The new telescope has finally arrived! I'm off to the Chamber. Would you care to join me?"

"Most definitely. I'll join you in a few moments." She waved, then watched Hubert head toward the old barn that he'd converted into his laboratory several years ago. Sammie left her bedchamber and walked toward the stairs, excited at the prospect of seeing the new telescope. As she approached the landing, Mama's voice drifted upward.

"How lovely of you to call, my lord. And such beautiful flowers! Chester, please escort his lordship to the parlor. I'll see to this bouquet and inform Samantha she has a guest."

"Yes, Mrs. Briggeham," intoned Chester in his deep, butler voice.

Botheration! No doubt the "my lord" currently on his way to the parlor was that annoying Viscount Carsdale, come to discuss the weather. Sammie leaned against the wall and fought the urge to sprint back to her bedchamber and hide in her wardrobe. She'd have done just that if she'd thought there was any hope of avoiding Mama and her guest, but the swish of Mama's skirts and the tread of her feet upon the stairs indicated she was trapped. Drawing a bracing breath, she met Mama at the top of the stairs. Mama bore a large bouquet of summer flowers and a radiant smile.

"Samantha!" Mama said in an excited undertone. "You have a caller, darling. And you'll never guess who it is!"

"Viscount Carsdale?"

Mama's eyes widened. "Heavens, is he planning to call upon you as well? You *must* tell me these things, darling."

"What do you mean 'as well'? Who is Chester showing to the parlor?"

Mama leaned forward, her face alight with delight. "Lord *Wesley*." She breathed his name with a reverence normally reserved for saints and monarchs.

Much to her annoyance, a tingle that felt suspiciously like anticipation skittered down Sammie's spine. What on earth was he doing here? Did he wish to continue their discussion regarding the Bride Thief? If so, his visit would be brief, indeed, for she had no intention of answering any more of his questions or listening to any more unkind words issued toward the heroic man. Or had he perhaps called for some other reason? If so, she couldn't imagine what. And why had he brought her flowers?

Mama thrust the bouquet under Sammie's nose and said, "He brought you these. Aren't they magnificent? Oooh, flowers from an *earl*. . . . I cannot wait to tell Lydia." Her eyes quickly assessed Samantha's plain gray gown. "Dear, oh, dear, you really should change into one of your new gowns, but I suppose this will have to do. We do not want to keep his lordship waiting."

Commandeering Sammie's arm with a strength that belied her petite proportions, Mama all but propelled her down the stairs, then down the corridor toward the parlor, whispering terse instructions the entire way.

"Don't forget to smile, darling," Mama said, "and make sure you agree with everything the earl says."

"But—"

"And be sure to inquire after his health," Mama continued, "but do *not* broach any of those unladylike topics such as mathematics and science you are so fond of."

"But—"

"And whatever you do, do *not* mention Isadore, Cuthbert, or Warfinkle. It is not necessary that the earl be apprised of your . . . unusual pets." She cast Sammie a narrowed-eyed, sidelong glance. "They *are* outdoors, are they not?"

"Yes, but—"

"Excellent." They paused in front of the parlor door, and Mama patted her cheek. "I'm very happy for you, darling."

Before Sammie could even attempt to utter a word, Mama opened the parlor door and sailed across the threshold. "Here she is, Lord Wesley," she announced, nearly yanking Sammie off her feet. "I'll rejoin you in a few moments—just as soon as I've seen to these lovely flowers and arranged for some refreshments." She beamed an angelic smile, then withdrew, leaving the door properly ajar.

Although anxious to join Hubert and his new telescope as soon as possible, reluctant curiosity about the reason for the earl's call pulled at Sammie. Determined to be polite, she turned toward her guest.

He stood in the center of the diamond-patterned Axminster rug, tall, imposing, perfectly turned out in glossy black boots, fawn-colored riding breeches, and a midnight-blue jacket that hugged his masculine frame to perfection. For just an instant, she inexplicably, and uncharacteristically, wished she were wearing one of her new gowns.

The only aspects of his appearance that weren't perfect were his cravat, which looked as if he'd yanked upon it, and his dark hair, which looked as if he'd raked his hands through it. She admitted, albeit grudgingly, that these flaws in his appearance were somehow . . . endearing.

She nearly rolled her eyes at her choice of word. He wasn't in the least endearing. He was annoying. Questioning her regarding the Bride Thief in what could only be described as an underhanded manner, then scoffing at her desire to aid the heroic man, claiming to be concerned for her welfare. What enormous impudence! Well, the sooner she greeted him and discovered the reason for his call, the sooner she could show him on his way.

"Good afternoon, Lord Wesley," she said, attempting her best, for Mama's sake, to sound friendly.

"And the same to you, Miss Briggeham."

"Er, thank you for the flowers."

"You're welcome." His gaze swept over the room, taking in the abundance of bouquets that adorned every available surface. "Although, if I'd known that you already possessed so many floral tributes, I would have brought you something else."

Her gaze followed his, and she couldn't suppress a sigh. "Mama says a woman can never have too many flowers, yet I shudder to think of all the poor plants that have been beheaded for these bouquets." The instant the words left her mouth, she realized how impolite they must sound to a man who'd just presented her with flowers. Hoping to make up for her *faux pas*, she asked in her politest voice, "Would you care to sit down, my lord?"

"No, thank you." He walked toward her, his gaze resting on hers in a way that oddly unsettled her. When only several feet separated them, he said, "I prefer to stand to express my regrets that we parted company on a strained note last evening. I did not mean to upset you."

The warmth radiating from his velvety brown eyes indicated his sincerity, but she'd learned over the past few weeks that seemingly sincere words flowed from gentlemen's lips like honey from a hive.

"You did not upset me, Lord Wesley."

When he raised his brows in a manner that clearly indicated he didn't believe her, she clarified, "You *annoyed* me."

Something that looked like amusement flashed in his eyes. "Ah. Then please allow me to express my regrets for *annoying* you. In spite of how it may have appeared, I was not trying to glean information from you. And I merely wished to point out the extreme folly of your desire to aid a wanted criminal."

Her hands clenched. "You express your regrets for annoying me, my lord, yet you continue to do so by again offering your unsolicited opinion."

"I assure you I am—"

"I say, Sammie," Hubert's voice broke in from just beyond the doorway. "What's keeping you?" Turning, Sammie watched Hubert stride into the parlor, then stop dead at the sight of her guest. "Oh, I beg your pardon," he said, his face flushing red. "I didn't realize you were entertaining."

"No reason to apologize," she assured Hubert with a smile she hoped didn't betray her relief at his interruption. "The earl is a very busy man. I'm sure he won't wish to occupy himself with me much longer." From the corner of her eye she noticed a whisper of a smile pass the earl's lips.

Striving to keep her voice level, Sammie performed the necessary introductions, watching the earl closely, all her protective instincts for Hubert on alert. Last week, when Viscount Carsdale had called upon her, she'd introduced Hubert to the gentleman. Hubert's face had fallen when the viscount's gaze had flicked over him with dismissive disdain, flooding Sammie with the urge to slap the arrogant man. She was well-accustomed to social slights and had learned to disregard them, but Hubert was still sensitive to such cuts. If the earl acted in a similar fashion . . .

Surprise suffused her when Lord Wesley extended his hand in a friendly, unaffected manner. "A pleasure to meet you, lad," he said.

"The pleasure's mine, my lord," Hubert said, his face flushing deeper. He returned his attention to Sammie. "Sorry to interrupt, but when you didn't meet me in the Chamber as you'd promised, I grew concerned that the

Cricket had waylaid you." A grin flashed across his face. "Thought you might need rescuing."

I did indeed, but not from Mama. Before she could respond, Lord Wesley asked, "Chamber?"

"My Chamber of Experiments," Hubert said. "I converted the old barn into a laboratory."

Interest filled Lord Wesley's gaze. "Indeed? And what do you do there?"

"All manner of experiments." Hubert cast a quick, self-conscious glance toward Sammie, then continued. "I also use it for my inventions and my astronomy studies."

"I've an interest in astronomy myself," the earl said. "I'm hoping the weather will be clear this evening so I might view the stars."

Hubert's face lit up. "As am I. It's a fascinating science, is it not? Sammie . . . I mean, Samantha, loves it as well."

Lord Wesley's gaze shifted to her. "Do you, indeed, Miss Briggeham?"

"Yes," she said briskly. "In fact, I was about to join Hubert in his Chamber when you called." Surely the earl would realize her broad hint and take his leave.

"My new telescope just arrived from London," Hubert reported to the earl. "Perhaps you'd like to see it?"

Sammie barely squelched a horrified squeak. "I'm sure Lord Wesley has pressing matters awaiting him, Hubert."

There was no mistaking the amusement glittering in the earl's eyes. "I do?"

"Don't you?"

"Actually, I'd be very interested to see Hubert's telescope."

"Surely you don't wish to—"

"Oh, it's a very fine one, my lord," Hubert broke in. " 'Twould be an honor to show it to you."

"I accept your kind invitation. Thank you." Lord Wesley offered Sammie a smile that appeared distinctly smug, a fact that tensed her shoulders. Extending his arm toward her, he said, "Shall we, Miss Briggeham?"

Mentally cursing her beloved brother for including the bothersome man in their outing, she forced a smile. She debated ignoring his arm, but decided not to give him the satisfaction of acknowledging that his presence disturbed her in any way. Besides, Hubert was clearly excited at the prospect of showing off his telescope. Surely she could endure the earl's presence for a short time longer . . . provided he did not voice disparaging words about the Bride Thief again. If he did, she'd simply change the subject, then send him on his way with all deliberate speed. And after today, she'd most likely never see him again.

Yes, that was a very simple, logical, practical plan. Resting her hand lightly on Lord Wesley's sleeve, they followed Hubert from the room.

Eric strolled along a winding garden path flanked by a profusion of roses, and tried to hide the smile that tugged incessantly on his lips. Miss Briggeham's fingers rested on his sleeve with what appeared to be all the enthusiasm of one touching a large, hairy, potentially poisonous insect. He had to admit that her reaction to him piqued his interest and curiosity. Women were always only too pleased to receive, as well as seek, his company. Perhaps such would still be the case were he not an earl, but certainly being titled and wealthy guaranteed him an excess of female attention.

Except, obviously, for Miss Samantha Briggeham, who looked as if she'd just as soon toss him into the privet hedges than spend another minute with him. When her brother had invited him to view his telescope, Miss Briggeham had looked as if she'd swallowed her tongue—a fact that simultaneously annoyed and amused him.

Determined to break the silence between them, he remarked, "Your brother mentioned a 'Cricket' earlier. Who, or what, is that?"

A subtle blush stole over her cheeks. "It's merely a silly name we call our mother. She tends to chirp when overtaken by the vapors."

"I see," he murmured, recalling with amusement that Mrs. Briggeham had indeed chirped last evening when she'd claimed to feel faint—just before hauling Misters Babcock and Whitmore away.

They walked for nearly a full minute in silence, and for reasons he could not explain, Eric took perverse delight in deliberately keeping their pace at a near crawl to counteract Miss Briggeham's not-as-subtle-as-she-believed attempts to hurry him along. Noting Hubert was far enough ahead of them not to be able to hear their conversation, the devil inside him prompted him to say, "You didn't want me to join you. May I ask why?"

She turned quickly, peering at him through her thick spectacles before turning her attention once more to the path in front of them. When she didn't answer for several long seconds, he prompted, "Tell me. Do not fear you will hurt my tender feelings. I'm quite impervious to verbal barbs, I assure you."

"Very well, my lord. Since you insist, I shall be perfectly blunt. I don't believe I like you."

"I see. And therefore you do not relish the thought of my company."

"Precisely."

"I must say, Miss Briggeham, I don't believe anyone has ever said such a thing to me before."

She sent him an arch, sidelong glance. "I find that very difficult to believe, Lord Wesley."

He should have been appalled at her temerity—and at the unmistakable insult that was only slightly tempered by the glint of deviltry in her eyes. Instead, he was unexpectedly amused.

"Hard to believe or not, I'm afraid it's true," he said. "In fact, so many people so often make it a point to tell me how *much* they like me and enjoy my company, I often find myself suspicious of their motives. I find it rather refreshing that you think I'm . . . "

"Annoying?" she supplied in a helpful tone.

"Exactly. However, since your brother's invitation forces you to endure my company for a bit longer, I propose we call a truce of sorts."

"What do you mean?"

"Clearly any mention of the Bride Thief raises your hackles, and believe it or not, it distresses me to be thought of as an annoyance."

She turned toward him and cocked a brow. "You *did* ask for the truth, my lord. And I cannot imagine that my opinion of you would affect you one way or another."

You're right. It shouldn't. But damn it, for some inexplicable reason, it does.

Before he could reply, she continued, "So am I to understand that this truce you are proposing would require you not to express your opinions about the Bride Thief, and me to refrain from calling you annoying?"

"You've summed it up quite nicely, Miss Briggeham."

Unmistakable mischief glinted in her eyes. "May I continue to *think* of you as annoying?"

"Of course. However, you should be aware that by doing so, you present me with an irresistible challenge."

"Indeed? What is that?"

"Why, the need to prove you wrong, of course."

Laughter erupted from her lips, and her eyes twinkled up at him. "Do you think there's any chance of that?"

He clutched his hand over his heart. "You wound me, Miss Briggeham. I'll have you know I'm rarely wrong. In fact, now that I think upon it, I don't believe I have *ever* been wrong."

She made a *tsk*-ing sound and shook her head. "Dear me. Annoying *and* arrogant. So many words beginning with 'a' to describe one man. And that is just the start of the alphabet."

"There are other 'a' words one might use, such as—"

"Aggravating?"

He sizzled a mock frown at her. "I was going to say 'amiable.'"

A noise that could only be described as a snort escaped her. "If it is any consolation, I'm certain most people think you are, my lord."

"Yet, I distinctly recall you telling me last evening that you are not most people."

"I fear that is true."

A grin tugged at his lips. "Well, then, I shall simply have to change your mind and make you see the error of your ways."

She laughed, a delightful sound that spread warmth through him. "You're welcome to try."

"See how well our truce is working? Already you've issued me an invitation." He paused, drawing them to a stop, and gazed down at her. The sunlight coaxed deep reds and burnished golds from her hair, and her eyes sparkled from her laughter.

His gaze moved downward, settling on her extraordinary mouth and that alluring freckle dotting the corner of her upper lip. The warmth her laughter had inspired, instantly turned to heat.

"Here's to our truce," he murmured. Taking her hand, he raised it to his lips and lightly kissed her fingers. The scent of honey filled his senses, and he barely resisted the overwhelming desire to touch his tongue to her skin to see if she tasted as sweet as she smelled. Their eyes met, and he watched all vestiges of humor slowly ebb from hers, as he continued to hold her hand a hairsbreadth away from his lips.

Surprise flashed across her features, then turned to confusion that painted her cheeks a delightful rose. Her skin looked petal soft, and his fingers suddenly itched with the need to feel that beckoning smoothness. With his free hand, he reached out, slowly, like a man in a trance, toward that enticing blush-hued skin. Her eyes widened and her breath caught, an utterly feminine sound that charmed him.

"Are you coming, Sammie?" Hubert's voice boomed from just beyond the rose hedges.

Miss Briggeham gasped and stepped back, snatching her hand from his grasp as if he'd burned her. "Yes," she called, in a slightly breathless voice. Clasping her hands tightly in front of her, she indicated the path with a jerk of her head. "This way, Lord Wesley."

Eric fell into step beside her, his height allowing him to match her brisk strides without much effort. He made no attempt to offer her his arm, instinctively knowing she wouldn't accept it, and not at all certain he should touch her again anyway. The woman had the oddest effect on his senses.

Damn it all, the desire to touch her had nearly overridden his common sense. What the devil was wrong with him? He wasn't here to court Samantha Briggeham. He merely wanted to ensure she wasn't hatching some crazy scheme to aid the Bride Thief. And while she was clearly protective of the man, a fact that oddly pleased him, she was also obviously an intelligent, logical young woman. There was no need for him to be concerned about her welfare. In fact, as soon as he finished looking at the telescope, he would take his leave.

*   *   *

Sammie carefully observed Lord Wesley as Hubert conducted a tour of his Chamber of Experiments for their guest, waiting to see any signs of boredom or ridicule directed toward her brother.

Instead, his lordship appeared fascinated by Hubert's Chamber and its vast array of glass beakers, jars, and experiments in progress. He asked Hubert dozens of questions, *intelligent* questions, she had to admit. Clearly the man possessed not only an interest but a knowledge of chemistry. And he never once looked askance at Hubert or spoke to him in a tone that suggested he thought either her brother or his laboratory odd. In fact, no matter how she looked at it, his lordship was acting in a way that could only be described as . . .

Amiable.

Her brow collapsed in a frown. Blast it all, she did not want to find the man amiable. She much preferred to think of him as annoying and arrogant. But seeing him bend over to apply his eye to Hubert's microscope, then look up at the boy with a grin creasing his handsome face, she couldn't deny that another "a" word to describe Lord Wesley was . . . attractive.

"Sammie, why don't you show Lord Wesley your section, where you prepare your honey and beeswax lotions?"

Hubert's question jerked her from her disturbing musing, and she pressed her hands over her stomach to quiet the jitters fluttering through her insides. As much as her scientific nature urged her to join the gentlemen across the room, her feminine instincts warned her to stay where she was, as far away from Lord Wesley as she could be while they stood in the same room.

Forcing a smile, she pointed toward the far corner of the room and said, " 'Tis nothing exciting to see, my lord. Just those burners, pots and molds, and my few remaining jars of honey."

"She is being modest, Lord Wesley," Hubert said. "Sammie is a first-rate scientist and teacher as well. Indeed, she sparked my interest in my own studies, and she is my greatest source of encouragement and inspiration. Her experiments with creams and lotions are fascinating, and she may soon see a breakthrough."

Heat rose in Sammie's cheeks, and she fought the urge to clap her hand over Hubert's mouth. While she appreciated his enthusiasm and kind words, she had no desire to see the inevitable expression on Lord Wesley's face—the one showing his dismay, horror, disgust, boredom, disdain, or any combination thereof regarding her work. She turned to him, determined to adroitly change the subject, and was surprised to see him regarding her with unmistakable curiosity.

"What sort of experiments are you conducting, Miss Briggeham?"

Not a bit of mockery or sarcasm in his voice. Just keen interest. She hesitated a few seconds, then led him to her work area. "Last night I mentioned one of my friends, a Miss Waynesboro-Paxton—"

"The lady who could not attend the soiree due to illness," Lord Wesley broke in.

"Yes," Sammie said, surprised he remembered. "She suffers from severe joint pain, mostly in her fingers and knuckles. I noticed that two things help alleviate her pain: wrapping her hands in warm, moist towels, and massaging my honey cream into her hands. I am attempting to discover a way to make my honey cream self-heating."

Lord Wesley stroked his chin and nodded slowly. "Thus incorporating the warming properties directly into the cream. And you're close to success?"

"I've recently made some progress, but I fear I've still much work to do. Still, I am determined to succeed."

She raised her chin a notch, silently daring him to mock

her, to dismiss her as nothing more than a bluestocking, but only admiration shone in his eyes.

"Ingenious idea," he said, his gaze shifting to roam over her supplies. "I offer you my sincere best wishes for success. Tell me, do you harvest your own honey?"

"Yes. I keep a half-dozen skeps behind the Chamber."

"She's hoarding those last few jars like a miser," Hubert said in a teasing voice. "But once she harvests her skeps next month, I'll be able to nip off with a jar without her noticing it's missing. I fear I have a weakness for honey."

Lord Wesley returned his gaze to her, studying her with an unfathomable expression that tightened her stomach. "Yes, I fear I do as well," he murmured. He then once again focused his attention on Hubert, and Sammie nearly groaned with relief.

Good heavens above, the man had the strangest effect on her senses. It was as if his nearness brought them all alive and into sharp focus. The feel of his strong arm beneath her palm as he'd escorted her down the garden paths; the woodsy, clean scent of him that made her want to lean closer to him and simply breathe him in. Disturbing feelings she'd managed quite well to ignore.

Until he'd stopped walking and looked at her with that intense expression that had curled her toes inside her slippers, and heated her from the inside out.

Until he'd brushed his lips over her hand.

Warmth rushed into her cheeks, and she quickly walked to the telescope and pretended to inspect the instrument, to hide her confusion. And there was no denying the man confused her. She'd started out angry with him, but after he'd apologized, he'd somehow managed to disarm her and amuse her, just as he'd done at Mrs. Nordfield's soiree. She'd enjoyed their verbal sparring, but once they'd ceased talking, and he'd looked at her in that way . . . suddenly she hadn't felt like laughing. Suddenly she'd wanted nothing more than for him to touch her face, as he'd been about to do.

She caught herself in the act of heaving a long sigh, and mentally slapped herself. Heavens, what was she thinking? She couldn't possibly entertain romantic notions toward Lord Wesley. To do so would be the same as extending an engraved invitation to Heartbreak. She needed to keep her romantic fantasies focused on make-believe gentlemen who could not ever hold her heart in their hands. Or even on a man like the Bride Thief—one that existed only in her memory, and even there more as a heroic figure than a flesh-and-blood man.

The rumble of masculine voices drew her attention to the other side of the room where Hubert and Lord Wesley were engaged in conversation. Hubert's face was alight with the pleasurable glow that always suffused him when he discussed one of his experiments or inventions. It was a look normally focused on *her*, and an odd pang clutched her that it was currently focused on a man she wasn't certain she liked. . . . A man she wasn't certain was worthy of the admiration shining from Hubert's eyes. Or perhaps the problem was the niggling fear that she *could* like him, if she allowed herself, and that Hubert's admiration wasn't misplaced.

Her gaze shifted to Lord Wesley, who was nodding, his serious expression riveted on the liquid-filled beaker Hubert held aloft. She tried to pull her gaze away, but she found herself admiring the man's profile—the sweep of his forehead, his high cheekbones, straight nose, firm lips, and the strong line of his jaw. As if he felt the weight of her regard, he turned and looked directly into her eyes. Heat washed through her and she barely refrained from smacking herself on the forehead. Dear Lord, he'd caught her staring! Coughing to cover her embarrassment, she quickly applied her eye to the new telescope, praying her cheeks were not as red as they felt.

Peering through the lens, she adjusted the focus, more out of a need to regain her composure than to actually see anything. The image of the garden sharpened, and she marveled at the wonder of the instrument. Mama's roses appeared close enough to touch, and—

A flash of blue crossed her line of vision. Adjusting her position, she squinted into the lens. Mama, her blue day gown flying behind her, was dashing toward the Chamber with a speed Sammie would have thought her incapable of. Heavens above, she'd forgotten all about her mother arranging refreshments for Lord Wesley. She was probably in a panic, wondering where the earl had gone, praying he was anywhere but the Chamber.

No sooner had Sammie straightened than the Chamber door burst open. Mama stood on the threshold, and Sammie had to bite her lip to keep from laughing at the disheveled picture her always perfectly turned out mother presented. Her chest heaved from the exertion of her sprint through the gardens, her fichu drooped limply from her bodice on one side, and her elaborate topknot, clearly missing several pins, sat askew on her head.

"*There* you are, Lord Wesley," Mama managed between panting breaths. "I thought you'd escaped . . . er, left before we had a chance to visit. I couldn't imagine where you'd gone. I've looked for you all through the gardens, even down at the stables." She skewered Sammie with a horrified look that screamed *whatever were you thinking to bring him here,* instantly followed by her sternest *we'll discuss this later* glare.

Lord Wesley waved his hand in an arc, encompassing the Chamber. "Hubert generously offered to show me his new telescope. A fine piece it is. And his laboratory is nothing short of amazing. You must be very proud of him."

Mama's gaze shifted to Hubert, who seemed to grow two full inches at the earl's praise. A smile softened Mama's eyes as she gazed upon her undeniably brilliant son whom she fiercely loved, but did not understand one iota. "Very proud," she agreed briskly, somehow managing to smile and send Hubert a warning frown at the same time. "Although the dear boy tends to forget that he mustn't bore our guests with all his complicated scientific chatter."

"You need not worry, dear lady," the earl said smoothly. "Your son"—his gaze shifted briefly to Sammie—"and daughter are both delightful company. I've enjoyed myself immensely."

Uncertainty flashed across Mama's face, as if she couldn't quite decide how much of the earl's words were truthful and how much were merely politeness. Clearly deciding her best strategy was to get him back to the house, she offered him her best hostess smile and announced, "Tea and biscuits are set out in the parlor."

He pulled a watch fob from his waistcoat and consulted the time. "As much as I'd love to join you, I fear that I must leave."

Mama's face showed her acute disappointment. Certain that her mother was about to issue an invitation for the earl to join them for tea another day, Sammie opened her mouth to intervene. She did not want Mama to entertain for even a *second* the notion that the earl would favor them with a return visit, nor did she want her mother disappointed when he refused. She firmly pushed aside the disturbing thought that she herself would be disappointed.

Before she could utter a word, however, Lord Wesley turned to her. "A footman took charge of my mount when I arrived. Perhaps you would escort me to your stables, Miss Briggeham?"

"Ah, yes. Of course."

"I thank you for the tour of your Chamber," the earl said to Hubert, then turned to make Mama a formal bow. "And you, Mrs. Briggeham, for your kind hospitality."

"Oh, you're most welcome, my lord," Mama said. "In fact—"

"This way, Lord Wesley," Sammie broke in, forestalling Mama. She swiftly exited the Chamber, resisting the urge to tug on Lord Wesley's arm.

He fell into step beside her, and she strode briskly across the green lawn toward the stables. After several seconds, she heard him chuckle.

"Are we engaged in a race, Miss Briggeham?"

"I beg your pardon?"

"You're striding toward the stables as if pursued by the devil himself."

Without slowing her pace, she shot him a sidelong glance. "Perhaps I am."

His chuckle deepened into a full laugh. "I'm quite the opposite, I assure you."

"Are you trying to convince me that 'angelic' describes you?"

"Well, it is another 'a' word. . . ."

His voice trailed off into a chuckle, and for some inexplicable reason, Sammie felt the need to quicken her pace even more. The sooner he left, the better. This man unsettled her, in a dismaying way she was certain, or at least almost certain, that she did not like.

They reached the stables less than a minute later. While Cyril brought around Lord Wesley's mount, Sammie fought to catch her breath from their brisk near-trot across the lawns. When Cyril appeared leading a chocolate-brown gelding, she couldn't suppress the appreciative sound that escaped her.

"He's magnificent, Lord Wesley," she said, reaching out to touch the beast's glossy neck. The animal immediately turned and nuzzled her cupped hand, blowing out a warm whinny that tickled her palm. "What is his name?"

"Emperor." He swung gracefully into the saddle. Stepping back, she shaded her eyes and looked up at him. The warm breeze ruffled his dark hair. His hand held the reins and his muscular legs hugged the horse's body with an ease that marked him as an experienced horseman. He looked incredibly masculine sitting astride his beautiful horse, and she wished she possessed the artistic talent to capture him in a drawing. She could almost see him, galloping full bent across a meadow, sailing over a fence, at one with his mount.

"Thank you for your hospitality, Miss Briggeham," he said, dragging her from her reverie.

"You're welcome, my lord." A frisson of regret washed through her that their time together was over. He'd proved himself polite, humorous, and charming, and the fact that he'd shown such kindness to Hubert tugged at her in a way that she couldn't put words to. If only circumstances were different . . . if she were the sort of woman to attract his attention for more than a fleeting moment—

But of course, she wasn't. He was an earl, and she was merely a . . . passing curiosity. Lifting her chin, she said, "Thank you for the flowers."

He stared down at her with an unreadable expression for several seconds. It seemed as if he wished to say something, and her heart beat in slow thumps, waiting for him to speak. He merely inclined his head, however, and murmured, "You're welcome."

Inexplicable disappointment rushed through her. Forcing a smile, she said, "I bid you a safe journey, Lord Wesley. Good-bye."

" 'Til we meet again, Miss Briggeham," he said in a low, compelling voice. He set Emperor into motion and cantered down the path. Sammie watched him until he disappeared around the bend, trying quite unsuccessfully to calm her erratic pulse.

'Til we meet again. Surely he meant nothing by his

parting words. They were merely a form of saying good-bye. She'd be a fool to read too much into them, to think that he meant to call upon her again. And why would she want him to? While she now couldn't, in all honesty, continue to think badly of him, he certainly bore no resemblance to the swashbuckling sort of gentleman she'd always imagined would set her heart aflutter. No, "adventurous" was not an "a" word she'd use to describe the Earl of Wesley.

Therefore, logically, she'd be the worst sort of fool to wish for him to return.

Yet suddenly she felt like the worst sort of fool.

Chapter 7

From the *London Times*:

> **Several more outraged fathers have joined the Bride Thief Posse, all of them contributing to the reward money, which now stands at seven thousand pounds. Adam Straton, the magistrate where the last kidnapping occurred, stated that he has redoubled his efforts to solve the case, and he is confident he will apprehend the Bride Thief soon. "I will not rest until I see him hang for his crimes," Straton promised.**

Eric stared out the window of his private study. Normally the warmth of the golden sunshine shimmering through the trees, and the sight of his stables in the distance brought him pleasure and comfort. Today, however, they failed to soothe, as he strove for the hundredth time to forget the one thing he couldn't seem to erase from his mind.

Samantha Briggeham.

Three days had passed since he'd called upon her. Three days since her honesty, intelligence, and lack of guile had charmed him, as it had on the two other occasions he'd met her. Three days of wanting to see her again, to the point where he'd actually had to force himself not to call upon her.

Damn it all, there was no need to concern himself with her welfare any longer. She bore no ill effects from his botched kidnapping. Yet he simply could not dismiss her from his thoughts.

Why? What was it about her that attracted him so? Certainly he could lie to himself and claim his interest lay only in the fact that he'd accidentally kidnapped her. But lying to himself was a futile exercise.

No, there was something about Samantha Briggeham that touched him . . . in a way he couldn't explain. What was it? She certainly was not beautiful, yet the combination of her too large eyes and those too large lips fascinated him in a way that a classic beauty never had. He'd enjoyed the company of many gorgeous women—women whose physical beauty could leave a man breathless, but he'd found them all eminently forgettable. Indeed, he couldn't recall one of their faces. The face that filled his mind during the day and rendered him wide awake at night was not that of a diamond of the first water, but of an unassuming country miss who inexplicably attracted him as no woman ever had.

Crossing to the decanters, he poured a finger of brandy, then stared at the amber liquid as if it held the answer to this extremely vexing puzzle.

Very well, he found her unusual looks intriguing. Pleasing. But that did not fully explain this . . . *thing* he could not name . . . this preoccupation with her. Leaning his hips against his mahogany desk, he sipped his drink, enjoying the trail of warmth easing down his belly. A series of images of Miss Briggeham flashed through his mind. Hiding behind Mrs. Nordfield's potted palms. Laughing as they'd examined Mrs. Nordfield's dreadful paintings. Her initial fright when he'd kidnapped her, her wistful expression when she'd confided her longing for adventure to the Bride Thief . . . her desire to swim in the Adriatic . . .

Bloody hell, perhaps *that* was the problem. He knew things about Miss Samantha Briggeham that he shouldn't, *wouldn't* know if he hadn't met her as the Bride Thief. And not just her yearnings for adventure. He knew how she felt in his arms, her soft body pressed against him, the heady sensation of galloping through the darkness with her, her honey-scented skin teasing his senses.

Then there was her anger . . . no, her *annoyance* . . . when he'd dared utter a word against the Bride Thief, a man she clearly admired. Her obvious love for her brother, and indulgence toward her mother. Her ambition to develop a medicinal cream to help her friend. She was intelligent, kind, loyal, amusing, horribly outspoken, and . . .

He liked her.

He was about to enjoy another swallow of brandy when the realization dawned, halting his hand halfway to his lips.

Bloody hell, he *liked* her.

Liked her smile, her laugh, even her indignation. She in no way exuded the supercilious attitudes of so many women of his acquaintance. She harbored dreams of scientific success and adventure that went far beyond which gown to wear, or which bonnet to purchase.

And her eyes . . . those extraordinary aqua eyes were filled with hopes, unfulfilled desires, and they hinted at feelings and vulnerabilities that he wanted to learn about. Yes, *that's* all this preoccupation was: simply a desire to learn more about an interesting woman. Converse with her. Discover all those fascinating thoughts he sensed lurked behind her thick spectacles.

He savored another sip of brandy while employing the decision-making processes he'd honed in the Army. He'd identified the problem—half the battle right there: He couldn't dismiss Miss Briggeham because he liked her and wished to learn more about her.

But how to solve this problem?

Clearly he had two options. He could force her from his mind, but since he'd been unable to accomplish that since he'd met her, he quickly discarded that option. Therefore, the only other possibility was to see her again, to speak with her and discover more about her. Once he did, his curiosity would be satisfied. Then he'd be able to put this preoccupation with her in its proper perspective. Perfect.

He raised his glass to salute his brilliant logic and toast his infallible plan.

Eric reined Emperor to a halt behind a copse of oaks near the fringe of the woods. Squinting against the glare of the early-afternoon sun, he watched Miss Briggeham approach from the direction of the village. Instead of the brisk strides she'd employed when last they met, she walked slowly across the verdant clearing, lifting her face to the sun, clearly savoring the warm weather. Her bonnet hung down her back from its ribbons, and her chestnut hair glinted in the sun, as if capturing its golden glow. A smile lit her face, and she twirled once in a circle, swinging the basket she carried with a joyful abandon, then bent over to smell a grouping of wildflowers.

He suddenly envied the carefree, relaxed picture she made. When was the last time he'd simply enjoyed the sunshine? Taken pleasure in a lovely day, savored the scents and sounds of nature without the gravity of his responsibilities and obligations weighing on his mind?

Not since that last summer before he'd entered the Army, he realized after a moment's thought. He and Margaret had enjoyed long rides around the estate, often bringing bundles of food with them. On several occasions, they'd ventured no farther than the stables, spending the afternoon grooming horses with Arthur.

It had been too bloody long since he'd passed a free and easy afternoon, and the urge to join Miss Briggeham, to lift her in his arms and swirl in lighthearted circles with her, share in her delight, tugged at his insides.

Pushing away the desire to indulge in behavior totally unsuitable for an earl, he continued to watch her, a smile pulling at his lips when she leaped over a pile of rocks with an exuberance that reminded him of a puppy.

He remained hidden until only a short distance separated them. Then, touching his heels to Emperor's flanks, he stepped onto the path.

"Why, Miss Briggeham, how nice to see you again."

She halted as if she'd walked into a glass wall. Color rushed into her already pinkened cheeks, and a host of expressions streaked across her face. But while she was clearly surprised to see him, she did not appear displeased. "Lord Wesley," she said in a breathless voice. "How do you do?"

"Very well, thank you. Are you returning home from the village?" he asked, as if he hadn't been informed by Arthur that Miss Briggeham walked this path to the village nearly every day.

"Yes. I visited my friend, Miss Waynesboro-Paxton."

"And how is her joint pain today?"

"Worse, I'm afraid. I brought her another jar of my honey cream. I massaged some into her hands, and it offered some temporary relief to the aches in her fingers." Shading her eyes with her hand, she looked up at him. "Are you going to the village?"

"No, I was just exercising Emperor, enjoying this beautiful day." He smiled down at her. "As I believe Emperor has tired himself running, may I walk with you?"

Emperor laid his ears back, huffed out a whinny, then

pawed the ground once. She chuckled and said, "Of course. But it appears Emperor does not appreciate you casting aspersions on his stamina. In fact, I never knew a horse could look *indignant* until just now." Patting the gelding's neck, she said, "If you'd like, we can detour toward the lake so Emperor can enjoy a drink."

"A marvelous suggestion." Eric dismounted, then turned toward her intending to offer to carry her basket, but the words died in his throat as he looked at her. The sunlight reflected an enticing array of vibrant reds and hidden golds from her shiny hair. Her chignon was more than a little disheveled, obviously from all her twirling about. Yet it looked as if the strands might have been mussed by a man's hands . . . a man who'd given in to the impatient need to run his fingers through those silky-looking curls.

The bright light glinted off her spectacles, drawing his gaze to her eyes . . . eyes that looked at him with a mildly expectant expression, as if she were waiting for him to say something, a feat he seemed unable to perform.

Her skin glowed with sun-kissed color that bloomed on her cheeks like roses. His gaze lowered to her full lips, where a half-smile lingered, and he had to force himself to look away. He noted she wore a pale blue muslin gown, completely modest and unadorned, but from the slow roll his heart performed, she might have been wearing a lace negligee.

Instantly, an image of her wearing a lace negligee popped into his mind, her enticing curves barely covered with sheer material. Heat shot to his groin, and he barely suppressed the frustrated growl that rose in his throat.

Bloody hell, what was wrong with him? He shook his head to clear the disturbing image.

"Is something amiss, Lord Wesley?"

"Er, no."

She stepped closer to him and squinted up at his face.

The subtle scent of honey filled his head, and he clenched his teeth.

"Are you certain? You appear somewhat . . . flushed."

Flushed? Surely she was mistaken, although he did feel as if someone had lit a fire in his breeches. "It's merely rather warm. Here. In the sun." Damnation, was that gravelly sound his voice? Offering her his arm, he inclined his head toward the path leading into the woods. "Shall we?"

"Of course. It will be much cooler in the shade."

Yes, cooler. That was simply all he required. For some inexplicable reason, the sun seemed to be having an odd effect on him. Holding Emperor's reins in one hand, and with Miss Briggeham's hand resting lightly on his sleeve, they walked into the forest.

He exhaled in relief when the shade provided by the soaring trees swallowed the heat, offering the much needed coolness. Gentle sounds surrounded them as they strolled, the quiet rustle of leaves, the trill of a bird, the crunch of twigs beneath their feet, Emperor blowing out a soft breath.

He searched his mind for something to say, something clever to make her laugh or smile, but for reasons he could not decipher, he felt like a tongue-tied, green schoolboy. The only thing he could think to ask her was *Do you taste as sweet as you smell?* and he certainly couldn't say *that*. For the first time he could recall, his normally smooth sophistication abandoned him. If he'd had a free hand, he would have raked it through his hair. He'd wanted to see her, to talk to her, to find out more about her. Yet here she was, and he'd all but swallowed his tongue.

He was saved from trying to think up conversation, as they had arrived at the lake. The water shimmered dark blue, reflecting golden ribbons of sunlight. He released Emperor's reins, allowing the gelding to walk to the water's edge to drink. Miss Briggeham released his arm, leaving him with the urge to snatch her hand back. She strolled several yards away to lean against the trunk of a huge willow.

"The last several evenings have been particularly clear," she remarked, breaking the silence. "Have you taken advantage of the weather to observe the stars?"

He pounced on the topic as a dog would a meaty bone. "Indeed, I have. Tell me, is Hubert pleased with his new telescope?"

"Yes. It's a fine instrument, but he plans to someday build one of his own. He believes it's likely that more planets exist, and he wants to construct a telescope powerful enough to find out."

"Rather like William Herschel did when he discovered Uranus," Eric remarked.

She regarded him with pleased surprise. "Precisely. Hubert quite worships the man."

"My telescope is a Herschel."

"A Herschel? Oh!" She pushed her spectacles higher on her nose and gazed at him with an awed expression. "It must be wonderful."

"Indeed it is," Eric agreed. "I was fortunate enough to meet Sir William several years ago, and purchased it directly from him."

"Heavens, you've actually met him?"

"Yes. Fascinating fellow."

"Oh, he must be! His theory of binary star systems is utterly brilliant." Her entire face lit up as if he'd just presented her with a handful of pearls . . . or rather, stars. "Tell me, can you see Jupiter with your Herschel?"

"Yes." Ducking his head to avoid the hanging leaves, he joined her under the shady tree. "And last evening I observed several falling stars as well."

"As did I! Were they not marvelous?"

Nodding his agreement, he said, "They remind me of diamonds, streaking across the heavens, leaving a trail of jewel dust in their wake."

She smiled at him. "A very poetic description, my lord."

Captured by her enchanting smile, he took several steps closer to her. "And how would you describe them, Miss Briggeham?"

She didn't answer right away. Rather, she tipped her head back against the tree trunk and looked up at the ribbons of blue sky visible through the veil of willow leaves. "Angels' tears," she finally said, her voice soft. "I watch the stars fall and wonder who in heaven is weeping, and why." She lowered her gaze back to him, and his throat tightened at her wistful expression. "Why do you suppose an angel would cry?"

"I can't imagine."

The hint of a self-conscious smile flashed over her lips. "Angels' tears. Completely unscientific and illogical, I know."

"Yet a very apt, clear description. The next time I see a falling star, I too shall wonder if there's an angel who weeps."

Their gazes locked for the space of several heartbeats, and he swore some manner of invisible spark all but crackled in the air between them.

Did she feel it as well? Before he could decide, she averted her gaze and said, "I cannot wait to tell Hubert that you've met Sir William Herschel, and that you *own* one of his telescopes." A smile touched her lips. "Of course, perhaps I'd best not tell him. If I do, he'll ask you a thousand questions. And whichever ones he might not think of, I will."

"I'd be pleased to answer them," he assured her, surprised that he meant it. "I've no one who shares my interest in astronomy. In fact, perhaps you and Hubert would like to come to Wesley Manor to see my Herschel?"

Her eyes widened behind her glasses, and he clenched his hands to keep from plucking those spectacles from her face.

"Hubert would all but expire from the excitement, my lord," she said, her voice breathless.

"And you, Miss Briggeham . . . would you also all but expire?"

"Indeed," she said, her expression perfectly serious. "I never thought to have such a rare opportunity."

"Excellent." He looked toward the glimpses of cloudless, azure sky visible through the leaves. "It looks as if tonight might be clear. Are you free this evening?"

"Well, yes, but are you certain . . . ?" Her voice trailed off and she sent him a searching look.

"You appear quite astonished at my invitation, Miss Briggeham. And here I thought 'a' words were to be used to describe *me*."

Amusement flickered in her eyes at his teasing words, then she smiled—a shy, pleased smile that for some ridiculous reason set his heart thumping.

"I assure you," he said, "I'd enjoy having you and Hubert as my guests this evening."

"In that case, my lord, I can only thank you for your most 'agreeable' invitation. Hubert . . . and I . . . shall look forward to it."

"Excellent. I'll send my carriage for you. Shall we say at eight?"

"That would be lovely. Thank you."

He watched her full lips form the words, his attention fixed on that fascinating freckle gracing the corner of her mouth. Her lips puckered when she said "you" . . . as they might if she were about to be kissed.

Kissed. The word slammed into him like a punch to the gut. Bloody hell, her mouth was incredible. The most kissable he'd ever seen. Awareness pulsed through him, and those moist lips beckoned him like a siren's call. The urge to touch that alluring mouth with his own, just once, for an instant, overwhelmed him, overriding his normally fine-tuned common sense.

Like a man in a trance, he walked slowly toward her. She watched him, her eyes growing rounder with each step he took. When he paused directly in front of her, she looked up at him with confusion.

He braced one arm on the willow's trunk, next to her shoulder, and allowed his gaze to roam over her. His nearness obviously unnerved her, a fact that shouldn't have pleased him, but did. Clearly he was not the only one experiencing this . . . whatever it was.

Her magnified eyes reflected uncertainty, and her cheeks bloomed with color. Her pulse beat visibly at the base of her delicate throat, and her chest rose and fell with her increasingly rapid breaths. Her delicious scent filled his head, and he leaned closer to better capture that elusive fragrance.

"You smell like . . . porridge," he said softly.

She blinked twice, then her lips twitched. "Why, thank you, my lord. However, I'd best warn you that such flowery words might swell my head."

His brows pulled down. Had he just compared her to *porridge*? *How* did this woman manage to strip him of all his finesse? Unable to stop himself, he leaned closer, until only several inches separated them.

Breathing deeply, he murmured, "Porridge with honey drizzled over it. My favorite morning meal." His lips hovered a breath away from the fragrant curve of her neck. "Warm. Sweet. Delicious."

He inhaled once more, and his entire body tingled. God, she smelled good enough to eat. The desire pulsing through him was so strong, so unexpectedly heated, it smacked him like a brick to the head, rousing him from his stupor. *What the hell are you doing?* He'd clearly taken leave of his senses.

Beating back his desire, he pushed himself away from her, backing up several steps. Damn it, he hadn't even touched her, yet his breath puffed from his lungs as if he'd run a mile. And one look at her confirmed that she was as affected as he. Her eyes were aqua saucers, staring at him in dazed wonderment. Rapid breaths whooshed from her slightly parted lips, her chest rising and falling in a way that drew his gaze to her ample curves. He barely managed to swallow the groan that rose in his throat.

Why hadn't he kissed her? Simply pressed their lips together, taken a quick taste to satisfy his curiosity, and been done with it? Obviously because his common sense had come back to life and reminded him that Miss Briggeham was a respectable young woman, not one to be trifled with. But just as his common sense had spoken up, so now did his pesky inner voice. *You didn't kiss her because you know, deep down, that a quick taste wouldn't be enough.*

Bloody hell. Best to leave now, before he did something he'd regret. Like take her up on the almost irresistible invitation he doubted she realized glowed in her eyes. Forcing himself to take several more steps backwards, he offered her a formal bow. "I must go," he said, managing to ignore the beguiling blush that colored her silky cheeks. "But I shall see you this evening."

A frown yanked at his brows. Perhaps having her in his home was not a wise idea. But he instantly pushed aside the worry. They would be properly chaperoned by her brother, and surely he'd have no problem resisting whatever mild attraction he felt for her. Whatever odd notion had come over him moments ago was gone, and he was totally in control of himself. Miss Briggeham was perfectly safe with him.

She pushed her glasses higher on her nose and cleared her throat. " 'Til this evening," she said in a calm voice that somehow irked him. Of course, *he* had sounded perfectly calm . . . but he hadn't expected *her* to.

He strode to Emperor, then swung himself into the saddle. After nodding at Miss Briggeham, he headed down the path leading toward his home at a brisk trot.

Vexing woman. He must have been mad to invite her to his home. But no matter. It was only one evening. Just several hours in her company. Quite easy to get through.

After all, hadn't he just proven to himself that he could easily resist her?

Sammie remained leaning against the tree trunk, riveted in place, watching the path long after he'd disappeared from sight, her pulse pounding erratically.

Heavens above, he'd been about to kiss her. Kiss her, with those firm, lovely lips. A feminine sigh the likes of which she'd never heaved, puffed from her lips. Her eyes slid shut as she recalled the way he'd braced his arm on the tree trunk beside her, the way he'd leaned in close to her, surrounding her with his woodsy, clean scent. Heat had all but pulsed from him, and she'd had to press her palms to the scratchy willow bark to keep from touching him, to see if he was really as warm as he seemed.

Another dreamy sigh worked its way toward her throat. Just as she was about to expel it, however, sanity returned with a resounding *thump*.

Of course, she must be mistaken. Why on earth would Lord Wesley want to kiss her? No doubt he'd simply been curious about her fragrance, wondering why she smelled like *porridge*.

But the way he'd looked at her . . . with that intense

expression that had all but stolen her breath. Surely he hadn't meant to stand so close. No doubt he'd just wanted to stand more in the shade.

And what had she done? Acted like an utter idiot, rendered breathless and weak-kneed by his proximity, her heart pounding in anticipation, yearning for the touch of his lips on hers.

Embarrassment washed through her. Had he known? Had her longing shown in her eyes? She clapped her hands to her burning cheeks. He'd simply wanted to stand in the shade, and all her logic had scattered like ashes in a windstorm. Good heavens, what on earth had come over her? She did not know, but there was no denying that the man affected her in the most dismaying fashion.

Perhaps she shouldn't go to his home . . . out no, the lure of seeing a Herschel telescope was too strong. She couldn't deny herself or Hubert such a rare opportunity. And besides, Hubert would be with her to act as chaperone. There would be no reason for Lord Wesley to stand close to her, and therefore, logically, no reason for her heart to flutter or her breath to stall. She and Lord Wesley merely shared an interest in astronomy. Naturally she would feel a . . . kinship toward him. Why, it was really no different than discussing the stars with Hubert.

Satisfied with her logical explanation, she pushed off from the tree, then walked briskly down the path leading toward her house. With a sigh, she realized one possible problem with this visit to Lord Wesley's home would be Mama. She did not want her mother to misinterpret the earl's invitation as being anything more than what it was— a kind and generous gesture toward fellow enthusiasts to view a telescope made by the world's foremost living astronomer. Lord Wesley was simply being . . . amiable. In fact, he was so amiable, it was . . . alarming. Astonishing.

Yes, she'd have to be very certain that Mama understood

there was nothing more to it than that. Otherwise she suspected that Mama's matchmaking mind would leap with
impossible, hopeless thoughts.

*And you yourself would do well to remember that they're
hopeless, impossible thoughts.*

Yet while that stern inner warning stiffened her spine, it
did little to squelch the impossible longing that Lord
Wesley's nearness had kindled in her heart.

Chapter 8

"That's the third time ye've checked the mantel clock in the last ten minutes, my lord," Arthur Timstone noted in his husky voice from across the room. "Yer guests will arrive soon. Makes the time go slower when you watch it."

Eric turned from his position near the fireplace in his private study and looked at his faithful servant over the rim of his brandy snifter. Arthur was comfortably ensconced in his favorite chair next to Eric's mahogany desk, a half-filled tumbler of whiskey cradled between his work-roughened hands.

They met like this frequently in the evenings, sharing a drink while Arthur related any news he'd gleaned through the servant grapevine that might be of interest to Eric and the Bride Thief. Tonight, however, it seemed Eric himself was the focus of gossip.

"Quite a stir this invitation to Miz Sammie has caused at the Briggeham's," Arthur remarked. "Her ma is all a-twitter. She's already invited Missus Nordfield to tea tomorrow to discuss it."

Eric had suspected something of the sort might occur, but he was well-versed in the art of sidestepping matchmaking mothers. "There's nothing to discuss. I simply offered to show Miss Briggeham *and her brother* my telescope."

" 'Course that's all there is to it," Arthur agreed with a nod. "Anybody would be a fool to suggest ye'd be *interested* in Miz Sammie."

"Precisely. And both Cordelia Briggeham and Lydia Nordfield, along with everyone else, know damn well my long-standing views on marriage. They'd be fools to think I'd changed my mind."

"Bah, ye could shout it from the rooftops that ye've no wish to marry. Wouldn't matter to some. They'd just think it a challenge of sorts. They probably think ye're just bein' coy."

"Coy?" A bitter sound erupted from between Eric's lips. "After witnessing firsthand my parents' nightmare marriage, and knowing how unhappy Margaret is in hers, I've no intention of foisting such misery upon myself. And even if I were mad enough to consider marriage, I couldn't possibly subject a wife, or children, to the danger I face. If I were caught, their lives would be ruined."

"A wise decision," Arthur agreed. " 'Course them matchmakin' biddies have no way of knowin' *that* reason." He savored a sip of whiskey, then expelled a contented sigh. "Still, it's mad for them to think ye'd want Miz Sammie. She's not the sort of woman to attract a man like you."

"No, she's not," Eric agreed in a harsher tone than he'd meant. He tossed back his brandy and immediately poured another.

"Still, with all the attention comin' her way, she might catch some gent's eye. Ye'd think there'd be *one* bloke with enough smarts to see beyond her spectacles." Arthur shook his head and muttered a disgusted sound. "But bah, these young pups want nothin' more than pretty faces, coy smiles, and simperin' giggles. Wouldn't know a special woman if she jumped up and bit their arse. And special, that's wot Miz Sammie is." He jabbed a thick index finger in Eric's direction. "I tell ye, if I were a few years younger and a gentleman, I might court her meself."

Eric's hand froze halfway to his mouth. Slowly lowering his snifter, he asked, "I beg your pardon?"

Arthur waved his hand in a dismissive fashion. "Don't concern yerself. I'm arse over heels for my Sarah. Still, a man'd have to be blind not to notice Miz Sammie's smile. Or how pretty her hair is. Or how those big eyes of hers sort of . . . glow. And smart as a whip she is, too. Took young Hubert under her wing, and thanks to her teachings, he's now sharp as a nail. Yes, there's more to Miz Sammie than wot most people see."

Eric leaned against the marble mantel in a relaxed pose completely at odds with the inexplicable annoyance pumping through him. "I didn't know you were so . . . *aware* of Miss Briggeham and her charms."

The instant the sharply spoken words left his lips, he knew he'd made a mistake. Arthur blinked several times, then leaned forward and peered at Eric. Eric tried his damnedest to keep his expression impassive, but clearly he failed because Arthur said, "I'm old, not blind. And I didn't know *you* were aware she *had* any charms."

Eric raised his brows. "I'm neither old nor blind."

Arthur's expression slowly changed from confused to stunned. "Devil take me, surely ye're not casting yer eye at Miz Sammie!"

Eric opened his mouth to deny it, but before he could utter a word, Arthur's eyes rounded. "Damn it, boy, have ye lost yer mind? She's not the sort of woman for the likes of you."

Unexpectedly stung by the remark, Eric asked in a cool tone, "The likes of me? What does that mean?"

"Oh, get that stick out of yer arse. Ye know I love ye like

a son. It's just that . . ." His eyes turned troubled and his voice trailed off.

Eric cocked a brow. "Clearly there's something you wish to say to me, Arthur. Why not simply say it—as you always have?"

Arthur downed a hefty swallow of whiskey, then met Eric's gaze. "All right. Why exactly did you invite her here?"

He didn't pretend to misunderstand what Arthur was asking, yet how could he explain what he himself didn't understand? Setting his snifter on the mantel, he tunneled his fingers through his hair. "I suppose I feel a certain responsibility toward her, to make certain she doesn't suffer any social backlash because of her kidnapping."

"She hasn't. I told ye, she's been highly sought after ever since."

"I know. But . . ."

"She's gotten under yer skin."

Their eyes met and understanding flowed between them. Understanding born of years of sharing, first as boy to servant, then young man to mentor, then as man to man. Friend to friend. Confidant to confidant. And what Eric had always felt for Arthur was more like son to father than anything he'd ever had with his own sire.

"Under my skin," Eric repeated slowly. "Yes, I'm afraid she has."

A long breath expelled from Arthur's lips. "Well split my windpipe." He leaned back against the leather chair and regarded Eric through shrewd eyes. "Be a shame if she got hurt."

There was no denying the hurt that pricked Eric. "Why do you suddenly harbor this ill opinion of me? I have no intention of hurting her."

"I hold ye in higher regard than anyone, and ye know it," Arthur said, his gaze sharp and steady. "Ye wouldn't mean to hurt her, but Miz Sammie's not like yer usual sort of woman. She's not one of yer sophisticated widows or experienced actresses."

"Do you think I don't know that?" Eric again raked his hands through his hair. "Bloody hell, you make it sound as if I'm bent on seducing the woman. It's disturbing and insulting that you'd even think such a thing. Do you not trust me?"

Arthur's fierce expression softened. Rising on creaking knees, he crossed the room to stand before Eric, then laid a warm hand on his shoulder. " 'Course I do. With my life. Ye're the finest man I know. But sometimes a man's judgment can get clouded. Even the most well-intentioned man. Especially if there's a woman involved."

Understanding and concern flowed from Arthur's gaze. "Miz Sammie . . . she's kind. Decent. Even to folks who snicker about her behind her back. And she's innocent. Just the sort of woman who might read more meanin' into yer attentions than ye mean." He leveled a look on Eric that seemed to penetrate to his soul. "Unless of course ye truly mean them?"

A humorless sound emitted from Eric's throat. "It sounds as if you're asking me what my intentions toward Miss Briggeham are. Why? You've never shown such an interest in my private life before."

"I've always been interested. I've just never commented before."

"But you are now."

"Yes. Because I know Miz Sammie. And I like her."

"Has it occurred to you that perhaps I like her, too?"

"Truth be told, ye'd be a fool not to. Salt of the earth, Miz Sammie is. Guess I'm just hoping ye'll be . . . careful with her. She's got a kind heart. I'd hate to see it broken." Arthur squeezed his shoulder. "Ye've a good heart, too. Would please me mightily to see ye give it to someone before I'm too old to realize ye've done it."

Eric's eyes narrowed. "You're reading far too much into a simple invitation."

Arthur didn't answer for several seconds. He simply looked at Eric with that same penetrating expression that somehow made him want to squirm. "Yes, ye're probably right." He squeezed Eric's shoulder then headed toward the door. "Enjoy yer evening, my lord. I'm sure Miz Sammie and Master Hubert will enjoy yer fancy telescope."

The instant the door closed behind Arthur with a quiet click, Eric grabbed his brandy snifter and tossed back the contents. The heat burned down his belly, soothing the unsettling feeling jittering there.

A simple invitation, damn it. That's all this was. He had no intention of involving himself with Samantha Briggeham. He had responsibilities, a secret life. A price on his head.

There was no room for her in his world.

Standing in a spacious glass-walled alcove set in the corner of Lord Wesley's vast conservatory, Sammie watched Hubert approach the Herschel with an awed expression. The boy issued a rapturous *oh!* that brought a smile to her face, and she concentrated on Hubert's excited enthusiasm, a feeling she herself should be experiencing . . . not this aching, almost painful awareness of the tall, dark-haired man patiently answering the barrage of rapid-fire questions shooting from Hubert's lips.

Heavens, was it possible for a man to be breathtaking? She never would have thought so. Until now. Until she stood in his home, trying to focus her attention on his words, on his magnificent telescope, and failing utterly. Until he glanced her way and all the oxygen seemed to leave the air.

Dressed completely in black except for his snowy white

shirt and cravat, he looked elegant; yet at the same time he somehow exuded an air that underneath his polished veneer lurked a barely contained energy. A suppressed strength that hinted there was more to him than his well-bred appearance indicated.

"There's Sagittarius," Hubert said with breathless wonder, gazing through the eyepiece. "And Aquila. I've seen them before, but never like this! They look close enough to touch." Turning, he grabbed Sammie's hand and tugged her toward the telescope. "Look, Sammie. You've never seen the likes of this."

Forcing her gaze away from her disturbing host, she reminded herself that she was eager to experience the splendor of such a fine telescope and stepped up to the instrument. After a minute adjustment to the focus, she gasped in delight.

"It's as if the heavens are laid out before me, just slightly beyond my reach." The stars shimmered like diamonds against black velvet, twinkling with a close-up brilliance that coaxed her hand to reach out, as if she could gather them up and sift them through her fingers.

"The stars are indeed fabulous," Lord Wesley said from behind her, "but if you look just over here . . ."

His voice trailed off and the warmth of his body surrounded her as he stepped in close behind her. Resting one hand upon her shoulder, he reached around her with his free hand and slowly pivoted the telescope. "Now," he said, his deep voice close to her ear, "you should be able to see Jupiter."

She watched the jewel-studded sky shift as he adjusted the telescope, her breath trapped in her throat at the brush of his body against hers. His clean, masculine scent invaded her senses, and she had to fight the urge to lean back against him, to surround herself with him as she would with a warm, velvety blanket.

Tingles erupted on her skin where his hand rested on her shoulder, scissoring pinpricks of pleasure down her spine. Squeezing her eyes shut against the sensations swarming through her, she forced a deep breath into her lungs. This unscientific, illogical behavior on her part would simply not do at all. Opening her eyes, she blinked, then gasped.

"Oh, my," she breathed. "It's a miracle to see something that is so far away."

"Tell me what you see," Lord Wesley said softly.

"It's . . . incredible. Red. Burning. Mysterious. Too distant to even imagine what it's like there." With the heat of his body grazing her back, she gazed at the distant planet and tried, completely unsuccessfully, to convince herself that the rapid beating of her heart was strictly due to the thrill of scientific discovery.

She drew a bracing breath and inwardly scolded herself, then turned toward Hubert, who was all but bouncing with excitement. Pushing her spectacles higher on her nose, she offered him a smile that felt decidedly shaky.

"Is it grand, Sammie?" Hubert asked.

"The grandest thing you'll ever feel . . . I mean, see."

She stepped hastily aside and watched Hubert apply his eye to the glass. His exclamation of wonder echoed through the room, and she dared a peek at Lord Wesley. He was watching her, and when their gazes met, he offered her a smile.

"You're pleased?"

"Oh, very much so, my lord." Heavens above, was that breathless voice coming from her? She nodded her head toward her brother, who was completely absorbed. "And I think it's fair to say that if Hubert were any more excited, he'd leap right out of his shoes."

He chuckled. "Actually, I reacted the very same way the first time I looked through that telescope."

An image of Lord Wesley hopping about with boyish

abandon flashed through her mind, leaving a smile in its wake.

"By jingo, this is incredible," Hubert said in a hushed, reverent tone. Turning toward them, he reached inside his waistcoat and withdrew a small, leather-bound book. "Would you mind if I jotted down some notes, my lord?"

"Take your time and jot all you wish, lad," he invited, offering Hubert a warm smile. Returning his attention to her, he said, "Perhaps while Hubert is enjoying the Herschel, you'd like to see some more of my home, Miss Briggeham?"

Sammie hesitated. It was a completely innocent invitation, yet her heart skipped at the thought of being alone with him. Then she nearly laughed aloud at her own silliness. Of course they wouldn't be alone. A house this size would have dozens of servants. Besides, she didn't dare stay here to look through the telescope again and risk having him stand so close behind her. And she refused to drag Hubert away from the Herschel.

"Surely the prospect of touring my home is not such a weighty matter," he said in a teasing tone. Extending his elbow, he said, "Come. I've arranged for tea in the drawing room. On the way, I'll show you the portrait gallery and bore you to tears with tedious stories about my excess of ancestors."

Forcing a lightness into her voice she was far from feeling, she took his arm and murmured, "How could I possibly resist such a tempting invitation?" As they exited the conservatory, she fervently prayed that he would, indeed, bore her to tears. But she very much feared that she already found Lord Wesley far too fascinating.

They paused near the last group of portraits in the gallery.

"I take it this is your mother?" Miss Briggeham asked.

Eric stared at his mother's beautiful face, which smiled serenely back at him, her countenance not showing a trace of the bitter unhappiness she'd suffered. "Yes."

"She's lovely."

His throat tightened. "Yes, she was. She died when I was fifteen."

The small hand resting on his sleeve squeezed his arm with clear sympathy. "I'm sorry. There's no good time to lose a parent, but it must be especially difficult for a boy on the brink of manhood."

"Yes." He managed to push the single word through his tight throat. Memories assaulted him, as they did every time he looked at his mother's portrait. Voices raised in anger, his father lashing out with verbal barbs that cut deep wounds, and his mother, desperately miserable, a prisoner of unhappiness in her marriage.

"Who is this?" Miss Briggeham asked, yanking him from his disturbing reverie.

He gazed at the next portrait and the ache that always accompanied thoughts of Margaret gnawed at him. The painting had been done to commemorate her sixteenth birthday. She looked young and so sweetly innocent in her ivory muslin gown, and he vividly recalled visiting the library during her endless sittings to tease smiles from her. *What sort of face is that, Margaret? You look as if you've chewed on a sour pickle. Smile, or I'll steal some red paint and draw a big grin on you.* In retaliation, Margaret had sucked in her cheeks, making a fish-face. In spite of their foolishness, the artist had managed to capture Margaret with a serene smile and just a hint of deviltry in her eyes.

"That is my sister, Margaret."

He felt her start of surprise. "I didn't know you had a sister, my lord."

Turning his head, he gazed down at her. He'd wager that

nearly every other female in the village was acquainted with the family members of the peerage. "Margaret is Viscountess Darvin. She lives in Cornwall."

"I've always wished to see the Cornish coast. How long has she lived there?"

Since my sire sold her like a sack of flour. "Five years. Since her . . . marriage."

She clearly heard the tightness in his tone, for her eyes flooded with sympathy and she asked in a soft voice, "Is her marriage not happy?"

"No."

"I'm so sorry. It's too bad the Bride Thief couldn't have saved her."

Her words sizzled through him like a lightning bolt of guilt. "Yes. It's too bad."

"Do you see her often?"

"Not often enough, I'm afraid."

"I'd miss my sisters dreadfully if they lived so far away," Miss Briggeham remarked.

"You have three sisters, I believe?"

"Yes. They're all married. Lucille and Hermione live here in Tunbridge Wells. Emily, who recently married Baron Whitestead, lives only one hour's ride away. We all see each other frequently."

"I recall meeting your sisters at a musicale several years ago."

A smile flashed across her lips. "I daresay you wouldn't forget them. Individually, my sisters are all beautiful. But together as a trio, they are breathtaking."

He couldn't disagree. Yet *she* was the sister he found unforgettable.

"But what is most amazing and wonderful about my sisters," Miss Briggeham continued, "is that they are as lovely inside as they are on the outside."

He detected no envy in her voice, only fierce pride. He

studied her upturned face, debating whether to tell her that she was equally as lovely. Would she accept his compliment as his true feelings, or believe he'd merely uttered it as nothing more than polite gibberish?

Unable to decide, he let the moment pass. Turning, he led her to the drawing room where tea had been laid out. He closed the door behind them, watching her as she crossed the parquet floor to the center of the room. She turned in a slow circle, taking in the cream silk-covered walls, the overstuffed sofa, settee and wing chairs, royal-blue velvet draperies, brass sconces flanking the heavy mirror, cozy fire crackling in the grate, and the smattering of antique porcelains his mother had loved gracing the mahogany end tables.

"A lovely room, my lord," she said, completing her circle to face him once more. "As is your entire home."

"Thank you." He indicated the tea service. "Would you care for some tea? Or would you like something stronger? A sherry perhaps?"

She surprised him by accepting a sherry. While she settled herself on the settee, he poured her drink and a brandy for himself. He then joined her, sitting on the opposite end of the settee. She took a tiny sip of her sherry, drawing his gaze to her full lips. He instantly imagined leaning over and touching his tongue to her lower lip to sample the sweetness clinging there. He squeezed his eyes shut and tossed back his drink to banish the erotic image.

When he opened his eyes, he set his empty snifter on the low table in front of them, then picked up a glass jar resting next to the tea service. Extending the jar toward her, he said, "This is for you."

"For me?" She set her glass on the table, then reached out for the jar. Holding it aloft to capture the fire's light, she exclaimed, "Why, it looks like honey."

"It is. I recalled Hubert saying your supply was nearly

depleted, so I . . ." His voice trailed off as a delighted smile broke over her face. A smile that utterly enchanted him, washing warmth through him. A smile he already knew wasn't brought on by gifts of flowers, and he suspected couldn't be coaxed with any of the other trappings most females longed for.

"How incredibly thoughtful," she said. "Thank you."

"You're welcome. I must admit, however, that my gift comes with a request."

"I shall be pleased to grant it if I can."

"You said that the honey cream you make relieves the aches in your friend's hands."

"It seems to, yes, even without the warming properties I hope to add to it."

"My stableman suffers from stiff joints, and perhaps your cream could help him. I'll be happy to supply you with several more jars if you'd consent to make some cream for me to give him."

Her smile deepened. "I already supply Mr. Timstone with my cream."

"You do?"

"Yes. For several months now. While it's not a cure, of course, it affords him some temporary relief. I would be happy to make an extra batch for him. It is not necessary to give me more than one jar, my lord. One is more than generous. You're . . . very kind."

"I'm certain you don't mean to sound so surprised," he teased.

"I'm not surprised, my lord." Mischief twinkled behind her spectacles. "At least not *very* much." Her amusement slowly faded. "I appreciate your kindness toward me, but I wish to express my gratitude for the generosity you've shown Hubert." Reaching out, she lightly touched his arm. "Thank you."

" 'Twas no hardship. Hubert's a fine boy with a sharp, inquisitive mind."

"Yes, he is. But many people simply . . . dismiss him."

"Many people are fools."

A slow smile, filled with unmistakable admiration, eased over her face, and he felt as if he'd just been presented with a priceless gift. He glanced down at her small hand resting on his sleeve and marveled that such an innocent touch could ignite such a fire in him. Raising his gaze, he stared into her magnified eyes, which regarded him with a warmth that only served to further heat his blood.

Her gaze dropped to where her hand still rested on his sleeve. Issuing a self-conscious sound, she withdrew her hand, and he barely resisted the urge to grab her fingers back and press them against him.

The room suddenly felt too warm. Too confining. He needed to put some distance between them, but before he could move, she set the jar on the table, then rose. Had she felt it, too?

She approached the fireplace, where she looked up at the massive portrait hung above the marble mantel. "Your father?" she asked.

"Yes." Eric gazed dispassionately at the man who had sired him. Marcus Landsdowne had provided the seed to create his son, but that was the extent of his "fathering." He supposed many men would have removed the portrait, but he'd never considered doing so. His father's unforgivable treatment of Margaret was the driving force behind his mission as the Bride Thief, and he made certain he looked upon his father's face every day so he wouldn't forget . . . wouldn't forget how the greedy bastard had bartered away a beautiful young woman like a piece of chattel. Or how his reckless infidelities had shamed his mother. Or how he'd treated his son with a cruel combination of contempt and indifference.

No, he'd never forget the sort of man he'd vowed never to become.

Yet the portrait taunted him every time he gazed upon it, for there was no denying the physical resemblance between he and his father, a fact that rankled him. *I may look like you, but I'm nothing like you, you bastard.*

He glanced at Miss Briggeham, who was studying the portrait with great interest.

"I gather you see the resemblance," he said, bracing himself for the inevitable comparison, even as he again told himself it didn't matter. The resemblance was only physical.

"Actually," she said, turning to face him, "I don't."

Confusion assailed him. "You don't? Everyone says I look like my father."

She tapped her fingers on her jaw and studied him with a serious frown. "Physically, I suppose."

"What other way is there?"

A blush stole over her cheeks, and she averted her gaze. Rising, he moved to stand in front of her. The fire's glow backlighted her, casting her countenance into shadow. Reaching out, he lifted her chin with a gentle fingertip until their eyes met.

"Tell me," he said, perplexed by the strange need to know what she meant. "Please."

"I only meant that your father seems . . . that is, he appears to have possessed a . . . harshness to his character. It's there, in his eyes. Around his mouth. The way he holds himself. You don't have that severity of spirit."

"Indeed?" He refused to examine the slow roll his heart performed. Or the pleasure her words washed through him.

His surprise must have shown on his face, for she immediately looked stricken. "Forgive me, my lord. I fear I'm far too outspoken, but I meant no offense. What I was really trying to say is that you are much the handsomer."

"I see." The corner of his mouth tipped up and he couldn't resist teasing her. "You think me handsome, Miss Briggeham?"

Her eyes widened, and her tongue peeked out to moisten her lips. "Well, yes. I'm certain most people would agree that you're . . . pleasing to the eye. Certainly most *female* people."

"Ah. And you are undeniably female. But you are quite nearsighted are you not?"

"Yes, but—"

He cut off her words by giving into the urge that had gripped him since the first time he saw her, and slid her spectacles from her nose. Retreating several paces, he asked, "*Now* what do you think, Miss Briggeham?"

She squinted at him, then pressed her lips together as if suppressing a grin. "I'm certain you're still handsome, however, I can't see you clearly."

"Then come closer."

She took a hesitant inch-long step forward, then squinted again.

"Well?" he asked.

"I'm afraid you're still blurry, my lord. But scientific logic would indicate that your appearance is unchanged."

"Ah, but in science, one must always test theories." He drew one step closer to her. "Can you see me now?"

Her lips twitched. "Still a blurry blob, I fear."

Another step closer. No more than two feet now separated them. He gazed at her, prepared to see nervousness, expecting to see anxiety, hoping to see desire flare in her eyes. Instead, she simply stared at him steadily, with what appeared to be cool detachment, her brows slightly raised, as if he were some sort of . . . scientific specimen. Bloody hell! "Am I still a . . . what did you call me? Oh, yes. A blurry blob?"

"You're getting clearer, but you're still fuzzy about the edges."

"Well then, why don't you simply tell me when I'm in focus." He leaned forward, slowly, watching her intently, willing her to react to the heat he knew simmered in his gaze. He knew the exact second he came into focus. No more than six inches separated their faces. She drew in a sharp breath and her pupils dilated.

"Can you see me clearly now?" he asked softly.

She swallowed and nodded. "My, yes. There you are. Right . . . there. So very . . . close." Her voice held a breathless, husky note that stroked over him like a caress. And her eyes . . . yes, they now shimmered with awareness, with the dawning heat he wanted. Reaching out, he gently grasped her wrist, pleased that her pulse raced beneath his fingertips.

His gaze dropped to her mouth and desire hit him low and hard. The sweet scent of honey wafted over him, befuddling his senses. He simply had to know if she tasted as sweet as she smelled. Had to. Just once.

Before he could recall all the reasons he shouldn't, he lowered his head, brushing his lips lightly over hers. Soft. Honey. A hint of sherry. His curiosity not nearly satisfied, he drew her into his arms and kissed her again, his lips circling, teasing, tasting hers.

Warm. Sweet. More. Had to have more.

With the tip of his tongue, he traced her full bottom lip, coaxing her to open for him. A tiny, breathy sound escaped her, sending a rush of her warm, sherry-scented breath over him. With a groan, he slipped his tongue into the silky velvet of her mouth.

Heat. Honey. Heaven.

Her sweet taste filled him, and everything faded away except her. God, she tasted good enough to eat and the urge to simply devour her overwhelmed him. He gathered her closer, pressing her lush curves to him, savoring her softness, ignited by the breathtaking way she fit in his arms. As she'd fit against him when he'd abducted her. Only this embrace was so much more. Because this time she returned it—with a hesitant wonder that grew into a rapidly increasing enthusiasm, dissolving any remaining control he imagined he possessed.

She mimicked his every action, tentatively at first, like a student presented with a new puzzle, but she caught on quickly. With devastating results. As he tasted her, she explored his mouth with the same slow thoroughness, her soft tongue sliding against his. Even as his fingers delved into her silky hair, scattering pins, her fingers sifted through the hair at his nape. When his arms tightened around her, she drew up on her toes, lifting her mouth higher for him.

A low groan rumbled between them. His? Hers? He didn't know. All he knew was that she felt incredible. Tasted incredible. And that he wanted more.

With one hand holding her head, the other skimmed slowly down her back, reveling in her soft, womanly curves. He caressed his palm over her buttocks, then pressed her closer to him, knowing she had to feel his arousal. But instead of backing away, she strained closer to him.

A maelstrom of heat flashed through him, like a brush fire on dry kindling. His pulse roared through his veins, pounding in his ears, obliterating everything but her. The texture of her hair. The fragrance of her skin. The taste of her in his mouth.

More. Had to taste more. Dragging his lips from her, he pressed a trail of kisses down her neck, savoring the vibrations against his lips as she expelled a long, low, moan.

"Samantha . . ." Her name whispered past his lips, unable to be contained. He touched his tongue to the frantically beating pulse at the base of her throat. Honey. God, did she smell like honey everywhere? Taste like it all over? An image of them, naked, in his bed, flashed in his mind. Her, eyes glazed with need, legs splayed, wanting. Him, grasping her hips, touching his tongue to her moist flesh . . .

Sweat broke out on his forehead. He had to end this insanity. Now. While he still could. Drawing a shaky breath, he forced himself to straighten and end their kiss.

He looked down at her and swallowed a groan. Damn it, she was as aroused as he. Shallow breaths puffed from between her moist, swollen lips, which remained slightly parted, begging him to kiss her again. Her eyes were closed, and crimson colored her cheeks. His gaze dropped to the rapidly beating pulse at the base of her throat, then lowered to her breasts, which still pressed against his chest. He imagined her nipples were tight and hard, and he ached to slip his fingers inside her bodice, to touch her.

Her eyelids fluttered open, and his resolve nearly crumbled at her dazed, languorous expression. A tremor shuddered through her, and his arms tightened around her, absorbing the shiver, inducing one of his own that tingled down his spine. He brushed a tangled chestnut curl from her flushed cheek and waited for her slumberous gaze to focus on him. When it finally did, he gritted his teeth against the guileless wonder shining from her eyes.

"My heavens," she said. "That was . . ."

"Delicious. Delectable. Delightful." A smile pulled up one corner of his mouth. "So many 'd' words to describe one woman. Or perhaps 'l' words would be better."

"I cannot deny that lightheaded comes to mind."

A chuckle of pure masculine satisfaction rumbled in his throat. Touching his fingertip to that beguiling freckle at the corner of her upper lip, he murmured, "I was thinking of luscious. And lovely."

She went completely still. All vestiges of desire slowly faded from her eyes until she stared at him with a completely blank expression. No, not completely blank. Shades of disappointment shadowed her eyes. He could almost hear her saying *I'm not lovely. You're just like all the others who have spent the past weeks spouting insincere compliments.*

Her expression filled him with an ache he could not name. Before he could figure out a way to erase that disillusioned look from her eyes, she pressed her lips together, then stepped back, out of his embrace.

"May I have my spectacles, please?" she asked in a flat voice.

"Of course." Reaching behind him, he picked her glasses off the mantel, then placed them in her outstretched palm. She quickly slipped them on, then wrapped her arms around herself as if to ward off a sudden chill. She drew several deep breaths, then she lifted her chin and met his gaze squarely.

Guilt smacked him like a brick to the head. Damn it, what was he thinking, kissing her in such a passionate manner? Kissing her at all? A gentleman would never do such a thing, and he knew he should heartily beg her pardon. But how could he apologize for something that had felt so . . . right? And how to make her understand that *he* thought she was lovely? Achingly so.

Before he could decide, she said, "I think it would be best if I fetch Hubert and leave now, Lord Wesley."

She was right. Things between them had gotten totally out of hand, and he accepted full responsibility. But still an acute sense of loss flooded him at the coolness in her tone. As he watched her leave the room, his hands clenched. Yes, it was best that she leave. But damn it, everything inside him wanted her to stay. He couldn't deny it.

But what the hell could he do about it?

Chapter 9

From the *London Times*:

> The annual masquerade ball held at Countess Ringshire's country estate in Devon was, as always, a fabulous affair. Several gentlemen costumed themselves as the infamous Bride Thief, which led many guests to laughingly speculate that the real Bride Thief might be among them. Would he possibly be that daring? Many guests further noted that the Bride Thief has not been heard from for several weeks. One cannot help but wonder when and where he might strike next. Yet with every able-bodied man in England eager to collect the seven-thousand-pound price on his head, the Bride Thief's next kidnapping will most certainly be his last.

Eric tossed the newspaper onto the cherry wood table in the drawing room and heaved a sigh. All this speculation and interest in his activities was a double-edged sword. While it brought the plight of women who were bartered away in marriage like household possessions to attention, it made his efforts at rescuing them ever more dangerous. A reward of seven thousand pounds? No one could resist that. If he made even the smallest mistake, his life was over.

How was the investigation proceeding? Had any additional clues to the Bride Thief's identity been discovered? Arthur hadn't reported anything, but perhaps it was time to go directly to the source. Yes, a casual chat with the magistrate might be a wise plan. He and Adam Straton were long-standing acquaintances. Perhaps he'd ride into the village today or tomorrow. And on his way home . . .

His gaze wandered to the honey-filled glass jar set on the table next to the carelessly folded newspaper. Miss Briggeham had forgotten the jar in her haste to leave last evening. He'd considered reminding her, but had discarded the idea. Returning the jar to her was the perfect excuse to see her again. And as much as he wished otherwise, it was inexplicably necessary to see her again.

Rising, he paced across the parquet floor, his brows pulled down in a frown. Damn it all, how could a mere kiss—one that had lasted only a few *moments*—affect him so profoundly? He recalled every second of it. Every nuance of her taste, the imprint of her body pressed to his. The way her soft curves fit his hands.

Bloody hell, over the years he'd spent countless *hours* enjoying the sensuous charms of other women. Always, once their passion was spent, once the act was completed, he'd simply . . . forgotten them. Yet the kiss he'd shared with Samantha, that heated, breathless mating of mouths was embedded in his memory, as if branded there.

He'd barely slept last night. Lying in his bed, his body painfully aroused, he'd relived their kiss over and over. Then he'd further tortured himself by imagining what might have happened had she not left. With a groan, he grasped the mantel with both hands, then lowered his head to stare blindly into the dancing flames.

The images he'd tried all night to banish bombarded him, and he squeezed his eyes shut, willing them away. Instead he saw himself slowly removing her gown, exposing her soft skin inch by inch, her beautiful eyes at first wide with wonder, then drooping shut as he kissed her long and deep, their tongues intimately dancing. Carrying her to the sofa, he opened the jar of honey and dipped his fingertip inside. He then slowly blazed a golden circle around her distended nipple. With her husky moans echoing in his ears, he licked the delectable treat he'd just created. When he finally lifted his head and again dipped his finger into the jar, she looked up at him, a devilish gleam shining through the desire fogging her eyes.

What do you plan to taste next, my lord?

All of you. And then we'll—

A knock sounded on the door, jolting him from his erotic daydream. He dragged his hands down his overheated face. Looking down, he shook his head at the bulge tenting his breeches. Damn. The seemingly neversubsiding, Miss Briggeham-induced erection.

With a grimace he adjusted his confining breeches, then all but limped back to the sofa. Lowering himself to the cushion, he grabbed the newspaper and strategically arranged it across his lap. "Come in."

A footman entered, extending a silver salver bearing a sealed letter. "This just arrived, your lordship. The messenger indicated it was urgent and that he would wait for a reply."

Eric took the letter, his insides freezing when he recognized his name written in Margaret's distinctive, elegant hand. He dismissed the footman with a nod. "I'll ring when my reply is ready."

The instant the door closed behind the footman, Eric broke the wax seal. His hands trembled with dread as he unfolded the thick vellum. Had that bastard Darvin dared to hurt her again? *If so, he's a dead man.*

His heart beating hard, he quickly read the letter.

My dearest Eric,

I am writing to inform you that Darvin is dead, killed Wednesday last during a duel. His younger brother Charles will move into Darvin Manor as soon as his affairs are settled. Charles has indicated I may continue to live here, but I wish to leave as soon as possible. I am hoping the offer you made me still stands and that I might be welcome to stay at Wesley—at least until I can make other living arrangements.

I anxiously await your reply.

Yours, Margaret

The tension slowly eased from Eric's shoulders, and he blew out a long breath. Crossing to the desk, he extracted a piece of stationery bearing the Wesley crest and carefully penned two words to his sister.

Come home.

Sammie sat on her favorite flat rock, her chin resting on her up-drawn knees, her bare feet peeking out from beneath the hem of her comfortable old dark green gown. She contemplated the calm lake water for several seconds, then skimmed a handful of pebbles across the glassy surface. Dozens of rings fanned out, marring the indigo stillness, crisscrossing each other in a watery echo of the myriad emotions rippling through her.

Vivid images of last evening flashed through her mind, filling her with a contradictory combination of elation, disappointment, and embarrassment—emotional ingredients that mixed to create a recipe for aching confusion.

Squeezing her eyes shut, she tried to erase the memory of him . . . him touching her. Looking at her. Kissing her. Making her feel more alive than she ever had, while never-before-experienced sensations whirled through her, heating her body in that exhilarating way that rendered her breathless. Aching. Burning. Wanting more.

Then the cold slap of disillusionment.

With a groan, she turned her head, resting her cheek against the sun-warmed muslin of her gown. *Perhaps "l" words would be better. I was thinking of luscious . . . and lovely.*

He had flattered her, very much like the false admirers who had spent the last several weeks seeking out her company under one pretext or another to question her about the Bride Thief. Nearly all of them had slathered ridiculous compliments on her, calling her everything from adorable to gorgeous. She'd endured them all, somehow managing not to roll her eyes.

Lovely. Why, oh why, had he called her lovely? It was such a blatant lie. Did he think she didn't know she was as plain as a white wall? But somehow, hearing him utter that single word had had the effect of a bucket of icy water on her, bringing her abruptly, cruelly, to her senses.

Lovely. Yes, Lord Wesley had chosen the very word one of her new admirers, a Mr. Martin, had used to describe her at the very beginning of her newfound popularity. For one insane, surprised, pleased instant, she'd believed the young man . . . until she'd overheard him an hour later, laughing with another gentleman near the French windows, where she'd stepped outdoors for a breath of much-needed air.

"Homely as a burlap sack, that Miss Briggeham is," Mr. Martin had said.

"Oh, but I heard you call her 'lovely,' " his companion said with a chuckle.

"And never has a more glaring lie ever passed my lips," said Mr. Martin. "Nearly choked me to utter it."

And now the earl had called her lovely.

A single tear slipped down her cheek, and she impatiently rubbed it away. She simply hadn't expected such falsehoods from him . . . from the man who had set her foolish heart aflutter almost from the start. She'd thought he was different, but clearly insincere words dripped from his lips as easily as they did from all the others'.

For the first time in a long while, she indulged in the useless exercise of wishing she actually *were* lovely. The sort of woman to attract the attention of a man like him. She'd ruthlessly buried such futile feelings long ago. It was illogical to waste time wanting the impossible.

A frown pinched her brow as a thought suddenly occurred to her. While she questioned the sincerity of his compliment, there was no doubt that he *had* actually desired her. She was scientifically aware of the workings of the human body, and there could be no doubt as to the physical evidence of his arousal. Lovely or not, he had desired her. And heaven knows she'd desired him.

Sitting up straight, she pursed her lips and applied logic to the facts. Yes, he'd muttered untrue statements regarding her appearance, but should she fault him for being kind? Polite? Heavens, what was the man supposed to say? That she resembled a toad?

Until last evening, no man had ever indicated he desired her. Wanted to kiss her. Touch her. But this man had. And God help her, she wanted him to desire her again. She'd never dared hope that she might feel a man's passion. This might well be her only chance to ever experience an adventure her heart had always secretly yearned for—to *know* a man. In every way a woman could.

Could she truly contemplate becoming Lord Wesley's lover? Her heart skipped a beat and heat suffused her. *Yes. This is my chance to experience something I've always dreamed of. Passion. With a man who sets my blood on fire.*

Of course, marriage was out of the question. Lord Wesley would never consider *marrying* someone like her. He would marry a diamond of the first water. A fresh, young, malleable miss from the peerage, who possessed a beautiful face and a dowry to match. But his physical reaction last evening clearly indicated he was not adverse to making love to *her*.

Making love. The adventure of a lifetime. Her eyes drifted closed, and a long sigh escaped her. She'd always dreamed of adventure, but since her abduction by the Bride Thief, it seemed as if the floodgates had opened. Her previous vague yearnings had blossomed into deep aches of want. Yes, her work in the Chamber fulfilled her, but as she'd grown older, she'd recognized that although her mind was satisfied, something inside her wanted more. And she knew exactly what she wanted.

Lord Wesley.

She pressed her hands to her stomach to calm its wild fluttering. Lord Wesley's lover. Dear God, did she dare? Every long-suppressed desire inside her screamed *yes!*

But there was much to consider. Certainly much discretion would be needed to avoid a scandal for herself as well as her family. And what if she became with child? Even though their affair might remain secret, she couldn't very well hide a child. Of course, there were ways to prevent pregnancy. While she didn't know what they were, surely one of her sisters would. Best to only ask one of them, however. The fewer people she involved in her plan in any way, the better. Perhaps Lucille would be best. She always knew all the London gossip and seemed particularly fascinated by wicked liaisons. *I'll claim I merely wish to know for scientific research. Certainly Lucille would never suspect I want the information because I intend to take a lover.*

A thrill of exhilaration *zing*ed through her at the prospect of such an adventure. She wanted to discover the ways of passion . . . and at no one else's hands but his. Heavens, his kiss had nearly dissolved her knees. What would it be like to share further intimacies with him? Caress each other . . . join their bodies? She didn't know, but she desperately wanted to find out.

Would she find herself in his arms again? If so, she would make the most of the opportunity. She'd allow her desires . . . and his . . . to lead her.

The snap of a breaking stick startled her. She turned around and heat flashed through her.

Lord Wesley stood directly behind her.

Eric looked down at her and stilled at her expression. He'd hoped she wouldn't gaze at him with that same disappointed blankness in her eyes as last evening. She didn't. But he was unprepared for the sight that greeted him.

Bloody hell, she looked . . . aroused. Crimson-stained cheeks, labored breathing, unmistakable desire shimmering behind her spectacles. What the hell had she just been thinking?

She reached for a pair of worn slippers and slid her bare feet into them. He caught a glimpse of shapely ankle that affected his pulse far more than it should have.

Extending his hand to help her up, he said, "Good afternoon, Miss Briggeham."

"Lord Wesley." She accepted his hand, and warmth spread up his arm when her smooth palm met his. He helped her rise, then immediately had to squelch the groan that rose in his throat. She stood no more than a foot away, her chestnut curls delightfully disheveled, her honey scent wrapping around him like a fragrant web. The desire to taste her, feel her, slammed into him with knee-buckling intensity. Even while his brain told him to release her hand, he shifted his fingers to bring their palms into more intimate contact.

"I thought I might find you here," he said softly.

"You wished to speak to me?"

No. I wish to strip that gown from your luscious body, then run my tongue all over you. And when I've finished tasting you, I want to—

He shook his head to clear it. "Speak to you? Er, yes."

"About last evening?"

"Er, yes." Good God, he sounded like a nodcock, but he hadn't expected such forthrightness. Yet, he should have from her.

She nodded once, briskly. "Excellent, for I wish to discuss it as well. I should not have departed your home in so abrupt a manner. You'd shown great generosity to both myself and Hubert and I apologize."

"There is no need for you to—"

"I've thought extensively on the matter, and I quite understand why you said what you did."

"You do?"

"Yes. After all, you couldn't very well tell me the *truth*. Yet while I appreciate your effort to—"

He brushed a single finger over her lips, cutting off her words. "What do you mean by the *truth*? Are you suggesting I *lied* to you?"

She puckered her brow and pursed her lips, clearly considering his question. "Lied, I believe, is too strong a word. Fibbed is perhaps better. I realize you were only trying to be polite, but in the future, I would prefer you not utter such drivel."

He knew immediately what she referred to. How was it possible that this incredible, unique woman had no inkling of her own appeal?

"I did not lie to you. Or fib." Bringing her hand to his lips, he feathered a kiss across her fingers. Then, sliding his other arm around her, he drew her closer, until her breasts brushed his shirt.

"You *are* lovely," he said softly, watching her steadily, willing her to read the sincerity in his gaze, in his voice. Uncertainty flickered in her eyes, as if she wanted to believe him but could not, and he ached with the need to show her, tell her, make her understand. "I do not say that to be polite, but because it's true."

He drew both her hands to his chest, pressing her palms over his rapidly beating heart. Then, trailing a single fingertip slowly down her cheek, he murmured, "Take your skin, for example. It's smooth. Flawless. Like the finest silk."

"I have freckles on my nose."

A smile tugged at one corner of his mouth. "I know. And they're utterly charming." He captured a wayward curl between his fingers. "And your hair is—"

"Unruly."

"Shiny. Soft." He brought the curl to his face and inhaled. "Fragrant." Reaching out, he slowly removed her spectacles, tucking them in his jacket pocket. "And then there are your eyes. They're extraordinary. Large and expressive. Warm and intelligent. Did you know they sparkle like aquamarines when you smile? Did you know your smile could light a darkened room?" She stared at him, blinked twice, then simply shook her head.

His gaze wandered down to her mouth, and his pulse jumped. Slowly tracing the rim of her lips with a single fingertip, he whispered, "Your mouth is . . . fascinating. Luscious. Kissable." Leaning forward, he brushed his lips over hers, once, twice, then kissed a slow trail across her jaw.

When he reached her ear, he gently captured the lobe between his teeth, enjoying the shiver that rippled through her. Inhaling deeply, her fragrance infused him, seeping through him like a drug.

"Your scent," he whispered against her soft neck, "is beyond lovely. Even if I live to be one hundred, I shall never smell honey again and not think of you. It's tantalizing. Tempting." He touched his tongue to her fragrant skin and a groan escaped him. "Tormenting. So many 't' words to describe one woman."

A shaky moan rumbled in her throat, and he leaned back to gaze at her flushed face. "Lovely," he reiterated firmly. "In every way. Inside and out. Don't ever let anyone tell you otherwise. And don't *you* ever believe otherwise."

She stared at him, wide-eyed and silent. Her hands rested on his shirt, radiating heat across his chest, down his abdomen, and into his groin. With her soft body pressed against his from chest to knee, he knew she felt his arousal. But he wanted her to. Wanted her to feel the undeniable evidence of his desire, the physical proof of the sincerity of his words.

Her tongue darted out to moisten her lips. "No one has ever said such things to me before."

"I find that impossible to believe. But I recall we agreed last evening that most people are fools."

She didn't react for several seconds, but then a smile spread slowly over her face, as if the sun were dawning, heating him until he basked in its golden glow.

"I think you're lovely as well," she whispered.

Her simple compliment washed over him, touching him in a way no other woman's words ever had. Need pulsed through him, throbbing hot in his veins, overriding his common sense, pushing aside his better judgment. One word echoed through his mind—a mantra fueling his desire.

Mine. Mine. Mine.

Unable to stop himself, he tunneled his fingers through her hair, scattering pins onto the ground until her chestnut tresses sifted freely over his skin. The scent of her engulfed him, flooding his senses, drowning his reason. Lowering his head, he kissed her slowly, deeply, his tongue sliding into her silky mouth then retreating in a sensual dance his body ached to share with her. She responded to his every move, gliding her tongue against his, combing her fingers through his hair, straining her body closer, tighter to his.

Mine. Mine. Mine.

Without breaking their kiss, he moved backwards until his back bumped against a thick tree trunk. Bracing his weight against the sturdy tree, he pulled her closer, his hands slipping down to her rounded buttocks. Hauling her against his straining arousal, he slowly rubbed himself against her, shooting spears of white-hot heat through him. With a low, guttural groan burning in his throat, his hands slid up her rib cage, then forward to cup her breasts. Her soft muslin-covered flesh filled his hands, her hard nipples pressing against his palms.

Dragging his lips from hers, he pressed hot, open-mouthed kisses down her neck. Long, feminine moans of pleasure rumbled in her throat, and she arched against him, igniting him. He slipped his fingers inside her bodice and brushed them over her distended nipples. His groan mingled with hers, and raising his head, he devoured her mouth in another searing kiss. She squirmed against him and his erection jerked in response. God help him, he wanted her. Needed her. Now. *Mine. Mine. Mine.*

Reaching down, he caught the hem of her gown, gathering it slowly upward. He slid his hand beneath the material, trailing his palm up her silky bare thigh. She gasped against his mouth, and he leaned back to look at her, his vision hazy with desire.

Bloody hell, she was incredible. Flushed, aroused, her lips swollen from his ardent kisses, her nipples hard beneath the thin muslin of her gown, her chest rising and falling with her rapid breaths. She was everything a man could want, and she was his for the taking. If he moved his hand, just a few inches, he could caress her feminine flesh . . . heated folds he knew were soft and wet. For him. And then he'd—

And then you'll what? His conscience yelled, breaking through the sensual fog enveloping him. *Are you going to take her against the tree? A virgin? And if you do, then what do you plan to do with her? Marry her?*

And on the heels of his outraged conscience, Arthur's words came back to him. *She's innocent. Just the sort of woman who might read more meanin' into yer attentions than ye mean.*

Reality hit him like a cold, wet blanket. Easing his hand from beneath her gown, he gripped her by the waist and firmly set her away from him.

Sammie dragged a much needed breath into her lungs. Heat spiraled through her, pooling between her legs. Her feminine flesh felt moist and heavy, and throbbed with an ache she'd never before experienced. A delightful ache she wanted more of.

But with the thrilling hardness of his body no longer pressing against her, she forced her eyes open. He leaned against the tree trunk, holding her at arm's length by the waist. She squinted at him, and although he was blurry, she could easily discern his labored breathing and intense expression.

Thank goodness he still held her or else she would have simply slithered to the ground in a boneless heap. Drawing several deep breaths, she tried to slow her racing pulse and gather her scattered wits.

Finally finding her voice, she asked, "Why did you stop?"

His grip on her waist tightened. "Because if I hadn't stopped then, I wouldn't have been able to." A humorless laugh passed his lips. "Believe me, the effort nearly killed me. Do you have any idea how close I came to making love to you?"

Elation swept through Sammie. Drawing upon all her courage, she whispered, "Do you have any idea how much I wanted you to?"

He went perfectly still. "We can't do this," he said in a raspy voice.

She raised her chin a notch and said the words she prayed would set her on the greatest adventure of her life.

"Why not?"

Chapter 10

"Why not?" Eric stared at her in amazement. She watched him, her head cocked to one side, clearly waiting for him to elaborate. After what seemed an eternity, he finally cleared his throat and said, "Surely you know why we cannot take this any further. There could be repercussions—and I'm not in a position to offer you marriage."

She raised her brows. "I don't expect a proposal."

"Then what *do* you expect exactly?"

"That we'd share a wonderful adventure."

Eric's heart thumped so hard he could feel his blood pounding in his ears. He tried to draw a breath, but his lungs seemed compressed in his chest, as if a heavy rock sat on them.

Her response stunned him, elated him, and he wanted more than anything to share a sensual adventure with her. But how could he? His conscience would flog him alive. The silence stretched between them and he knew he had to respond.

"As flattered as I am by your willingness, I'm afraid we must stop."

She frowned, then her eyes widened. "Oh, dear. Do you already have a lover?"

A warm flush crept up his neck. "Not currently, no."

There was no mistaking her relief. Her gaze drifted down to his still-bulging manhood, then returned to his face. "You cannot deny you desire me."

"Obviously not. But there is much more involved here than simply satisfying my desires." His fingers tightened briefly on her wasit, then he released her and dragged his hands down his face. "Clearly you have not thought this through—"

"On the contrary, I have."

"Indeed? 'Tis clear you have not considered your reputation, which would be utterly ruined."

"Only if someone found out. I wouldn't tell anyone. Would you?"

"Of course not. But no matter how discreet we might try to be, someone would suspect and gossip. A servant, a neighbor, someone in your family. It would be impossible to hide an affair in a close-knit village like Tunbridge Wells."

"I disagree." Drawing a deep breath, she clasped her hands in front of her. "I am regarded in this village as an odd, eccentric, homely, firmly-on-the-shelf bluestocking. No one would credit for an instant that any man, let alone a man such as yourself, would grant me more than a passing glance. I find it nearly impossible to credit myself. Indeed, I would go so far as to say that even if we stood in a crowded room and *announced* to one and all that we'd become lovers, no one would believe us."

The fact that she was most likely correct rushed a surge of anger through him toward every dolt who had ever dismissed her. Damnable idiots.

"I am rapidly approaching my twenty-sixth birthday,"

she continued. "I accepted long ago the limitations put upon me by my appearance and unusual interests, but that has never stopped me from yearning for adventure. And passion."

Fragile hope and longing flickered in her eyes, tightening his throat. Damn it, he had to convince her that taking him as a lover was a bad idea—and somehow manage to convince her without crushing her. But it was damn difficult to recall why when his loins ached with need and it seemed he'd lost his voice.

Needing to touch her, he reached out, took her hand, and entwined their fingers. Warmth eased up his arm at her touch, and it required a great deal of willpower not to simply yank her against him and consign his bloody conscience to the devil.

"Ever since my encounter with the Bride Thief," she said softly, "I've been unable to suppress my need for adventure. It's as if he burst a dam inside me."

He froze. "The *Bride Thief*? What has he to do with this?"

"He made me feel . . . alive. Made me realize how very much I wanted . . . things."

His jaw hardened and he narrowed his eyes. "Things such as a lover?"

She met his gaze unflinchingly. "Yes."

Unreasonable, irrational jealousy pumped through him, and he abruptly released her hand. "Then perhaps you should approach the Bride Thief with your offer."

Color rushed into her cheeks, and he gritted his teeth. He hadn't considered that she might be harboring . . . *lover-like* feelings for his alter personality.

"It is unlikely I shall ever see him again," she said.

Damned unlikely. "And if you did?"

"He did not give me any indication that he . . . desired me."

Bloody hell, what did she mean by *that?* Did she *want* to experience passion with the Bride Thief? The thought of her wanting another man, regardless of the fact that the other man was in reality *him*, edged his vision with a red haze.

Swallowing his mounting anger, he said coolly, "Have you considered that your *adventure* could result in pregnancy?"

"Yes, but I understand that there are ways to prevent such an occurrence."

"And do you know what they are?"

"No . . . not yet."

"Yet?" He raked a hand through his hair. "How do you intend to find out?"

She raised her brows. "Do *you* know?"

"Of course. I've no wish to father any by-blows."

A smile of unmistakable relief touched her lips. "Excellent. You can tell me everything I need to know."

"I'll do nothing of the sort. You do not require such information as I will not be your lover." He rubbed his hand over his face, shaking his head. "What if you decide to marry in the future?" The instant the words passed his lips, another image of her, wrapped in some faceless man's arms, filled his mind, almost choking him.

"I have no desire to marry. My scientific work fulfills me, and I hope to someday travel. If I'd wanted to be a wife, I could have agreed to a match my parents recently tried to arrange. You have my word that I shall not attempt to extract an offer of marriage from you."

"That is wise, as I've no intention of ever marrying. And I would never want to be forced into marriage."

"Nor would I. But what of your title?"

"It will die with me," he said, his voice stiff with cold finality.

"I see." She expelled a long breath, then said, "Well,

now that we've discussed and dismissed all the obstacles . . ."

God knew he ached to make love to her. But with his damned conscience all but hammering him in the head, he felt compelled to save her from herself. For in spite of her protestations, she obviously didn't realize how much she stood to lose.

Forcing aside the need that threatened to overwhelm his good intentions, he took her by the shoulders and looked into her eyes. Praying she would see the depth of his regret, he said, "I cannot be your lover. Not because I don't want you, because I do." A humorless laugh escaped him. "Desperately. But I cannot, *will* not be responsible for your social ruin."

She lifted her chin a notch higher. "I've told you I would not hold you responsible for any adverse effects stemming from our association."

"I understand. But I am not the sort of man who can simply walk away from or ignore my responsibilities."

Confusion flashed in her eyes. "But what of your previous lovers? Were you not concerned for their reputations?"

Tenderness washed through him. Cupping her heart-shaped face between his hands, he brushed his thumbs over her smooth cheeks. "None of my previous lovers were innocents. Any association with me, or any other man, would not harm their social standing. *You* would be ruined. I cannot do it."

His words drained all the expression from her eyes. "I see." She stepped jerkily backward and his hands slipped from her face. "In that case, I suppose it's best if I go home. May I have my spectacles, please?"

"Of course." He extracted her glasses from his jacket pocket and handed them to her. He watched her slip them on, his insides aching with a sharp pang of loss.

After adjusting her glasses, she offered him a formal

nod. "I bid you good-bye, Lord Wesley." Turning on her heel, she headed down the path toward her home.

Good-bye. There was no mistaking her meaning or her tone. This was clearly the last she expected to see of him.

It was for the best. He should be happy. But damn it, his heart bloody well hurt at the thought of not seeing her ever again. Seeing her smile. Hearing her laugh. Touching her. Kissing her. Making love to her.

He pressed his lips together to keep from calling her name, planted his feet firmly in the dirt to keep from running after her, clenched his hands into tight fists to keep from grabbing her. Then he squeezed his eyes shut so he wouldn't have to watch her walking away from him.

He'd done the right thing. The noble thing. For her. Although where he'd found the strength to resist her offer, he'd never know.

Never know. Yes, now he'd never know what it would have felt like to have Samantha Briggeham under him. Over him. Wrapped around him. Moaning his name. Awakening her to the passion she longed to experience . . . and had wanted to share with him.

He opened his eyes. The path she'd taken was now deserted. Forcing himself to move, he turned to leave, but his footsteps halted as his gaze riveted on the jar of honey. He'd set it down near a clump of bushes before he'd approached her. Instantly a swarm of images bombarded him. Her pleasure at his gift. Her desire-glazed eyes after he'd kissed her. Her earnest, achingly hopeful expression as she asked him to become her lover.

A humorless sound emerged from his throat.

Yes, he certainly was noble.

A noble idiot with an ache in his heart that he feared might not ever subside.

* * *

Sammie sat at her escritoire, drumming her fingers against the polished cherry wood surface. *He refused. I must put the idea out of my mind.*

Unfortunately her mind was not cooperating at all.

Pursing her lips, she blew out a slow breath. His refusal should have left her embarrassed. Humiliated. Chastened. Instead she was frustrated. Disappointed.

And more determined than ever to have her way.

But how? How to convince him . . . entice him . . . seduce him? Why did he have to be so excruciatingly *noble*?

Yet even as she asked herself that question, she had to admit that she admired him even more for his concern for her welfare and reputation. If he weren't so honorable, she suspected he would not appeal to her so much. Still, she could not let this opportunity to experience passion pass her by. She could not imagine wanting to share such intimacies with anyone other than Lord Wesley, and if she failed to convince him, she feared she'd grow old without ever knowing what physical love was like. Perhaps if she hadn't met Lord Wesley she might have remained content to simply record such dreams in her journal.

But now that she'd tasted his kiss, knew the strength of his arms around her, felt the heat of his desire, she had to know more. And since she was determined to proceed, she needed to learn how to prevent pregnancy.

Pulling a clean sheet of vellum from the top drawer, she penned a quick note to Lucille asking if she could visit her this evening after dinner. Folding the missive, she sealed it with wax, then headed downstairs to find Hubert. She knew he would be happy to deliver the letter to their sister's house in the village, as Lucille always kept a jar filled with Hubert's favorite honey biscuits in her pantry.

While she waited for Lucille's reply, she'd formulate a logical list of questions to ask her sister regarding ways to prevent pregnancy.

And hope she would have a reason to make use of the information.

At nine o'clock that evening Sammie entered Lucille's cozy drawing room, but froze in the doorway as she met the inquisitive stares of three pairs of eyes.

"Good evening, Sammie," Lucille, Hermione, and Emily chimed in unison.

Oh, dear. This was not at all what she'd had in mind. Normally she'd be happy to spend an evening with all her sisters, but these were not normal circumstances. Clearly she'd have to wait to discuss the topic uppermost on her mind until another time, but she chafed at the delay. Swallowing her disappointment, she walked into the room and hugged her sisters.

Once the greetings were complete, they settled themselves on chintz-covered chairs around the fireplace. As Lucille poured generous glasses of sherry, she asked, "All right, out with it, Sammie. What's going on with him?"

Sammie's hand froze in the act of reaching for her glass. "I beg your pardon?"

"Oh, don't be coy," Hermione scolded, scooting her chair closer to Sammie. "We're absolutely dying to know all about it."

Sammie took her sherry and immediately quaffed a hefty mouthful. Oh, dear. She had a sinking feeling she knew which "him" and "it" her sisters referred to. Her suspicions were confirmed when Emily, who shared the settee with her, shifted so close she nearly sat in Sammie's lap. "Oh, he's ever so handsome, Sammie," Emily said, her eyes shining. "And wealthy and—"

"Titled," Lucille cut in, setting the decanter on the table next to her chair. "A very impressive lineage. He's the *eighth* earl, you know."

"No, I didn't know," Sammie murmured. "But—"

"The earl's aversion to marriage is well known, but it appears he's changed his mind about taking a wife if he's courting our Sammie," Hermione said, accepting a tray filled with sweet biscuits from Lucille.

Sammie nearly spewed a mouthful of sherry. Instead she swallowed the liquor and nearly choked. While she knew no one else would believe the earl was pursuing her, she should have known her loyal sisters would accept such an unlikely notion.

Emily thumped her on the back several times and added, "Imagine him claiming he'd never marry. What nonsense. We all *knew* he'd change his mind when he found the right woman." Tears shimmered in her eyes, and she gazed at Sammie with something akin to awe. "We just never knew you would be the right woman."

Sammie coughed and frantically waved her hand in front of her watering eyes. "No," she gasped. "Not right."

"Pass me her glass to refill, Emily," Lucille instructed. "And keep thumping on her back. Look there, her color's returning."

"When is he planning to call upon you again?" Hermione asked, accepting more sherry while Lucille was pouring. "You must make it a point not to be available every time he calls."

"Hermie's right," Emily said. "And make certain you keep him waiting at *least* a quarter hour before you appear. Don't worry that he won't wait. A sophisticated gentleman such as the earl is quite used to such things."

"And," chimed in Lucille, "you must spend at least a half hour a day practicing your flirtatious looks in the mirror. The one that always worked best for me was this." Lowering her chin, she cast her gaze demurely downward. Then she slowly raised her gaze and fluttered her lashes.

"Oh, marvelously done," Emily said, nodding her approval. "Or peek at him over the edge of your fan—"

"—and pout your lips like this," Hermie said, puckering her mouth into a perfect o. "And be sure to—"

Sammie held up her palm. "Stop. Cease. You must listen to me."

Her sisters fell silent and looked at her with a trio of eager, inquisitive, rapt expressions. Heavens, what a tangle. She needed to nip this disastrous state of affairs in the bud before it bloomed into a full garden. Shoving her spectacles back into place from where they'd slid down her nose during her coughing fit, she said, "You've quite misinterpreted the situation. There is nothing going on between me and the earl."

"But Mama said he called upon you and brought you flowers," Lucille protested.

"Every unmarried gentleman in the village has done the same since my abduction, all seeking to question me about the Bride Thief. Lord Weslcy is not besotted. Like all the others, he is merely a curiosity seeker."

Emily emptied her sherry glass, then held it out for a refill. "But Mama said he invited you to his home and—"

"Sent his carriage for you," Lucille finished.

"Then surely Mama told you the earl invited both *Hubert* and I for the sole purpose of viewing his Herschel telescope. His invitation was purely scientific in nature."

A frown crinkled Hermione's perfect brow. "Has he called upon you since?"

"No," Sammie said, quickly rationalizing that him finding her at the lake today did not qualify as calling upon her. "Nor would I expect him to. Mama has read far too much into his actions." *Good lord, if Mama even suspected what half the earl's "actions" had included, she'd chirp herself into a real faint.*

Emily's lovely smile collapsed with obvious disappointment. "Then you mean he's not—"

"You mean he hasn't—" cut in Lucille, her expression matching Emily's.

"Indeed not," Sammie said in her briskest tone. "There is absolutely nothing between me and Lord Wesley." She pursed her lips and settled her features into her most prim expression, praying the flush heating her face wouldn't give evidence of her blatant lie. "I suggest you dismiss the matter from your minds."

Although obviously let down by this turn of events, her sisters all mumbled their consent. Then Emily reached out and squeezed her hand. "Well, if Lord Wesley spent an evening in your company yet failed to recognize how special you are, well, then the man is simply . . ."

"A dolt," supplied Hermie, laying her hand on top of theirs.

"An ass," Lucille pronounced in a too-loud whisper, followed immediately by an unladylike hiccup. "More sherry, anyone?"

They all held out their empty glasses. As Lucille refilled their drinks, she said, "If you didn't want to discuss your relationship with the earl—"

"There is no relationship to discuss," Sammie managed through gritted teeth.

"Right. Then why did you wish to speak to us?"

She did not bother to point out that she hadn't wanted to speak to *all* of them—only Lucille. But clearly Lucille had dispatched messages fetching their sisters with the promise of finding out the details of Sammie's relationship with the earl. She was tempted to abandon her entire scheme, but her sisters were her only hope of gaining the information she sought. So long as she made it crystal clear she wished to know simply for scientific reasons, all should go well.

After swallowing another bracing mouthful of sherry,

she said, "Actually I need your assistance on a scientific matter."

Her announcement was met by three completely blank expressions. "We know nothing about such things," Emily said after taking a dainty bite of biscuit. "You should ask Hubert."

Sammie prayed her embarrassment didn't show. "The topic is one I'm afraid I cannot discuss with a . . . man."

Hermione frowned. "Then perhaps Mama could help you."

Sammie somehow managed not to wince at the suggestion. "I don't think so. You know how excitable Mama is, and I fear she would misinterpret the meaning behind my questions."

"You may ask us anything," Lucille said with an encouraging smile.

"Excellent. I need to know how one goes about preventing pregnancy."

Three completely slack-jawed, bug-eyed expressions met her announcement. Her heart sank. Botheration. Did her sisters not know? But surely they must, as they were all married. Didn't *all* married women know such things? The three of them exchanged odd glances, then returned their attention to her. Sammie suddenly felt like a specimen under a microscope.

Lucille took a healthy sip of her sherry. "I thought you said there was nothing going on . . ."

Emily gulped her sherry. "Between you . . ."

Hermione tossed the remainder of her drink down her throat. "And the earl."

Heat rushed through Sammie like wildfire until even the tips of her ears burned. "There *is* nothing between us." *Yet.* "My inquiry is strictly to gather information for a scientific experiment I wish to conduct. Of course I realize this is a highly sensitive topic, and I couldn't ask just anyone."

"It's highly improper to discuss such things with an unmarried woman," Emily said with a frown, her words slightly slurred.

"Yes," agreed Hermione. "What sort of experiment would require such information?"

Adopting the monotone she knew bored her sisters to tears, she stated, "I wish to conduct a comparative study of the reproductive cycles of several species, among them frogs, snakes, and mice, as they relate to humans." As if on cue, at the mention of frogs, snakes, and mice, her sisters immediately looked as if they'd all bitten into the same sour lemon. Pretending to warm to her subject, she continued. "Take for instance, the snake. After it sheds its skin—"

"Fascinating stuff, Sammie," Lucille broke in quickly, "but it's not necessary to go into detail." She shoved the platter of biscuits at Sammie.

Sammie accepted a sweet, and swallowed her guilt at manipulating her sisters in such a shameful manner.

Emily cleared her throat, then imparted in an undertone, "Well, so long as it's for science, I heard that some women wash themselves *you know where* with vinegar afterwards."

Sammie stared at her in stunned surprise. Finding her voice, she murmured, "Is that so? And, er, why would they do that?"

"To wash away the *you know what*." Emily's face turned crimson, and she quickly reached for another biscuit.

Fascinated, Sammie opened her mouth to question Emily further, but Lucille interjected, "Well, *I* heard . . ." She paused, glancing quickly around the room as if to ensure no one had entered, then leaned forward. Her rapt audience strained forward, Sammie leaning so far she nearly slid off the cushion. Lowering her voice to a whisper, Lucille continued, "*some* women go so far as to *douche* themselves with vinegar."

Emily's eyes rounded. "Never say so!"

"Or lemon juice," Hermione added, nodding. "Although that is more difficult to come by." She picked up the decanter and refilled everyone's glass to the rim. "But *I* heard tell of some women using sea sponges."

"What do they do with them?" Sammie asked, wondering where on earth she might obtain a sea sponge.

"Soak them in vinegar—"

"Or brandy," Emily broke in.

"Then insert them *you know where*," Hermione finished.

"And, um, what does that do?" Sammie asked, hoping *you know where* was where she thought it was.

A delicate burp escaped Emily's bow lips. "It prevents the *you know what* from going *you know where* and making a baby."

"Oh, yes, I understand that's quite common," Lucille said, "But *I* also heard that there's a device *gentlemen* can put on their *you know what* that keeps the *you know what* from going *you know where*." She waved her hand in front of her face and loosened her lace fichu. "My goodness, it's *hot* in here!"

"Well, *I* heard," Emily said, "about a method that requires the man to remove himself from *you know where* before he *you know whats*."

The group froze for several seconds, then Hermione collapsed into giggles. "Good heavens, Emily, I'm not certain I wanted to know that!"

A spurt of laughter sprang from Emily's lips, and she clapped her hand over her mouth. Her giggles were contagious, and within seconds the four of them were bent double with laughter.

"Well, I for one would not dream of employing any of those methods," Lucille said, wiping tears of mirth from her cheeks with the hem of her gown. "I very much want to be a mother."

"As do I," said Hermione. "Although the thought of giving birth is more than a little scary. One of us needs to have a baby so she can tell the rest of us how it feels. Emily, I vote you go first."

"Me?" Emily glared at her sister. "Why don't *you* go first?"

Hermione turned to Lucille. "You've been married the longest, Lucille. *You* should have the first baby."

"All right. Since you insist, I shall give birth before the year is finished."

"Oh, but that's impossible," Emily scoffed. "It takes nine months and it's now already July."

Lucille simply raised her brows, a small smile playing around the corners of her mouth. Realization dawned in Sammie and she gasped.

"It's not impossible," Sammie said, looking at Lucille with wonder, "if she's already with child."

Silence reigned for several seconds, then pandemonium broke loose as they all squealed in unison, laughing, crying, hugging, and talking all at once.

"How long have you known?"

"How are you feeling?"

"You don't *look* like you're with child!"

"Does Mama know?"

Lucille laughed. "Heavens, slow down! I've known for several weeks, but I wanted to tell Richard first, and he didn't return from visiting his mother until yesterday."

"Is that why you didn't go with him?" Hermie asked.

Lucille nodded. "We suspected I might be with child, and we did not want to risk me taking such a long trip. The doctor confirmed our suspicions while Richard was away. As for the rest, I'm feeling marvelous and my condition will become obvious within the next several weeks. I told Mama the good news earlier today, but I made her promise not to tell you, as I wished to do so myself."

Another round of hugs ensued, then Sammie sat back and listened to Emily and Hermione bombard Lucille with questions.

A pang of longing resonated through her, and she wrapped her arms around herself. How would it feel to carry the child of the man you loved inside your body, feeling it grow? A child you'd created together? Based on Lucille's radiant face, it was a beautiful, wondrous feeling.

Having a child. How marvelous that it was the best news in the world for Lucille.

How sad that it would be an utter disaster for her.

For a moment her heart flooded with yearning for a loving husband and a child, but she ruthlessly pushed back such impossible desires into the deepest recesses of her soul. Her choices were to become a dried-up spinster or to pursue a passionate adventure—and now that she knew how to prevent pregnancy, there was nothing to stop her.

Except Lord Wesley.

But surely she could convince him.

Couldn't she?

Yes, by informing him in a logical manner of all the reasons they should enter into a liaison, coupled with the information she'd gleaned from her sisters, she would surely convince him.

But just in case, she supposed it couldn't hurt to practice flirtatious looks in the mirror.

Chapter 11

From the *London Times*:

> **The Bride Thief Posse reports that in order to cover more territory, they are allowing any man with a marriage-age daughter to join their ranks. Gentlemen seeking to join must make a monetary contribution to the reward offered for the Bride Thief's capture.**

All Sammie's plans regarding Lord Wesley went awry the next morning. Just as she finished her solitary breakfast—forced upon her by uncharacteristically oversleeping, which she attributed to a bit too much celebrating the evening before with her sisters—Hubert dashed into the breakfast room. His footfalls thumping against the parquet floor set up an unholy pounding in her head, and she pressed her fingers to her temples in a feeble attempt to stem the throbbing.

Before she could beg him to tiptoe, he thrust a wax-sealed envelope at her and said breathlessly, "This just arrived for you. 'Twas given to Cyril at the stables by a lad he'd never seen before."

"Indeed?" Her name was neatly scripted on the front in an unfamiliar hand. "Who is it from?"

"I don't know, but perhaps it's from him."

Sammie stilled. "Him?"

"Lord Wesley. Wouldn't it be grand if this were an invitation to use his Herschel again?"

The hope shining behind Hubert's spectacles tugged at her heart. Setting the note on the table, she grasped both his hands and squeezed. Carefully choosing her words, she said, "You shouldn't set your heart on him inviting us back, Hubert. While he was very kind—"

"Oh, but he told me I was welcome to return."

"He did? When?"

"When we left his home, as you settled yourself in the coach. He said he was sorry we had to leave so soon, especially since I clearly hadn't finished taking my notes. He said I was welcome to return any time to finish." A flush brightened his cheeks. "I'm anxious to do so, but I hesitate without him specifying a date and time."

A lump settled in her throat, and she swallowed to clear it. "That was most generous of Lord Wesley."

"He's a fine gentleman," Hubert agreed, his breathing returned to normal. "Even with his title and position, he was . . ." he shrugged his thin shoulders and averted his gaze.

"Kind to us," Sammie said softly.

Their eyes met and understanding flowed between them, two people more accustomed to ridicule than acceptance. His Adam's apple bobbed in his thin neck. "Yes. I think that's why I like him—besides him owning a Herschel. It's because he was nice to you."

Dear Hubert. Heavens, could she love the boy any more than she already did? She squeezed his hands again and smiled at him. "What a coincidence. *I* like him because he was nice to *you*."

A lopsided grin pulled at one corner of his mouth. "Well, everyone says we think alike." He jerked his head toward the letter. "Are you going to read it?"

"Of course." She reached for the missive while Hubert seated himself opposite her and spread strawberry jam on a thick slice of bread for a second breakfast. After breaking the envelope's wax seal, she withdrew two ivory vellum sheets.

Dear Miss Briggeham,

   My name is Anne Barrow and I live in a small village about an hour's ride north of Tunbridge Wells. Although we've never met, I am writing to ask, nay plead, for your help. I have been so very desperate, you see. When word of your abduction by the Bride Thief reached my ears, I knew you were my last chance.

   My father has arranged for me to marry a man I loathe. I have begged and pleaded with Papa, but he refuses to listen. My betrothed is a cruel, ruthless man who has already tried to force himself upon me. In exchange for me, my betrothed will pay Papa's huge gambling debts. I am devastated that my own father would sell me like this. He will not stop gambling and drinking, and even though I do not wish debtor's prison on him, I cannot marry this man. Papa made his choice, and now I must make mine.

   Please, Miss Briggeham, you are the only person who can help me. I've nowhere else to turn. My mother is dead, and I have no relatives other than Papa. Can you contact the Bride Thief and tell him how desperately I need his help? I greatly fear there is little chance that the Bride Thief would hear of my plight on his own as Papa has kept the betrothal quiet, perhaps in fear of a rescue actually taking

*place. I will go anywhere, do anything, to escape the
nightmare my life will become if I am forced to wed
this man. I would attempt to contact the Bride Thief
myself, but Papa has gone so far as to lock me in my
room, and even if I were free, I would not know how
to reach the man. I am praying that this note even
reaches you.*

*I am scheduled to travel to my betrothed's home
two nights from now. Enclosed is a map I have drawn
of the exact route my coach will take. Please, I beg of
you to pass this information on to the Bride Thief so
he will know how to find me. I realize this is a great
deal for a stranger to ask, but I would not impose myself upon you if I were not desperate. Please help me
save my life.*

Forever in your debt.
Anne Barrow

A second sheet contained the drawing of the coach's
route. Sammie laid the papers on the table and drew a
shaky breath.

Hubert's eyes clouded with concern. "I say, Sammie,
you're white as chalk. What's wrong? Is the note from Lord
Wesley?"

"No." Wordlessly she pushed the letter across the table
to Hubert, knowing she could never convince him nothing
was amiss.

Hubert scanned the contents, then looked at her over the
rim of the vellum, his blue eyes wide behind his spectacles.
"Upon my word, this is dreadful."

"Indeed it is. I must help this poor girl." Rising, she
paced the length of the breakfast room. "It is imperative
that I get this information to the Bride Thief. But how?"

Hubert rose and paced along with her, on the opposite
side of the long mahogany table. "If we could find the

cottage he brought you to, perhaps we could leave him a message there. I examined some hair and leaf samples I removed from your clothing the morning after your abduction, but—"

Sammie stopped pacing and stared at him. "You did *what*?"

Color rushed into his thin cheeks. "I was looking for evidence as to his identity. Unfortunately all I was able to determine was what you'd already said: he rode a black horse, and you'd traveled through the woods."

"But why would you wish to know his identity? Surely you wouldn't be trying to collect the reward offered for his capture?"

"Of course not. Although I wouldn't hesitate if he'd hurt you in any way. No, I quite agree with you that the man is noble and is fighting a just cause. I merely wished to match my wits against his." A sheepish grin curved his lips. "You know I cannot ignore an unsolved puzzle."

"Indeed I do, but in this case you must." Setting her palms on the table, she leaned toward him. "Not only might pursuing the answer prove dangerous for you, but for him as well. Once his identity is known, his life is over. And you might be hurt in the process."

Hubert reached out and patted her hand. "Not to worry, Sammie. I simply conducted a few experiments in the Chamber, and they amounted to nothing. And even if I learned his identity, I wouldn't tell the magistrate."

She read the earnestness in his gaze and nodded. Resuming her pacing, she said, "About finding the cottage— it's a good suggestion, but it could take weeks, months, to locate, assuming we'd even be successful. It was dark, and without my glasses, I lost all sense of direction. No, we must think of something else." Tapping her fingers against her chin, she continued to pace. "Let's apply logic to this.

We need for the Bride Thief to find out about this girl's plight. How does he find out about the upcoming marriages of *any* woman he rescues?"

Hubert frowned and nodded thoughtfully. "Yes, how does he? Seems unlikely that he would personally know all of them."

"Precisely. And how did he find out about *me*? How did he know I did not want to marry Major Wilshire? My betrothal had not yet been announced, and even Mama wouldn't risk gossiping about it before it was formally agreed upon."

They both paused, staring at each other across the table.

"Then there's only one way—" Hubert said.

"It must have been through—"

"The servants' gossip grapevine," they said in unison.

Sammie clasped her hands together. "Yes, that's the only logical explanation. I don't know why I didn't think of it before."

"Most likely because you weren't trying to figure out a way to contact your abductor."

Snatching up the letter and the map, Sammie rounded the table. "The gossip could only have started in our household or Major Wilshire's." She drummed her fingers on the table, her mind racing. "I must immediately spread word of this girl's plight to the servants. Here at home, and at Major Wilshire's residence. There's not a moment to lose if we hope for the news to reach the Bride Thief in time."

"I'll visit at the Major's," Hubert offered. "I share an acquaintance with his coachman's son. But Sammie, what if the magistrate hears the gossip and sets a trap to catch the Bride Thief?"

"We shall do our best to contain the rumor to the two households . . . and pray we're successful. 'Tis a dangerous plan, but the Bride Thief is clever, and we must try to help this girl."

"And what if word doesn't reach the Bride Thief in time?"

She clutched the letter in her hands, her heart aching for Anne Barrow. She well understood the poor girl's desperation. "I was fortunate that I was able to extricate myself from an unwanted marriage, but so many women cannot do so. If the Bride Thief can't help her, then we must devise another plan."

"How?"

A frown pulled her brows. "I'm not certain, but I'll think of something."

With Hubert on his way to Major Wilshire's home, Sammie sought out Mama, who could spread gossip faster than weeds grew in the sunshine. After telling her mother of Anne Barrow's plight, she visited the kitchen and shared the news with Sarah, the cook. Confident that the entire household would know within the hour, she donned her shawl and bonnet. On her way to the village for her daily visit, she paused at the stables to tell Cyril the story.

She spent several hours visiting with Miss Waynesboro-Paxton. Sammie read to her from a well-worn edition of *Sense and Sensibility,* then massaged the aging woman's stiff hands with honey cream. After enjoying a restorative cup of tea, she took her leave, anxious to return home and find out how Hubert had fared at the Major's house.

Walking home with the late-afternoon sun angling through the trees, she offered up a prayer that her plan would work and word of Anne Barrow's forced marriage would reach the Bride Thief's ears—and not the magistrate's. By purposely spreading the rumor, she was straddling a tense line between possibly endangering the Bride Thief and trying to secure freedom for a desperate woman. But critical situations called for desperate measures.

Of course, it was highly likely that word would not reach the Bride Thief in time to help Miss Barrow. She did not doubt for a moment that he would rescue her if he knew of her plight, but he could not rescue her if he didn't know. She had to ensure that Miss Barrow was freed from her upcoming marriage. But how?

An image of the dashing Bride Thief flashed in her mind, and an idea slammed into her with a lightning-like jolt. Her footsteps halted and she quickly turned the idea over, mentally weighing, measuring it from every angle. It was terribly risky, but a woman's life was at stake. Her mind warned her that a hundred things could go wrong.

Her heart told her one thing could go right. Miss Barrow would be free.

If the Bride Thief did not show up to rescue Miss Barrow, then Sammie would rescue her herself.

Eric alternated his gaze between Emperor, who grazed near the lake, and the path leading through the woods from the village. Pulling his watch fob from his waistcoat pocket, he frowned at the timepiece. Damn, had he missed her? It seemed unlikely, as he'd been waiting for over an hour. Perhaps she had not walked to the village today. Perhaps she was ill—

The cracking of a twig snapped his attention back to the path. When he caught sight of her, he released a breath he hadn't realized he held, a fact that annoyed him. The sudden leap his heart performed, further annoyed him. Bloody hell, he was behaving like a wet-behind-the-ears schoolboy. Standing in the woods, holding a jar of honey like a besotted fool. *You are a besotted fool,* his inner voice informed him.

Clenching his jaw, he banished his irritating—not to mention incorrect—inner voice to perdition. He wasn't besotted. He was merely . . .

His brows collapsed in a frown. He didn't know what the hell he was. Other than inexplicably irritated. At himself for wanting her. At her for looking so utterly . . .

Samantha-like.

If he weren't feeling so unsettled, he would have laughed at himself when desire hit him low and hard at the sight of her modest blue gown and shawl. She walked briskly along the path with her purposeful strides, her lips pursed and brows pulled down as if in deep thought. She swung her bonnet from its ribbons as if it were a reticule, and her shiny hair appeared more disheveled than usual. With an unconscious gesture, she pushed her spectacles higher on her nose—certainly not an action that should have pumped heat through his veins. But it instantly brought to mind an image of him slipping off her glasses and losing himself in her beautiful eyes.

A grunt escaped him, and he ran a hand over his face. He shouldn't have come here. Shouldn't have waited for her. Why in blazes had he? *Because you couldn't stay away.*

His annoyance level notched up another step at the undeniable truth. But how the hell was he supposed to stay away from a woman who fascinated him? Charmed him? And all without an ounce of artifice or coyness or even effort on her part? A woman who wished to become his lover? He didn't know, but clearly lying in wait for her in the forest was *not* the way to dismiss her from his thoughts.

He'd simply give her the jar of honey. This was an errand of honor. He'd promised her the honey and give it to her he would. Then he'd immediately remove himself from her distracting presence. Yes, that was an excellent plan.

When she was only a few yards away, he stepped from beneath the low-hanging willow leaves, onto the path.

She halted and gasped. "Good heavens, Lord Wesley, you startled me."

"Forgive me. I did not mean to."

The most deafening silence he'd ever heard stretched between them. She twisted her bonnet ribbons between her fingers, clearly waiting for him to speak, but it was as if her presence rendered him witless. He simply looked at her, his question from yesterday echoing through his mind. *Do you have any idea how close I came to making love to you?* And her heartstopping reply. *Do you have any idea how much I wanted you to?* Good God, how had he managed to let her walk away?

Finally she cleared her throat. "Well, it was lovely seeing you again, my lord. If you'll excuse me . . ." She inclined her head then started to move around him.

He caught her arm as she passed him. "Wait. I wanted to give you this." He held out the jar of honey. "You forgot it the other evening."

A blush stained her cheeks, and he wondered if she was thinking about the heated kiss they'd shared after he'd given her the honey at his home.

She took the jar from him. "Thank you. I'll see to it that Mr. Timstone receives his cream. And now if you'll excuse me . . ." She tried to pull her arm away, but his fingers flexed, keeping her in place.

She peered up at him with a quizzical expression. "Was there something else, my lord?"

His eyes narrowed, and he studied her upturned face. There was nothing even resembling desire in her eyes. In fact, she was regarding him with nothing more heated than cool detachment. Bloody hell, she looked downright *disinterested*.

Damn inconsistent woman. One moment she wanted

him as a lover, now it seemed she couldn't get away from him fast enough. His common sense told him this was good. Every other part of him rebelled against it. Why this sudden change? Even though he'd refused to become her lover, *his* desire had not lessened. Not one damn bit.

"Is something amiss at home, Miss Briggeham? You seem in a hurry."

"No, my lord. But there's a . . . project I need to start on as quickly as possible."

"What sort of project?"

She lowered her gaze, apparently fascinated by something on the ground. "Nothing that would interest you."

An acute sense of loss flooded him. She didn't want to share the details with him—details of a project that was clearly important to her, as she couldn't wait to get home to start on it. Hell, he hadn't anticipated that he would so sorely miss the easy camaraderie they'd shared. He should let her simply walk away.

But he couldn't.

Moving to stand directly in front of her, he tipped her chin up until their eyes met. "About our discussion yesterday . . ."

Crimson flooded her cheeks. "Have you changed your mind?"

Yes. "No." A scowl pulled down his brows. "But I was hoping that we could remain . . . friends."

Whatever reaction he'd expected from her, it certainly wasn't the flash of temper that ignited in her eyes.

"Friends?" she repeated, raising her brows. "Yes, I suppose we can remain friends. Lord knows I do not have so many that I can turn one away."

"Yet you're angry with me."

"No, I'm disappointed. However, I *am* angry at the situation I'm in. The same situation thousands of women are in. Because we're not beautiful or witty or heiresses—or for whatever reason—we are forced into celibate spinster-hood. Forced to live our lives without ever experiencing a man's touch." Sparks all but flew from her eyes. "A woman should be able to choose. Good lord, it's just as bad as be-ing forced into an unwanted marriage."

He stilled. "It's not the same—"

"Yes, it is. It's *exactly* the same." Yanking her arm from his suddenly lax fingers, she stepped away from him. "The Bride Thief would understand."

His every muscle tensed. "The Bride Thief? What rub-bish. He's nothing more than a common criminal, abscond-ing with women who—"

"*Have no choice.* Who are being forced into a life they *do not want.*" Her voice shook with feeling. "He gives women a choice. And offers them the priceless gift of free-dom. 'Tis more than a woman like me shall ever have."

His heart ached for her, as there was no denying the truth of her words. Women's choices were severely limited. He, too, railed against such unfairness, but not in a way he could ever share with her.

Fisting his hands at his sides to keep from touching her, he said, "Even if the Bride Thief did understand, you'll never see him again."

The determined look she gave him snaked an icy chill of foreboding down his spine. "That's what *you* think," she said in a tight voice. Before he could recover himself, she brushed past him and stalked down the path.

He stared after her, stunned. Surely she was merely spouting nonsense in a moment of pique, as women were wont to do. But the instant the thought entered his mind, he dismissed it. Samantha Briggeham was the most forth-right woman he'd ever encountered. He couldn't imagine her making such a statement unless she believed it to be true.

Clearly she intended—or at the very least *hoped*—to see

the Bride Thief again. Of course she couldn't very well accomplish that without his cooperation, but *she* did not know that.

Apprehension filled him. For her. And himself.

Bloody hell, what was she planning?

Chapter 12

By the time Eric arrived back at his stables, he still had not figured out what Miss Briggeham might be planning. Distracted, he dismounted and handed Emperor's reins to Arthur.

"We need to talk," Arthur said in an undertone.

His gaze snapped to Arthur's, and his heart thumped against his ribs as he instantly recognized the look in the older man's eyes. Eric nodded. "We'll meet in the usual place in half an hour."

Thirty minutes later, Eric entered the gazebo near the rear of the gardens. Arthur paced inside the marble structure, his weathered face taut with worry.

"I've heard word of another who needs help," Arthur said without preamble.

Eric leaned his hips against the balustrade and crossed his arms over his chest. "I'm listening."

"Chit named Anne Barrow. Seems like the usual scenario, but . . ."

When Arthur didn't elaborate, Eric prompted, "Something is bothering you?"

"Well, I just think it's damned odd how I heard about it."

His gaze locked onto Eric's. "It seems Miz Sammie's the one wot started the gossip."

Eric froze. "I beg your pardon?"

"Surprised me, too, it did, 'cause Miz Sammie's not one to carry tales. But I heard it straight from Sarah, the Briggeham's cook. Told me Miz Sammie came into the kitchens this mornin' and told her about this Anne Barrow bein' forced to wed a horrid man, and wouldn't it be wonderful if the Bride Thief rescued her? Even went on to say how she would be traveling along a certain route two nights from now." Arthur scowled and scratched his head. "Damned odd if you ask me. Where do you suppose Miz Sammie would hear such a thing?"

"I'm not certain," Eric said slowly. "Has anyone else carried the tale to you?"

"No. And that's also strange. Story like this usually makes its way to me from several sources."

"Tell me exactly what Sarah told you."

Arthur obliged, then said, "This Bride Thief Posse is gainin' in numbers, and they're determined to catch ye. The magistrate, too. This whole story could be a trap. What are ye going to do?"

"I'll let you know as soon as I decide. In the meanwhile, quietly see what you can find out about this Anne Barrow."

Eric strode into his private study and immediately poured himself a brandy. Tipping back his head, he drained the potent liquor down his throat, enjoying the heated path it burned through his chilled insides. He poured another, then walked to the fireplace where he stared into the low-burning flames while his mind spun with questions.

Why had Samantha spread the news about Miss Barrow? By her own admission she wasn't interested in gossip. Had she merely stumbled upon the news, or been told by some-one else and was simply passing it on? If so, why hadn't she told *him* when they'd spoken by the lake? Had a member of the ever-growing Bride Thief Posse told her the story, hoping to start the rumor as a trap for the Thief? Perhaps. Still, why use Samantha? It didn't make sense. Unless . . .

Had someone hoped she'd carry the tale to him? Did someone suspect him?

But if he were under suspicion, why hadn't someone brought the tale directly to him, to *ensure* he knew of Miss Barrow's plight rather than relying on the unpredictability of the gossip grapevine—especially if a trap was being set?

Setting his snifter on the mantel, he dragged his hands down his face and considered the other possibility . . . the one he'd pushed aside but could ignore no longer.

Had Samantha made up the entire tale as a way to lure out the Bride Thief so she could see him again? Could that be the "project" she'd spoken of? He recalled the words she'd spoken at the lake when he'd said she would never see the Bride Thief again. *That's what* you *think.* Damn it all, was there really a girl who needed rescuing or was it just a ruse? And if there was a girl in need, how did Samantha fit into the situation?

Part of him instantly rebelled against the idea that she would lie and spread a false story for her own means. She was too honest and straightforward.

But another part of him taunted: *How else could she ever hope to see the Bride Thief again? It's a smart plan, and she's a smart woman. . . . A woman who clearly admires your alter personality. A woman who wants to experience adventure.*

A woman who wants a lover.

Searing jealousy pulsed through him and a bitter laugh

escaped him. Bloody hell, he was losing his mind. He was burning up with jealousy—over himself. But there was one way to fix that.

After taking extra precautions to ensure his safety, the Bride Thief would rescue Miss Anne Barrow—if indeed she existed.

And if Miss Samantha Briggeham happened to be involved, he'd see just how familiar she hoped to become with the Bride Thief.

The following afternoon Eric reined Emperor to a halt and tipped his hat to the magistrate riding toward him.

"Good afternoon, Straton," he greeted. "Fine afternoon for a pleasurable ride."

Adam Straton tipped his hat in return. "A fine afternoon indeed, Lord Wesley. However, I'm not on a pleasure ride. I'm on my way to London. I've several new leads to follow."

Eric raised his brows. "Oh? For a new investigation or one already in progress?"

"They concern the Bride Thief investigation."

"Indeed? Have you caught the brigand?"

"Not yet. But some new information has come to my attention that I'm hoping will lead to his capture."

"Excellent. Bad having a scoundrel like him roaming about—although I haven't heard that he's stolen any brides lately."

"Last victim was Miss Briggeham," Straton agreed, "and he botched that one." His lips tightened into a grim line. "If I'd arrived only minutes earlier I might have apprehended him. Unfortunately Miss Briggeham proved a rather uncooperative witness."

"Did she?"

"Yes. Kept glaring at me and insisting the man's actions

were *heroic*. Rather than being outraged at *him*, she was annoyed with *me* for casting aspersions on his character." He shook his head. "A most unusual woman."

Eric fought to suppress a smile. "Obviously."

"You mark my words, my lord, the Bride Thief won't be at large much longer. The botched Briggeham kidnapping proves he's growing careless. He's bound to make another mistake, and when he does, I'll be waiting."

"I wish you the best of luck, and I hope your new information proves helpful."

"As do I." Straton spent several seconds adjusting his gloves, then asked, "How is your sister faring, my lord?"

"She's coming home. I expect her within the next several days. Darvin passed away."

Straton seemed to freeze in place. He swallowed once, then said in a strained voice, "I'm sorry for her loss."

Eric didn't bother to point out that Darvin's death was no loss to anyone, least of all Margaret. "I'll be certain to pass along your condolences."

"Thank you. Good afternoon, Lord Wesley." With a curt nod, Straton applied his heels to his horse's flanks and trotted down the road leading toward London.

Filled with grim satisfaction, Eric turned Emperor toward the path leading to Wesley Manor. It would take Adam Straton at least two days in London to investigate the "information" Eric had arranged for him to receive about the Bride Thief.

It was more than enough time for Eric to carry out everything he needed to accomplish without the magistrate's sharp eyes nearby. He disliked tricking Adam, for he admired the hardworking man's honesty and integrity. But since success for Adam on this particular matter meant the hangman's noose for Eric, he managed to bury his guilt.

Just before he entered the dense forest, Eric glanced back over his shoulder. The sight of a carriage appearing from around the bend in the road leading to London made him rein Emperor to a halt. Shielding his eyes against the sun's glare, he studied the vehicle. His entire body tensed when he recognized not only the vehicle but the chestnut-haired figure inside.

What the hell was Samantha Briggeham doing riding back from London?

Hubert pounced on Sammie the instant she entered the Chamber.

"Well?" he demanded. "Were you successful?"

She patted her reticule and nodded. "I have everything right here. The money, and a ticket for passage aboard the *Lady Seafarer*, departing for America tomorrow morning."

"Did Cyril suspect anything?"

Guilt suffused Sammie for deceiving the loyal coachman. "No. The dear man believed I was in the bookstore the entire time."

Hubert nodded his approval. "Now let's go over the plan one more time to make sure you're prepared."

"All right." She paced in front of Hubert, ticking off each item on her fingers. "After dinner I shall claim fatigue and go to my bedchamber. Cyril retires at nine. At half after, you and I shall meet in the stables, where you'll help me saddle the horses. I'll ride Sugarcane and lead Dancer to the spot Miss Barrow indicated in her letter. I estimate it will take an hour to an hour and a half to arrive—sufficient time, as Miss Barrow is not scheduled to pass by until after midnight."

Hubert nodded. "Excellent. Go on."

"When I arrive, I'll tether Dancer so she's close to the road, but hidden from view. I'll then hide and wait for Miss Barrow's coach to approach. If the Bride Thief appears to rescue her, I'll simply remain hidden and then come home.

If he doesn't appear, I'll stop the coach, claiming my horse has gone lame, and ask for help. While her coachman examines Sugarcane, I'll slip the money and ticket to Miss Barrow and tell her where to find Dancer. I'll then distract the coachman for as long as possible to give her a chance to escape."

"Have you written the directions to the ship and the instructions about where she should leave Dancer, so Cyril can retrieve her?"

"Not yet, but I shall do so before dinner. According to the agent who sold me the ticket, there is a livery within sight of the dock. Miss Barrow should have no trouble finding it." She pushed her glasses higher on her nose. "Did we leave anything out?"

"I did think of a potential problem, Sammie." His eyes turned troubled. "What if you are not able to distract the coachman long enough for Miss Barrow to escape? And even if she does manage to get away, what if he realizes she's gone? He might suspect you aided her, and then there's no telling what he might do to you."

"An excellent point." She tapped her fingers against her chin. "But what can I do? I wouldn't want to cosh the fellow."

"Indeed not. You might not hit him hard enough."

"I was actually thinking I might strike him *too* hard."

Hubert blinked. "Oh. Well, that would be equally as disastrous I suppose."

A wry smile curved her lips. "It's too bad he wouldn't voluntarily take a little nap until Miss Barrow was safely gone."

The instant the words left her mouth she stilled. Her eyes met Hubert's startled gaze and a long look passed between them.

"I could give you something," Hubert said, his voice low and excited. "It's derived from a combination of herbs that

I developed based on my studies of South American tribes. It's very useful for putting animals such as chipmunks temporarily to sleep so I can examine them without risking injury to myself or them. It would ensure the coachman takes a nap."

"It wouldn't harm him?"

Hubert shook his head. "He'd simply fall asleep. For an hour or two."

Sammie raised her brows. "But how would I give it to him? I can't very well hand him a cup and say *drink this*."

"Do you have a hat pin?"

"A *hat pin*? Why on earth would I—"

"I'll coat the pin with the substance. All you'd have to do is stick him with it."

"And you don't think he'd notice?" she asked, unable to keep the incredulity from her voice.

"By the time he realizes it wasn't a bee sting, he'll be asleep."

A slow smile pulled at Sammie's lips. "Why, Hubert. I believe you're a genius."

A pleasure-filled flush colored his cheeks. Peering at her over the rims of his glasses he asked, "Did you ever doubt it?"

"Not for a moment." Reaching out, she ruffled his unruly hair. "I believe we have now thought of everything."

"Yes . . . except for the fact that I'll worry horribly about you. I wish you would allow me to come with you—"

"Absolutely not. I need you to remain here to distract Mama should she discover my absence." She didn't add that she couldn't risk involving him in an outing that might prove dangerous. She grasped his hands and squeezed them tightly. "I love you for wanting to protect me, but I'll be fine. All I'm going to do is give Miss Barrow the money, instructions and ticket, and if the Bride Thief shows up, that won't even be necessary."

"In that case, it's not fair that you get to have all the fun," Hubert mumbled. "You've already seen the Bride Thief."

"And *if* I see him again tonight, it shall be at a distance. You make it sound as if we'll be sitting about, chatting and visiting, sipping tea and nibbling biscuits."

Hubert ducked his head and scuffed the floor with the toe of his shoe. "I know it won't be like that, but I'd still like to come."

"But you cannot." Sammie drew a deep breath. "Now that that's settled, I'm going to go write out the instructions. I'll see you at dinner." She left, closing the door gently behind her.

Hubert planted his hands on the long wooden table and blew out a long breath. He knew the real reason Sammie didn't want him to accompany her—she didn't want anything to happen to him. But devil take it, what sort of man would he be if he allowed his sister to traipse through the woods at night unescorted? Why, no sort of man at all. Something could just as easily happen to *her*, and then he'd never forgive himself.

Therefore, the only logical thing to do was to follow her without her knowledge. That way, he'd not only be able to protect her, but he'd have himself a grand adventure. And perhaps even learn the answer to the question that had haunted him since Sammie's kidnapping.

His gaze rested on the experiment he'd been working on for weeks. Would his idea work? He didn't know, but he'd find out tonight.

And if it did, he would discover the identity of the Bride Thief.

Chapter 13

Sammie stood hidden behind a tall clump of bushes near the side of the road, running her hands gently over Sugercane's neck to keep her quiet. So far everything had gone according to plan. Her heart slapped against her ribs with such a wild combination of exhilaration and trepidation, she marveled that it simply didn't leap from her chest to land at her feet. Clouds obscured the moon, suiting her purposes perfectly. Crickets hummed nearby, and a gentle earth-scented breeze cooled her heated skin.

One way or another, within the next few minutes, Miss Barrow would be on her way to freedom. She drew several deep breaths, and a sense of anticipation tempered by calm purpose settled over her. She was doing the right thing. A young woman's life hung in the balance. Dancer was tethered to a tree several yards away, completely hidden from view. From her position behind the bushes, Sammie could see the road, but it would be nearly impossible for anyone to see her. Clutching her reticule, which contained the hat pin and all Miss Barrow would need, she peeked over the bushes and scanned the area around her.

Would the Bride Thief show up? A tingle raced through

her at the thought of seeing the heroic adventurer again. For Miss Barrow's sake, she prayed he would. But if he did not, she would do her best to aid the woman.

Now all she could do was wait.

And pray all went well.

Dressed in his Bride Thief mask, cape, and gloves, Eric sat astride Champion, hidden behind a dense clump of tall hedges, all his finely honed senses on alert. The combination of exhilaration and caution that accompanied all his rescue missions pumped through him, making him keenly aware of his surroundings—for tonight there would be a rescue. According to the information Arthur had gathered, Miss Barrow's story was indeed legitimate.

He scanned the area, searching for any sound or movement, and even though he detected nothing amiss, his instincts warned him something was not quite right. Out of place. Before he could decide what was bothering him, he heard the approaching squeak of a carriage wheel.

Forcing his unease aside, he moved Champion forward through the shadows until he was in perfect position at the side of the road to dash in front of the coach when it rounded the bend—if indeed it bore the Barrow family insignia. The squeak grew ever closer, and Eric patted Champion's neck. "Get ready, my friend," he whispered. Champion laid his ears back in acknowledgment.

Eric leaned forward, every muscle ready, his eyes trained on the bend in the road. A coach drawn by a pair of matching bays came into view. He peered at the coat of arms on the door. It matched the description Arthur had given him. Drawing a deep breath, he set Champion in motion, expertly calculating his speed. When the coach pulled alongside him, he reached out and grabbed the reins from the startled coachman, then forced the coach to a halt.

Reaching inside his cape, he tossed his signature bouquet and attached note on the leather seat next to the coachman.

"Stap my vitals," the coachman said. "You're the bloody Bride Thief."

"Silence," Eric commanded in the Bride Thief's raspy brogue. "Cooperate and no harm will come to ye. Now I—"

His words sliced off as a movement across the road caught his attention. Turning, his gaze swept the area. Trees. Thicket. More trees. Wild hedges.

Samantha Briggeham peeking at him over the top of a bush.

His hands fisted in his gloves. Bloody hell, she *was* involved in this! But how? He didn't know, but by damn, he was going to find out. But first he had to deal with the coachman.

He turned his attention back to the man, and instantly cursed his grave error. In those few seconds he'd been distracted, the coachman had acted. He now wielded a stout wooden stick and his face bore a fierce expression. Eric tried to deflect the oncoming blow, but he was too late.

The stick slammed into the side of his head, the impact jarring him from the saddle. He landed on the road with a stinging thud, white-hot pain searing through him.

"Got you, you devil," he heard as if from a great distance.

Then blackness washed over him and he heard no more.

Sammie stood behind the bushes and watched in horror as the coachman swung a wooden stick and knocked the Bride Thief from his mount, rendering him senseless.

"Got you, you devil," the coachman said. "Try to steal me employer's daughter, will ye?"

The coach door rattled loudly and a muffled feminine voice came from within.

"Not to worry, Miz Barrow," the coachman called. "Ye're locked up in there good and tight. Yer Pa's orders." He reached under his seat and pulled out a length of rope. Jumping to the ground, he approached the still form of the Bride Thief. "I figgered ye might try to abscond with Miz Barrow, ye blackhearted thief, and I was ready for ye. And now I'll truss ye up all tidy, deliver ye to the magistrate, and collect meself that nice, fat reward wot's bein' offered for ye."

Sammie clapped her hands over her mouth to contain her gasp. If she didn't act quickly that dreadful man was going to turn the Bride Thief over to the authorities.

Grim determination filled her. She couldn't allow such a thing to happen. But with the coachman already binding the unconscious Bride Thief, there was only one way to stop him.

Opening her reticule, she carefully removed the hat pin Hubert had prepared. She then pulled up her hood to hide her face as much as possible. Holding the long pin in front of her like a sword, she crouched low and inched forward. The coachman was murmuring to himself, completely absorbed in his task of tying the Bride Thief's hands and feet with a sturdy piece of rope.

Keeping one eye on the coachman, she silently crept up behind him. Praying that Hubert's potion would work, she jabbed the pin into the man's buttocks.

"Ouch!" Dropping the ropes, he pressed his hand to his abused flesh and spun around. Sammie jumped to her feet and scooted backwards until her back bumped into the coach's door. The coachman's eyes narrowed on her, and he took two menacing steps forward. "Who the 'ell are you?"

Her heart pounding, she fumbled to hide the hat pin between the folds in her dark gown while her mind screamed *Go to sleep!*

As if he heard her silent plea, his eyes rolled back, his knees folded, and he crumpled to the ground, landing face up next to the Bride Thief. Sammie stared at the man for several seconds, her heart in her throat. Then she leaned over him. Soft snores emitted from between his lax lips and relief surged through her. By jove, Hubert really was a genius!

Moving swiftly, she dropped to her knees next to the Bride Thief and pressed her fingers to his neck. When she felt the strong thump of his pulse beating against her skin, she nearly swooned with relief. Before she could assist him, however, the coach door rattled once more.

"Please, let me out," came the cry from within.

Crawling to the coachman, Sammie slipped her fingers into his waistcoat pocket. She encountered cool metal and swiftly withdrew what she prayed was the correct key. Several seconds later she yanked open the coach door, and a wide-eyed, disheveled young woman stumbled out.

"Who are—?"

"Samantha Briggeham. Your coachman has injured the Bride Thief. I've temporarily disabled your man, but we must hurry."

Miss Barrow's gaze flew to the two fallen men. "Dear God. What can we do?"

Sammie walked swiftly to the pair and dropped to her knees next to the Bride Thief. "You work on untying him and I shall try to bring him around."

Without another word, Miss Barrow knelt beside the Bride Thief and applied herself to the knots binding his wrists. Sammie ran gentle hands over the silk mask that covered his head, pausing when she encountered an egg-sized lump just above his ear.

Alternately tapping his silk-covered cheek and gently shaking his shoulder, she asked, "Can you hear me, sir? Please wake up."

Eric heard a voice as if through a thick, pain-filled fog.

He slowly became aware of the sensation of gentle hands smoothing over his face. Touching his head. Running across his shoulders. He inhaled and smelled honey.

"Can you hear me, sir?"

Eric turned slowly toward her voice, a breath hissing between his teeth as shafts of pain ricocheted through his head. He forced his eyes open, then blinked several times, trying to align the trio of figures swimming before his eyes into one entity. When he finally succeeded, he found himself staring up into Samantha Briggeham's anxious face.

When his gaze locked on hers, she squeezed her eyes shut for a brief second and exhaled. "Thank God you're all right." She offered him a tremulous smile, then added, "You've nothing to fear, sir. 'Tis I, your friend, Samantha Briggeham."

He tried to lift his head, but immediately thought better of it when a battalion of hammer-wielding devils set up an unholy rhythm in his temples. A groan escaped him.

She laid her palms against his chest. "Don't try to move yet. Rest for a few more moments."

"I've untied him," came an unfamiliar feminine voice. "How is he?"

"Coming around," Samantha said. "Why don't you use those ropes to bind the coachman in case he awakens?"

"My pleasure," came the soft reply.

Coachman? Were they out for a ride? "What happened?" he whispered. His tongue felt like shoe leather.

"Miss Barrow's coachman struck you." Her bespectacled eyes reflected grave concern. "Do you not remember? You were about to perform a rescue."

Rescue? He raised a hand to his pounding head. His leather glove rasped against silk, and his memory returned in a rush. Mask. Bride Thief. Rescue. Seeing Samantha across the road. Distracted. Coachman wielding a stick. And now sizzling pain shooting through his head.

Recalling to speak in his raspy brogue, he said, "I remember. Where's the coachman?"

"He's unconscious. Miss Barrow is tying him up."

A wave of dizzy nausea rolled through him, and he squeezed his eyes shut and drew in slow, deep breaths. She clasped his gloved hand with one of her hers, and continued to stroke soothing fingers over his masked face and shoulders. After a moment, the dizziness subsided and his wits returned—along with a heaviness that settled in his gut like a rock.

What an untenable mess this was. He had to get away from here as quickly as possible—Miss Briggeham and Miss Barrow as well—before the coachman regained consciousness and decided to unmask him and turn him over to the magistrate. Or before someone else happened along the road and decided to do the same.

Or had his identity already been discovered?

Opening his eyes, he looked directly at her. "Did the coachman remove my mask?"

"No."

Relief eased through him. "Did ye?"

Her eyes widened, and she shook her head. "No."

Some of the tension left his body. She didn't know who he was. Thank God. She squeezed his hand and he returned the pressure.

"Do not fear, sir," she whispered. "I shall see to it that no further harm comes to you." She laid her free hand along his masked jaw and offered him a gentle smile.

His eyes narrowed. She certainly was being solicitous of the Bride Thief. Holding his hand, touching him. Yes, she was being all too much familiar with his person, damn it.

"Do you hurt anywhere else?" she asked with a tender concern that rankled him.

Bloody hell, he hurt everywhere, but he'd be damned if

he'd tell *her*. She'd no doubt offer to massage away all the Bride Thief's aches and pains.

"I'm fine," he rasped. "I want to sit up." After he pushed himself up onto his elbows, she grasped him by his forearms and helped him slowly move into a sitting position. The earth spun around him, and he held his head between his gloved hands, wincing when his fingers encountered an egg-sized lump. After a moment the dizziness passed, and he lowered his hands.

Moistening his lips, he whispered in his brogue, "Why are ye here?"

"The same reason you are. To help Miss Barrow."

"Did ye not trust me to do so?"

She pushed her spectacles higher on her nose, then gazed at him through serious eyes. "I would trust you with my life, sir. But Miss Barrow asked for my assistance. As I had no way of knowing if word of her plight would reach you, I had to be prepared to help her myself."

"And how did ye plan to do that?"

In a terse voice she outlined a plan that simultaneously filled him with admiration and fury. His gaze wandered to the sleeping coachman, whom Miss Barrow was still trussing up like a goose. Bloody hell, he wished he'd been awake to see Samantha stab the bastard in the arse. "Blast it, lass. Don't ye realize the danger ye put yourself in?"

"No more danger than you put yourself in, sir. I assure you I did not undertake this adventure without extensive, logical thought, and I carefully weighed the risks involved. But as you understand only too well, I could not ignore Miss Barrow's plea for help."

"But what if ye'd been hurt?" The thought of her injured, lying in the woods, at the mercy of that stick-wielding bastard or someone else, sent a tremor of fear and fury down his spine.

"I knew there were risks, of course. But as I'm sure you'll agree, the wanted outcome makes them worthwhile." She rose, then held out her hands. "Let's get you on your feet. Slowly now."

He grasped her outstretched hands and moved first to his knees, where he remained for a moment while another wave of dizziness hit him. Then with her assistance, he gained his feet. His knees wobbled a bit, and he braced his hands on her shoulders, closed his eyes, and drew deep breaths until his equilibrium returned.

"Are you all right?" she asked, her voice tight with concern.

He opened his eyes and gazed at her tense face. "Yes, lass."

"I'm so relieved. I nearly died when that horrid man struck you." A shy note entered her voice. "It was my honor to assist you, sir. I . . . I would gladly do so again."

His blood ran cold at her words. Good God, if he didn't take drastic measures, he could well imagine her donning a mask and cape of her own, trotting through the forest with a sack full of hat pins. Tightening his grip on her shoulders, he barely refrained from shaking her. "Your loyalty humbles me, lass, and you'll forever have my gratitude for rescuing me this night. But in truth, if it weren't for your interference, the rescue would have taken place without a problem."

A stricken look entered her eyes, and he knew he'd hit the intended mark. "I never meant—"

"It matters not. Your presence distracted me, affording the coachman the opportunity to strike me. 'Twas a mistake that could well have cost me my life."

Her eyes widened with unmistakable horror and a sheen that, damn it all, looked suspiciously like tears. Guilt gnawed at him for being so hard on her, and unable to stop himself, he reached out and trailed his gloved fingertips down her cheek. "It could have cost ye your life as well, lass. I'd never be able to bear the guilt if harm befell ye. I want your promise that ye won't try to help me in my mission again. 'Tis far too dangerous."

"But—"

"Your promise, Miss Briggeham. I'll not leave here until I have it."

She hesitated, then jerked her head in a stiff nod. "Very well, I promise. But I want you to know . . ." She slowly reached up and laid her hand against his masked cheek. "I hold you in the deepest admiration."

Warmth washed through him, and it required all his will not to turn his face and press his lips to her honey-scented palm.

"And the deepest affection," she added softly.

He froze as if she'd thrown a bucket of icy water over him. *Affection?* And not just *any* affection, but the *deepest* affection? Bloody hell, he didn't want her holding another man in the deepest affection—even if that man happened to be *him!*

Miss Barrow joined them and he forced his unreasonable, not to mention annoying, jealousy aside. "Is your coachman securely bound?" he asked the young woman.

She cast a look of disgust down at the man. "Yes, sir."

"Do ye still wish for me to help ye to escape, Miss Barrow?"

"More than anything, sir."

"Then we must be off. Gather any belongings ye wish to bring." He turned to Samantha. "Fetch your mount and the horse ye brought for Miss Barrow."

As they did as he bid, he walked to where Champion stood several yards away and reassured himself the stallion was uninjured. He then returned to where the coachman lay. He bent down, wincing at the pain in his head, and checked the coachman's bindings. A humorless smile touched his lips. Miss Barrow had indeed tied up the bastard tightly.

Miss Barrow emerged from the coach carrying a small traveling case. "Wait right there," he instructed her. He then turned to Samantha, who was emerging from the woods leading two mounts. "Miss Barrow will ride with me. Ye lead your other horse, and I shall accompany ye back to the woods near your home."

"No," she protested, accepting his hand up into the saddle. "You must be off."

"And I shall be. As soon as I see ye safely back to your home. 'Tis more than an hour's journey, much too far for ye to travel alone, especially at this time of night. I'll not argue with ye, lass."

A disgruntled sound came from her throat. "Then at least take this." She pressed her reticule into his hand. "It contains the funds and passage aboard the *Lady Seafarer* I'd arranged for Miss Barrow." He opened his mouth to protest, but she pressed it more firmly into his hand. "Please take it. It would mean a great deal to me to be able to help her."

It took all his strength not to pull her into his arms and kiss her. "I've made my own arrangements for Miss Barrow. Since it is your wish, I shall give her the funds, but I will destroy the ticket. I want no evidence that could lead back to ye. And when ye return home ye must make certain ye destroy anything that could implicate ye. Do ye understand?"

"Yes."

"Then let us be gone."

He strode to Champion, and after assisting Miss Barrow into the saddle, swung himself up behind her. He then turned Champion around and led the way into the forest, heading back toward Samantha's home.

* * *

Hubert jabbed his spectacles higher on his nose and resisted the fierce urge to kick a tree trunk in frustration. What had started off as a grand adventure had somehow turned into an utter fiasco. Based on the information provided in Miss Barrow's letter, he knew where he was supposed to eventually be, but unfortunately he hadn't a clue how to get there.

How could he possibly have lost sight of Sammie? One minute she'd been no more than ten yards ahead of him, and the next she was gone. As if she'd vanished into a puff of smoke.

Irritation rippled through him. Dash it, how was he to protect her if he couldn't find her? And how could he hope to test his experiment to discover the Bride Thief's identity? He simply had to find her.

Continuing through the unfamiliar woods in the direction where he'd last seen her, he walked along, pausing every few minutes to strain his ears. After nearly a quarter hour, he halted at the sound of muffled voices in the distance. Crouching low, he moved cautiously forward. His heart jumped with relief when he spied Sammie sitting upon Sugarcane. His relief turned to excitement when he discerned a figure speaking to her—a masked man who could only be the notorious Bride Thief.

He had come! His gaze swept the area. A woman who was surely Miss Barrow stood by a coach, a traveling case clutched in her hands. A huge black horse stood near the side of the road. Based on what Sammie had told him, he deduced this was the Bride Thief's mount. His elation quickly turned to dismay when he realized the group was about to depart the area. He had to act immediately if he had any hope of testing his experiment.

Keeping one eye on the Bride Thief, he moved toward

the black horse. With his heart pounding against his ribs, he opened the leather pouch clutched in his hand. He quickly sprinkled the contents over the animal's saddle, reins, and stirrups, then withdrew, hiding behind a dense clump of hedges.

Frustration mixed with exhilaration pumped through him. If only he'd had more time! Then he could have emptied his powder inside the Bride Thief's saddlebag and snipped a small hole in the leather to leave a trail he could follow. He cursed the failure of his original plan, but at least by spreading the powder as he did, he'd see if its long-term phosphorescent properties worked. And perhaps the Bride Thief might lead him to the cottage where he'd brought Sammie!

Seconds later the Bride Thief helped Miss Barrow into the saddle, swung up behind her, then led the way into the woods.

Making certain to keep Sammie in his sights, he followed behind the group. Disappointment filled him when after a time it became obvious they were heading toward Brigge-ham Manor, dashing his hopes of finding the Bride Thief's cottage. Fustian! Simply everything had gone wrong! Just before the woods thinned into the clearing that led to his house, the group stopped. On stealthy feet he moved closer.

"This is where we part company, Miss Briggeham," the Bride Thief said in a low, raspy brogue. "I thank ye again for your assistance and remind ye of your promise."

"And I thank you as well, Miss Briggeham," said Miss Barrow.

"God speed to you both," came Sammie's reply.

No sooner had the words left her mouth, than the Bride Thief turned his mount and raced with Miss Barrow through the woods. Seconds later the darkness swallowed them, and they were lost from sight.

Hubert watched a slow smile ease over Sammie's face, then she closed her eyes and blew out the sort of long, drawn-out sigh his other sisters usually heaved. She then headed toward the stables.

The instant she was gone from view, he dashed across the clearing toward the house. In spite of his experiment not going as planned, he was barely able to contain his excitement over his adventure. He'd actually seen the infamous Bride Thief! Heard his voice!

Would he also, by some stroke of luck, learn the Bride Thief's identity?

Chapter 14

From the *London Times*:

The Bride Thief strikes again! The infamous Bride Thief's latest kidnapping two nights past answered the burning question, When will he strike again? Stolen was Miss Anne Barrow of Kent, betrothed of Mr. Lucien Fowler. Miss Barrow's coachman, Nigel Grenway, informed the magistrate that just before he fell victim to an inexplicable malady, a hooded figure appeared behind him, leading to speculation that the Bride Thief has an accomplice. The investigation has intensified, and the magistrate has vowed to bring the kidnapper, as well as any other involved parties, to justice.

In related news, the Bride Thief Posse reports that since allowing any man with a marriage-aged daughter to join their ranks, their membership has swelled to two hundred and is growing daily. The newest member is the latest victim's father, Mr. Walter Barrow. The reward now stands at nine thousand pounds.

Eric stared at the words that cramped his stomach: *speculation that the Bride Thief has an accomplice.* Tossing the newspaper onto his desk, he pinched the bridge of his nose. An accomplice. Bloody hell. Had the coachman discerned, in spite of the darkness, that the hooded figure was a woman? Had he provided the magistrate with a description of Samantha?

Rising, he paced the length of his study. Damn it all, if this Grenway identified Samantha . . .

His gut knotted tighter and his hands fisted. Fear more potent than any he'd ever felt for his own safety pumped through him. He had to protect Samantha. But in order to do so, he needed to know what Grenway had told the magistrate. It seemed another conversation with Adam Straton was in order.

And based on the outcome of their talk, he'd then decide if he needed to provide Adam with some additional "helpful" information.

In the meanwhile, he—or rather the Bride Thief—had to warn Samantha to watch her words should the magistrate call upon her. He squeezed his eyes shut, picturing her earnest, concerned face as she'd helped him in the woods. He'd been at her mercy, and she easily could have turned him in. The reward on his head would have made her a wealthy woman. At the very least, she could have satisfied her curiosity and lifted his mask.

Instead she'd risked her reputation, her freedom, her very life to help him. To help Miss Barrow. He was furious with her. Frightened for her.

And so damn proud of her.

Frowning, he pushed that disturbing thought away. He needed to concentrate on the fact that she'd poked her nose where she had no business meddling. Yet one phrase kept running through his mind. *What an incredible woman.*

Blowing out a weary sigh, he raked his hands through his hair, avoiding the still-tender spot above his ear. Yes, she was incredible. But if the magistrate discovered she'd assisted the Bride Thief, she'd face criminal charges. *Not so long as there's a breath in my body.*

Stalking to his desk, he pulled a piece of vellum from the top drawer and prepared to write the most important letter of his life.

Sammie stood in the drawing room and stared at her name neatly scrawled on the thick ivory vellum. Somehow she knew the letter was from the Bride Thief. The unfamiliar, bold print. The way it had mysteriously appeared on the front step, as if left there by a ghostly hand.

With her heart beating in slow, heavy thumps, she broke the wax seal.

> *My dear Miss Briggeham,*
> *I write to warn ye. The coachman has informed the magistrate that the Bride Thief may have an accomplice. I do not know if the man was able to offer any description of ye, but ye must prepare yourself for the possibility that the magistrate may call upon ye, either in reference to the other evening, or to question ye further regarding our first meeting.*
> *For your safety, I remind ye of your promise not to attempt to aid me again. I also remind ye to destroy anything that could possibly link ye to the other evening. Needless to say, ye must burn this note as soon as ye finish reading it. Ye will be happy to know that our friend is safely on her way to a new life of freedom. Please take care of yourself.*

There was no signature, but of course there was no doubt as to who had sent the note. Her eyes drifted shut, and she pressed the letter against her heart.

Miss Barrow was safe. And free. Embarking on a brand-new life filled with adventure. Happiness, tinged with a pang of envy, filled her as she mentally wished the young woman a long, happy life.

The Bride Thief was also clearly safe, thank God, but for how long? A shudder ran through her as an image of him lying helpless on the ground flashed through her mind. He could have been killed. Or captured. She offered a silent prayer of thanks that the rescue had turned out successfully, but what if his next one did not? According to *The Times*, the Bride Thief Posse was growing daily, along with the price on the Bride Thief's head. How much longer could his luck possibly hold out? Her stomach turned over at the thought of that vital man swinging from a hangman's noose.

That vital man. An involuntary sigh escaped her lips as she recalled the feel of his solid shoulders and muscular arms. Warmth eased through her, and she pressed his letter closer to her heart. For the second time, he'd provided her with a grand adventure, the memories of which she'd always treasure. A heated blush rose up her cheeks when she thought of him gently touching her face with his gloved hand. He was tender and caring. Utterly heroic. Kind and gentle. Just like . . .

She blew out a long breath. Just like Lord Wesley. But just like the Bride Thief, Lord Wesley was lost to her—albeit for different reasons. The Bride Thief didn't want her help with his missions, and Lord Wesley simply didn't want her. At least not in the same way she wanted him.

The memory of their passionate kisses rushed through her, leaving a trail of heat in its wake. The sensation of his body pressed against hers, his hands caressing her breasts. *All right, clearly he* does *want me, but unlike me, he is unwilling to undertake the risks involved.* If only Lord Wesley were as daring as the Bride Thief!

Of course, Lord Wesley had offered her friendship, which was more than any other man had ever offered her. And while she would accept and cherish his friendship, a portion of her heart still wished for more from him. His kiss. His embrace.

But for right now, she needed to stop thinking about both Lord Wesley and the Bride Thief, and burn this incriminating letter. The vellum crinkled against her bodice and sadness swept through her. She hated to destroy her only memento of the man, but for safety's sake she must. By her own promise, she'd never see him again, a vow that lay heavy on her heart, but that she wouldn't break. She had to keep him, and herself, safe.

Opening her eyes, she turned toward the fireplace, then froze.

Lord Wesley stood in the open doorway, regarding her with an intense expression.

Heat singed her, as if she'd set herself on fire. Thrusting the Bride Thief's letter behind her, she inched backwards toward the desk. "Lord Wesley, what are you doing here?"

He closed the door, then walked slowly toward her, like a sleek cat stalking its prey, his dark gaze riveted on her. "I wished to speak to you. Your butler advised me you were in the drawing room and I offered to announce myself."

The back of her legs bumped into the desk and she swiftly turned, thrusting the letter into the top drawer, then slamming it shut. The bang reverberated through the quiet room, then silence reigned.

Eric walked across the room, not stopping until he stood directly in front of her. He fisted his hands to contain the hot jealousy pumping through him. He'd stood in the doorway for at least two minutes watching her before she'd noticed his presence. Watching her clutch the Bride Thief's letter to her heart, her eyes closed, heaving dreamy sighs, her color high. She'd looked innocent and beguiling. And utterly aroused. For another man.

Damn it all to hell and back. He'd called upon her to make certain she'd suffered no ill-effects from her adventure, and to hopefully discover if Adam Straton had visited to question her. But every thought had drained from his head when he saw her holding that damn letter. Every thought except the one that chanted *Mine. Mine. Mine.*

And it was about damn time he did something about it.

Leaning forward, he braced his palms on the desk on either side of her, bracketing her in. Her eyes widened and she leaned back slightly, but otherwise did not attempt to escape. Good. Now he had her right where he wanted her. Trapped.

"What did you thrust so hastily into the drawer, Miss Briggeham?" he asked in a silky voice.

"Oh, just a letter."

"It seemed like an important letter."

She swallowed once. "It was from a . . . friend."

"Indeed? Was it from a . . . gentleman friend?"

She lifted her chin and cocked a brow. "Why do you wish to know?"

Because I don't want you thinking about any other man, even if the other bloody man is me. He raised his hand and trailed his fingertips down her crimson-stained cheeks. "You're blushing. I was wondering if your letter was the cause."

"If I'm blushing it's merely because it's very warm in here. And because you're standing . . . so close."

He looked down, carefully assessing the several inches that remained between them. His gaze wandered slowly upward, pausing on the generous swell of her breasts that even her modest neckline could not hide. He drew a deep breath, and her honey-sweet scent filled his head, overwhelming him with the urge to bury his face in her fragrant flesh. Raising his gaze back to hers, he asked, "And if I were to move even closer?"

Her tongue peeked out to moisten her lips, and his groin tightened in immediate response. "I imagine I would grow warmer still."

His eyes intent on hers, he deliberately moved forward, erasing the few inches between them. Her scent fully enveloped him, and it took every ounce of his rapidly deteriorating control not to simply yank her into his arms and devour her. Lowering his head, he brushed his mouth across her jaw.

"Warmer?" he whispered against her ear. He flicked his tongue over her delicate lobe, then captured it gently between his teeth, enjoying her gasp of feminine pleasure.

"Very much warmer," she said in a breathless voice.

Leaning back just enough to look at her, he barely managed to swallow the growl that rose in his throat. Desire dilated her aqua eyes, and her lush mouth begged to be kissed.

He wanted her with an intensity he'd never experienced for any other woman. His entire body pulsed with a need that demanded to be met. A need he knew only she would satisfy. All the reasons he shouldn't make love to her flashed through his mind, but he squashed them like bothersome insects. He would protect her. Employ the discretion that ruled every other facet of his life. And she would be his.

Tipping up her chin with his fingers, he met her gaze. "I want you more than warm," he said softly. "I want you hot. Melting. Burning. For me. With me." He watched her absorb his words, her skin flushing deeper, the pulse at the base of her neck quickening. "Are you still willing?"

"*I* was never unwilling."

Heat scorched him at her reply. Stepping back, he ran

his hands down her arms and entwined their fingers. "Unfortunately, this is not the time or place." He wanted no interruptions when he took Samantha Briggeham on the biggest adventure of her life. And erased all thoughts of any other man from her mind. And satisfied his hunger for her.

Raising her hand to his lips, he pressed a kiss against her honey-scented palm. "Meet me tonight. At midnight. At the lake."

A long look passed between them, and his heart thumped in slow, hard beats as he awaited her reply.

"All right," she whispered.

He refused to examine the relief that washed through him at her consent.

"How do you propose we go about . . ." her voice dropped even lower, *"you know what?"*

"I'm not certain I know which *you know what* you are referring to."

She drew what appeared to be a bracing breath, then rushed out with, "Which method of preventing pregnancy shall we employ?"

He stared at her, completely nonplussed. No woman had ever asked him such a thing.

"I've researched the various ways—"

"Researched?" Thank God his jaw was firmly attached or it would have dropped to the floor with a thud. "How did you do *that*?"

"I discussed the matter with my sisters."

A feeling he could only describe as horror pierced him. "Your *sisters*?" Good God, there went all hope for discretion. She was ruined before they'd begun.

Before he could find his voice, she continued, "They were quite knowledgeable on the subject, although I'm afraid they did not tell me exactly *where* I could secure a sea sponge such as they described." She looked up at him with a hopeful expression. "I don't suppose you would know?"

Bloody hell, could this conversation possibly get any worse? When he simply continued to stare at her, she clarified in a conspiratorial whisper, "The sort of sponge that keeps the *you know what* from going *you know where.*"

Jesus. It apparently *could* get worse. Releasing her hands, he dragged his fingers down his face. "Samantha. Why did you discuss something of such an intimate nature with your sisters?"

"They were the logical choice, my lord, as I could not very well ask my mother. I needed information . . . information that you were unwilling to provide—"

"Because at that time you did not need such knowledge. Surely they were shocked when you questioned them."

"They were somewhat surprised, but I assured them that I wished to know for purely scientific research reasons."

"Scientific research?"

"Yes. When I explained I wished to conduct a comparative study of the reproductive cycles of several species, among them frogs, snakes, and mice, as they relate to humans, they were quite willing to discuss the matter with me. Believe me, there is no need to worry that they suspected the true reason I wished to know."

"But surely they thought your questions . . . *odd.*"

"There is not much I could do, especially concerning scientific matters, that my sisters would consider odd. They're quite accustomed to my inquisitive nature. We've nothing to fear from them." Her lips twitched slightly. "So you may now remove that aghast and alarmed expression from your face."

He instantly rearranged his facial muscles, annoyed that he'd allowed his feelings to show so clearly. Could she really be correct in her assessment of her sisters' reaction to her inquiries? Did they really believe she only wished to know for scientific reasons? If any other woman had made such a claim, he'd have laughed at her. But Samantha . . . well, he had to admit such a claim somehow seemed reasonable coming from her. His shoulders relaxed a fraction. Frogs, snakes, and mice? Yes, that sounded like Samantha.

But then a thought occurred to him that narrowed his eyes. Bloody hell, had she considered taking another man as a lover? Like perhaps the Bride Thief? "If we'd already decided not to become lovers, why did you still seek such information?"

A decidedly guilty-looking flush washed over her cheeks, and his hands fisted at his sides. But rather than averting her gaze, she raised her chin a notch and met his stare. "Actually, my lord, *you* had decided we should not become lovers. I was hoping you would change your mind, and I wished to be prepared in case you did."

She'd sought the information for him, then, not some other man. She'd hoped he'd change his mind, and by God, he had. A combination of relief and heat surged through him. Reaching out, he once again entwined their fingers. "In that case," he said softly, "I'm glad you know what to expect."

"Well, actually I don't. Which method do you suggest we employ?"

He stepped closer to her, until their bodies just touched. "I shall withdraw myself from your body before I spill my seed." An image of them, naked, locked in a sensual embrace, her legs wrapped around him, his erection buried in her velvet warmth, flashed through him like a lightning bolt. Blood pooled in his groin, and he nearly groaned aloud at his strong reaction. Hell, if he did not depart her company immediately, he knew he stood in danger of kissing her again . . . and not being able to stop.

"You have my word that I shall protect you, Samantha." He squeezed her fingers, then reluctantly released her.

"Until midnight." Wide-eyed, she nodded her assent, and forcing his feet to move, he walked to the door.

He had only to wait until tonight. Twelve more hours. Then she'd be his. His conscience tried to speak, but he ruthlessly beat his inner voice back. He wanted her. She wanted him. They would have each other.

Closing the door softly behind him, he strode swiftly toward the foyer where he encountered Hubert.

"Good afternoon, Lord Wesley," the boy greeted him with a broad grin.

He smiled in return. "Hello, Hubert. Are you off to your Chamber?"

"Yes. I'm finishing a new invention. A cutting machine for the kitchen staff to assist them in food preparation." A hopeful light came into his eyes. "Would you like to see it?"

"I'd be very interested, but I'm afraid I have another appointment right now. May I stop by tomorrow to see it?"

The boy's face flushed with pleasure. "Of course, my lord."

"Excellent. Shall we say around two o'clock?"

"I'll await you in the Chamber." He dipped his chin shyly downward. "Perhaps you'd also like to see . . ." His voice trailed off as his gaze riveted on Eric's riding boots. The boy frowned, then pushed his glasses higher on his nose. After blinking several times, he jerked his head upward and stared at Eric with an utterly confused expression.

"Is something amiss, lad?"

"I . . . no." Hubert shook his head so vigorously, his spectacles slid to the tip of his nose. He again looked at Eric's feet, staring at them as if he'd never seen riding boots before.

Eric's gaze followed Hubert's, but he saw nothing unusual, except perhaps that his boots appeared unusually dusty. A grin pulled at his lips. "Looks as if my valet polished these in the dark," he remarked. Opening the door, he walked out into the warm sunshine, followed by Hubert. Emperor stood tethered to a nearby tree, and Eric swung himself into the saddle. As he pulled on his riding gloves, Hubert slowly approached the horse, his gaze alternating between the saddle, the reins, and the stirrups. His face appeared pinched and pale, and bore an unmistakably worried frown.

Concerned, Eric asked, "Are you certain you're all right, Hubert? You look as if you've seen a ghost."

The boy slowly raised his somber gaze to Eric's. He swallowed audibly, then jerked his head in a nod. "I'm fine, my lord. I'm merely . . . puzzled."

"Oh? Anything I can help you with?"

"I don't believe so."

"And you're certain you're not feeling ill?"

"Positive, my lord."

Eric smiled at him. "Well, then, let me know if you change your mind about needing my help. Of course, you're an extremely bright lad. I'm certain you'll figure out your puzzle. I'll see you tomorrow." With that, he turned Emperor and trotted away.

Hubert stared after him, a whirlwind of disturbing questions storming through his mind. But one question glared brighter than all the others.

Why did Lord Wesley's boots, saddle, stirrups, and reins bear unmistakable traces of the phosphorescent powder he'd made and sprinkled on the Bride Thief's belongings?

He searched for a reasonable, plausible explanation— actually *any* explanation—but his logic screamed that there was only one conclusion to be drawn from the irrefutable evidence.

Lord Wesley was the Bride Thief.

But even as the thought entered his mind, another part of him tried to refute it. How could that be? Lord Wesley was a *gentleman!* Not a swashbuckling rescuer of damsels in distress. He was titled and wealthy. What earthly reason could he possibly have to undertake such a dangerous enterprise?

Deeply troubled, he started to walk toward the Chamber, but froze when a disturbing thought hit him with the force of a brick. Good God, did Sammie know? Did she realize the man she'd befriended was England's Most Notorious Kidnapper? He pressed his hands to his churning stomach.

No. Impossible. Sammie would have confided in him. And she hadn't known how to get in touch with the Bride Thief when she'd received Miss Barrow's letter. He had to discuss this with her. Perhaps she could offer him a plausible explanation for how the Bride Thief's powder was on Lord Wesley.

Turning, he strode swiftly into the house. He found Sammie in the drawing room staring into the fire. She signaled him to close the door behind him. When he'd done so, she grabbed his hand and pulled him toward the settee.

"I received a note from the Bride Thief," she whispered once they were seated. "His rescue of Miss Barrow was successful." Her gaze wandered to the fireplace. "I'd let you read the note, but I just burned it."

"A wise decision. I'm glad all went well." He wiped his moist palms on his breeches and cleared his throat. "Um, Sammie, have you ever wondered who the Bride Thief is under the mask?"

Sammie pursed her lips. "I must admit I've speculated more than once about what he looks like, but it is really not important. It's his work, his mission that matters." Reaching out, she gave his hand a quick sympathetic squeeze. "I know your questioning nature must chafe at the mystery, but you must put the matter from your mind. If anyone were to discover the man's identity, his life would be in grave danger."

A sick feeling settled in the pit of Hubert's stomach. He cleared his throat, then said, "I saw Lord Wesley leaving a few moments ago."

A deep flush raced into Sammie's cheeks, and she fidgeted with the lace on her gown. "Indeed?"

"Yes." Watching her closely, he asked, "Do you like him?"

Her blush deepened. "Of course. He's a very fine gentleman."

He shook his head, frustrated at his inability to ask the correct questions. "No, I meant, do you have . . . *feelings* for him?"

He wouldn't have thought it possible for her face to flame any brighter, but it did. "I'm sorry to ask you something so personal," he said in a rush. "It's just that I, well, I . . . I only want your happiness," he finished lamely.

Tenderness filled her gaze and she laid her palm against his cheek. "I'm very happy, Hubert. My work in the Chamber fulfills and challenges me, and I enjoy assisting you. *You* make me happy."

"And Lord Wesley . . . does he make you happy as well?"

The sort of dreamy expression he was well accustomed to seeing from his other sisters' entered Sammie's eyes. "Yes," she said softly. "My friendship with Lord Wesley pleases me."

Hubert pressed his lips together. It did not take a genius to deduce that Sammie's friendship with Lord Wesley pleased her a *great deal*. And from what he'd witnessed, Lord Wesley seemed to care for Sammie as well. Dash it, how could he possibly risk discussing the evidence of the powder with her? What if he were wrong? Or even worse—what if he were *right*?

Perhaps Lord Wesley meant to tell her himself. Or perhaps he meant to retire from his Bride Thief activities. Or perhaps there was nothing to tell or retire from. If he told Sammie of his suspicions, he might ruin any chance she and Lord Wesley might have at happiness . . . at a life together.

But what if Lord Wesley really was the Bride Thief?

"Sammie, what would you do if you found out a suitor hadn't been entirely . . . truthful with you?" he asked in what he prayed was a casual voice.

She frowned, but then understanding dawned in her eyes. "Why, is there a young lady you're interested in?"

Hubert nearly swallowed his tongue. Heat swamped his face and neck. Before he could find his voice to reply, she grasped his hands between hers. "Do you wish to talk to me about it?"

He mutely shook his head.

"All right. But remember, honesty is crucial, Hubert. I know you would never speak untruthfully to a young lady, and I pray she would return the courtesy. Lies destroy trust, and without trust there is nothing. I would never consider a future with someone who deceived me."

Unease rippled down his spine. No, he couldn't talk to Sammie about the evidence of the powder. At least not without verifying his suspicions first. And there was only one way to do that.

He'd have to confront Lord Wesley.

Chapter 15

Sammie arrived at the lake at half after ten that evening. She hadn't planned to arrive so early, but she hadn't been able to remain indoors another moment. The cool night air beckoned her, as did the nocturnal sounds and moist scents of the forest.

He would arrive in less than two hours. The man who would be her *lover*. And she would embark on the most thrilling adventure of her life. With a man who had unquestionably become very . . . important. A man she undeniably . . . cared for deeply.

Her eyes drifted closed, and her heart beat a wild rhythm as it had all day. What would it be like? *Wonderful. Like everything you've already shared with him, only more.* Heat shimmered through her as she recalled his touch, his kiss, the way he looked at her. A long sigh drifted from her lips. He'd already made her feel things she'd never known existed, and by doing so had awakened her hunger for more. She could only hope that her inexperience would not tarnish their liaison for him.

She wandered to her favorite area, a small private cove secluded by an outcropping of rocks and an abundance of tall hedges. Lowering herself onto a large, flat-topped rock, she trailed her hand in the water. The coolness felt like a welcome balm against her heated skin.

She slipped off her shoes, then rolled down her stockings. When she couldn't stand pacing in her bedchamber another moment, she'd grabbed an extra chemise, then made her way to the lake, knowing nothing soothed her like a dip in the water. There was plenty of time to dry and redress before Lord Wesley arrived.

She shimmied out of her gown, then folded it carefully on the rock. She removed her spectacles, placing them inside her shoe. Dressed only in her chemise, she waded into the cool water until it lapped at her waist. She breathed in the scent of moist earth, and blew out a contented sigh. Trailing her hands through the glasslike surface, she closed her eyes and turned in slow circles, allowing the quiet stillness to relax her muscles, soothe and calm her.

A twig cracked. Her eyes snapped open, and she squinted toward the sound. A blurry blob stood on the shore. Her heart jumped, but before she could say a word, his deep, smooth voice reached her ears.

"It appears we're both early."

Eric stood frozen in place at the sight of her, standing in the privacy of the secluded cove, waist-deep in the water, dressed only in her chemise, moonlight reflecting off her shoulders. He'd come early, unable to remain in his empty house, thinking about her, wanting her. He'd hoped she might arrive a few minutes early, but he hadn't dared to hope for . . . this. It was as if the gods had placed his fantasy before him, like a banquet feast.

Without moving his gaze from hers, he removed his jacket, allowing it to fall to the ground. Next he untied and removed his cravat. Then, without the slightest hesitation, he walked into the lake, not stopping until he stood directly in front of her. She stared up at him with a dazed, startled expression.

He took her hands, entwining their fingers, then lowered his head until their foreheads touched. "I trust I am no longer blurry."

She shook her head and their noses bumped. "No. But you've ruined your clothing. Your boots."

"I have others." He leaned back, drinking in the sight of her. A simple ribbon held her hair back from her face. Her eyes appeared enormous, filled with a nearly heartbreaking combination of longing and trepidation. Her mouth appeared to tremble, and the need to touch her, kiss her, slammed into him with such intensity he nearly groaned.

He placed her wet hands against his shirt, pressing her palms to his chest. "Someone told me that you swam in this lake," he whispered.

There was no mistaking the embarrassment that passed over her features. "The gossips often remark upon what they consider my eccentric behavior. I'm certain you were properly scandalized."

"No. I was fascinated." His gaze wandered down to her breasts which pushed against the thin material of her chemise. "You cannot know how many times I've imagined you like this. Wet. Waiting. For me."

"You have?"

"Yes." *Almost constantly.* Reaching out, he trailed a single fingertip slowly across her cheek, over her jaw, down her neck, watching the play of emotions flare in her eyes. Any questions he might have entertained regarding her still wanting to follow through with their plans evaporated by the desire he read in her eyes.

His hand continued its lazy journey, brushing over her collarbone, then slipping downward to caress the swell of her breasts. When a tiny gasp escaped her, he cupped his hands in the water, then drizzled a trail of cool water over her shoulder. A thin wet path meandered down her chest. Entranced, he repeated his action several times, allowing ribbons of water to drip off his fingers onto her moonlight-dusted skin.

"Everywhere the water touches you," he said softly, "your skin gleams like silver."

She clutched at his shirt. "Newton's law," she murmured in a breathless voice. "To every action there is an equal and opposite reaction."

"Ah. So when I touch you like this . . . ?" He filled his wet palms with her full breasts. "What is your reaction?"

"I . . . shiver."

"And when I do this . . . ?" He caressed her nipples through her wet chemise, tugging gently as he molded her soft flesh to his palms.

"Oh, my." Her head tipped back and a long moan escaped her. "I tremble. Everywhere."

"And this?" He slowly slipped the thin cotton straps down her arms, exposing high, rounded breasts topped with aroused nipples.

"I . . . I forget how to breathe."

Desire, sharp as a knife, stabbed him. With a low groan, he dipped his head, circling first one aroused peak, then the other with his tongue. She squirmed against him, still clutching his shirt as if it were a lifeline. Slipping one arm around her hips and cupping her head with the other, he leaned her back, drawing a plump nipple into his mouth. His lips and tongue caressed her, tasting her satiny, honey-scented skin, reveling in her quick intake of breath, followed by an earthy moan that aroused him beyond bearing. His hand slipped down to her rounded buttocks, and he pulled her tight against him, her feminine softness pressing against his hardness.

An inferno of need suffused him, and he lost all sense of

time and place. *Mine, mine, mine* echoed through his mind as his teeth tugged her chemise lower. His wet fingers traced over her revealed skin as he trailed a hot path of kisses up to her neck, then fused his mouth to hers.

Blood rushed through him so hard that he felt it pounding in his ears. No woman, ever, had tasted like this. So sweet. So hot and silky. So delicious that he felt as if he could kiss her for days and still not have satisfied his hunger for her. He explored all the warm secrets of her satiny mouth, memorizing each tantalizing texture, as his hands wandered with increasing urgency up and down her back.

He needed to slow down, to savor each of her moans, but as she'd done before, she robbed him of his finesse. He hadn't planned to make love to her for the first time standing in the lake, but he couldn't seem to stop. Hell, he couldn't even slow down. His heart slammed against his ribs like a hammer. He felt as if his skin had shrunk two sizes, all but strangling him. He wanted, needed, her hands on him.

Breaking their kiss, he drew a ragged breath into his lungs. "Touch me, Samantha. Don't be afraid."

Uncertainty glimmered in her eyes. "I don't know what to do. I don't want to displease you."

He would have laughed if he'd been able. "There's not much chance of that." With one hand, he quickly unfastened his shirt, then glided her palm across his chest. A low growl rumbled in his throat. Releasing her hand, he said, "Do it again."

She brushed her hand across his chest, and his muscles contracted under her light touch. "Do you like that?" she asked, splaying her fingers against his skin, her eyes alight with wonder.

"God, yes."

Growing bolder, she lifted her other hand to his chest,

and slowly eased her fingers downward, over his ribcage. "What is your reaction when I do that?" she asked.

It took every bit of his concentration to remain still and allow her to explore. "My heart pounds."

She ran her hands upwards, brushing over his nipples. "And that?"

He moved slightly, rubbing his erection against her. "It arouses me."

Her eyes widened. Taking one of her hands, he slid it down his chest, over his abdomen, then slipped it under the water. He pressed his rigid arousal against her palm. "You arouse me. Undeniably. Unequivocally. In a way that is nearly unbearable. So many 'u' words to describe what you do to me."

Her fingers closed around him, and his teeth clenched against the pleasure. He stood in an agony of sweet torment while she ran her fingers up and down his rigid length, learning him through his breeches. Her gaze remained steadily on his, and he watched her absorb the feel of him, along with the white-hot desire he knew burned in his eyes.

Without breaking their gaze, he unfastened his breeches, freeing his aching arousal. Her fingers closed over him, and his breath stalled. The cool water in no way tempered his ardor, and her hand enveloped him like a warm glove.

God help him, he didn't know how much of this he could stand. Her fingers moved over him, each caress killing him with pleasure. But when she squeezed him gently, he grasped her wrist.

"Did I hurt you?" she asked in a stricken voice.

His fingers tightened on her skin. "No. But when you do that . . ." he swallowed hard.

Feminine understanding suddenly gleamed in her eyes. "How do you react?" she asked in a voice he could only describe as smoky.

"It makes me forget to go slow with you. Makes me forget your innocence."

She flexed her fingers over his aching flesh and he groaned. "I do not feel very innocent," she whispered. "I feel decadent. And wicked. And . . . wanting."

God, he knew all about wanting. Wanting until he felt as if he'd caught on fire. Wanting, needing, until he burned from the inside out.

"I want to touch you more," she whispered.

Unable to deny either of them, he released her wrist. She glided her hand up and down, over him, igniting him until any semblance of control he might have imagined he still possessed, disappeared. Gone was his sophistication, his experience, his mastery over his own body. His hands trembled and his damn knees felt weak. All from her. Nothing existed except her. The touch of her hands. The feel of her skin. The need to be inside her overwhelmed him. Now. Before he exploded in her hands.

Slipping one hand under the water, he grabbed the hem of her chemise and drew it upward.

"Hold onto my shoulders and wrap your legs around my hips," he ground out in a barely recognizable voice.

She did as he bid, opening herself up to him. His hand slipped between them, under her chemise. He caressed her with a slow circular motion, watching her eyes slip shut. Her fingers bit into his shoulder muscles, her breaths long and deep.

"Look at me," he commanded.

Her eyelids fluttered open and pure male satisfaction slammed into him at her languorous, bemused expression. When she focused on his face, he said, "Say my name."

Her lips parted and she sighed out, "Lord Wesley."

"No. My given name. Eric." He parted her plump folds, teasing her gently, then eased one finger just inside her. "Say it."

"Eric," she whispered.

Her velvety warmth surrounded his fingertip, and his erection jerked in response. She was so tight. So warm. So ready. And he could wait no longer.

He slowly slipped his finger from her, and a soft moan of protest rumbled from her. With his gaze locked on hers, he grasped her hips, then guided himself slowly into her welcoming heat. When her maidenhead halted his progress, he stilled, the significance of his actions ramming into him like a brick to his head. He was about to take her innocence—irrevocably ruin her. But God help him, unless she begged him to stop, there was no turning back now.

"We're not . . . finished, are we?" she asked in a tone that conveyed such suppressed dismay he would have chuckled had he been able.

Instead, he offered up a prayer of thanks that she hadn't asked him to stop. "No, sweetheart. We're not finished. But when I breach your maidenhead, it will probably hurt for a moment."

She brushed her wet fingertips over his face. "It couldn't possibly hurt worse than the thought of not sharing this with you. Don't stop. I want to know everything . . . every sensation. Every touch."

Praying he wouldn't hurt her, he tightened his grip on her hips, surging upward as he pressed her downward. Her eyes widened and she gasped, a sound that pierced his heart.

"God, I'm sorry," he said, forcing himself not to move. "Are you all right?" Damn it, had he been too rough? He should have taken more care. More time. But she'd driven him nearly insane—

"I'm . . . fine."

Thank God. But his relief instantly turned to sensual torture. Her feminine softness enveloped him like a tight silk glove, and he suddenly questioned his ability to withdraw from her when the time came. Gritting his teeth against the nearly unbearable pleasure, he remained motionless to give her time to adjust to the feel of him. A myriad of emotions flickered across her face . . . surprise, wonder, then pleasure, seconds later giving way to desire.

"In fact I'm . . ." She moved her hips, and he touched her a bit deeper, her liquid heat caressing him. Her fingers dug into his shoulders, and a long sigh escaped her as her lids drifted shut. "Oh, my."

Gripping her hips, he moved within her with an excruciating slowness that nearly killed him, easing nearly all the way out of her, only to slide smoothly back, filling her. Each time it seemed he caressed her deeper, she clenched him tighter, until he shook with burning need. His breathing turned into short, ragged, pants that matched her staccato gasps as his thrusts grew faster, stronger, the water swirling around them, slapping at their writhing bodies. He feared his intensity might frighten her, but she moved with him, her breaths as choppy as his.

"Eric," she moaned. Her legs clamped around his hips like a vise, and she wrapped her arms around his neck, pressing her breasts to his chest. He captured her against him, holding her so tightly, he didn't know where her skin ended and his began. He felt her orgasm tremble through her with his entire body. Her heart pounded against his, her hips bucked, and her sleek walls spasmed around him, drowning him in the same vortex that took her down.

The instant she sagged against him, he withdrew from her, helpless to hold back his climax another second. Clutching her to him, he buried his face against her fragrant neck, his arousal pressed tightly between them as his release shuddered through him.

He had no idea how many minutes passed before his

breathing returned to normal and he could lift his head. When he did, she leaned back as far as his binding arms would permit and their gazes collided.

Pure incredulity glowed from her eyes. "Good heavens," she whispered. "That was . . ." her voice trailed off into a vaporous sigh.

"Incredible," he offered.

"Indescribable," she agreed.

"Intoxicating."

She reached out and traced his mouth with a single fingertip. "So many 'i' words to describe what you did to me, Eric."

He kissed her finger, then drew it slowly into his mouth, circling it with his tongue before releasing it. "So many 'i' words to describe *you*, Samantha," he corrected.

She lowered her lashes, and he knew his words brought a blush to her cheeks. "I didn't know people did . . . *this* in the water."

"Neither did I."

Her gaze flew to his. "You mean you've never . . . ?"

"In a lake? No. This was a first for me."

A smile of unadulterated delight lit her face, and his throat tightened at the enchanting, sensual picture she made.

"I'm glad this was an adventure for you as well," she said. "I feared my lack of knowledge might bore you."

For an instant the area around his heart went hollow, then flooded with a tenderness he'd never before experienced. How could she not know that she was nothing less than fascinating? In every way? *Because so many fools overlook what is right in front of them.* Idiots. Yet, he selfishly couldn't deny that what others failed to recognize and admire in her somehow made her seem more *his*.

Brushing a damp tendril from her cheek, he said, "I assure you, I have never been less bored in my life. Indeed, boredom is not a feeling you have ever once inspired in me. And you are not lacking, Samantha. In any way."

He again sensed her blush, and she glanced downward. "I couldn't help but notice that you withdrew before you . . ."

"I promised you I would." *And you have no idea how the effort nearly killed me.*

Raising her gaze to his, she whispered, "I didn't realize that a man's seed was so . . . warm."

Warm? Hell, scalding was closer to the truth. He'd felt hot enough to heat the entire damn lake. Just recalling the sensation of her wrapped around him, his flesh buried deep inside her, pumped renewed desire through him.

"I think we'd best exit the lake before we become water-logged." *Before I make love to you again.* "I hadn't meant to make love to you for the first time in the *water.*"

Interest flared in her eyes. "Oh? What *had* you planned?"

"Bringing you to a small lodge on my property." He gazed into her eyes, and his blood stirred. "Would you like to accompany me there now?"

She only said one word, but it was the only word he wanted to hear.

"Yes."

Chapter 16

The following morning, before joining her parents and Hubert in the breakfast room, Sammie peered at herself in the cheval glass in her bedchamber.

How was it possible that she looked the same when everything was so completely, irrevocably *different*? How could it be that all the extraordinary things she was feeling on the inside did not show on the outside, except perhaps for the color staining her cheeks?

Hugging her arms around herself, she closed her eyes, allowing memories from last night to wash over her. Never in her wildest dreams could she have imagined the intimacies she and Eric had shared, first at the lake, then at his lodge. The indescribable sensation of lying naked before a man who slowly explored her body with his hands and lips, eliciting a passion in her that she had never suspected herself capable of.

Then, the sheer beauty of exploring his naked body in return as he reclined before the hearth, the fire's glow illuminating a fascinating display of masculine planes and muscles. Endless caresses and whispering as he taught her how to please him, and discovered what pleased her. Long, slow, deep kisses that touched her soul. It had indeed been the adventure of her life . . . yet so much more.

Opening her eyes, she stared at the unremarkable woman reflected in the glass. What did he see in her? He'd worshipped her last night as if she were a queen, yet there was no denying a man like him could have any woman he wanted. For right now, incredible as it was, he wanted her.

But for how long?

Don't think about it, her heart warned, but her mind refused to listen. She'd be a fool to entertain the notion that she could hold his interest for any length of time. How long before he tired of her? A week? A month? Sharp pain knifed through her at the thought of them parting company. Of never seeing him again. Or worse, seeing him and having to pretend that nothing had ever passed between them. Knowing that he was enjoying the intimacies they'd shared with another woman.

Waves of helpless jealousy washed over her at the thought of him caressing another woman . . . of someone else touching him. Arousing him. Pleasing him. She pressed her hands to her stomach and fought back the hot tears that pooled behind her eyes, valiantly trying to banish the thought before her heart broke in two. *You fool, This was supposed to be an adventure. And look what you've done. You've fallen in love with him.*

Why hadn't she warned herself against such a disastrous occurrence? Prepared herself? Why hadn't it occurred to her how utterly *logical* it was for her to lose her heart to him? He not only possessed every trait she admired in a person, he filled every corner of her mind with romantic dreams that she should dismiss as ridiculous and illogical, but that instead suffused her with . . . love.

A strangled sound erupted from her throat, and she staggered the few steps to her escritoire, dropping down into the hard wooden chair. She tried to deny her inner voice's words, but there was no point. She loved him. Helplessly. Hopelessly. *So many "h" words to describe my feelings for him.* And of course there was one more 'h' word—the one that would describe her when their affair ended.

Heartbroken.

He would continue on to the next woman, and she would be left with nothing more than the memories of their time together, for she could not envision ever taking another lover. Not when her heart and soul belonged to Eric.

Rising, she paced the length of the room. The longer she allowed their liaison to continue, the worse her heartbreak would be when it ended. She knew with sinking finality that she would only fall deeper in love with him—and she wouldn't be able to hide her feelings from him for she was not a good actress.

She paused in her pacing and buried her face in her hands. Dear God, how humiliating if he knew . . . if he pitied her for her hopeless feelings. But what else could he do *except* pity her? There was no chance that he would return her feelings. He might treat her kindly, hold her in some affection, but he would never fall in love with her. Never want to marry her and spend his life with her. His earlier words reverberated through her mind. *I've no intention of ever marrying.*

She'd had no desire to marry either, a decision that had been simple to accept before today. Why would she wish to spend her life with someone who did not respect her dedication to her scientific studies? She hoped to someday make an important contribution to medicine with her honey cream—something Eric *did* respect. Now, for the first time, she could see that she would not have to give up her dreams in order to appease a man.

But the man she wanted had made his aversion to marriage very clear. Why did he feel so strongly about it? She shook her head. Although she was curious, in the end his reasons did not matter. He did not wish to marry, and that was that. And even if he should some day change his mind, he would of course choose a beautiful, young wife from the peerage.

Her common sense told her to end things between them. Immediately. Before she further risked her heart. But her heart rebelled, urging her to grasp whatever time she could with him, and to enjoy it while it lasted. She'd have a lifetime to mend her heart.

Perhaps. Yet she suspected her heart would never mend. And she could never bear his pity. And she'd never successfully hide her feelings from him. For her own sake, to save herself from falling so far in love with him that she would never recover, she had to end their affair.

Still, she could not bear the thought of not seeing him one more time. She had to hold him, touch him, just once more. To store up the memories that would have to last her for all the empty, lonely nights ahead. They'd agreed to meet again tonight, at the garden gate at eleven o'clock, then depart for his lodge. She would cherish him one more time, then pray she'd find the strength to let him go.

Eric stood in front of the windows in his private study, sipping his morning coffee. His gaze wandered to the mantel clock and a wry smile twisted his lips. Exactly three minutes had passed since he'd last checked the time.

Fourteen hours until he saw her again. No, actually

fourteen hours and thirty-seven minutes. How the hell was he going to fill the time? He glanced at his desk. Several dozen pieces of correspondence required his attention, as did the accounts for his Norfolk estate.

He expelled a long, frustrated breath. No matter how he might try to engross himself in work, nothing would banish the memories of last night. The feel of her under him. Over him. Wrapped around him. The sound of his name on her lips as she climaxed in his arms. Discovering all the fascinating secrets of her body. Her wide-eyed, wondrous exploration of his. The white-hot intensity tempered by the laughter they'd shared.

None of his previous sexual encounters had prepared him for what he'd experienced with Samantha. Never before had he felt this overwhelming rush of fierce protectiveness. This chest-aching tenderness. This sharp-edged desire to know everything about her . . . her mind as well as her body. This raw need to please her in every way. To hold her to him and simply not let her go.

Draining his last sip of coffee, he set the china cup on his desk, then pressed his fingers to his temples in a vain attempt to relieve the unsettling emotions scraping at him. Damn it all, he felt edgy, yet at the same time, uncharacteristically vulnerable. And he didn't like it one bit. How had she—an innocent in the ways of love—managed to arouse and enchant him as no experienced woman ever had? Why wasn't last night proving to be like all the other nights he'd spent in a lover's arms—delightful while it lasted, yet eminently forgettable once the act was completed?

A dozen words to describe last night jumped into his mind, but forgettable was not one of them. A humorless laugh rumbled in his throat as he recalled how less than a fortnight ago he'd entertained the notion that he could see Samantha Briggeham one more time and then forget her. What a raging jest on him! He hadn't been able to push the woman from his thoughts *before* he'd made love to her. Now she occupied every corner of his brain.

Forget her? How could he hope to do so when the feel of her, the scent of her, was indelibly etched in his mind? And, he feared, more than his mind. It was as if she'd engraved her name across his heart. And soul. A disturbing development to be sure.

This desire, this need for her, sorely tested his control, a facet of himself he'd always prided himself on. It had required a Herculean effort keep from spilling his seed in her last night. In truth, he'd barely managed to withdraw in time.

His gut clenched, and he mentally cursed himself. How had he allowed their relationship to progress to this point? Why had he pursued something so utterly impossible? *Because you're a selfish bastard and you couldn't keep your hands off her.* As much as it shamed him, he couldn't deny the truth of his inner voice. And there was only one way to fix what his selfishness had wrought.

He would have to end their affair.

Everything in him cringed in protest, and he swore his heart screamed *No!* But damn it all, these . . . *feelings*, these soft and tender emotions she generated in him did more than unsettle him. They frightened him. He could not offer her the sort of future she deserved. Indeed, *any* long-term liaison with him might possibly place her in danger.

Their affair would have to end sooner or later. For both their sakes, he needed to make it sooner.

But God, not just yet.

He had to see her again. One more time. To memorize every look, every touch, every inch of her. Because he knew, in his suddenly heavy heart, that he would never meet another woman like Samantha Briggeham.

His thoughts were interrupted by a knock at the study door.

"Come in."

Eversley entered, his normally impassive butler's face showing unprecedented animation. "You've a guest, my lord."

His heart jumped. Had Samantha come to him? Forcing his voice to remain impassive, he asked, "Who is here?"

An unmistakable sheen glinted in Eversley's eyes. " 'Tis Lady Darvin, my lord."

At that moment, his sister, Margaret, appeared behind Eversley. Perfectly coiffed dark hair surrounded her face, which in spite of showing signs of strain and fatigue, was still beautiful. Tears shimmered in her dark eyes that exactly matched his own. He searched her gaze, relieved that no suffering lingered in her eyes, although it was painfully obvious she remained haunted and pitifully unsure of herself.

Her bottom lip trembled. "Hello, Eric. Thank you for—"

He reached her in three long strides, catching her against him in a fierce hug that cut off her words. Her arms slipped around his waist, and with her hands fisted against his back, she buried her face against his shirt. Long shudders racked her body, and he tightened his arms around her, prepared to stand there all day and absorb her tears if that's what she needed.

A lump lodged in his throat, and he cursed his inability to absorb her suffering as well. Damn, she felt so small and fragile in his arms, yet he knew she possessed an inner strength that defied her delicate appearance. He nodded to Eversley who discreetly withdrew. The instant the door closed behind the butler, Eric lowered his head, resting his cheek against her soft hair.

A smile touched his lips. She still smelled of roses. She always had, even as a little girl. Even at the age of ten, when she'd escaped the watchful eye of her governess and played in the mud. She'd returned to the house utterly filthy and bedraggled, but by damn, she'd still smelled like roses.

After several minutes, her shudders subsided. Lifting her head, she looked up at him through damp, spiky lashes. The bleak emptiness shadowing her eyes squeezed his heart like a fist. It was a look he vowed to erase.

"Are you all right?" he asked quietly.

She nodded slowly. "I'm sorry I fell apart like that. I'm just so glad to see you. And to be here."

He dropped a quick kiss on her forehead. "You have no idea how good it is to have you here. This is your home, Margaret. You are welcome to live here as long as you wish." He offered her a smile. "It's been lonely here without you."

She did not return his smile, and his gut clenched at the reminder that this was not the same bright-eyed, laughing girl from his youth. He inwardly cursed their father and the man he'd forced her to marry, for stealing her laughter and joy. *By God, I'll do everything in my power to see that you are never sad again.*

"Actually, this is *your* home, Eric," she said, "and I am grateful for your generosity."

"'Tis no hardship to enjoy the company of my favorite sister."

She did not smile, but he thought he detected a tiny glint of amusement in her eyes. "I am your *only* sister."

"Ah, but even if I had a dozen others, I know you would still be my favorite."

Instead of the laugh he'd hoped for, she stepped back from his embrace. Walking to the window, she looked out at the flowering garden. "I'd forgotten how . . . beautiful it is here."

His hands fisted. The catch in her voice broke his heart. Forcing his own voice to be cheery, he asked, "Why don't we stroll through the gardens, and I'll bring you up to date on all the local news. Then, this afternoon, perhaps you'd care to accompany me on a visit."

She turned to face him. "Who are you visiting?"

"The Briggehams. Do you remember them?"

Pursing her lips, she considered for several seconds, then nodded. "Yes. There are several daughters and a young son, I believe."

"Four daughters, all married except the eldest. Actually, it's the son, Hubert, whom I'm calling upon. An incredibly intelligent lad. He's made a fascinating laboratory he calls the Chamber, in the old barn. I promised to look at an invention he's working on." He joined her by the window and gently clasped her hands. "Come with me. You'll enjoy meeting Hubert, and his sister and his parents as well, if they are home. I believe you'd quite like Miss Briggeham. The two of you are of similar ages and—"

"Thank you, Eric, but I do not feel up to answering questions about . . ." Her voice trailed off and her gaze dropped to the floor.

Placing his fingers under her chin, he lifted her face until their eyes met. "I have no intention of subjecting you to pain, Margaret. Samantha . . . I mean, Miss Briggeham, is not prone to gossip. She's kind, and like you, she could use a friend."

He suddenly froze as in a flash it occurred to him what he'd just done. He'd offered to introduce his sister to his *mistress*. Suggested they befriend each other. Bloody hell! Never before would he have considered such a breach of propriety toward Margaret, but he simply hadn't considered Samantha in those terms. Damn it, she was his . . . friend.

The enormity of what he'd done to Samantha crashed down on his head like a boulder dropped from the sky. He'd made her his *mistress*. As far as Society was concerned, her actions would render her no better than a harlot. Fury rushed through him at the idea that anyone might ever think of her like that. She was a loving, intelligent, kind, generous young woman who deserved so much more than he'd given her.

Just another compelling reason to end their affair. Tonight. But now he realized that in order to retain any of his tarnished honor and not subject her to further disrespect, he'd have to end things *before* he made love to her again. A sick feeling settled in the pit of his stomach, knowing he wouldn't have the opportunity to touch her again. But what drove a knife of pain through his heart was the realization that by taking her as a lover, he'd destroyed any true hope of them remaining friends. He could not envision being able to go back to the casual camaraderie they'd once enjoyed. Not when he'd want her with every ounce of his being.

Margaret's voice jerked him from his thoughts. "All right, I'll accompany you to the Briggehams'." She searched his gaze for several seconds, her eyes dark and serious. "Eric, I know you do not want my gratitude, but I must thank you. Not only for allowing me to live here, but for not . . . pressing me for details."

"I won't question you," he said, "but know that I am willing to listen should you care to talk to me."

A single tear slid down her cheek, clenching his heart. "Thank you. It's been so long since . . ." Pressing her lips together, she swallowed hard. "I do not want to talk about . . . him. He's gone." Some deep emotion flickered in her eyes. "I cannot mourn him. His death freed me."

Her words, her fervent tone, pumped rage through his veins. Not only at Darvin, but at himself. "I should have killed the bastard," he bit out. "If only I'd—"

She pressed her fingers to his lips, cutting off his words. "No. Then you would have hung for murder, and he was

not worth losing you. I made marriage vows before God
and it was my duty to honor them."

"*He* did not. I should have—"

"But you didn't. Because I asked you not to. You honored my wishes above your own, and I'm grateful." Determination fired in her gaze. "I've spent the last five years in
darkness, Eric. I want to enjoy the sunshine again."

He grasped her hands, squeezing them tightly. "Then let
us go outdoors immediately and frolic in the sun."

The barest ghost of a smile touched her lips, and his
heart turned over.

"I believe," she said, "that is the best invitation I've received in a very long time."

Eric and Margaret stood in Hubert's Chamber, listening
with interest as Hubert explained his latest invention, a device he called The Guillotine Slicer.

"Several weeks ago, our cook Sarah cut herself slicing
potatoes," Hubert said. "The knife slipped right out of her
hand, the blade nearly cutting her foot as well when it fell
to the floor. With my slicer, this ceases to be a problem.
Observe." He stuck a round metal disk studded with a
dozen short prongs into the end of a potato. Slipping his
hand through a leather strap attached to the disk, he then
set the potato on his invention, which indeed resembled a
horizontal guillotine set on sturdy, six-inch wooden legs.

"The blade is fixed in place," Hubert explained. "I hold
the metal disk so as not to cut my fingers, then simply run
the potato over the blade." Holding the slicer steady with
his free hand, he demonstrated. Within seconds, a stack of
uniformly sliced potatoes sat on the plate beneath the
slicer.

Pointing to a knob on the side of the device, he said,
"I'm working on adding a feature so you can adjust it here

to vary the thickness of the slices. Once I perfect that, I'm hoping to develop a larger version based on the same principles, to cut meats."

"Very impressive," Eric said, examining a perfect slice.

A crimson flush of pleasure washed over Hubert's cheeks. Laying a hand on the boy's shoulder, Eric said, "I'd be interested in purchasing one of these for my own cook."

Hubert's eyes widened behind his spectacles. "Oh, I would gladly give you one, Lord Wesley."

"Thank you, lad, but I insist upon paying for it. In fact, I daresay that if this were available for purchase, hordes of people would buy them." He turned toward Margaret. "What do you think?"

She was clearly stunned to be asked her opinion. "I . . . I think it's an ingenious invention that would be a welcome addition to any household."

Eric smiled at her, then shifted his attention back to Hubert. "I honestly believe this is a machine with great potential, Hubert. Should you decide you'd like to sell them—"

"You mean like a *business*?"

"Precisely. I have several contacts in London who I could speak to on your behalf. And I myself would be willing to invest funds should you decide to proceed, with your father's permission, of course."

Eric's offer clearly flabbergasted the boy. "That is very kind, my lord, but I do not consider the design completed. Besides, I am a scientist, not a tradesman."

"Then you might wish to consider selling your idea to a third party. At any rate, my offer stands. Think upon it, discuss it with your father, and let me know what you decide. If you'd like, I'll speak to your father as well."

"All right. Thank you." Hubert pushed his glasses higher on his nose, then shuffled his feet. "Actually, there is something else I wished to discuss with you, my lord." He cast an embarrassed glance toward Margaret.

Margaret, clearly sensing the boy's need for privacy, inclined her head. "Thank you for showing me your machine, Hubert. If you'll excuse me, I'd like to stroll through your gardens and enjoy the lovely weather . . . if you do not mind."

"Not at all, Lady Darvin." A flush stained his cheeks. "I hope I did not bore you. Mama always warns me not to harangue our guests."

"On the contrary, I greatly enjoyed my visit with you." A tentative smile slowly spread across her features, as if she'd forgotten her face could move in such a way. Seconds later, she offered Hubert a full, genuine smile, and a breath he hadn't realized he held, escaped Eric. God, that show of happiness was a balm to his heart. Gratitude toward Hubert filled him, for giving Margaret a reason to smile.

She slipped outside, closing the Chamber door quietly behind her. Eric turned toward Hubert, surprised by the troubled expression creasing the boy's face. "Is something amiss, lad?"

"I need to ask you something, my lord."

Eric studied him for several seconds. The boy looked as if he bore the weight of the world on his thin shoulders. A trickle of unease slid down his spine. Did Hubert's obvious distress in some way concern Samantha? Damn, could the boy have seen them last night at the lake?

"You may ask me anything," Eric assured him, praying for the best, but bracing himself nonetheless.

Hubert pulled open a drawer and withdrew a black leather pouch. Opening the drawstring, he sprinkled a small amount of a powdery substance into his hand. "This is a powder containing special phosphorescent properties that I developed myself," Hubert said in a quiet voice. "To the best of my knowledge, no one else possesses such a powder."

Relief punched Eric along with confusion. Leaning closer, he peered at the substance. "What does it do?"

"It casts a slight glow that lends it a distinctive adhering quality." Setting the pouch down on the wooden table, he wiped his powdery hand over his black breeches. He then attempted to brush the powder from his breeches, but was not completely successful. "It is actually the glow, rather than the powder itself that cannot be fully removed from the cloth."

Eric stared at Hubert's breeches and recognition shot through him. He recalled recently observing that same odd, dusty glow on his boots.

Straightening, he met Eric's eyes. "The other evening, I sprinkled this powder on the saddle, reins, and stirrups of a certain gentleman's horse."

Something in Hubert's steadfast gaze edged a chill of foreboding through Eric. "On which gentleman's horse?"

"The Bride Thief's."

The name hung in the air between them for several seconds. Keeping his face carefully blank, Eric asked, "What makes you think this horse belonged to the Bride Thief?"

"I saw him. In the woods. Dressed all in black, with a full head mask. He rescued Miss Barrow."

For the space of a heartbeat, everything in Eric froze. His breath. His blood. His heart. Then, he raised his brows, and said in a controlled voice, "Surely you are mistaken—"

"There is no mistake," Hubert broke in, shaking his head. "I saw him with my sister and Miss Barrow. And before he mounted his horse to ride away with Miss Barrow, I sprinkled my powder on his saddle, reins, and stirrups. And the next day . . . yesterday . . . you called on Sammie. Traces of my powder were on your boots. Your mount's saddle, reins, and stirrups as well."

"My boots and riding equipment merely collected dust on the way here."

"It was not dust, Lord Wesley. It was my powder. I would recognize it anywhere. But just to confirm my observations, I wiped a bit from your saddle. It was a perfect match."

Jesus. Eric barely managed to swallow his bark of incredulous laughter. Every damn official in England, along with the Bride Thief Posse, and hundreds of other people eager to collect the price on his head wanted to capture the Bride Thief—and a fourteen-year-old had succeeded where they all had failed. If he weren't so stunned and alarmed, he'd offer Hubert his heartiest congratulations on a job well done. Unfortunately, Hubert's brilliance could very well cost him his life.

He quickly considered several falsehoods he could try to foist upon the boy, but just as quickly realized the futility of such a plan. Hubert was not only keenly intelligent, he was tenacious as well. Clearly he stood a better chance of trusting him rather than attempting to deceive him, but he had several points to make first.

"You're asking if I'm the Bride Thief."

Hubert nodded, his Adam's apple bobbing.

"Are you looking to collect the reward for his capture?"

The boy's eyes filled with shocked distress. "Egad, no, my lord. I have the greatest respect for your . . . his . . . your mission. You are the personification of bravery and heroism. I mean, he is. Er, you are." His face flushed crimson. "Um, you both are."

Eric narrowed his eyes. "You realize that if the Bride Thief is caught, he will hang."

The crimson drained from Hubert's cheeks. "I swear, upon my soul, that I will never tell anyone. Ever. I would never do anything to harm you, my lord. You've been a good friend to me. And to Sammie as well."

At the mention of her name, Eric's hands fisted. "Have you spoken of this to her?"

Hubert shook his head so hard he nearly dislodged his spectacles. "No, my lord. And you have my word of honor that I will not." He cleared his throat. "And I suggest that you not consider confiding in her either."

"You do realize that if the magistrate discovers Samantha aided the Bride Thief in his rescue of Miss Barrow, she could be brought up on charges."

Hubert's complexion whitened to chalk. "The magistrate will hear nothing from me. But I meant you should not tell Sammie because I think the news would anger her. You see, she told me . . ." His voice trailed off and he frowned.

Eric's heart jumped into double time. "What did she tell you?"

"She said honesty is crucial and that lies destroy trust." His voice dropped to a whisper. "She said that without trust, there is nothing."

Eric clenched his teeth against the pain of Hubert's words. There was, of course, no hope that he and Samantha could ever share a future, due to his work as the Bride Thief. Nor would he ever risk her safety by telling her his identity. Yet, even if, for one wild, impossible moment he'd considered doing so, he'd clearly lose her anyway for deceiving her. *Without trust there is nothing.*

Hubert squared his shoulders and met his gaze unflinchingly. "I do not want my sister hurt, Lord Wesley."

"Nor do I, Hubert. I give you my word of honor that I will allow nothing to harm her."

Lifting his chin a notch, Hubert added, "She cares for you. Do not be careless with her feelings."

Admiration for the boy filled Eric even as his words slapped him with guilt. *She cares for you.* God help him, but he cared for her as well. Too much.

"I'll not hurt her," he assured Hubert. "I fully understand and respect your wish to protect your sister. I feel the same way about my sister. She is the reason I do . . . what I do."

Hubert's eyes widened. "I must say, I'd wondered why."

"Our father forced her to marry. I couldn't save her, so I save others."

Understanding dawned in Hubert's gaze and they shared a long, measuring look. Then Eric slowly extended his hand. "I believe we understand each other."

Hubert firmly shook his proffered hand. "We do. And may I say that it is an honor to know you."

Some of the tension drained from Eric's shoulders. "Odd. I was just about to say the same thing to you." He released the boy's hand, then inclined his head toward the door. "I'd like to introduce our sisters. Is Miss Briggeham at home?"

"She was reading in the drawing room when I came to the Chamber."

"Excellent." Eric led the way outside, blinking to adjust his eyes to the bright sunshine. He spied Margaret sitting on a stone bench in the garden, and raised his hand in greeting. She returned his wave, then stood. She had covered half the distance between them when she halted. Her eyes widened and appeared riveted on something behind him. Turning, he looked in the direction of her fixed stare and froze. He sensed Hubert coming to stand beside him and heard the boy's quick intake of breath.

Walking toward them, her expression grim, was Samantha. Alongside her walked Adam Straton, the magistrate.

Chapter 17

As Sammie and the magistrate approached the Chamber, she tried to mask the disquiet niggling at her nerves. Mr. Straton's unannounced visit to question her further about her abduction by the Bride Thief had left her decidedly unsettled. Although his queries gave no firm indication that he suspected her of wrongdoing, she couldn't help but wonder if he'd somehow discovered her part in Miss Barrow's rescue. She'd been relieved when he'd announced his intention to leave, but as she'd escorted him toward the stables to fetch his mount, they'd spied Lord Wesley and Hubert emerging from the Chamber.

Her heart had jumped at the sight of Eric, but to her consternation, Mr. Straton had immediately changed his course and headed toward the Chamber, murmuring that he'd like a word with the earl. Struggling to keep up with his long-legged strides, Sammie noticed a woman step from the garden path to stand alongside Eric. There was no mistaking the resemblance between them, and she instantly recognized her as Eric's sister from the portrait she'd seen at Wesley Manor. She was dressed in black, and sympathy tugged at Sammie. Just this morning Mama had mentioned that Lord Wesley's sister was recently widowed.

When she and Mr. Straton joined the trio in front of the Chamber, the entire group stood motionless for several seconds, a silent tableau with a quintet of differing expressions.

Samantha tried to hide her own discomfort, but was not certain she succeeded. Hubert, she noticed, was staring at Mr. Straton, as if he'd seen a ghost. Eric's features were completely devoid of expression as he, too, looked at the magistrate. Like Hubert and Eric, his sister's gaze was riveted on the magistrate, her eyes wide, her face pale. Sammie glanced toward Mr. Straton and observed that his attention was focused on Eric's sister. For some reason the air surrounding the entire group seemed charged with tension—or perhaps it was only *her* anxiety making it seem so.

Eric broke the silence. Inclining his head toward her and the magistrate, he said, "Good afternoon. May I introduce my sister, Lady Darvin. This is Miss Samantha Briggeham, and I believe you already know Mr. Straton, the magistrate."

Sammie performed a curtsy then offered the woman a smile. "A pleasure to meet you."

There was no mistaking the sadness in the half-smile Lady Darvin gave her, and compassion washed over Sammie, not only for the loss of her husband, but because she recalled Eric saying his sister's marriage had not been a happy one.

"A pleasure for me as well, Miss Briggeham," said Lady Darvin, "although I believe we may have met each other years ago at some soiree or another."

Mr. Straton stepped forward and performed a stiff bow. "An honor to see you again, Lady Darvin."

Color suffused Lady Darvin's pale cheeks, and she lowered her gaze to the ground. "And you, Mr. Straton."

"My condolences on the loss of your husband."

"Thank you."

Another awkward silence fell over the group, and Sammie wondered why Eric had not mentioned his brother-in-law's death or his sister's visit, to her.

Finally Eric spoke up. "What brings you to the Briggeham home, Straton?"

"I wished to ask Miss Briggeham several more questions regarding her encounter with the Bride Thief."

Sammie bit the inside of her cheek and prayed her feelings did not show. It would never do for Mr. Straton to suspect that she knew a great deal more than she would ever tell him.

"How did those leads you were following work out?" asked Eric.

"They proved useless. But I have received new information that appears most promising."

Eric's brows rose. "Indeed? Anything you can share?"

"One of the victims who was abducted last year wrote to her family. Her father brought me the letter this morning. In it she reassured her family that she was all right. She did not reveal her whereabouts other than to say she was living in America and had recently married. The most interesting information was that she traveled to America on passage and funds provided to her by the Bride Thief the night she was kidnapped." Mr. Straton stroked his jaw. "I must say I am relieved. This new evidence at least shows that the Bride Thief did not murder the girl."

An impatient sound erupted from Sammie's lips. "Good heavens, Mr. Straton. Surely you do not believe the Bride Thief harms the women he helps. He leaves behind a note explaining as much."

He fixed a penetrating look on her. "Yes, he does. But until this letter, there's been no trace of any of his victims. I've had no proof that any of them are actually still alive—except a handful of notes from a wanted criminal."

She raised her chin a notch. "I believe *I* am evidence, Mr. Straton. As you can plainly see, the Bride Thief did not harm me. In fact, he took every precaution with my safety."

"Except for snatching you in the first place."

Irritation snaked through her. She opened her mouth to argue further, but Eric broke in, saying, "Surely you can use the woman's letter to locate her so she can be questioned."

Sammie's gaze snapped to Eric, dismay filling her.

The magistrate's countenance hardened. "I have already taken steps toward that end. The Bride Thief has escaped thus far, but he'll be caught soon. I'll comb the countryside until I find him."

A barely audible, yet familiar sound, caught Sammie's attention, and she glanced toward Hubert. His face appeared unnaturally pale, and he stood ramrod straight and motionless—except for the rhythmic flexing of his fingers, which produced a muffled cracking noise. It was a habit he only indulged in when greatly distressed. Clearly the magistrate's words had agitated him, a feeling she fully shared.

"The countryside?" asked Eric. "I would have thought a criminal like he would hide himself in London. There's literally thousands of buildings and alleyways in which to secret oneself. The scoundrel no doubt skulks about in the rookery or down by the docks."

Sammie clamped her lips together to keep quiet, and prayed her disappointment and distress at Eric's words did not show. Why did he have to think of the Bride Thief as a criminal and make suggestions that might lead to the man's capture? While she longed to voice her opinion, she dared not utter another word as she feared she might say too much and make the situation worse.

"I previously believed the Bride Thief would be found in London myself," Mr. Straton said, "but I'm beginning to suspect that he's a country fellow. Someone with the financial means and connections to buy these women passage to another country and provide them with enough funds to establish a new life. By all descriptions, his mount—a magnificent all-black stallion—is worth a king's ransom, and despite the huge price on his head, no one has come forward claiming to board such an animal. That leads me to believe that he has his own stable."

Eric stroked his chin and nodded slowly. "An interesting theory." A wry smile touched his lips. "I do not envy you the job of poking into every stable in the English countryside."

"I'm hoping that will not be necessary. Based on the locations where the majority of the kidnappings have occurred, I believe it's entirely possible that the brigand operates from somewhere in this general vicinity, most likely within a fifty-mile radius. With the aid of the ever-growing Bride Thief Posse, it shouldn't prove difficult to search the area."

Sammie's stomach knotted. It sounded as if the hunt were indeed tightening. If only she could somehow warn the Bride Thief . . . but she couldn't break her promise to him. And of course he did not need her to tell him the dangers he faced. He already knew.

"I'm considering soliciting several volunteers to assist me personally in my scrutiny of the area," Mr. Straton said, giving Eric a speculative look. "Are you interested, Lord Wesley?"

"Glad to help in any way I can," Eric said without hesitation. "I have contacts at a number of stables in the area, and many between here and Brighton. I'd be happy to make inquiries for you."

Sammie's heart plummeted. Eric was taking an active role in capturing the Bride Thief! Offering logical suggestions, the benefit of his contacts, and a willingness to volunteer. Thank goodness she'd never confided in him about her meetings with the Bride Thief.

Anguish and alarm gripped her, along with the realization that she'd made an awful mistake. How could she have fallen in love with a man whose beliefs were so opposite from her own? A man so willing to destroy the Bride Thief? And why, in spite of their divergent opinion on the matter of the Bride Thief, did she still love him? *Because in every other way he's wonderful. He has never met the Bride Thief. He does not know him as you do. Perhaps if he did, he'd see him as a hero, too.*

But one look at his set profile withered that hope.

Dear God, she'd never felt so torn in her life. The investigation surrounding her hero was tightening like a noose, with the man she loved assisting in the execution. An image of the Bride Thief approaching the gallows flashed in her mind, and foreboding trembled through her.

Hubert cleared his throat, yanking her attention back. "If you will excuse me, I promised my father a game of chess and I'm already late."

Everyone bid him good-bye, and he departed, walking at twice his normal speed toward the house. Sammie looked after him, filled with concern. He was clearly upset, and knowing he regarded the Bride Thief as a noble man fighting a just cause, he was obviously anxious to escape the conversation. She could hardly blame him. She longed to do so herself. But first she had several things to say to Eric.

She turned toward him . . . and discovered him staring at her with a concentration that stalled her breath in her lungs—that same white-hot intensity he'd focused on her as he'd explored her body. Instantly the memory of him, naked, fully aroused, kneeling between her splayed thighs flashed in her mind. Heat engulfed her as if she'd lit a match to her gown. She cast a surreptitious glance toward Lady Darvin and Mr. Straton and was relieved to note that they were busy admiring one of Mama's nearby rose-bushes. Leaning as close to Eric as she dared, she whispered, "I need to speak with you. Privately."

Straightening, she suppressed a frustrated sigh. As much as she wished to converse with Eric immediately, hospitality dictated that she offer refreshments. She would simply have to draw Eric aside before he departed. "Would you all like to come up to the house for some tea?"

"Thank you, Miss Briggeham," Lady Darvin said, "but I fear the exhaustion from my long journey has caught up with me. I believe I'll start for home, but I'd be happy to join you another day." Concern immediately flared in her brother's eyes, and she laid her gloved hand on his sleeve. "I'm fine. Just fatigued. I know the way back to Wesley Manor. Please enjoy your visit." She turned back to Sammie. "It was a pleasure to be reacquainted with you, Miss Briggeham, and to meet your brother."

"Thank you, Lady Darvin. I shall look forward to seeing you again soon."

Eric alternated a quick look between Sammie and his sister. "I do not want you going home alone, Margaret."

"I would be honored to escort Lady Darvin home in my curricle," Mr. Straton interjected.

"That is not necessary," Lady Darvin protested in a tight-sounding voice.

Eric smiled down at her. "Perhaps not necessary, but it would relieve my mind to know you were escorted safely to the door. I'll lead your mount home when I depart."

Lady Darvin looked as if she were going to refuse, but then she jerked her head in acquiescence. After saying good-bye, Mr. Straton extended his elbow toward her. Lady Darvin rested her fingertips on his sleeve, and they headed down the path leading toward the stables.

The instant they disappeared from view, Eric grabbed Sammie's hand and tugged her toward the Chamber. Good. She did not want to risk their conversation being overheard. She followed him inside the laboratory. He closed the door behind them, then leaned against the wood, watching her through hooded eyes. She returned his stare, ignoring the heat pulsing through her. How did he manage to affect her so with a mere *look*? 'Twas most illogical. And most vexing.

He pushed off from the door and approached her slowly, not stopping until only several feet separated them. "You wished to speak to me?"

Forcing herself to concentrate despite his disturbing nearness, she nodded. "Concerning what you said to Mr. Straton just now about the Bride Thief."

"I see. And is the Bride Thief what you and Mr. Straton discussed during his visit?"

"Yes. He made much the same manner of queries as the night I was mistakenly abducted. Naturally I was unable to throw further light on the subject. But about what you said to him regarding helping him to capture the Bride Thief, and offering to make inquiries . . ."

"Yes?"

Reaching out, she laid her hand over his heart. "Please do not." Some emotion she could not identify flashed in his eyes, disappearing as quickly as it had appeared. "I would not ask you were it not important to me. I know most people believe the Bride Thief is a criminal—"

"He *is* a criminal, Samantha. Kidnapping is against the law."

"But he is not kidnapping! He does not force women to

go with him. He does not hurt them or demand a ransom. He returned me safely home when he'd realized his error in taking me, at great risk to himself I might add." She searched his face, dismayed by his cool expression. "Trust me when I say he is not the brigand people make him out to be. He is honorable and seeks only to help those women he takes. To offer them a choice. I know I have no right to ask you not to aid in his capture, but I'm asking you anyway. Please don't."

Eric looked at her, her eyes so earnest behind her spectacles, and fear iced his blood. Damn it to hell, didn't she realize the danger she placed herself in by making such a request? What if she asked someone else the same thing and Adam Straton heard of it? What if Straton discovered her involvement in the Bride Thief's last rescue? That she'd purchased a passage to America? The consequences were too horrible to even contemplate. Her family would be utterly destroyed. *She* would be destroyed. And that would destroy him.

Grasping her shoulders, he looked into her eyes and resisted the urge to shake her. "Samantha. Listen to me. You must leave this matter of the Bride Thief alone. The man is dangerous."

Blue fire flared in her eyes. "He is *not*."

"He is. His very *life* is dangerous, in ways you do not understand. There is an enormous price on his head, and anyone around him, anyone who might try to help him could find themselves in danger as well. I want your promise that you shall do nothing to aid him."

"I am not trying to aid him. I am merely asking that *you* not assist in capturing him."

"Do you not see that *is* helping him, however indirectly?" He tightened his hold on her shoulders. "Promise me you will leave this matter alone."

She studied him for several seconds, her gaze searching and serious. "Will you promise me not to assist the magistrate any further?"

"I cannot make such a promise."

The hurt and disappointment shimmering from her eyes nearly undid him. "Then I'm afraid I cannot make any promises to you."

The trembling finality in her voice struck him like a blow. She attempted to step away from him, but he held on to her shoulders. He couldn't let her go. Not like this.

"Don't you see," he said, fighting the desperation gnawing at him, "that I'm concerned for your safety? I cannot stand the thought of you in danger."

Before she could reply, a distant call came from outside. "Samantha . . . where are you?"

Her eyes widened. "Good heavens, that's Mama. Come quickly." Pulling from his grasp, she walked swiftly to the door. He followed her outside, closing the Chamber door softly behind him. Samantha led him toward the gardens. They'd barely set foot on the path when Cordelia Briggeham came upon them.

"There you are, dear! And Lord Wesley, too." She dropped into a curtsy in front of Eric. "The instant Hubert mentioned you'd stopped by with your sister, I knew I had to find you. You both simply *must* stay for tea, *especially* since you begged off during your last visit." She craned her neck around. "Where *is* Lady Darvin?"

"I'm afraid you just missed her," Eric said, injecting just the right amount of regret into his voice. "She was fatigued from her long journey and returned home to rest." Knowing he was trapped into staying, he commanded his mouth to smile and extended his elbow. "I, however, would be delighted to take tea with you."

Mrs. Briggeham's sharp gaze bounced swiftly between

him and Samantha, then she smiled. "Well, that would be lovely, wouldn't it?"

If the heaviness dragging on his heart was any indication, he suspected that "lovely" was most likely not going to be the case.

Adam's curricle moved slowly along the tree-lined path. Sunlight dappled through the leaves, casting shadows that cooled the afternoon warmth. The only sound breaking the silence was the twittering of birds and the faint squeak of the leather seat. From the corner of his eye, he stole a glance at his passenger, trying his damnedest to think of something, *anything*, to say to her, but his tongue remained as tied as a knotted string.

By God, she was lovely. He had not laid eyes on her in five years. *Five years, two months, and sixteen days.* He wouldn't have believed it possible that she could be more beautiful than the image he held in his heart, but she was. Yet he could easily see that the carefree young girl he'd fallen so deeply in love with was gone. Losing her husband had clearly left her bereft.

He inhaled, then pressed his lips tightly together. Damn, she still smelled of roses. In his foolish youth, when he'd tortured himself with useless dreams that an untitled man like him could court an earl's daughter, he'd planted a dozen rosebushes in the corner of his mother's garden. Every year he'd wait impatiently for them to bloom, then he'd sit on the stone garden bench with his eyes closed, breathing in their delicate scent, picturing Lady Margaret's smiling face. After he'd learned she was to marry Lord Darvin, he'd never visited that part of the garden again.

"It is good to be home," she said, her soft voice breaking through his thoughts.

Relieved that she'd started a conversation, he seized the opportunity to ask, "How long are you planning to visit?"

"I'm here to stay."

His heart slammed against his ribs at those four simple words. Elation pumped through him, only to be instantly replaced by dread. He turned toward her and their eyes met. Feelings he'd thought he'd successfully buried rushed through him like a brushfire. Want. Need. And a love so fierce and hopeless it nearly choked him. He hadn't managed to forget her, even after she'd moved to her husband's estate in Cornwall. How could he possibly hope to function normally when she was here? Close enough to see. To touch. Yet never to claim as his own.

Tearing his gaze from hers, he returned his attention to the road. Having her return to Tunbridge Wells would only mean torture for him. The years had changed nothing. He was still a commoner, she a lady. A viscountess.

Realizing the silence between them had grown heavy, he asked, "Did you enjoy living in Cornwall?"

"I hated it," she said in such an implacable tone, he turned back to her in surprise, not quite certain how to respond. She stared straight ahead, her face pale, her gloved hands fisted in her lap. "I used to spend time on the cliffs, looking out at the sea. Wondering . . ."

"Wondering what?"

She turned and looked directly into his eyes with a bleak expression that sent a chill through him. "How it would feel to jump from the cliff. To fall into that churning, frigid water."

Shocked, he pulled the horses to a halt. He searched her face, looking for any indication she might be speaking in jest, but there was no mistaking the horrible truth to her words.

He swallowed hard. "I'm sorry," he said, inwardly cringing at the inadequacy of his words. "I had no idea. All these years . . . I thought you were happy."

"The only thing that brought me happiness was thoughts of home. Of one day being able to return here."

Questions buzzed through his mind. What had happened in Cornwall to make her so unhappy? Clearly the separation from her home and her brother had greatly affected her. He cursed his own stupidity for not considering such a possibility, but he'd just assumed she would flourish in her new surroundings. He'd pictured her presiding over elegant soirees, being feted and admired by all of Society. And even if he *had* considered that she might not be happy, what could he possibly have done? Nothing.

Although her marriage had broken his heart, she had to marry in accordance with her father's wishes. 'Twas only right that she do so. He'd wished her well, secure in the knowledge that she would be pampered by a wealthy nobleman who would worship the ground she walked upon.

Yet she'd been unhappy. Had Lord Darvin not showered her with affection? It seemed impossible to credit. What man would not love her to distraction? No, it must be something else—

The answer hit him like a punch in the gut. No doubt the fact that she had not borne a child was the source of her unhappiness. He recalled her saying on more than one occasion how she longed for a large family some day, and how he'd hidden his misery behind a smile, knowing he could never marry her and therefore be the one to provide her with the children she wanted.

Pity gripped him, and without thinking, he reached out and covered her clenched hands with one of his own. Her eyes widened slightly, but she made no move to pull away from his touch. With his heart pounding as if he'd run a mile, he said, "I hope being home brings you the happiness you deserve, Lady Darvin."

She studied him for several seconds with an expression he could not decipher, then murmured, "Thank you." She then returned her gaze back to the path in front of them. "I'd like to go home now."

"Of course." He reluctantly withdrew his hand from atop hers, knowing he'd never have another opportunity to touch her so intimately again. Filled with a maelstrom of conflicting emotions, he grasped the reins, then set the horses in motion toward Wesley Manor.

Sammie thought the hour Eric spent drinking tea with her and her parents in the drawing room had passed innocently enough. The moment he departed, however, she realized her naiveté.

"Oh, did you see that, Charles?" Mama asked breathlessly.

Papa looked at her over the top of his bifocals. "See what?"

"Why, Lord Wesley, courting our daughter."

Sammie nearly choked on a mouthful of tea. While she attempted to catch her breath, Papa frowned and said, "Well of course I saw Wesley. Impossible to miss the fellow, especially since he sat directly across from me. But all *I* saw him doing was drinking tea and enjoying these biscuits. Very good biscuits, by the way."

Mama waved an impatient hand at him. "Lord Wesley would not take tea with us for no reason. He was courting, I tell you. Oh, I cannot wait to tell Lydia—"

"Mama," Sammie gasped out. She coughed several times, finally managing to catch her breath. "Lord Wesley is *not* courting me."

"Of course he is." She clapped her hands in front of her, and her face took on a rapturous expression. "Oh my word, Charles, our darling Samantha shall be a *countess*!"

Alarm raced through Sammie. Good heavens, why hadn't she anticipated such a reaction from Mama? No doubt because the magistrate's visit, coupled with her disturbing conversation with Eric in the Chamber, had interrupted her logical thought processes. Besides, she'd dismissed the possibility of anyone believing Eric would court her as completely illogical—yet here it was, staring her in the face. Something was horribly wrong with her logic of late, and the timing could not have been worse.

Well, she had to stop this at once. Before Mama started planning a wedding that would never occur. Rising from the settee, she strode across the room to her mother and grasped both her hands.

"Mama. Lord Wesley came today at *Hubert's* invitation. To see *Hubert*. To look at *Hubert's* latest invention. Do you understand?"

Mama sent her an exasperated look. "Well, of course I understand, Samantha. But clearly his visit with Hubert was simply a ruse to see *you*." A sly gleam flashed in her eyes. "I watched him very closely and caught him looking at you one time with an expression that could only be described as 'interested.' "

"I'm certain he merely had dust in his eye," Sammie said, trying to hold the desperate note creeping into her voice at bay.

"Nonsense." Mama reached out and patted Sammie's cheek. "Trust me, darling. A mother knows these things."

Sammie drew a deep, calming breath. "Mama, I assure you the earl has *no interest whatsoever* in making me his countess." That, at least, was the truth. "I beg you not to misinterpret what is nothing more than simple politeness on his part. If you do, he will no doubt withdraw his friendship from Hubert. I know your intentions are good, but surely you can see how embarrassing it would be for both Lord Wesley and myself if it were suggested he were a suitor."

"I see nothing of the sort. Indeed, what *I* see is that one of the most eligible bachelors in England has taken a fancy to my daughter. Do you not agree, Charles?" She shot her husband an annoyed glare when he did not answer. "Charles?"

Sammie's father, slumped comfortably in his favorite chair, awakened with a snort. "Eh? What's that?"

"Do you not agree that Samantha would make an admirable countess?"

"Mama, I would make an *appalling* countess."

"Heavens, I only dozed for a moment. Did I miss a proposal?" Papa asked, blinking behind his bifocals.

"No!" Sammie all but shouted. Dear God, this situation had gotten totally out of hand, and only served to strengthen her resolve to end things with Eric tonight—before Mama arranged to announce the banns. "There is nothing between Lord Wesley and I." *Or there won't be after tonight.* "Do *not* even *consider* spreading tales that the man is interested in me. I'll not have this interference."

Mama stared at her with a stunned expression. "I'm not interfering—"

"You are. And it will accomplish nothing except causing me embarrassment. Is that what you want?"

"Certainly not," Mama all but huffed. "But—"

"No 'buts', Mama. And no more matchmaking." Sammie blew out a deep breath. "Now, if you'll excuse me, I have several letters to write." She left the drawing room, closing the door behind her with a smart snap.

Cordelia stared at the closed door and *whoosh*ed out a frustrated breath. She turned toward her husband and treated him to a narrow-eyed stare when he muttered something that sounded suspiciously like "well done, Sammie."

Oh, what a vexing situation! Here was an *earl*, practically *sitting* on their doorstep like a gift from above, and *she* was the only one who recognized this golden opportunity. Well, of course recognizing such opportunities was a mother's responsibility, but how both Sammie and Charles could be so obtuse was a mystery of gargantuan proportions.

Well, *she* had seen that hungry look in Lord Wesley's eye when he'd thought himself unobserved. He was smitten with Samantha, she'd stake her life on it. Oooh, just the thought of lauding a proposal from an earl over Lydia's head shivered anticipation down her spine. Lord Wesley was a fine gentleman who she knew would make Samantha very happy. What woman in her right mind wouldn't find the dashing nobleman attractive? And even if he weren't terribly attractive, he was terribly wealthy. And well-connected.

Oh, it was a mother's dream come true! The possibilities were all but dizzying. Indeed, now that she thought of it, she felt rather lightheaded. She glanced over at Charles, then pursed her lips. Drat. No point having a spell when her hartshorn-fetcher was snoring.

Well, nevermind. There was no time to indulge in the vapors anyway—not when so many plans needed to be made. For regardless of her protests, Samantha had hooked one of the largest fishes in England.

Now all that was necessary was reeling him in to the shore.

Chapter 18

Margaret lifted her gaze from her book and observed her brother pace the length of the paneled library. Brandy snifter in hand, he crossed from the fireplace to the floor-to-ceiling bookcases, his steps muffled by the thick Persian rug. Back and forth, again and again, pausing each time at the mantel to stare with a brooding expression into the flames, only to continue on.

After a quarter hour of watching him, she lowered her book to the chintz settee where she sat. She'd observed him carefully this afternoon, and she suspected she knew exactly what was troubling him. When next he halted by the fire, she asked, "Are you all right, Eric?"

He turned toward her, blinking with unmistakable surprise. Clearly he'd forgotten her presence. A sheepish grin pulled up one corner of his mouth. "Forgive me. I'm being a dreadful bore."

Rising, she walked to the fireplace, enjoying the warmth emanating from the low-burning fire. Large and drafty though it was, the library somehow possessed a cozy air and had always been her favorite room. Much more so than the drawing room where her father's portrait hung above the mantel. A shudder had run through her when she'd seen his cold-eyed countenance staring down from the canvas earlier today. She ruthlessly shoved the image aside. Like her husband, her father was dead. Neither one could hurt her anymore.

Looking up at Eric, she laid her hand on his sleeve, marveling at how good it felt to be able to touch someone. "Something is troubling you," she said softly. "Do you wish to talk about it?"

Tender weariness filled his gaze. "I'm fine, Margaret."

He wasn't, but clearly he did not want to burden her—a kindhearted but unnecessary gesture on his part that sparked a flare of annoyance in her. He returned his gaze to the fire, obviously considering the discussion closed. Foolish man.

Adopting a casual tone, she remarked, "I enjoyed meeting your friends today. Young Hubert is quite ingenious, and Miss Briggeham was . . ."

His gaze whipped back to hers so quickly she swore she heard his muscles snap. "Was what?"

Any doubts she may have harbored about the source of his preoccupation instantly vanished. "I thought her quite interesting."

"Indeed? In what way?"

"I admired her spirit in stating her opinions to Mr. Straton regarding the Bride Thief. I also could plainly see that she is devoted to her brother—a feeling I can well understand."

He acknowledged her remark with a smile. "She and Hubert are very close."

"She is not the sort of woman who normally captures your interest."

His entire body stilled for an instant. Then, with a casual air that would no doubt fool anyone except her, he asked, "What do you mean?"

"There's no point denying it to me, Eric. I know you too well. I saw the way you looked at her."

"And what way was that?"

She gently squeezed his arm. "The way every woman dreams of being looked at."

He said nothing, just stood, watching her with an unreadable expression. She wondered if she'd pushed too much, and perhaps she had, but she could not stand to see him so troubled. "She cares for you as well, you know," she said softly. "I could see it, even in those few moments we spent together."

A tortured sound rumbled in his throat, and he squeezed his eyes shut.

"Why are you not happy? You should thank God that as a man you're not trapped by the confines that dictated my fate. You have the freedom to pursue your heart's desire. To marry whom you choose."

He opened his eyes and pierced her with a look that made her wonder if she'd made a terrible error in her assessment. "You know how I feel about that. I have no intention of marrying. Ever."

His harsh reply took her aback. "I'd assumed your feelings on the subject would have changed over the years, and certainly by now, as you clearly have feelings for Miss Briggeham." When he remained silent, she felt compelled to add, "She is the sort of woman a man *marries*, Eric."

A muscle clenched in his jaw. "I realize that."

"Surely you want a son to inherit the title."

"I care nothing about perpetuating my title." He swept his hand in a wide arc encompassing the room. "While I cannot deny that I prefer living like this as opposed to residing in the slums of London, my title has not brought me happiness." He pinned her with a penetrating stare. "Any more than your title brought you."

His words cut through her like a steel blade. "But surely a wife, a family, *would* bring you happiness."

A short, humorless laugh erupted from him. "I am frankly amazed that you, of all people, would recommend marriage." He tossed back his brandy, then set the empty snifter on the mantel with a sharp click of crystal against the marble. "Our parents' union was nothing short of hell, as was yours to that bastard Darvin. Why would you wish such misery on me?"

"I want only your happiness. And I learned that marriage *can* be beautiful if two people care for each other as you and Miss Briggeham seem to. I knew a woman in Cornwall named Sally. She lived in the village and worked in the kitchens at Darvin Hall. She was the same age as me and married to a local shopkeeper. Oh, Eric, they were so much in love. . . ." Her voice trailed off, and she looked into the fire. "And so incredibly happy, in a way that filled me with joy for them, but also with envy. Because I so desperately wanted what they shared."

Raising her gaze back to his, she whispered, "I was in love like that once. If I'd been allowed to choose the man I wanted, I might have enjoyed the contentment Sally knew."

Confusion flickered in his dark eyes. "I did not know you'd cared for someone."

"It happened after you left home for the Army."

"Why did this man not offer for you?"

Hot tears pushed behind her eyes, and she looked up at the ceiling to keep them from falling. "Many reasons. He never gave me any indication he cared for me as anything more than a friend. And even if he had, Father never would have allowed it." She lowered her chin and met his questioning gaze. "He was not titled. Or wealthy. But he owned my heart." Her voice dropped to a whisper. "He still does."

Eric stared at her, stunned by her revelation. Then a slow

burn of anger seeped through him. Damn it, she'd not only been sold into marriage, she'd been ripped away from the man she'd loved. A single tear eased down her pale cheek and guilt flayed him once again for failing her. *If only I'd known. If only I hadn't been away at war.* But by her own admission she still loved this man. *By God, I won't fail her again. She shall have the man she wants.*

Taking her by the shoulders, he asked gently, "Who is he?"

"It matters not."

"Tell me. Please."

She pressed her lips together, then whispered, "Mr. Straton."

Eric felt as if the floor gave way beneath him. "Adam Straton? The *magistrate*?"

She jerked her head in a nod. A single sob escaped her, and he gathered her into his arms. Hot tears wet his shirt, her shoulders quaking as he helplessly patted her back and allowed her to purge her anguish.

The magistrate. If he weren't so stunned he would have laughed himself into a seizure at the irony. Of all the men in England to choose from, Margaret had to love the man determined to see him hang!

Tipping his head back, he squeezed his eyes shut. He could well imagine the hopelessness she'd felt at her situation. Had Adam loved Margaret as well? He didn't know, but of course it would not have mattered. Their father never would have allowed a commoner to court Margaret. And Eric could not imagine the strictly law-abiding Adam Straton ever thrusting aside Society's rules and declaring himself to an earl's daughter.

Well, this was one hell of a bloody mess. God knows he wanted Margaret's happiness, yet how could he encourage her to consider a relationship that would involve Straton more closely in his life?

Margaret's sobs quieted, and she leaned back to look at

him. Spiky, tear-wet lashes surrounded dark eyes that pleaded with him. "Please, Eric. It is too late for me—but not for you. You've found someone to care for, who returns your affection. Do not throw it away. Love is so very precious. And rare. Don't allow the unhappiness and bitterness that defined our parents' lives to destroy your chance for a happy future."

Drawing a deep breath, she continued, "In spite of the sadness we knew here at Father's hands, you and I managed to carve out a cheerful existence for ourselves. Imagine how wonderful Wesley could be if it were filled with love and laughter and children born of a loving relationship. You would be an incredible father, Eric. Kind. Patient. Caring. Nothing like him. And I would be delighted and proud to call a woman you loved my sister, and to be an aunt to your children." Rising up on her toes, she pressed a kiss to his cheek. "I'm afraid I must retire now as I'm completely exhausted. Please, please think about what I've said."

She exited the room, and as soon as the door closed behind her, Eric dragged his hands down his face and huffed out a long, slow breath.

You've found someone to care for.

Yes, it seemed he had indeed. A woman who appealed to him on every level. He loved the look of her. The feel of her. The scent and taste of her. Loved her laugh and her intelligence, her wit and caring nature. He loved her loyalty and . . .

He loved her.

A groan rose in his throat, and he plopped down in a wing chair with a thud. Propping his elbows on his knees, he lowered his face into unsteady hands. God help him, he loved Samantha.

How had he allowed such a thing to happen? He'd always carefully guarded his heart, but in truth, no woman had ever come close to touching it. It was not difficult to protect a citadel that had never been stormed. But Samantha had somehow reached inside him, scaled his walls, and grabbed his heart in her fist.

Damn it, he never should have made love to her. If he hadn't, he might have avoided this debacle. Yet even as the thought entered his mind, he realized it was untrue. He hadn't fallen in love with her because of last night. Last night's lovemaking had happened *because* he loved her.

Yet how could he have fallen in love and not realized it until now? When had it happened? He tried to pinpoint the exact moment he'd tumbled into this emotional abyss and could not. He'd been fascinated with her from the beginning, unable to forget her in spite of his best efforts to do so.

She cares for you as well. Margaret's words reverberated through him, and he rubbed his throbbing temples with his palms. He knew Samantha cared for him, but hell, she cared for everyone. *But she's never made love with anyone but you.* Was it possible she loved him?

He turned the matter over and over in his mind, but finally decided no. She'd wanted an adventure, nothing more. And it was good that she didn't love him. He would not want to leave her heartbroken, as he would be. For even if she did love him, and for her sake he prayed she didn't, a future for them together was impossible.

Marriage was not in his plans. He'd seen it cause nothing but misery. Yet, if he believed Margaret, if two people loved each other, then marriage could be wonderful. For one impossible minute he allowed himself to consider the unthinkable. Samantha as his wife. Sharing his life and his bed every night. Bearing his children.

An ache of loss such as he'd never known rushed through him, and for the second time that evening, the irony of a situation hit him like a backhanded slap.

Bloody hell, he *wanted* all that. Love. Children. He *wanted* to marry her.

But the life he'd chosen as the Bride Thief made it impossible. Even if he never rescued another woman, he could still hang for the abductions he'd already committed. He could not subject Samantha to the horror her life would become if her husband were arrested and hanged. And their children would never escape the shame of having an executed criminal for a father.

No, he could never marry. The farther away he remained from Samantha the better for her. But God, how would he bear the rest of his life without her?

Lifting his head, he glanced at the mantel clock. Two hours until he was supposed to meet her at the garden gate.

Two hours until he told her their affair was over.

Two hours until his heart broke.

Sammie breathed in the cool night air, allowing the flowery fragrances of the garden to infuse her ruffled nerves as she walked along the path leading to the rear gate. Ten minutes remained until she was to meet Eric, but she'd had to escape the stifling confines of her bedchamber. Shortly after dinner, Mrs. Nordfield had arrived for an evening of cards and gossip. As Sammie rarely participated in such gatherings, no one thought it odd when she retired early.

Indeed, she'd detected a gleam in Mama's eyes that made it clear she could not wait to inform Mrs. Nordfield about today's guest for tea. Sammie could only pray that Mama would heed her pleas and not hint that the earl was courting her. Of course, she could well imagine Mama not directly *saying* the man was a suitor, but alluding as much with a well-timed lift of her brows. And naturally Mama would not disabuse Mrs. Nordfield of any incorrect notions she might inadvertently assume.

The potential for humiliation was overwhelming. She could hear the gossips now. *Oh, how utterly ridiculous that poor, odd, Samantha Briggeham and her mother would entertain the notion that Wesley would pay court to that plain chit!* No doubt the gossip would reach Eric's ears, and a deep ache of mortification throbbed through her at his inevitable response: *Court Miss Briggeham? What nonsense. Why on earth would I do that?* Oh, he would try to couch his denial in kinder terms than that, but the end result would be the same.

Shame burned her, and she hurried along the flower-lined path. She arrived at the gate several minutes later, out of breath. Settling herself on a stone bench flanked by fragrant rose bushes, she closed her eyes. A series of images from last night instantly bombarded her, and she buried her heated face in her hands.

Lord above, what have I done? She'd only wanted to share the wonders of passion, with the only man who had ever inspired them. A man she respected and admired. A man who had been her friend.

But he was also a man, as she'd discovered today, who held some basic beliefs that were diametrically opposed to her own. Just one more reason to end their affair.

A half-sob, half-laugh erupted from between her lips as she blessed her luck that no one suspected the true extent of her relationship with Eric. Good heavens, the man had simply taken afternoon tea with her family, and now Mama clearly hoped for a marriage between her bookworm daughter and an earl. If Eric were to call upon her again for any reason . . . well, there would be no stopping Mama. As it was, Mama's inevitable disappointment would reverberate through the halls of Briggeham Manor, no doubt for decades.

If only she hadn't fallen in love with him! Yes, she would have her memories, but she'd also condemned herself to the agony of a broken heart. Lowering her hands, she drew a shaky breath. Clearly she could not risk another night with Eric. When he arrived, she had to tell him immediately their affair was over—for both their sakes.

Her heart rose into her throat and she fought back the hot tears flooding her eyes. There would be no last night of passion spent in his arms. No chance to touch him again. Taste his kiss. Show him, with the words she could not say, how much she loved him. No one more time to make the memories to sustain her for a lifetime. They had no future. He was the wrong man for her in every way.

Her passionate adventure was over—and she'd paid for it with her heart and soul.

In the drawing room, Cordelia Briggeham gazed at an extremely out-of-sorts Lydia Nordfield and expertly hid her smug smile behind her teacup. The evening had gone even better than she could have hoped. Not only was Lydia all but seething about Lord Wesley's visit and his interest in Samantha, Cordelia had also soundly trounced her nemesis at piquet. She peeked at Lydia from under her lashes and swiftly took another sip of tea to swallow her mirth. Indeed, Lydia resembled a cat who'd just been given a most unwanted bath.

With her triumph rendering her unable to sit still, Cordelia rose and crossed to the French windows. A cool, flower-scented breeze drifted toward her from the gardens. A flash of color caught her eye, and she turned toward a side path leading into the gardens. Her teacup froze halfway to her lips and a frown bunched her brows. What on earth was Samantha doing traipsing about in the gardens at this time of night? Why was she not asleep as she'd retired several hours ago?

Fustian, the girl and her unorthodox behavior would be the death of a mother. No doubt she'd take a chill and be ill the next time Lord Wesley called upon her. . . .

Peering through the darkness at her daughter, Cordelia's heart skipped a beat. There was something decidedly odd—and perhaps furtive?—about this late-night stroll. Cordelia's eyes narrowed briefly, but then she mentally scolded herself for her untoward suspicions. Surely Sammie would never . . . and Lord Wesley wouldn't think to . . .

No, an assignation was out of the question. Wasn't it? Of course, if they'd made arrangements to meet, why that would be positively wonderful—er, worrisome.

Walking swiftly back to the settee, she set her cup on the mahogany table. "Lydia, it is a lovely evening. Let us go for a walk."

Lydia stared at her as if she'd grown a third eye in the center of her forehead. "A *walk*? It's nearly eleven o'clock!"

"Hubert planted a new flower in my garden—something he developed in his Chamber. I quite forget the name of it, but it supposedly only blossoms at night. I'm most anxious to see if it has bloomed."

"A night-blooming flower?" Lydia asked, interest sparking in her eyes.

"Yes. If it has flowered, I'll supply you with some clippings." Surely such enticement would convince Lydia. It would kill the woman if Cordelia possessed a flower she did not.

"Well, I suppose as long as we brought lanterns we'd be safe from turned ankles—"

"We absolutely can*not* bring lanterns. Nor can we talk above a whisper. Any such light or noise and *pffth*!" She snapped her fingers under Lydia's nose. "The flowers will instantly close up."

When Lydia hesitated, Cordelia heaved an exaggerated sigh. "Oh, well I suppose if you're too weary, Lydia . . . quite understandable for a woman of your advancing years."

Lydia popped to her feet as if a giant spring were attached to her buttocks. "I am merely two years older than you, Cordelia. I assure you I am very fit."

"Of course you are, dear. Now why don't you just sit down again before you injure your delicate self." She reached out a helping hand toward Lydia, who nimbly sidestepped her and shot her a dark glare.

"I most certainly will *not* sit down. Your suggestion of a walk merely startled me. Now that I've thought upon it, I believe a silent, unlit stroll in the gardens to search for night-blooming flowers is a smashing idea."

"Well, if you insist, Lydia . . ."

"I most certainly do."

Lydia lifted her chin, then sailed toward the door like a queen approaching her throne. Cordelia followed close behind, biting the inside of her cheeks to stifle her triumphant smile.

At precisely eleven o'clock, Eric dismounted Emperor, tethering him to a tree a short distance from the Briggehams' garden gate. As he approached the garden, he caught sight of Samantha sitting on a stone bench, and he paused. She seemed lost in thought. Was she thinking about last night? He stared at her profile, allowing the memories of their passionate evening to fill his mind. Every sensual touch, every exquisite taste, replayed in his brain, simultaneously filling him with longing and a thudding ache of loss.

He resumed walking toward her. He'd nearly reached her when a twig snapped beneath his boot, and she jumped to her feet, turning toward him. She stood bathed in a pale shaft of moonlight, and his heart performed a crazy roll as his gaze roamed slowly downward, taking in her slightly disheveled chignon and her modest muslin gown. He then returned his gaze to her face. She peered at him through her thick spectacles with serious eyes. Her tongue peeked out to wet her lips, and he involuntarily mirrored the gesture, imagining her honey-sweet taste.

He walked slowly toward her, stopping when only two feet separated them. His pulse pumped through him at double its normal pace as his hungry gaze devoured her . . . the woman he loved. The woman he could not have. The woman he would most likely never see again after he walked away from her tonight.

God help him, he wanted nothing more than to drag her into his arms and take her away. Repeat the passion and pleasure they'd shared last night. He looked into her eyes and felt his resolve slipping like sand through a sieve. He had to tell her their affair was over. Now. Before the wants and needs of his heart overrode everything else.

"I have something to tell you," they said in unison.

They stared at each other for several surprised seconds. Then, relieved to postpone the inevitable for a few more moments, he inclined his head. "Ladies first, my dear."

"All right." She drew a deep breath and looked up at him with emotion-filled eyes. "I've spent hours trying to find the right words, but I'm not certain they exist, so I shall have to simply say it. I wish to end our . . . liaison."

Eric felt as if the air had been knocked from his lungs. *She* wished to end their affair? Here he'd been agonizing, so concerned about hurting her, and *she* no longer wanted *him*! A bark of stunned disbelief lodged in his throat, and he would have laughed at his own conceit if he'd been able.

Certainly he should be relieved by this unexpected turn of events, which released him from the responsibility of breaking off their relationship. All he needed to do was agree, then walk away. He stood motionless, waiting for the happiness he should be feeling to wash over him, but happy was definitely not the "h" word to describe the emotions roiling through him. *Hurt* was much closer to the mark, damn it.

"May I ask why?" he asked stiffly.

She clasped her hands in front of her, then pivoted to face a tall, perfectly pruned hedge, leaving him to stare at her back. At her nape. At the delicate curve of her neck that he knew tasted like honey and felt like silk.

"Many reasons. I fear we risk discovery if we prolong our affair, and as it was only a temporary arrangement anyway . . ." She paused and squared her shoulders. "Your visit today gave my mother false hope that you are pursuing me. I did my best to convince her that she was wrong, but Mama is most persistent in these matters. In addition, I have been neglecting my work in the Chamber. I wish to devote my energies to furthering my experiments, and perhaps even plan a trip to the Continent. Therefore, I believe it is the wisest, and most logical, decision for us to no longer see each other. In any capacity."

Unreasonable, unjustified anger gripped him like a vice. "Look at me," he grated out through clenched teeth.

She slowly turned around until she faced him. Her eyes appeared huge, but she seemed otherwise perfectly composed, a fact that annoyed him further.

"So you wish for our friendship, as well as our affair to end?" he asked.

Her head bobbed in a jerky nod. " 'Tis for the best."

Silence fell between them. She was perfectly right, of course. His mind told him to bid her farewell and depart, but his voice and body refused to cooperate.

After what felt like an eternity but was surely no more than half a minute, she asked, "What did *you* wish to tell *me*?"

That I love you. That I want you to be my wife. My love.
The mother of my children. I want to see the world with you
and share all those adventures you dream of. Explore the
ruins of Pompeii. Trek through the Colosseum, visit the Uf-
fizi, and view the works of Bernini and Michaelangelo.
Swim in the warm waters of the Adriatic. . . . I want to tell
you that I do not want one day of my life to pass without
seeing your smile, hearing your laugh, and touching your
skin. And that I'm dying inside knowing that I shall never
have those things with you.

He attempted to force his features into a sheepish expression, completely unsure if he succeeded. "Oddly enough, I'd intended to suggest we end our liaison . . . for much the same reasons as those you gave."

"I . . . I see." She looked at the ground for the space of several heartbeats, then raised her chin and offered him a small smile. "Well, then, it appears we are agreed. I wish you a long and prosperous life. It has been my . . . very great pleasure to know you."

She moved, clearly intending to leave him like that. Simply wish him well then saunter away.

Before his better judgment could stop him, his hand shot out, grasping her upper arm as she walked by him. Raw hurt seethed through him, scraping his insides. How could she just *walk away*?

She glanced down at his restraining hand, then raised her gaze to his. "Was there something else, my lord?"

Something inside him snapped at her dispassionate tone and her formal use of his title. Damn it, he wanted to hear *his name* pass her lips. As she'd whispered it last night, heavy with want and need for him. When he'd been deep inside her. Before the world and its dictates and his responsibilities conspired to rob him of her.

"Yes, Samantha, there is something else." Hauling her

up against him, he covered her lips in a searing, explosive, angry kiss.

She stood motionless and unresponsive for several seconds, but then she moaned, rose up on her toes, and returned his kiss. Sanity fled as he wrapped his arms around her in an iron grip, reveling in the feel of her soft curves crushed against his body. He explored her mouth with a rough possession and utter lack of finesse that under other circumstances would have appalled him. His tongue stroked hers with a rhythmic desperation that matched the mantra pumping through his head. *Mine. Mine. Mine.*

He had no sense of how much time passed before their kiss changed from that out of control meeting of lips, breath, and tongue, to a slow, languid, deep mating that pumped thick, hot need through his every vein. He eased one hand up her nape and into her hair, scattering pins that fell silently onto the ground. Her soft, fragrant curls sifted over his fingers as his other hand drifted down to caress the feminine curves of her buttocks. A pleasure-filled moan sounded in her throat. She moved against him, and his erection jerked in response.

"Samantha," he whispered against her lips. "I—"

A loud gasp cut off his words. He and Samantha turned toward the sound.

Cordelia Briggeham and Lydia Nordfield stood not ten feet away, both ladies slack-jawed and bug-eyed.

Samantha drew in a sharp breath and jerked from his embrace as if he'd burned her. But the damage was done.

Mrs. Briggeham's lips formed a perfect O from which puffed a series of staccato chirping sounds. Touching the back of one hand dramatically to her brow, she staggered a few feet to the curved stone bench, then flowed downward in a graceful, chirping faint.

Chapter 19

Sammie stared at her artfully fainted mother in horror. Humiliation and shame crashed upon her like rocks falling from the sky, crushing her until she could barely draw a breath. She wanted to scream denials, claim misunderstandings, but there was no refuting the damning evidence. Even if she and Eric had not been caught in a passionate embrace, neither could disguise their disheveled hair and clothing.

"Charles, my hartshorn," Mama called, waving her hand weakly to and fro.

Eric approached Mama. "I fear your husband is not within earshot, madam, and I am fresh out of hartshorn," he said in a distinctly dry tone. "May I assist you? Or perhaps we should call for a physician?"

Mama blinked and sat up straight. "A physician? Oh, no, that's quite unnecessary. I'm certain I shall recover in a moment. I was merely overcome for a moment by the good news."

Mrs. Nordfield stepped forward and issued a derisive snort. "*Good news?* Lud, Cordelia, you're a candidate for Bedlam." She favored both Eric and Sammie with a scathing head-to-toe glare. "This is scandalous. Horrifying. Outrageous. Completely beyond the pale."

Mama propelled to her feet with an amazing agility for one who'd just swooned. "Good news," she repeated firmly. She turned her attention to Eric and bestowed a smile so angelic upon him, Sammie could almost see a halo encircling Mama's head. "I had no idea you'd decided to propose so soon, my lord." She pulled a lace hanky from the pocket of her gown and dabbed her eyes. "I'm so very happy for you both."

A full minute of the most deafening silence Sammie had ever heard, ensued. Mortification singed her from head to toe. She prayed for the ground to open and swallow her. She squeezed her eyes shut and prayed that she'd open them and this tableau would be nothing more than a dreadful nightmare. She prayed for lightning to strike her.

A smug smile curved Mrs. Nordfield's lips. "Clearly you have misinterpreted the situation, Cordelia."

"Of course I haven't," Mama said with a breezy wave of her handkerchief. "The earl is an honorable man and never would have kissed Samantha in such a . . . vigorous manner unless he'd proposed to her." She shook her index finger at Eric in mock reproof. "Of course it was very naughty of you not to seek Mr. Briggeham's permission for Samantha's hand first, my lord, but naturally you have our blessing."

"I do not believe we interrupted a proposal at all," said Mrs. Nordfield, treating the entire group to a collective glare down her long nose. "No, 'tis obvious that in our quest to locate night-blooming flowers, we inadvertently stumbled upon an illicit assignation. Why on earth would the earl propose at this time of night? Gentlemen propose during the day, in a properly chaperoned setting such as the drawing room." A sly look entered her eyes. "But fear not, Cordelia. I would not *dream* of repeating a word of this scandal."

Mama raised her chin to its most regal height. "'Tis *not* a scandal. 'Tis a proposal. And of course you will tell everyone as much." She turned her imperious stare on Eric. "Well, Lord Wesley? What have you to say for yourself?"

Sammie slanted Eric a glance from the corner of her eyes. He stood straight and tall, seemingly calm, but a muscle ticked in his clenched jaw and he appeared pale.

"Miss Briggeham and I will marry," he ground out in a voice that resembled broken glass.

Nausea gripped her and her brain screamed a long, agonized, silent *NO!* In her deepest, secret dreams she'd longed for his proposal, but dear God, she did not want him like *this*. Trapped. Unwilling. His earlier words ate at her like acid. *I'm in no position to offer you marriage. I've no intention of ever marrying. . . . I would never want to be forced into marriage.*

Mama's smile could have illuminated the entire kingdom. "My husband and I shall expect to hear from you on the morrow regarding the plans." She slanted a glance toward Mrs. Nordfield. "Lydia, you may be the first to offer congratulations and best wishes to his lordship and my daughter."

Mrs. Nordfield's puckered countenance indicated she'd prefer lying on a bed of hot coals. Her jaw sawed back and forth several times, then she said, "My felicitations to you both." She then muttered something under her breath that sounded suspiciously like *damn it all to hell and back again.*

Still beaming, Mama turned to Sammie, grabbing her firmly by the arm. "Come along now, Samantha."

Too numb to argue, she allowed her mother to pull her along the path leading back to the house, Mrs. Nordfield following close behind.

* * *

Eric arrived back at his stables needing two things: a miracle and a stiff brandy. Miracles, he knew from experience, were impossible to come by. Luckily he possessed an abundance of brandy.

Arthur emerged through the stable's double wooden doors just as Eric dismounted. "We need to talk," Eric said, handing him Emperor's reins. "Meet me in my study in thirty minutes."

By the time Arthur arrived, Eric was working his way through his second brandy. After the stableman settled himself in his favorite chair along with a glass of whiskey, Eric tersely related the afternoon's conversation with Adam Straton. When he finished, Arthur shook his head.

"Looks to me like yer rescuin' days are done. We knew ye'd hafta quit someday, and 'tis too risky now for ye to go on. Even though Champion's stall is hidden behind the false door in the stables, someone real sharp like Straton— someone who was lookin'—might find him."

Arthur rose and crossed the few steps to where Eric leaned his hips against the edge of his desk. Clamping a work-worn hand on his shoulder, he said, "Lady Margaret ain't married no more. Ye've saved many women and should be proud of yerself, as I'm proud of ye. Ye've paid yer debt. 'Tis time to let go of yer guilt and stop. Now." He tightened his grasp. "I've no desire to see ye hang."

A humorless laugh puffed from Eric's lips. "I've no desire to see me hang, either."

"'Tis decided then." Arthur lifted his glass in salute. "Here's to yer retirement. May it be prosperous. And lengthy."

Eric did not raise his snifter. "I've more news, although between your connection to the Briggeham household and the way gossip travels, you may have already heard. Samantha Briggeham is getting married."

Arthur's brow creased in a puzzled frown. "Wot's this?

Miz Sammie gettin' married? Bah, must be another mistake. I'd have heard tell of it."

"Trust me, there's no mistake."

Anger bristled from Arthur. "And just wot idiotic dolt is her pa foisting on her this time?"

This time Eric did raise his glass. "That idiotic dolt would be me."

If the situation hadn't been so dire, Eric would have laughed at Arthur's stunned and utterly bewildered expression. "You! But . . . but . . . how? Why?"

"Earlier this evening her mother and Lydia Nordfield discovered us in a compromising position."

Surely if Arthur's eyes bugged out any farther they would simply pop from their sockets. "Ye *compromised* Miz Sammie?"

Eric tossed back his brandy. "Thoroughly."

Arthur stepped backwards until the backs of his knees hit his chair. Then his legs folded and he flopped down with a plop, staring at Eric with amazement that quickly turned to anger.

"Devil take me, we talked about this very thing," Arthur ground out. "Wot the hell were ye thinkin'? Why didn't ye just seek out one of yer actresses or widows?"

"I'm in love with her."

If he'd thought his softly spoken admission would garner him any sympathy from Arthur, he was sadly mistaken. "Then ye should have done the honorable thing and married her first."

Eric slammed his empty snifter on his desk. "And condemn her to a life of danger with a husband who could be dragged off in chains to the gallows at any moment? A life where she could be suspected of conspiracy simply by her association with me?"

"Then ye should have kept yer damn hands off her. But since ye didn't, now ye'll make it right and marry her."

Eric met Arthur's outraged glare, then dragged his hands wearily down his face. "I want to. More than anything. If my situation were different, I would gladly wed her and spend the next several decades making heirs." A humorless laugh scraped his throat. "Although a difference in my situation wouldn't even matter as the lady does not want to marry me."

"Bosh. Why wouldn't she want to? Any woman would trade her teeth to marry ye."

"I think we can agree that Samantha falls well outside the category of 'any woman.' Just before her mother discovered us, she'd made it clear she did not wish to see me anymore. In any capacity. She wants to devote herself to her scientific studies and travel abroad."

"Don't matter no more wot the gel wants. She's gotta marry ye or be ruined."

"Damn it, what she wants *does* matter. More than anything. She shouldn't be forced into a marriage she doesn't want, any more than any woman should . . ."

His voice trailed off and he froze.

Arthur's eyes narrowed. "Ye've got that look about ye that shivers a chill down me spine. Wot are ye thinkin'?"

"I'm thinking that there will be one more rescue before I retire," Eric said slowly, his mind whirling.

Arthur scratched his head, a puzzled frown creasing his forehead. "Another rescue? Damnation, 'tis too dangerous with Straton and that damnable posse sniffin' about. Why risk it?"

Eric met his gaze. "Because Samantha Briggeham is worth the risk."

Understanding dawned, and Arthur's brows disappeared into his hairline. "Ye're mad! Just marry her."

Pushing off from his desk, he paced in front of Arthur. "Think about it. The easy thing, the selfish thing, would be to simply marry her. Force her into a union she doesn't want. Love her and enjoy her until my past catches up with me, then go to the gallows and leave her, and perhaps some children, behind to face Society's scorn. I cannot take that chance."

He paused by the windows and looked out at the darkness. Laying his forehead against the cool glass, he closed his eyes, trying not to think about the dark, bleak days facing him once she was gone. "I love her enough to let her go. The Bride Thief will rescue her." Hurt stabbed him like steely blades, and his voice lowered to a husky whisper. "Free her from a marriage she does not want. Give her the adventure she *does* want."

Turning away from the window, he faced Arthur, looking into his old friend's troubled eyes. "And I am, or rather the Bride Thief is, the only man who can free her. I refuse to force her. And I cannot stand the thought of her in danger. If Straton were to ever discover that she aided me during my last rescue, she'd be charged with conspiracy."

"As her husband, ye could protect her."

"As her husband, I could *destroy* her."

Arthur heaved out a long breath. "Bloody bit of an irony, that is."

Eric's throat tightened. Unable to speak, he merely nodded his agreement. He knew what he had to do. For her. He'd arrange for her to explore all of Italy, the entire damn Continent if she wished. Set up a laboratory anywhere she chose. She'd have the adventures she'd always longed for, and he'd see to it that she never lacked for anything.

All he needed to do was supply the passage and funds, a simple enough task. But by God, he didn't have any idea where he'd find the strength to let her go.

Sammie descended the stairs at ten the next morning, tired beyond compare but filled with resolve. After spending a sleepless night punctuated by several useless bouts of tears, she'd decided upon a course of action. Even though she did not feel the least bit hungry, she headed toward the dining room, knowing she would require all her strength for the battle that would erupt when she spoke to her parents.

Hubert greeted her when she entered the dining room. "Good morning, Sammie. I say, are you all right? You look peaked."

She forced a smile. "I'm fine. Have you seen Mama and Papa?"

"Yes. They're in the drawing room with Lord Wesley."

Her stomach tumbled over. "Lord Wesley is here? So early?"

"Arrived over an hour ago. I saw him from my bed-chamber window. He looked quite grim I must say."

Over an hour ago! Good heavens, this was a disaster. She fled from the room, racing down the corridor. She skidded to a halt when the drawing room door opened. Out stepped Papa bearing a contented expression, followed closely by Mama who resembled a cat just presented with a bowl of cream *and* a rasher of fish.

Eric then emerged. His gaze collided with Sammie's and her heart shattered. He was so beautiful. So trapped. And so clearly unhappy.

"Samantha, darling," Mama cooed, lacing her arm through Sammie's. "How delightful you're awake. We have dozens of plans to make and very little time. How I shall manage to arrange a wedding in less than a week I cannot say, but—"

"I need to discuss that very matter with both you and Papa," Sammie said, "but first, I would like a word with Lord Wesley."

Mama made a *tsk*-ing noise. "Well, I suppose we can spare a few moments—"

"A *private* word, Mama."

Mama blinked several times, then she inclined her head in her most gracious manner. "Well, I suppose it wouldn't be *too* improper for you to spend several moments alone with your *fiancé*." Turning toward her husband, she said, "Come along, Charles. We shall enjoy a cup of tea while the earl and *his future countess* conduct their first conversation as a betrothed couple." She glided down the corridor as if floating on air, Papa following meekly in her wake.

Sammie walked quickly into the drawing room, crossing to the center of the room. With her hands clasped tightly at her waist, she stared out the window, waiting until she heard Eric enter and close the door behind him. She drew several bracing breaths then turned to face him, startled to find him standing only several feet away from her.

His gaze locked onto hers and sorrow washed through her at his obvious fatigue. Sunlight poured through the window, bathing him in a golden glow that highlighted the weary lines bracketing his eyes and mouth.

He stepped closer to her, out of the column of sunshine. He reached out and ran a gentle finger across her cheek, a tender gesture that nearly brought tears to her eyes. "Are you all right?" he asked.

"In truth, no. I'm sorry I was not about when you arrived, but I did not expect you until later this afternoon."

"I saw no reason to delay meeting with your father. I set the necessary proceedings to procure a special license in motion early this morning."

"Those proceedings are precisely what I need to discuss with you," she said, proud that her voice sounded so steady. "I wish for you to cancel them."

A tired smile touched one corner of his mouth. "I'm afraid that is impossible, as we shall need the special license to marry on such short notice."

Dear God, did he have any idea how exhausted and resigned he appeared? "I'm sorry," she whispered. "So incredibly sorry—"

He brushed two fingers against her lips, cutting off her words. "You have nothing to apologize for, Samantha."

"But you are so upset, and rightfully so."

"Not at you." He clasped her shoulders and looked into her eyes. "Never at you."

"Well, you should be. This entire debacle is my fault."

"On the contrary, it is completely my fault. I never should have stolen your innocence."

"You took nothing that I did not freely, willingly give you. And that is why I cannot accept your offer."

A frown formed between his brows. "I beg your pardon?"

She squared her shoulders and raised her chin. "I am releasing you from your obligation to marry me."

He slowly released her shoulders, his dark eyes wiped clean of all expression. "I see. Even facing ruin you don't wish to marry me."

Her heart went numb at that flatly spoken statement. Her throat burned with the words aching to burst forth, that she loved him and wanted more than anything to be his wife, but she forced them back. "You made your position on marriage quite clear before our liaison began, my lord."

"As did you."

"And my views have not changed. Neither of us wishes to marry, most especially under these circumstances."

"Be that as it may, I'm afraid our actions leave us with no choice."

"That is why I am releasing you from your obligation. I refuse to force you."

"Your parents and I have already agreed to terms."

"Then you can all simply un-agree."

"Un-agree?" An incredulous sound rumbled in his

throat. "Have you considered your reputation would be irrevocably ruined?"

"I shall plan an extended trip to the Continent. . . . The sort of trip I've always wanted. By the time I return, the gossip will have died."

"The gossip will *never* die. The scandal will shadow you your entire life and attach itself to every member of your family. Clearly you have not thought of that. Nor of the blight it would cast upon my honor should I not marry you."

"It would not impugn your honor if *I* were the one to cry off."

He advanced a step, and she forced herself not to back up. "And how many people," he asked in a soft voice completely at odds with the dark emotions flickering in his eyes, "do you think would believe that you turned down the opportunity to become my countess?" Before she could reply, he continued, "I'll tell you how many. None. It would not matter what you claimed, everyone would believe that I'd ruined you, then refused to marry you."

She swallowed. "I . . . I hadn't thought of it that way, but of course you are correct. No one would credit that a woman like me would refuse a man like you."

Eric looked down at her, at her stricken eyes behind her glasses, and his anger withered. *Damn it, a man like me would give every last bloody thing he owned for a woman like you. Including his heart.* He knew what she was trying to do for him, and he loved her for it, but her solution was impossible.

Taking her hands, he squeezed them gently. "Samantha, we've no choice but to marry. Gossip is already spreading about our scandalous behavior and upcoming nuptials."

"Surely not."

"My butler congratulated me this morning on my upcoming marriage," he said in a dust-dry tone.

Her shoulders slumped, and she looked down at the floor. "Oh, dear. I'm so sorry. I never meant for something like this to happen to you. To me. To us."

He tipped her chin up until she looked at him. The defeat and sadness swimming in her eyes nearly brought him to his knees. He brushed a wayward chestnut curl off her pale cheek, then cradled her face between his hands. "Samantha. Everything will be all right, you have my word. Will you trust me?"

She gazed at him with solemn eyes glittering with unshed tears. "Yes, I will trust you."

"And you will agree to be my wife?"

The reluctance flashing through her eyes slapped his ego, and an inexplicable urge to laugh at his own conceit hit him. Bloody hell, granted he'd never planned to marry, but he certainly hadn't ever considered that he'd encounter such difficulty getting a woman to agree to become his countess.

She finally jerked her head in a nod. "I will marry you."

A breath he hadn't realized he held pushed from his lungs. He gathered her into his arms, then brushed a kiss against her head. "I promise you," he whispered against her soft, honey-scented hair, "that all your dreams will come true."

Eric had nearly reached the Briggeham's stables to collect Emperor and head for home, when Hubert's breathless voice halted him.

"Lord Wesley, may I speak to you, please?"

Turning, Eric waited for the lad racing across the lawns toward him. "What is it, Hubert?" he asked when the panting boy reached his side.

"Mama just told me that you and Samantha are going to be married. Is that true?"

"Your sister has agreed to be my wife, yes," he said carefully, not wanting to lie to him.

A frown creased Hubert's thin face. "Does she know?"

Eric didn't pretend to misunderstand. "No."

"You must tell her, my lord. Before you're married. 'Tis only fair that she know the truth."

After studying his flushed countenance for several seconds, Eric asked, "And what if, once she knew, she refused to be my wife?"

Hubert seriously pondered the question. "I don't think that will happen. I believe that she will initially be upset, but after considering the matter, she would understand why you hadn't told her previously and appreciate that you trusted her enough to share your secret *before* you married."

A shudder ran through Eric as a life-size image of Sammie accepting his role as the Bride Thief, rose in his mind. Good God, she'd want to help him, share in his every adventure. No doubt she'd want a mask and cape of her own.

Hubert pushed his glasses higher on his nose. "I would be happy to put in a good word for you should the need arise, my lord." Scuffing his booted toe against the grass, he added, "You'd make an admirable husband for Sammie, and, well, I'd be honored to have you as a brother. But you must tell her."

A rush of affection for the loyal lad swept through Eric, tightening his throat. Reaching out, he clapped his hand on the boy's shoulder.

"Do not worry, Hubert. I promise I shall take care of everything."

Chapter 20

From the *London Times*:

> The search for the Bride Thief is intensifying, as the reward for his capture has grown to eleven thousand pounds. The Bride Thief Posse boasts nearly six hundred members, and it has been reported that wagers are flying fast and furious in White's betting book that the Thief will be apprehended before the week is out, even sooner should he attempt another rescue.

Two days later, Sammie stood still as a statue in her sunlit bedchamber while the seamstress tucked and pinned, making final adjustments to her wedding gown. The hum of female voices floated toward her from where her sisters and Mama sat perched along the edge of her bed, resembling a quartet of pastel-hued doves. They alternately discussed the plans for the wedding, pointed out places where the hem appeared uneven—earning them reproving glares from the seamstress—and beamed at Sammie with a pride that would indicate she'd done something wonderful, when in actuality, she'd trapped an unwilling earl into marriage.

Sammie turned a deaf ear to their excited chattering, an art form she'd perfected long ago, and stifled a sigh. She glanced in the cheval glass, and a lump lodged in her throat. The gown was beautiful, a simple creation of cream silk with short, puffed sleeves. A delicate satin ivory ribbon tied beneath the bust, trailing down the unadorned skirt. Mama had wanted a much fancier dress, covered with lace and flounces, but Sammie had adamantly refused.

She wondered if Eric would like the gown, and a blush immediately heated her cheeks. The day after tomorrow she would be his *wife*. Sadness washed over her when she considered how different, how joyous this occasion would be if he loved her and actually wanted to marry her, instead of being forced to do so. But over the past two days, since her last conversation with him in the drawing room, she'd realized that while their situation was perhaps not heaven-made, it was not completely hellish either. She loved him. They were friends and shared common interests. He was kind and generous, patient and intelligent. Surely many marriages were based on less. And the way he kissed her, touched her . . .

A breathy sigh puffed from her lips. Good heavens, sharing his bed would be no hardship. He did not love her, but she would try her very best to be a good wife to him. Of course being a good wife to him entailed becoming a countess, and her stomach knotted at the daunting prospect. Trying to fit into his social world would be like attempting to shove a square peg into a round hole.

She cringed at the thought of all the blunders she knew awaited her, and offered up a prayer that she wouldn't bring shame upon him. Hopefully her sisters and Mama could instruct her, thus enabling her to sidestep total disaster. Eric deserved happiness and a wife he could be proud of, yet she seriously questioned her ability to be that woman. But she would try. For him. And perhaps, given time and a very large miracle, the friendship he felt for her would blossom into something deeper.

Hugging that hope close to her heart, she glanced toward her escritoire. Her pulse leapt as she thought of the note hidden in the top drawer. The missive had arrived this morning, containing a single line scripted in an elegant, yet obviously masculine hand: Please come to the lake tonight at midnight.

Her pulse involuntarily jumped at the thought of seeing Eric, and she shifted her gaze toward her mantel clock. Only ten more hours to wait. Looking toward the bed, she encountered four beaming, proud smiles and knew it was going to be a very *long* ten hours.

Early that afternoon, Lady Darvin called on Sammie. As they settled themselves in the drawing room, Sammie hoped her unease did not show. Although Eric's sister appeared perfectly pleasant, Sammie wondered about the purpose behind this visit. Did Lady Darvin know the truth behind Eric's proposal? Would she accuse Sammie of trapping Eric into marriage?

Once they were seated on the settee, Lady Darvin reached out and squeezed Sammie's hand. "I know you are busy preparing for the wedding, so I won't take much of your time. I just came to extend my best wishes to you. I realize we barely know each other, but I'm hoping that will change. I've always wanted a sister."

Relief flooded Sammie, and she offered Eric's sister a smile. "Thank you, Lady Darvin."

"Please, call me Margaret. And may I call you Samantha?"

"Of course. And I am honored I shall soon be your sister."

"Thank you. Although, I know nothing about being a

sister to a *sister*, I'm afraid. But since you already have three, I'm certain you can teach me everything I need to know."

"I shall do my utmost." Then, determined to allay any concerns Margaret might harbor, Sammie said, "I want you to know I shall also do my utmost to be a good wife to Eric and make him happy and proud of me."

A gentle smile curved Margaret's lips. "You've already succeeded in making him happy, and I know he's proud of you. He told me in glowing terms about your experiments, and your hopes to develop a warming cream. I think that such a pursuit is fascinating. And very commendable." Sadness clouded her expression. "I wish I'd had something useful like that to occupy my time when I lived in Cornwall. Oh, I tended my garden and embroidered countless handkerchiefs, but nothing of any importance."

Sympathy washed over Sammie. Hoping she was not overstepping, she clasped one of Margaret's hands between both of her own. "Would you like to learn how to make the honey cream?"

A combination of uncertainty and pleased surprise shimmered in Margaret's eyes. "Do you suppose I could learn?"

"But of course. If you have the fortitude to embroider, you can master making hand cream in no time. In my experience, science is not nearly as complicated as working with a needle and thread."

There was no mistaking the gratitude in the half-smile Margaret offered her. "I shall look forward to our first lesson." She studied Sammie for several seconds, then said, "I cannot tell you how pleased I am that Eric took my advice."

"What advice is that?"

Margaret hesitated, then instead of answering, she asked, "Has Eric spoken to you about our parents?"

"No. I only know that your mother died when Eric was fifteen."

"Yes. She was very beautiful. And desperately unhappy." Her gaze bore into Sammie's. "Our father was a greedy, selfish man. He humiliated our mother with his indiscreet liaisons and gambling debts. He set impossibly high standards for Eric, yet would fly into rages when Eric exceeded his expectations. As for me, I was a useless girl, and therefore Father roundly ignored me . . . until he decided I was to marry Viscount Darvin, another greedy, selfish man whom I disliked from the moment I met him."

Sammie squeezed Margaret's hands. "I'm so very sorry."

"As am I. But because the two marriages Eric was most exposed to—our parents' and mine—were both unhappy, he'd convinced himself he did not ever want to marry. Even as a young boy, he found the idea of marriage distasteful, and when our mother died, he swore he would never enter into matrimony.

"Still, when I saw the way he looked at you, saw that he cared for you, I told him not to allow those two miserable marriages to destroy his future happiness." A smile curved her lips. "He took my advice, and I'm so very glad he did. He brought joy into what otherwise would have been a miserable childhood for me, and he deserves every happiness. He has always been a wonderful, caring brother. I'm certain he'll be the same sort of husband. And father."

Sammie forced herself to return Margaret's smile, but her insides churned with turmoil and guilt. Margaret clearly thought Eric had proposed out of an actual desire to have a wife. How horribly wrong she was. And only now did Sammie understand exactly how horribly wrong.

Dear God, he'd hated the idea of marriage *his entire life!* His deep-seated honor would bring him to the altar, yet the idea of marrying *had* to be torturous for him.

Now more than ever, she loathed the thought of trapping him.

But there was nothing she could do to free him.

Dressed for his final rescue in his black cape and mask, Eric sat astride Champion, concealed behind a wild thicket of bushes. Crickets chirped all around him, and an occasional owl's hoot sounded. He kept his gaze steadfastly trained on the path, refusing to look at the lake, unwilling to relive the memories the sight induced. He'd have the rest of his life for those memories . . . after she was gone.

At that instant, a figure rounded the bend. He could not distinguish the features, but he'd recognize that purposeful stride anywhere. As she drew closer, he noted her nondescript dark-colored gown with a wry half-smile. Only his Samantha would dress so plainly for an illicit rendezvous.

His Samantha. His lips compressed and a dull ache thudded in his chest. After tonight he would never see his Samantha again. At the moment, the fact that she would be safe and free offered little consolation to the pain squeezing his heart.

She paused near the huge willow, her gaze riveted on the water, and his mind filled with the memory of standing beneath that tree the first day he'd come across her at the lake. He'd ached to kiss her, just once, believing a single taste of her would satisfy his appetite. He couldn't recall a time in his entire life when he'd been more wrong.

He watched her for a moment, his insides clenching when she briefly buried her face in her hands. Damn it, it killed him to see her so unhappy. The time had come to free her.

He dismounted then approached her on silent feet. Clearly

occupied with her thoughts, he stood almost directly behind her before she detected his presence. Her shoulders stiffened and she appeared to draw a bracing breath.

"You are early, my lord," she said, then turned around. A gasp escaped her, and she stumbled back a step, her hand flying to her throat.

He grabbed her upper arm to steady her. "Do not be afraid, lass," he whispered in his raspy brogue.

"I—I'm not afraid, sir. You merely startled me."

"Forgive me. Ye were lost in thought."

Even the darkness could not obscure the sadness that passed over her features. "Yes." She suddenly glanced quickly around. Grabbing his hand, she pulled him under the willow, concealing them behind a curtain of voluminous leaves. "Why are you here, sir? It is dangerous for you to be about. The magistrate has new information—"

He pressed a gloved fingertip against her lips. "I am aware of this information, lass. Fear not." Moving a step closer to her, he whispered, "Just now . . . were ye thinking about your upcoming marriage?"

She stared up at him, her eyes shining like two pools of distress. "You know about my wedding?"

Before he could answer, an owl hooted nearby and she started, looking wildly about. "I am supposed to meet my fiancé here, and he is as intent upon capturing you as the magistrate. You must leave at once."

"*I* wrote ye the note." Her expression turned to surprise, then confusion. Her hand still clutched his, and he flexed his fingers, savoring the contact. "Your wedding . . . 'tis the reason I am here, lass. To save ye from it."

"Save me . . . ?" Confusion filled her gaze, followed by stunned amazement as comprehension dawned. "You're here to help me escape."

"I offer ye the gift I've offered the other women, Miss

Briggeham. Freedom from an unwanted marriage." His voice grew raspier. "Ye shall have all those adventures ye told me about."

Her eyes widened to saucers. "I . . . I don't know what to say. I must think on this. Logically." Releasing his hand, she pressed her fingers to her temples and proceeded to pace in front of him with short, jerky steps. "I never considered I'd have such an opportunity to free him. I hate the thought of leaving my family . . . but dear God, for me to disappear would certainly be the best thing for him. The best gift I could give him."

A frown formed behind Eric's mask. " 'Tis *ye* I'm seeking to free, lass."

She paused in front of him. "I understand. But it's actually Lord Wesley you'd be freeing."

"What are ye talking about?"

Looking at the ground, she said, "He is only marrying me because Society dictates he must."

"He compromised ye," Eric rasped in a harsh tone.

Her head jerked up. "He did nothing I did not want. . . . Nothing I did not ask him to do," she whispered fiercely. "Yet he is shouldering all the consequences by being forced into a marriage he does not want."

"That *ye* do not want either," he said, then waited for her to confirm it.

Instead, moisture that looked suspiciously like tears glistened behind her spectacles. Then, pressing her lips together, she averted her gaze. "What makes you think that, sir? Indeed, I have to wonder why you're here. It never occurred to me that you would attempt to rescue me again as you only help unwilling brides."

An odd feeling he could not name prickled through him. Touching his gloved fingertips under her chin, he gently brought her gaze back to his. "That first night, ye told me ye had no desire to ever marry. Have ye changed your mind since then?"

A single tear trailed down her cheek. "I'm afraid so."

Confusion broke over him like a tidal wave. "Are ye saying ye *want* to marry the earl?"

"More than anything."

Bloody hell, he might have been more shocked in his lifetime, but he'd be hard-pressed to recall the time. "But why?"

"Because I love him."

Time seemed to halt, bringing his breath and his heart along with it. Her words reverberated through his brain like the echo in a cave. *I love him. I love him.*

By God, he hadn't thought he could be more shocked than when she'd said she wanted to marry him, but this . . . this knocked him sideways like a blow to the head. Damn it, he actually felt a strong need to sit down. But first he had to clarify a few things.

He grasped her by the shoulders. "Ye love the earl," he stated, thankful he remembered to speak in his raspy brogue.

"Completely."

"Ye want to marry him."

"Desperately."

Elation flashed through him like a bolt of lightning.

"But," she said, "*he* doesn't wish to marry *me*. He's only doing so because he must. To save my reputation. He is kind and decent and honorable. . . ." A sad half-smile curved her lips. "Those are only a few of the reasons I love him so much."

She drew a deep breath, then bobbed her head with a single, decisive nod. "I would have tried my best to make him happy, to be a good wife, but you have given me the unexpected opportunity to free him." A tremor ran through her, and her voice dropped to an aching whisper. "Even though it breaks my heart to do so, I love him enough to let him go."

He could do nothing but stare at her, emotions stabbing him from all sides, ambushing him like a brigade of bayonet-wielding soldiers. The enormity of her words, of what she was willing to sacrifice for him—her family, her entire existence—humbled him in a way that left him shaking. Overwhelmed.

"Samantha," he whispered around the lump clogging his throat. "God, Samantha . . ." Her name ended on a groan, and he hauled her into his arms and kissed her with all the passion and need hammering through him. She gasped, effectively parting her lips, and his tongue possessed her mouth with desperate demand. He crushed her closer, his arms wrapped around her like bands of steel. She melted against him with a low moan, returning his urgent kiss, and his blood pounded through his body.

Mine. Mine. Mine.

Nothing existed except her. . . . This woman in his arms. This woman he loved so much he trembled with it.

This woman who loved him.

Ending their kiss, he gently cradled her face. . . . The unique, imperfect face that had captured him, fascinated him from the start.

Her eyes slowly slid open and their gazes collided. She blinked several times, then frowned. Very slowly she lifted her hand and touched his face. His *masked* face.

At that instant sanity returned, and he recalled where he was. *Who* he was.

Damn it to hell! What was he thinking? Obviously he *wasn't* thinking. But what the hell was *she* thinking? Kissing another man like that, seconds after she'd professed to love *him*.

He released her as if she'd turned into a column of fire

and took two hasty steps backward. "Forgive me, lass," he rasped. "I don't know what came over me."

She simply stared at him, eyes round with shock, somehow managing to appear still as a statue yet limp as an overcooked noodle at the same time.

He braced himself, waiting for her outrage, for a barrage of angry words. But she merely looked at him with tears slowly rolling down her cheeks, and whispered one word.

"Eric."

Chapter 21

Sammie had to fight to pull a breath into her lungs. The edges of her vision blurred, and for an instant she actually believed she might faint.

This masked man standing in front of her, the Bride Thief, was *Eric*. There was not a trace of doubt. The instant he'd pulled her into his arms, her body, her mind had recognized him.

She squeezed her eyes shut, trying to apply logic, but her brain seemed frozen. How was this possible? *Why?* She needed to ask him, but she could barely form a coherent thought, let alone speak.

Opening her eyes, she looked at him, standing motionless, swathed from head to toe in black, only his eyes and mouth uncovered. Even so, now that she knew the truth, she recognized him instantly. His height, the breadth of his shoulders, his commanding air. How could she not have realized the truth sooner? *Because you had no reason to believe he was anything more than what he appeared. You had no reason to suspect he was lying to you.*

And indeed, that one fact pushed its way through the

morass of thoughts jumbling her brain. He'd lied to her. Repeatedly.

Anger smacked her like a two-fisted blow, and she nearly reeled from the impact. Clenching her hands at her side, she approached him on shaking legs.

"Take off that mask," she demanded, proud that she managed to keep her voice steady.

When he hesitated, her anger turned to full-blown fury, and for the first time in her life she had to fight the urge to hit someone. Unable to completely suppress the impulse, she jabbed his chest with her index finger. "I know it is you behind that mask, Eric. I would recognize your kiss, your taste, anywhere. Take. It. Off." She punctuated her demand with three more sharp jabs to his chest.

They stared at each other for what felt, to Sammie, like an eternity. Finally, he reached up and slowly pulled off the black silk that covered his head and face.

Shock sizzled through her even though she knew she'd see Eric's face. He watched her, his dark hair mussed from the confines of the mask, his countenance unreadable. Silence stretched between them until she felt as if her head would explode.

Fighting to control the tumult roiling through her, she asked, "Can you please explain this to me?"

"What more do you wish to know?"

"*More?* I know nothing! Except that you've deceived me."

He stepped toward her, and she backed away from him. A frown creased his brow, but he ventured no closer. "Surely you can understand the necessity to protect my identity, Samantha."

"Does anyone else know?"

"Only Arthur Timstone. And your brother."

She felt as if the ground moved beneath her feet. *"Hubert?"*

"He followed you the night I rescued Miss Barrow and

sprinkled a special powder he'd concocted on the Bride Thief's saddle and stirrups. When I—Lord Wesley—came to your home the next day, my boots and saddle still bore traces of his powder. I couldn't deny it when he confronted me with such irrefutable evidence."

She locked her knees to keep from sinking to the ground. "I cannot believe he did not tell me."

"I asked for his word to keep my identity a secret. If I'm discovered . . ."

His voice trailed off and an image of him with a noose around his neck flashed through her mind.

"You shall hang," she finished for him, her stomach churning at the mere thought. "You know I believe strongly in your cause, but what made you—?" But even as she started to ask the question, the answer came to her. "Your sister," she whispered. "You told me someone you loved was forced to marry—"

"Yes. I failed to save her. But there were so many others I *could* help." He raked his hands through his mussed hair. "But now, with the magistrate's investigation tightening, it seems I shall have to retire."

"Yet in spite of the danger, you came here tonight."

A muscle ticked in his jaw. "Yes."

The significance of that trickled into her brain, slowly at first, then gaining momentum until it galloped at her full speed. A half-laugh, half-sob rose in her throat, and she forced her lips together to contain the cry. She'd known he hadn't wanted to marry her, but God in heaven she hadn't suspected the lengths he would go to to keep from doing so. In spite of the threat he faced from the magistrate and the Bride Thief Posse, he'd risked his life to offer her freedom.

And by freeing her, he would liberate *himself*.

Eric looked down at her, trying to make sense of his wildly conflicting emotions. She loved him. He briefly squeezed his eyes closed as warmth coursed through him, and he savored the incredible feeling. A series of images flickered through his mind, of what their life might have been like . . . sharing their love, making each other's dreams come true, raising their children.

He nearly exploded with the need to tell her he loved her, loved her so much he ached with it, but he forcibly clamped down the desire. The danger he faced was still all too real, and now that she knew his identity, the threat to her had worsened. If he told her he loved her, as loyal as she was, she would never leave him. He would never be able to get her away from him to safety. Indeed, he knew without a doubt that she would walk through fire for him, a fact which simultaneously pleased, humbled, and terrified him. He had no right to love her or marry her. But to not marry her would ruin her. He dragged his hands slowly down his face. What the bloody hell was he going to do?

Sammie looked at his tortured expression and her insides curdled. He was clearly torn and confused; didn't know what to say or do. He didn't want to marry her, but he wouldn't, *couldn't* honorably send her away. He didn't want her, yet he did not wish to hurt her. And now that she'd blurted out her feelings . . .

Humiliation settled on her with a weight so heavy she nearly collapsed beneath the burden. Their conversation rushed back at her like a river raging out of control. How she'd bared her heart and soul. Confessed her love for him. And her response when he'd asked if she wanted to marry the earl. *Desperately.*

Her entire body turned cold with mortification. He reached out a hand toward her, but she took a shaky step back from him. Wrapping her arms around herself, she whispered, "Don't touch me."

He slowly lowered his hand, looking shaken, but she could do nothing, say nothing to comfort him. Not when it took every last ounce of her strength and concentration to keep from falling apart in front of him. And she could not do that. She *would* not do that.

A soft nicker drew her attention and she looked toward a nearby thicket.

"Don't worry," he said. "It is only my horse, Champion."

Her mind whirled, and further realization fell upon her like a down-pouring of rain. "Champion . . . your horse . . . you offered to help Mr. Straton locate *your own horse*. All those things you said, suggestions you made to help capture the Bride Thief, they were merely more lies. Every word from your mouth is nothing but a *lie*."

"I do what I must to keep myself free, Samantha."

Those softly spoken words knifed directly through her heart. "Yes," she agreed tonelessly. "That much is obvious."

"I came here tonight to give you your freedom."

Sammie inwardly cringed. *Yes, which in turn would give you* your *freedom.*

He stared off into the darkness for several seconds, his brows bunched in thought, then began pacing in front of her. Just when she didn't think she could stand the silence any longer, he said, "An idea has just occurred to me. . . . Perhaps there is another way," he said. He paced several more times, frowning, clearly working something through his mind. Then he nodded decisively and paused in front of her.

"I believe I have arrived at a solution. We can marry, and go abroad immediately after the ceremony. Live on the Continent or in America—somewhere the magistrate can't find us. Somewhere no one has ever heard of the Bride Thief."

Despair clutched her. Dear God, now that he knew she loved him, he was nobly offering to give up everything— his home, his birthright, his place in Society, his entire way of life—all in the name of honor. For a woman he didn't love.

"I know it is a great deal to ask of you," he said in a quiet voice. "You'd have to leave your family, your home—"

"As would you."

"Yes. But us marrying and leaving the country would solve the problem."

The problem. Yes, that's what she was to him. An acute sense of loss washed through her, coupled with an almost insane desire to laugh. She'd never thought she'd find a man to love, and what happened when she did? He was *two* men—and while she admired his courage and believed fervently in his cause, she clearly didn't really know him. Or did she? His entire life was based on lies, and he'd deceived her from the start. How could she possibly love such a man? Yet in her heart, she knew she did. She rubbed her throbbing temples with her fingertips, in a vain attempt to dispel some of her confusion.

"It would work, Samantha," he said, his voice jerking her back.

She slowly shook her head, inching away from him. "I need time to think. I have no idea who you are. And obviously you had no intention of ever telling me. Or did you? Would you ever have told me the truth?"

His gaze bore into hers, and silence stretched between them for nearly half a minute before he shook his head and said, "I do not know, but for your own protection . . . probably not."

"I . . . see." Her voice broke and she cleared her throat. Then, raising her chin she whispered, "I said things to you, the Bride Thief you, that I would not have had I known to whom I was really speaking. I truly do not know who you are, but I do know that you are not the man I thought you were. Either of you." A bitter, humorless laugh nearly choked her. "My God, I don't even know who I'm talking to."

Gathering the last fragile remnants of her control, she drew a shuddering breath. "I must go." She started to walk from underneath the tree.

He grasped her arm. "Samantha, wait. I cannot let you leave like this. We must talk."

She tried to jerk from his hold, but could not. "I have nothing to say to you. Not now. I want, I *need* to be alone. Away from you. So I can think. Decide what to do." The tight rein she'd held on her emotions slipped another notch. "I gave everything to you. My respectability, my innocence." *My heart. My soul.* "Let me leave without surrendering my dignity as well. Please."

He slowly released her arm. "I *will* be at the church the day after tomorrow."

Choking back a sob, she inched away from him. "I'm afraid I cannot promise the same." Without another word, she lifted her skirts and walked away, her strides quickening with each step until she ran as if the devil pursued her.

Eric stood rooted to the spot and watched the darkness swallow her running form. His mind screamed to go after her, but he honored her request, her broken words branded in his brain. *I gave everything to you.*

No, Samantha, I took *everything from you.* Self-hatred battered him, and he sank to his knees, the moist earth seeping through his breeches. Squeezing his eyes shut, he rested his forehead on his clenched fists. How the hell was it possible to feel so numb, yet hurt so excruciatingly bad at the same time?

Somehow, without looking for it or even realizing he'd wanted it, a treasure had miraculously been handed to him. A woman who touched him deeply, profoundly, in parts of his heart and soul he hadn't known existed.

But like a handful of sand, he'd let Samantha slip

through his fingers, although, in truth, nothing he could have done would have stopped their inevitable parting—except never going near her in the first place. Bloody hell, what a selfish bastard he was! He'd had no right to want her, to touch her, to love her, knowing he couldn't offer her the sort of future she deserved. If he'd left her alone, another man, one without a price on his head, might have courted her. Fallen in love with her and married her.

A bolt of white-hot jealousy streaked through him at the mere thought of another man touching her. She was his, damn it. But the choice had to be hers. Would she come to the church and marry him? A bitter laugh rose in his throat. *Are you mad?* Why would she marry a man she viewed as a liar? One who would no doubt hang and embroil her in scandal? *If I were her, I'd simply want to settle in a new life, as far away from me as possible.* Well, if that was what she wanted, he'd do everything in his power to make it happen.

The decision was out his hands. All he could do now was wait. She was better off without him, but his selfish heart prayed she would show up for their wedding.

Sammie did not stop running until she entered her bedchamber. Closing the door behind her, she stumbled to her bed and crawled under the covers, aching all over like a wounded animal. She curled into a tight ball and finally allowed the tears to flow. She'd never known it was possible to hurt so much, as if her heart had been ripped from her chest, then tossed on the floor.

Burying her face in her pillow to muffle her sobs, she cried until her gritty eyes were nearly swollen shut, her mind replaying every minute she'd spent with Eric, punctuated with silent screams of *liar!*

But as dawn broke and tentative shafts of sunlight filtered through her window, she breathed out a long, weary sigh. After hours of soul searching, she could not fault Eric for his lies. He'd done what was necessary to protect himself. Her feelings toward the Bride Thief, her deep admiration for his courage and commitment to his cause, remained unchanged. And in a moment of harsh self-honesty, she admitted that it was thrilling to know that the man she loved was in truth the masked hero.

The man she loved. Humiliation hit her again. The man she loved had risked his life to give her freedom. Or was it more to free himself? Did it really matter? Nothing could change the fact that he harbored a deeply ingrained repugnance toward marriage. He'd never wanted to marry, and while she tried to take comfort in the fact that he'd never wanted to marry *anyone*—not necessarily her in particular—it was cold comfort indeed.

If Eric had wanted her, she would have sacrificed anything to marry him. Instead he'd offered her freedom, thereby freeing himself. Freedom was the one thing he wanted, and she was the only person who could give it to him.

And that was exactly what she planned to do.

Immediately after breakfast, she would begin making arrangements. She would purchase her own passage abroad, would prepare to leave her home forever.

There would be no need for him to wait at the church tomorrow.

Chapter 22

From the *London Times*:

With the Bride Thief Posse growing daily and expanding their extensive search, and with the price on his head now at fifteen thousand pounds, the Bride Thief is as good as dead.

Adam Straton walked briskly along a little-traveled path running along the west perimeter of the village, which led into the dense forest that marked the rear boundary of Lord Wesley's vast property. He tried to enjoy the cool, morning air, but his nerves were far too rattled by the prospect of his errand. Pausing before entering the forest, he attempted to quiet his conscience.

He really shouldn't cut through Lord Wesley's property, but . . . He glanced down at the bouquet of roses clutched in his hand and grimaced. If he didn't take this shortcut, the flowers he'd purchased for Lady Darvin would be wilted, not to mention strangled. Immediately his nerves jangled, and his better judgment and common sense fired a few more volleys in the battle they'd waged ever since he'd purchased the flowers in the village a half hour ago. Drawing a determined breath, he strode into the forest.

He had no business calling upon Lady Darvin, claimed his better judgment. But his common sense scoffed. Of course he should call upon her. They were friends. Acquaintances of long standing. There was absolutely no reason not to visit her. Especially in light of their conversation, when she'd revealed the depth of her unhappiness. He was merely a concerned friend making sure she was all right.

His better judgment snickered. Merely a concerned friend? Then why was his heart slapping against his ribs and his stomach tied in knots at the prospect of seeing her? Why had he spent his weekly laundry budget on roses instead of his clothing? And why did the idea of her unhappiness fill him with an overwhelming need to make her smile?

Because, you beef-witted booby, common sense chimed in, *you're hopelessly in love with her.*

Adam halted on the path and raked his free hand through his hair. He absolutely should not call upon her, but he had to know if she was all right. He nodded decisively. Yes, it was his duty to visit her. In fact—

A slight movement in his peripheral vision halted his thoughts and he turned. Peering through the trees, he observed a man leading a black horse toward Lord Wesley's stables. Moving closer to allow himself a clearer view, Adam recognized the man as Arthur Timstone, the earl's stableman.

He did not, however, recognize the horse. It might have been a gelding, but judging by its height and restless manner, he decided the animal was most likely a stallion. In fact, as he watched Arthur calm the horse then lead him into the stable, he was certain.

A frown pulled at Adam's brow. To the best of his knowledge, Lord Wesley did not own such an animal. Of course, the earl might have recently purchased the beast.

His pulse jumped as he considered another possibility. Had Lord Wesley perhaps located this animal in his effort to assist in the Bride Thief investigation? The horse certainly matched the description of the Bride Thief's mount. Excitement raced through him, and he immediately headed toward the stables, intent upon speaking to Arthur.

When he arrived slightly out of breath at the large wooden structure, he stepped inside the doorway. It took his vision a moment to adjust to the shadowy interior. When it had, he noted that the Wesley stables were vast and immaculate.

"Hello?" he called, walking in farther. "Are you about, Timstone?"

Silence, at least of the human kind, greeted his query. Clearly Arthur had departed after settling the black horse in its stall, no doubt to the kitchens for a bite to eat. Well, he'd just snatch a look at the animal before walking up to the house to call upon Lady Darvin. With any luck the earl would also be home, and he could ask him about the black stallion.

Adam walked slowly through the stables, peering into each stall. When he looked into the last stall, he stilled. Lord Wesley owned some exceptionally fine horseflesh. But there was not a black stallion among them.

Lord Wesley's dour-faced butler opened one half of Wesley Manor's massive double oak doors in response to Adam's knock.

"May I help you, sir?" the butler asked.

Adam handed him his card. "I would like to speak to Lord Wesley or his sister, please. Both of them, if possible."

"I'm afraid it's quite impossible, Mr. Straton, as they left early this morning to travel to London for the day."

"I see. Do you have any idea when they plan to return?"

"No, however as the earl is scheduled to be married at ten tomorrow morning, I would assume they shall return prior to that time."

"Er, yes. Of course. Do you know the reason for their journey?"

The butler sniffed with clear disapproval at the question. "His lordship is not required to explain his comings and goings to the staff."

In other words, the servant didn't know. Or wasn't telling. Reaching out, Adam handed the bouquet of roses to the butler. "I brought these for Lady Darvin. To help her spirits."

The butler's stern countenance relaxed a bit as he took the roses. "That was very thoughtful, sir. I'll see that she gets them."

"Thank you, Mr . . . ?"

"Eversley, sir."

"Tell me, Eversley, have you seen Arthur Timstone about? He wasn't at the stables, and I was hoping to have a word with him."

"If he's not in the stables, then he's most likely in the kitchen eating. Would you like me to fetch him?"

"Does he return to the stables after breakfast?"

"Yes, sir."

"Then don't disturb his meal. I'll walk back to the stables and await him there."

"Very well, sir."

Adam started to walk away, but then turned back. "One more thing, Eversley. Would you happen to know if the earl owns a black stallion?"

Eversley appeared startled by the question. "The horses

are Timstone's area, sir, but I cannot say I recall ever seeing such an animal or the earl ever mentioning one."

"Thank you, Eversley."

The butler nodded, then closed the door. Frowning, Adam strode back across the expanse of perfectly manicured lawns toward the stables, determined to await Arthur Timstone's return. Something very odd was going on and he had no intention of leaving until—

A gruff voice hailed his name. Pausing, he turned and saw Arthur walking toward him. Excellent. He'd have his answers sooner than he'd anticipated.

"Mornin', Mr. Straton," Arthur said once the older man reached him. "What brings ye to Wesley Manor?"

"I'd intended to pay a condolence call upon Lady Darvin, but I was informed she and the earl traveled to London for the day."

"That's right."

"Do you know the reason for this trip? Or when they're expected home?"

"Don't know for certain, but I'd guess the earl went to buy some bauble or another for his bride and asked for Lady Darvin's assistance. Probably be home by dinner time."

"I see. I'd also hoped to ask the earl if he'd had any success with some inquiries he was making for me regarding an all-black stallion." Adam offered the man a friendly smile. "Has Lord Wesley located such an animal?"

"Not that he's mentioned."

"Indeed? Does he perhaps *own* such an animal?"

Arthur's face scrunched into a perplexed frown and he scratched his head. "A black stallion? No, sir. Lord Wesley has no such horse."

"A black gelding, then?"

"No, sir. Only pure black horse his lordship owns is a mare name of Midnight."

Adam shook his head. The horse he'd seen had most definitely not been a mare. "Perhaps the earl is boarding the stallion for someone? I'm speaking of the horse I saw you leading into the stables approximately thirty minutes ago."

Arthur's face cleared and he chuckled. "The earl don't take in no boarders, so ye must mean Emperor. I walked him about a bit before me breakfast. But yer eyesight's failin' ye, Mr. Straton. Emperor's coat ain't black, 'tis dark brown. An easy mistake to make. Sunlight and shadows must have played tricks on ye."

"Yes, I suppose so."

"Well, if ye'll excuse me, I've a lot o' work to get to."

Adam smiled. "Of course. Have a nice day, Timstone."

"Same to ye, sir." The stableman departed, continuing across the lawn toward the stables.

Adam's eyes narrowed on the man's retreating back. Although Timstone had been convincing, there was no doubt he'd lied. But why? Adam had seen the animal clearly, and no trick of sunlight had made that horse's coat turn from brown to black.

And somehow, this mysterious black stallion that Lord Wesley seemed not to own, had disappeared somewhere between the stable doors and its stall. Was it possible there was a stall he'd missed? No, he'd been quite thorough . . . unless there was a hidden stall somewhere behind a door. A stall no one was meant to see.

Adam's heart started to beat in slow, hard thumps as he allowed the full ramifications to fall into place. Why would Timstone lie about the horse unless he had something to hide . . . like perhaps the Bride Thief's mount? But if that black stallion did indeed belong to the Bride Thief, Adam could not envision Arthur as the man behind the mask. No, the Bride Thief was much younger and stronger. . . .

A sense of shock stilled him. Good God, could *Wesley* be the Bride Thief? He tried to discard the possibility as ridiculous, but could not. Indeed, he could almost hear the puzzle pieces clicking into place in his brain. Wesley certainly had the financial means. His estate afforded him privacy. He was an expert horseman. And who would ever suspect him?

Adam recalled the earl's willingness to help in the investigation. Was it help—or sabotage? He exhaled a long breath and attempted to calm his racing thoughts. Had the man he'd sought all this time been practically under his nose? Was his investigation nearing an end?

His jaw clenched. Damn it, he'd always liked Wesley. Of course, like him or not, he'd bring the earl to justice if he proved to be the Bride Thief. His hands fisted at his sides at the thought of Margaret suffering the loss of her brother, and the idea that her name would be blackened by the scandal. *If her brother hung and her name was besmirched, I could comfort her. I could—*

He sliced the thought off, appalled at himself. He would never abuse his position as magistrate to further his own personal wants. Besides, Margaret would no doubt hate him for arresting her brother. But justice had to be served. And the Bride Thief had to be stopped. What he needed now was proof.

His gaze settled once again on the stables. Timstone stood in the doorway, watching him, and Adam raised his hand in a friendly wave. Timstone returned the gesture, and Adam forced his feet to move toward the path leading back to the village.

He needed to get into the earl's stables again, but he couldn't conduct the sort of search he needed to under Timstone's watchful eye. *Tonight. I'll return after Timstone retires and see if I can't find that horse.*

That decided, his thoughts drifted to Samantha Briggeham. Did she have any idea the man she was about to marry might very well be England's Most Notorious Man? She had, after all, been carried off by him that night. Had she recognized him?

He didn't know, but by God, he was going to find out. When he reached the fork in the path, he turned away from the village and headed toward Briggeham Manor.

Sammie sat at her usual place in the dining room and forced a forkful of breakfast into her mouth. It might have been eggs she chewed, but she wasn't certain. Her gaze drifted between Mama, Papa, and Hubert, and all she could think was that after today she did not know when, or even if, she would ever see them again.

A lump lodged in her throat and hot tears pushed at her eyes, and she quickly lifted her teacup in an attempt to hide her distress. Mama was chattering away about the wedding, her lovely face wreathed in smiles. Mama could be exasperating at times, but Sammie would miss her dreadfully. Her quick laugh, her antics, her chirping.

Her gaze wandered to Papa and warmth filled her. Papa who loved her even though he often didn't understand her, and possessed more patience than any dozen men combined—although he could hold his own with Mama when the need arose. As a child she'd loved to curl up in his lap with a book and listen to his deep voice as he read to her. When she was older, she and Papa would sit together in the drawing room on the overstuffed settee cushions and applaud enthusiastically after Lucille, Hermione, and Emily sang one of their many impromptu family concerts.

Her mind drifted to her sisters and her lips trembled. They'd shared so many wonderful times, so much laughter as they'd banded together to deflect Mama's more outrageous ideas, or when the three beauties good-naturedly tried to turn Sammie into the swan she would never become, heatedly defending her when others scoffed at her.

Sadness swamped Sammie that she would not share in the birth of Lucille's child, perhaps never know her niece or nephew.

Hubert asked Mama a question, his voice drawing Sammie's gaze to his serious bespectacled face. An ache such as she'd never known, squeezed her. Dear God, how could she bear leaving Hubert? She'd loved him from the moment he was born and had delighted in each stage of his development like a proud mother. And now look at him—a young man, so intelligent and full of promise. It broke her heart that she wouldn't see him grow into the wonderful man he was destined to become.

At least she would say a proper good-bye to Hubert. She'd considered not confiding her plans to him, but she simply could not face leaving without doing so. She'd tell him everything once her arrangements were in place. He'd proven he could keep a secret, and she trusted him implicitly.

Her thoughts switched to those very arrangements and what she needed to do directly after breakfast. A trip to London to secure her passage to . . . where she was not sure. It would depend on which ships were setting sail on the morrow. But before she headed to London, she planned to stop at Wesley Manor. She needed to inform Eric of her decision.

Her heart ached with loss at the prospect of calling upon Eric. It would take every last ounce of strength she possessed to say the words that would set him free . . . and then to leave him.

And when she arrived home from London, she needed to gather the belongings she wished to bring with her. Much of her wardrobe was already packed for what everyone believed would be her wedding trip, but there were her books, her journals, and personal mementos she could not bear to leave behind.

Mama's voice pulled her from her reverie. "Don't you agree, Sammie darling?"

Sammie looked at her mother's beaming face and tried to smile, but failed completely. Instead her lips trembled, and to her mortification, a huge tear plopped into her teacup.

Mama's eyes filled with concern. "Why, whatever is the matter, darling? Oh dear, it's those pre-marriage nerves." Mama rose, and in a rustle of muslin walked quickly to Sammie's chair. Wrapping an arm around her shoulder, Mama said gently, "Don't fret, Sammie. All brides feel unsettled the day before their wedding. But after tomorrow . . ." Mama heaved a blissful sigh. "Your entire life will be different."

Sammie squeezed her eyes shut to contain her tears, and leaned into her mother's comforting embrace. Indeed, after tomorrow her entire life would be different.

Dressed in her most comfortable blue walking gown and shoes, Sammie closed the front door behind her, then hurried down the sunlit flagstone porch steps. The sooner her visit with Eric was over, the better.

She'd only taken a half-dozen paces when her footsteps faltered at the unwelcome sight of the magistrate approaching. She remained in place, trying to appear outwardly calm, while her heart thudded painfully and surely loudly enough for him to hear. Why was he here? Did he have further news on his investigation, or more questions? Dear God, had he discovered the truth?

When he'd nearly reached her, she forced a smile. "Good morning, Mr. Straton."

"The same to you, Miss Briggeham. Are you on your way out?"

Deciding it was best if he not know her plans, she said,

"Yes, as a matter of fact I am on my way to the village. If you'll excuse me." She moved around him, but he simply fell into step beside her.

"I have several questions to ask you. Perhaps you'd permit me to walk with you?"

As she had no intention of walking to the village, nor did she want to remain in his company that long, she halted and offered him a regretful smile. "I fear my mother would not approve of me walking such an extended distance with a man, unchaperoned."

"Of course." He looked around, then indicated a stone bench a short distance away, near the pathway leading into the garden. "Why don't we sit for a moment. I promise not to take too much of your time."

Suppressing the urge to refuse, she nodded her consent.

Once they were seated, Mr. Straton offered her a smile. "I trust all the arrangements are in place for tomorrow's wedding?"

Sammie's stomach clenched, but she managed to return his smile. "Yes."

"Excellent. I'm relieved to know Lord Wesley's trip to London isn't because of some last minute problem."

Clearly her expression indicated her surprised dismay at this news, because he asked, "You didn't know the earl was in London for the day?"

For the day? How was she going to speak to him? "No, I did not know."

"According to his butler, the earl and his sister departed early this morning. I'd hoped you might know why they'd gone."

Sammie lifted her chin and met his searching gaze. "I'm sure I don't know. Perhaps Lady Darvin ordered a dress for the wedding. Or perhaps Lord Wesley wished to purchase a wedding gift for me."

"Ah, that is no doubt the case," the magistrate agreed.

"Tell me, Miss Briggeham, have you ever had the occasion to visit Lord Wesley's stables?"

A feeling of sick foreboding slithered through Sammie, and it required a great effort not to show her alarm. "No, however I'm certain they are very well run. I am acquainted with his stableman, Mr. Timstone, and he is very knowledgeable."

"Have you ever seen Lord Wesley ride a black stallion?"

Her heart skipped a beat. *Dear God.* She pursed her lips and pretended to ponder the question, then shook her head. "I've only ever seen him ride a brown gelding. A beautiful, spirited mount named Emperor." She curved her lips upward in what she prayed passed for an impish grin. "I'm hoping to cajole him into allowing me to ride the beast."

Mr. Straton merely nodded at her reply, his dark watchful gaze boring into her like a drill. An interminable ten seconds of dead silence passed. Unable to stand his scrutiny any longer, Sammie started to rise.

"If that is all, Mr. Straton—"

"Actually, I have some news regarding the Bride Thief."

Sammie slowly sank back down, her stomach knotting. "Indeed?"

"Yes. New evidence has come to light, and I am confident I shall be making an arrest very soon. Hopefully within the next twenty-four hours."

Sammie actually felt the blood drain from her face.

Mr. Straton's eyes clouded with concern. "I say, Miss Briggeham, are you all right? You're looking quite pale."

"I . . . I'm fine. Your news simply surprised me." She moistened her dry lips. "So you've discovered the Bride Thief's identity?"

"We're following up on several promising leads. When the man strikes again, he will be apprehended, if not before." With that, he stood. Looking down at her, he made her a bow. "Well, I won't keep you any longer, Miss

Briggeham. Enjoy the rest of your day. I shall see you at the church tomorrow."

Paralyzed with shock and numb with fear, Sammie remained on the bench, watching him saunter away in the direction of the village as if he hadn't a care in the world.

When he disappeared from view, she forced her watery legs to stand, then move with studied calm back toward the house. She had to appear relaxed and normal in case he watched her from the dense foliage and trees, waiting to see her reaction. A chill edged down her spine, and she indeed had the sensation that his intense gaze was upon her.

Mr. Straton clearly suspected Eric, and she greatly feared that her involuntary reaction to the magistrate's announcement regarding an imminent arrest might have furthered the man's suspicions.

She had to warn Eric. But how could she when he was in London? And how to do so without arousing suspicion? Mr. Straton no doubt planned to watch her, and Eric as well. She dared not send a note as it might get intercepted, nor did she dare go to Wesley Manor. Any effort of her part to contact him might be construed as suspect.

She pressed her hands to her rolling stomach. What on earth was she going to do?

Hidden behind a thick hedge, Adam watched Miss Briggeham walk slowly toward her front door. He raised his brows. Apparently she'd forgotten about her trip to the village.

She'd tried to act nonchalant at his questions, and indeed he had to give her credit for her fine performance, but he'd noted several flickers of fear in her eyes. And when he'd announced that he expected to make an arrest, her face had turned to chalk.

Yes, Miss Briggeham's reactions not only reinforced his

suspicions regarding Lord Wesley, they led him to believe she knew, or at least suspected, her betrothed was the Bride Thief. Now all he had to do was prove it.

And a plan was forming in his mind of how to do just that.

Chapter 23

At ten that evening, Eric strode down the dark corridor toward his study, wanting nothing more than solitude and a stiff brandy. While he'd enjoyed Margaret's company on their outing to London, he was relieved to be home where he could be alone with his thoughts.

His thoughts. Bloody hell, Samantha had occupied them the entire day. On the coach rides to and from Town. While he'd awaited Margaret at the dressmaker's. As he'd secured passage for two aboard the *Sea Maiden* departing for the Continent the next evening, then again during his meeting with his solicitor, where he'd updated his Will to include provisions for her and any children resulting from their marriage—a marriage he wasn't certain would even take place.

He entered his study, closing the door behind him. Heading toward the crystal decanters, he halted halfway across the room at the sight of Arthur sitting in his usual chair, a tumbler of whiskey cradled between his work-roughened hands.

"We need to talk," Arthur said in a tone that set Eric's

nerve endings on alert. Jerking his head toward the decanters, Arthur added, "Pour yerself a long one. Ye'll need it."

Twenty minutes later, with Arthur's disturbing words about Adam Straton's visit echoing in his ears, Eric poured himself a second hefty drink. Standing in front of the fire, he lifted his snifter in a wry salute. "Well, that's not particularly good news."

Concern flashed in the older man's eyes. "It's nothin' but *bad* news. The man is suspicious of ye. He'll be like a bloody dog with a bone, searchin' and pryin' til he sees ye swingin' from a noose. I think ye should take yerself on an extended trip. Somewhere far away."

"Actually, I've made plans to do just that. Under the guise of a wedding trip, I've purchased passage for Samantha and I to leave England after the wedding—provided she shows up for the wedding."

Arthur nodded slowly. "Right smart plan. Ain't unusual for yer class to be gone months on a weddin' trip. Years even."

"Exactly. I've made all the necessary arrangements, but I would ask that you keep an eye on Margaret for me. Make certain she settles in here and that she's . . . happy. Unless, of course, I'm still here."

"Ye know I will. But ye must leave no matter what— even if Miz Sammie leaves ye at the altar. Say ye're leavin' England to mend yer broken heart. The reason don't matter none, just so long as ye *go*."

"I can't do that. I couldn't leave Samantha to face the scandal alone. If she doesn't show up, I'll . . ." he dragged a hand through his hair and blew out a long breath. "Bloody hell, I don't know what I'll do. I'll just have to come up with another plan."

"They'll kill ye if ye don't leave." Tears glistened in Arthur's eyes. "I'll never forgive meself fer bein' so bloody careless, walkin' Champion that way. This entire mess lays on me."

Eric set his snifter on the mantel then crossed to Arthur. Crouching down until they were on eye level, he squeezed the distraught man's shoulder then pinned him with a steady stare.

"Stop blaming yourself. You had no way of knowing Straton was watching you. I've known and accepted from the beginning the consequences of my actions, and that is what they are—*my* actions. And I shall take responsibility for them. As for Straton, he can be as suspicious as he wants, but he can do nothing without proof. Even if he were to locate Champion's stall, that doesn't prove I'm the man he seeks."

"No, but the bastard could make yer life miserable. We'll have to make sure he finds no evidence against ye. And that means ye absolutely can't risk another rescue. Ever."

Eric nodded slowly, then offered what he hoped passed for an encouraging smile. "Agreed." But in his heart he suspected it was already too late.

The next morning Eric stood in an alcove tucked away to the right of the church's altar and glanced at his watch fob. Thirty minutes until the wedding ceremony was scheduled to begin.

Would Samantha show up?

Clutching the fob in one hand, he paced in the confining space. Would she show up—bloody hell, he'd asked himself that question a thousand times since he'd last seen her. The fact that she hadn't contacted him—did that mean she meant to marry him? Or that she'd cut him out of her life, scandal be damned?

Muted voices reached his ears and he parted the heavy green velvet drapes concealing the alcove enough to allow him to observe the gathering guests while remaining hidden.

It seemed as if every person in the village was turning up at the church to see the Earl of Wesley make Samantha Briggeham his countess. He scanned the growing crowd, noting Lydia Nordfield sitting on a long wooden pew, flanked by her daughters and sons-in-law. Arthur, Eversley, and a dozen long-time members of his staff occupied a rear pew.

His gaze roved over the crowd, noting names and faces, then settled on Margaret. She sat in the first pew, staring at her gloved hands clenched in her lap.

His heart twisted with sympathy and concern. She was no doubt thinking of her own wedding to that bastard Darvin. He considered going to her, but decided to give her some time with her private thoughts. Perhaps being here, in this church, was a good way for her to exorcise the demons haunting her.

He continued to hopefully scan the guests, but not one member of Samantha's family entered the church. Releasing the drape, he consulted his watch fob. Twenty-three minutes until the ceremony began.

Would Samantha show up?

Adam Straton walked toward the church, his heart pounding with conflicting emotions, his mind whirling. Last night, after observing Arthur Timstone head to the main house, he'd searched the Wesley stables. Noting that the building seemed longer on the outside than on the inside, he concentrated his efforts on the rear of the structure. Ten minutes later he located a cleverly hidden door. Pulling it open, he found himself in a spacious stall with a window fitted into the ceiling rather than the wall. Holding his low-lit lantern aloft, triumph pulsed through him. In the far corner stood the magnificent black horse.

There was no longer any doubt in his mind that Lord Wesley was the Bride Thief, but he needed more proof. He had no intention of arresting the man only to have him released due to a lack of evidence. And with any luck, that evidence would be presented to him within the hour. He slipped his timepiece from his waistcoat pocket, noting the time with satisfaction. His most trusted man, Farnsworth, was right now searching the earl's home. With Wesley Manor all but deserted while most of the staff attended the wedding, Farnsworth would hopefully locate the necessary evidence.

Replacing his watch fob, he increased his pace, his gaze settling on the guests entering the church. Yes, today would most likely see the end to the most perplexing, frustrating case of his career—a career rife with countless possibilities once he apprehended the notorious Bride Thief. Yet, while he should have felt nothing but triumph, his imminent victory somehow felt hollow. He liked Wesley. And he loved Margaret. He hated the thought of her losing her brother.

But he had to uphold the law.

Chapter 24

Eric paced in the alcove like a caged animal, his heart growing heavier with each passing second.

She was ten minutes late.

He couldn't bear to look at his timepiece again, couldn't stand to gaze upon its mocking face.

The velvet drapes parted and he turned sharply. The visibly nervous vicar joined him.

"Is she here?" Eric asked.

"No, my lord." Extracting a handkerchief from the folds of his voluminous robe, the vicar wiped his perspiring forehead.

Eric lifted a single brow. "Then I suggest," he said in a carefully controlled tone, "that you keep watch for her and advise me the instant she arrives."

The vicar's vigorous nod set his double chins in motion, and he hastily backed away. "Yes, my lord." He exited through the drapery.

Alone again, Eric closed his eyes, desolation crushing him. She wasn't coming. She didn't want him. She'd rather face scandal than marry him.

Damn it, that *hurt*. In a way nothing else had ever hurt

him. And it angered him as well—that she hadn't even had the courtesy to tell him her decision. If she wasn't going to marry him, she could bloody well tell him to his face. And if she wouldn't come here to tell him, he'd go to her and make her say it.

He turned to stride through the drapery, but before he could take a step, the heavy curtain parted to reveal the vicar's face.

"Miss Briggeham has arrived, my lord. However, she insists upon speaking to you privately—*before* the ceremony. *Most* irregular." The vicar's lips puckered with disapproval. "She awaits you in my office."

Sammie paced the worn rug in the vicar's small office located off the vestibule. When a knock sounded at the door, she called, "Come in."

Eric entered the room, softly closing the door behind him. Their eyes met, and her breath stalled at the sight of him. Dressed in his formal wedding attire, from his perfectly knotted cravat and snowy shirt, cream waistcoat, to his Devonshire brown coat and fawn breeches, he was simply the most beautiful man she'd ever beheld. And for a short, incredibly lovely moment in time, he'd been hers.

"Thank you for agreeing to meet me in here," she said. "I must speak with you."

He leaned against the door and regarded her through hooded eyes. "You're late."

"I'm sorry. There are so many details to see to when one is leaving home forever."

He squeezed his eyes shut for several seconds, muttering something that sounded like *thank God*.

"I had to say good-bye to Hubert," she said, her voice hitching on his name. "I could not leave without explaining things to him."

Pushing off from the door, he approached her. When he stood before her, his gaze swept her slowly from head to foot. Then he looked at her with an expression that heated her from the inside out. "You're beautiful, Samantha."

Warmth rushed into her cheeks, and she looked down at her wedding gown. "Thank you. The dress *is* lovely."

He lifted her chin with his fingers. "Yes. But I was referring to the bride wearing it."

The sincerity in his voice, in his eyes, made her want to throw her arms around him and pretend no obstacles stood between them. But time was short, and with so many things to tell him, she couldn't waste another minute.

Drawing a resolute breath, she said, "I am not here to become a bride, Eric. Indeed, I am here to release you from your obligation to marry me. I have made arrangements to travel abroad, to live my own life. You need not concern yourself with my welfare any longer."

His hand slowly lowered from her chin, and his eyes went blank. "I see."

She grasped his arm and shook it. "No, you don't. I wanted to speak to you yesterday, but I did not dare. Eric, Adam Straton knows who you are. He came to my home yesterday and questioned me." She quickly repeated her conversation with the magistrate. "He *knows*, Eric. He's going to arrest you and see you hang." Her voice broke and tears flooded her eyes. "You must take this opportunity to escape. Now. Immediately. I will distract the vicar and guests as long as I possibly can to give you a head start. I have this terrible, awful feeling inside that there isn't a moment to lose."

He clasped her by the shoulders. "Samantha, I cannot abandon you here."

"Yes, you can. You have my full blessing to do so."

"Then allow me to rephrase that. I *will not* abandon you here."

Desperation washed over her and she clutched at his jacket. "You must. Please. I can face anything—a scandal, ridicule, scorn. But I cannot face you being captured." Hot tears spilled onto her cheeks. "I cannot bear to see you die."

"Then marry me. And we'll leave together. All the arrangements are in place for us to do so." He cradled her face between his hands, his dark eyes serious and intense. "I don't want to live without you, Samantha. I want to share my life—my new *law-abiding* life—with you. We can continue to offer women a choice, but we'll do it together, legally, through financial channels. Set up a trust of some sort—whatever we decide upon. Together."

Her ability to speak, indeed her ability to breathe, abandoned her, and she simply stared at him, trying to absorb his words. *I don't want to live without you.*

Lowering his head, he rested his forehead on hers. "I love you, Samantha. So much I ache with it." He raised his head and pinned her with a deep gaze. "All those things I believed I never wanted . . . marriage, a family . . . things I thought I could never have . . . love changed all that. *You* changed all that. I want you for my wife. My lover. The mother of my children. I cannot deny there's a risk of me being arrested for the rescues I've performed, but we can leave England immediately following the ceremony."

She attempted to moisten her dust-dry lips with her equally dust-dry tongue, and failed miserably. "Say that again," she croaked.

"We can leave England—"

She laid a finger on his lips. "Not that. The 'I love you, Samantha' part."

Grasping the hand that had silenced his words, he pressed a kiss into her palm, his gaze boring into hers. "I love you." He lowered her hand to his chest, and his heartbeat thumped hard against her palm. "Feel that. It beats for

you. If you want me, you'll make me the happiest man in
the world. If you don't . . ." He pressed her palm tighter
against him. "Then there will simply be a hole here. My
heart is yours to take . . . or to break. Every woman deserves to choose. The choice is yours."

Sammie stared at him, her own heart pounding so hard
she could feel the drumming in her temples. He loved her.
Plain, odd, eccentric Sammie. Impossible. He must be daft.
Or inebriated. She discreetly sniffed, but there was no odor
of spirits about him. Only his clean, warm, masculine
scent. And there was no doubting the sincerity in his gaze.
Or the love burning from his dark eyes.

Still, just in case the poor man's wits were addled, she
felt compelled to point out, "You realize I would make a
frightful countess."

"No. You'd be a charming countess. Captivating. Caring.
Clever and considerate. Courageous." He brushed gentle
fingertips over her cheeks. "So many 'c' words to describe
my extraordinary Samantha."

She locked her knees to remain upright and tried to
gather her thoughts, but him loving her simply defied logic.
Before she could even begin to corral her scattered emotions, a knock sounded.

They both turned toward the door. "Come in," Eric said.

The vicar entered, his questioning gaze bouncing between them. "Are we ready to begin?" he asked.

Eric turned back to her and their eyes met. He said nothing, merely watched her, waiting for her, allowing her to
choose, praying she would want him.

With her gaze locked with his, she spoke to the vicar.

"Yes, we're ready to begin."

Exhilaration and joy swelled in Eric. He and Samantha
would be together—as husband and wife.

Everything was going to work out perfectly.

* * *

Farnsworth, the magistrate's most trusted man, slipped into the Earl of Wesley's bedchamber, closing the door softly behind him. Looking about the spacious, luxurious room, he quickly made his way to the cherry-wood desk near the window. Hopefully he would find something here. His search of the earl's private study and the library had yielded nothing, and time was running short.

He checked through the drawers, but found nothing. Crouching down, he ran his hands lightly over the glossy wood. Underneath one of the legs, his fingers encountered a round knob. Scarcely daring to breathe, he twisted it. A faint click sounded and he was able to push aside a panel on the bottom. Something soft fell into his palm.

Sliding out his hand, he gazed at a black silk mask.

Triumph pulsed through him. This was just the evidence the magistrate needed. All Farnsworth had to do was deliver it to him.

Chapter 25

Eric stood at the altar and watched Samantha walk slowly down the aisle, her hand resting on her beaming father's sleeve. While the quiet hum of the crowd filled the church, her gaze remained steady on his, her spectacles magnifying the love shining from her eyes.

Love hit him like a punch in the heart, radiating warmth through his entire system. She joined him at the altar, a shy smile trembling on her lush lips, her gaze brimming with the same emotions swarming through him.

Fifteen minutes later, after they repeated the vows that joined them for life, the vicar blessed them, his rotund face wreathed with pride. Eric turned to his wife—his *wife*— and a surge of happiness nearly knocked him off his feet. He brushed a chaste kiss against her upturned lips, and need overwhelmed his senses. He had to touch her, kiss her deeply. Now. Away from prying eyes. Tucking her hand through his elbow, he propelled her down the aisle. He practically ran through the vestibule, then outside, pulling her around the corner, into the shadows.

"Good heavens, Eric," she said in a breathless voice. "I—"

He yanked her into his arms and covered her mouth with his. A tiny sound of pleasure rumbled in her throat, and she parted her lips. His tongue slid into her welcoming honey-flavored warmth, his entire body humming with satisfaction. And nearly inconceivable happiness.

Sammie slid her arms around his waist, eagerly accepting the onslaught of his kiss . . . a kiss filled with love and promise and deep passion. When he finally lifted his head, she clung to him limply and vaguely wondered where she'd placed her missing knees. She slowly opened her eyes and saw nothing but white. As she blinked rapidly to clear her vision, she felt her spectacles being removed. As soon as he'd slid them off, she saw him. Her *husband*. And the heat blazing from her husband's loving gaze seared through her like an inferno. Several seconds of silence passed, then a wry smile touched one corner of his mouth.

"I'm afraid we fogged up your spectacles."

"I thought I was seeing clouds. As if I'd died and gone to heaven."

"Heaven. Yes, that's what you feel like." He traced her bottom lip with his fingertip, the tickling sensation curling her toes inside her slippers. The sound of voices reached them as guests exited the church. He smiled down at her, warming her like the sun. "Come, my charming countess. Let us accept the best wishes and congratulations of our guests."

"Indeed, before they discover us kissing behind the bushes." Inclining her head in what she hoped was a countess-like fashion, she slipped her hand through his arm. Laughter rumbled in his throat, and they rounded the corner, prepared to face their guests.

Adam exited the church, squinting against the sun's sudden glare. He looked at the crowd gathering around the bride and groom, and he craned his neck higher, hoping for a glimpse of Margaret. As if the mere thought of Margaret conjured her up, he noticed her standing beneath the shade of the huge oak in the churchyard. She stood alone, head bent, hands clasped in front of her. Drawn to her like iron to a magnet, he veered away from the throng and approached her.

"Good morning, Lady Darvin," he said, stepping beneath the oak's umbrella of shade.

She turned toward him, and he stilled at her utterly bleak expression and the tortured look in her eyes.

Driven by deep concern, he dismissed propriety. Reaching out, he gently grasped her upper arm, then maneuvered himself so his back blocked her from any curious glances that might be cast their way. "What is wrong?"

She seemed to look right through him, her thoughts clearly far away. "The wedding ceremony . . . I was just remembering. I tried so hard not to, but sitting in that church . . ." A shudder ran through her. "I have not been inside it since my own wedding day."

He instantly recalled that day in vivid detail. He'd sat on his bed, sick with loss, staring at the clock, knowing with each passing minute the woman he loved was exchanging vows with another man. When the church bells had chimed in the distance, signifying the end of the ceremony, he'd opened a bottle of whiskey and proceeded for the first time in his life to get deliberately, blindly drunk. He'd stayed drunk for two days, then spent another two days suffering the worst hangover in the history of hangovers. After that, he'd simply . . . lived, believing she was happy.

One look at her stricken face disabused him of that notion. She looked so . . . haunted. So distraught. Her eyes shimmered with tears, but there was no mistaking them as the happy sort women often shed at weddings.

Was there something more to her unhappiness than he'd previously thought? Was there more involved than missing her home and her brother? More than the fact that she hadn't had children? Releasing her arm, he pulled his handkerchief from his pocket and pressed it into her hand.

Dabbing her wet eyes, she said, "Thank you. And forgive me. This is a happy day, yet here I am sniffling. I'm afraid I allowed my memories to distress me."

Her words disturbed him, and a sick uneasiness slithered down his spine. "Your husband . . ." He hesitated, not certain how to phrase what he wanted to ask her. "Was he . . . unkind?"

A humorless sound erupted from her lips, and she averted her gaze. Even as his mind told him not to, he grasped her gloved hand and gently squeezed her fingers.

She turned back to him, and he was taken aback by the fire burning in her eyes. "Unkind?" she repeated in an awful voice he didn't recognize. "Yes, he was *unkind*."

As suddenly as her anger appeared, it vanished, as if doused by cold water, to be replaced by a broken, lost expression. Tremors shook her and she squeezed her eyes shut. A single tear rolled down her pale cheek, silently landing on his white shirt cuff. He watched the droplet soak into the linen.

Hell and damnation, that bastard had *hurt* her. Hurt her mind and spirit. God Almighty, had he hurt her body as well? A red haze veiled his vision, and violence such as he'd never felt before gripped him.

A sense of unreality overwhelmed him. The news of her marriage to Darvin had nearly brought him to his knees, but he'd accepted the inevitable with stoic resignation. As much as he loved her, he'd known he could never so much as court, let alone marry her. He had nothing to offer an earl's daughter.

Except love. And kindness. Her words raced through his mind. *I used to spend time on the cliffs, looking out at the sea, wondering how it would feel to jump. . . .*

Nausea gripped him at the thought of Darvin mistreating her. To the point where she'd contemplated suicide. God in heaven. If only he'd known—

What would you have done? he asked himself. *What could you have done?* But he knew without question. He knew in his soul that he—a man who dedicated his life to upholding the law—would have killed the bastard. And why the hell hadn't her brother done so?

She opened her eyes and looked at him. His feelings must have shown, for a look of unmistakable tenderness filled her gaze, stealing his breath. "I appreciate your outrage on my behalf. You were always such a stalwart friend. There was nothing you could have done."

A stalwart friend. Did she have any idea he would have given anything to be more? "Your brother," he managed past his tight throat. "Did he not know?"

"He knew I was unhappy, but not the extent of my misery, and I dared not tell him. He visited me when he returned from the war. He saw bruises on my arms. I told him I'd fallen, but apparently he'd heard of Darvin's proclivities, and he did not believe me."

He clenched his teeth against his mounting rage. "Why on earth did you protect such a monster?"

"I wasn't protecting Darvin. It was my brother I sought to protect. He would have killed Darvin and hung for his efforts. As it was, he beat Darvin nearly unconscious and threatened to finish the deed if he ever dared hurt me again."

"And did he?"

Her eyes went totally flat. "Yes. But not as often. I . . . I never told Eric. When I finally stopped fighting Darvin, he eventually lost interest in me and turned to other women.

Eric only knows that Darvin was unfaithful, not about
the . . . other things."

Every cell in his body screamed with impotent fury
against her suffering and the man who'd caused it. He'd
hurt her. Humiliated her. Been unfaithful to her . . . this
gentle, lovely creature he'd loved from the first moment
he'd laid eyes on her when they were both little more than
children. His heart shattered, aching for her. For himself.
Bile burned his throat, and he pressed his lips together, trying to calm his heaving insides.

He squeezed her hand, fighting the overwhelming urge
to pull her into his arms, to protect her. To let her know he'd
never allow anyone to ever hurt her again. "Why didn't you
leave him?"

"I did, a month after our marriage. He found me at an
inn fifty miles from Cornwall. He told me if I ever left him
again he would kill my brother." Her gaze searched his, her
eyes troubled and confused. "I . . . I never meant to tell you.
I don't know why I did."

A tempest of emotions consumed him, and he could not
force away the image of her bruised and crying, from his
mind. He looked into her haunted eyes, shadowed with
dark memories of sufferings he could not begin to imagine.
Rage erupted in him, and he fought to clamp it down, contain it. Control it. Darvin was dead, yet he wanted nothing
more than to dig up the bastard and kill him again. How the
hell had her brother kept from strangling Darvin with his
bare hands?

Her brother. Everything in him shifted, then stilled as realization clicked into place. No, her brother hadn't killed
Darvin. Instead he'd channeled his rage elsewhere, and
risked his life to save other women from a similar life of
misery.

He moistened his dry lips. "Tell me . . . if you'd had the
chance to run away, even if leaving meant never seeing

your family or friends again, would you have done so to avoid marrying him?"

She didn't even hesitate. "Yes."

That single word, barely more than a whisper, rocked his very foundation. He'd devoted the last five years of his life to capturing the Bride Thief. The man was a criminal. A kidnapper. He tore families apart and ruined planned marriages. Yet Margaret clearly would have accepted his help to escape marrying Darvin. *And she would have been spared those years of horror and despair.*

Confusion assailed him. There was no curtailing the law. He prided himself on his honesty and integrity. The punishment for kidnapping was the gallows. If he failed to see justice carried through, how could he call himself a man of the law?

He swallowed to dislodge his heart from his throat. "You said you'd never meant to tell me. Why not?"

She looked at the ground. "I . . . I didn't want you to think badly of me."

He swore he actually felt his heart break in two. His hand shook as he reached out and lifted her chin with his fingertips. "I could never think badly of you. Of the man who hurt you, yes. Of you, no." God, he longed to tell her that it would be impossible for him to think any more highly of her, but he didn't dare. "I'm so very sorry for what you suffered."

"Thank you. But I'm free now. And I'm back at the home I love, with my brother."

Guilt hit him like a blow to the gut. Within an hour's time he hoped to have her brother in custody.

A fleeting smile touched her lips. "And this very day I have gained a sister, so there is much to be happy about." She gently eased her hand from his. "I'd best go offer my congratulations. Would you care to join me?"

Before he could reply, he heard a discreet cough behind him.

"Begging your pardon, Mr. Straton, but I need to speak with you."

Adam's every muscle tensed as he recognized Farnsworth's voice. Offering Lady Darvin a bow, Adam said, "I'll be along in a few moments."

She inclined her head, then moved past him, walking toward the crowd of well-wishers. Once he was certain she could not overhear, he turned to Farnsworth.

"Well?" he asked.

Farnsworth pulled a piece of black material from his pocket and handed it to Adam. "I found this in Lord Wesley's bedchamber, sir. Behind a hidden panel under his desk. No question it's the Bride Thief's mask."

Adam stared at the black silk mask. In his hands he held the evidence he'd sought for five long years. He now had everything he needed to arrest the Bride Thief.

Sammie and Eric no sooner rounded the corner after their passionate kiss than Mama descended upon them.

"There you are, darling!" She engulfed Sammie in a rib-squeezing hug that Sammie nonetheless relished, as it would be the last time she felt her mother's arms around her. "I'm so happy for you," Mama said with a sniffle. Then into Sammie's ear she whispered, "I'm sorry we didn't have time to discuss . . . *you know what*, but I'm certain the earl will know what do to."

Stepping back, Mama dabbed her eyes with a lacy handkerchief and emitted a trio of chirping sounds. She glanced quickly about, but obviously realizing that no benches were in "fainting" distance, Mama drew a deep breath and recovered herself. Indeed, she lit up like a dozen candles when

Lydia Nordfield and her daughter Daphne approached, both women wearing similar puckered expressions.

"Lydia!" Mama exclaimed. She embraced her nemesis with an enthusiasm that brought a wince to Mrs. Nordfield's already pinched features. Leaning back, Mama's face became the personification of concern. "Now don't you worry, Lydia. I'm *certain* Daphne will find a nice gentleman. Someday."

A choking sound erupted from Mrs. Nordfield, and the smile she leveled upon Mama was glacial. Mrs. Nordfield and Daphne then offered Sammie stilted best wishes. The woman's narrow-eyed gaze bounced between her daughter and Sammie several times. Sammie bit the insides of her cheeks to hide her amusement, for she could almost hear Mrs. Nordfield saying, *If Samantha Briggeham can become a countess, surely my Daphne can become a marchioness or a duchess.*

"Perhaps if *you* had spectacles, Daphne dear," Mrs. Nordfield mused as she led her pinch-faced daughter away. "They do have a certain charm. . . ."

Hermione, Lucille, and Emily came next, and Sammie embraced them each in turn, committing their glowing faces to her memory. How was it possible to feel such sadness and such joy at the same time? Such regret for the times they would not share, yet such anticipation for the future?

Papa followed, kissing both her cheeks. "Always knew some lucky fellow would find you, Sammie. I told your mother so." He patted her on the head as if she were his favorite hound, then moved on.

And then Hubert stood before her. They'd already said their good-byes earlier this morning, and although she smiled at him, tears still misted her eyes. Reaching up, she tousled his unruly hair, and their gazes met. His Adam's apple bobbed, and a lump lodged painfully in her throat.

Sadness lingered in his eyes, but his lips curved upward in a lopsided grin. He then wrapped her in an awkward, bony hug and their spectacles smacked into each other. Laughing, they separated.

"Nice show, Sammie," he said, adjusting his glasses. "You're the most beautiful countess I've ever seen."

Swallowing her melancholy, she laughed at him. "I am the *only* countess you've ever seen."

"Well, *I've* seen a great many countesses"—interjected Eric—"and I must agree with Hubert. Beautiful." Taking her hand, he raised it to his lips, his dark eyes sending her a message that shot heat down to her toes.

Hubert moved on, and what seemed like an endless stream of well-wishers followed. Finally Margaret stood before her, extending both her hands. "We're officially sisters now," she said, tears shimmering in her eyes. "And you're officially a countess."

Sammie squeezed her hands and smiled to hide her sorrow that she would not have the opportunity to get to know Margaret better. "Indeed we are sisters. And good heavens, I am a countess—a prospect I find a bit . . . daunting."

Margaret shifted a quick glance at her brother, then offered Sammie a genuine smile. "Not to worry. You have already mastered a countess's most important task. You've made the earl very, very happy."

Sammie felt Eric's warm hand at her back. "Indeed she has," he said.

She watched Eric hug his sister, her heart tugging when his eyes squeezed shut to savor what would be their last embrace. She turned to the next person waiting to extend best wishes.

Adam Straton stood before her. Another man she did not recognize stood next to Mr. Straton. She judged Mr. Straton's companion to be in his mid-thirties, well-built, with dark blond hair, and a tight-lipped, serious air. Both men appeared tense, with no signs of well-wishes in their gazes. Their attention was riveted on Eric, who was smiling down at his sister.

Sammie's heart started drumming in slow, hard thumps, dread spreading through her with each beat, while her stomach seemed to fall like a dead weight to her feet. Forcing what she hoped passed for a cordial smile, she opened her mouth to speak, but before she could utter a word, Mr. Straton spoke to Eric.

"Would you mind stepping inside with me for a moment, Lord Wesley? My man Farnsworth here and I need to speak to you. Privately."

Eric and the magistrate exchanged a long look, then Eric nodded slowly. "Of course." He slid his arm around Sammie's waist and gave her what she guessed was supposed to be an encouraging squeeze. Leaning down, he brushed a kiss across her cheek. "Don't ever forget," he whispered in her ear, "how much I love you." He released her, and she bit her lips together to contain the agonized *No!* threatening to spill from her throat.

Fingers of ice-cold fear clutched her, freezing her as the trio of men entered the shadowy church interior and disappeared from her view.

"I wonder what that is all about," Margaret murmured.

Sammie's stomach heaved with panic.

She suspected she knew.

With his heart pounding at thrice its normal speed, Eric stood in the vicar's office and regarded Straton and Farnsworth with studied detachment. After several seconds of silence, Eric crossed his arms over his chest and raised his brows. "What did you wish to discuss with me?" he asked, injecting a bit of impatience into his voice.

Straton slowly pulled a piece of black material from his

pocket and handed it to Eric. The familiar smooth silk felt cool against his palm, in complete contrast to the heated sense of dread thumping through him. Keeping his expression carefully blank, he asked, "What is this?"

Farnsworth cleared his throat, drawing his attention. "It is the Bride Thief's mask. I found it hidden in the desk in your bedchamber, my lord."

The words reverberated in his mind, and he clamped his jaw to contain the anguished roar threatening to erupt. *Not now!* Not when he'd just been handed happiness on a golden platter. Not when he and Samantha were so close to escaping.

Not when he had so much to live for.

He shifted his gaze to Straton, expecting to meet a hard-edged stare. Instead, the magistrate was looking out the window with an expression that Eric could only describe as troubled. Following his gaze, Eric realized Straton's attention was riveted on Margaret, who stood alone, a short distance away, in the shade beneath a huge oak tree.

With his hands clenched, one fist crumpling the soft silk, Eric stood still as a statue, every muscle tense as he waited to be arrested. There was no refuting the evidence in his hand, and he even had to give Straton and Farnsworth his grudging respect for their cleverness.

His thoughts switched to Samantha and a muscle ticked in his jaw. Damn it, she was no doubt frantic. Regret weighed upon him for what she would face in the wake of his arrest and hanging. Regret that he would never have the chance to be her husband. To laugh and love with her. At least he'd secured her financial future. The Countess of Wesley was an extremely wealthy woman. He prayed she would depart England. Leave the scandal behind and start a new life.

His attention focused once again on the magistrate. Straton continued to stare out the window. His face appeared pale, and his hands were fisted at his sides in a white-knuckled grip. Nearly a full minute of deafening silence passed.

Finally Straton turned to his subordinate. "Excellent work, Farnsworth," he said. "You passed the test in an extremely admirable fashion."

Eric felt the same puzzlement that blanketed Farnsworth's face.

"Test, sir?" Farnsworth asked, scratching his head.

"Yes. I've had my eye on you for quite some time now for a promotion, but it was necessary for me to test your skills, as I'm sure you understand."

"Er, actually, no—"

"Lord Wesley, who has shown great generosity in offering his assistance during this investigation, was kind enough to lend me the use of his home."

Straton clasped his hands behind his back and continued, "As per my instructions, the earl hid this mask, which is a replica of the Bride Thief's I fashioned based on descriptions from witnesses, at Wesley Manor. I knew if your deductive skills were honed enough to locate the mask, Farnsworth, you deserved the promotion." He turned to Eric. "A secret panel under your desk, my lord? Fiendishly clever hiding spot. I thank you for your help."

Shock rippled through Eric. Only a lifetime of keeping his emotions in check kept him from showing the same slack-jawed reaction as Farnsworth. Surely his hearing was afflicted. What the hell was Straton talking about?

Turning back to Farnsworth, Adam extended his hand. "Congratulations, Farnsworth. Your promotion entails you heading up a new case concerning suspected smugglers. I'll brief you on your assignment tomorrow morning."

His face now wreathed in a smiling combination of flushed pride and bemusement, Farnsworth shook his boss's hand. "Thank you, sir! I'm quite overwhelmed." His smile faded. "Of course the bad news is that we still haven't apprehended the Bride Thief." He turned a sheepish look on Eric. "I thought we had our man with you, Lord Wesley. My apologies."

Not trusting his voice, Eric merely inclined his head in reply.

"Yes, unfortunately the Bride Thief is still at large," Straton said. He turned to Eric and pinned him with a dead-serious stare. "However, I vow that I will not tolerate any further kidnappings. If the Bride Thief should make the mistake of striking again, I shall see that he hangs."

The unbelievable truth slowly worked its way through Eric's confusion.

He'd been set free.

While there was no mistaking the magistrate's warning regarding further kidnappings, there was also no denying the fact that Straton had saved his life.

Farnsworth laid a comforting hand on Straton's shoulder. "That's the spirit, sir. You'll capture the Bride Thief when he shows himself again."

Straton and Eric shared a long look. Then the magistrate said, "We won't keep you any further, your lordship. Our best wishes to you and your wife."

Eric somehow managed to find his voice. "Thank you."

Farnsworth opened the door, then stepped from the office. As the magistrate made to follow, Eric said, "I'd like a word with you, Straton."

The magistrate paused in the doorway, then turned back into the room, closing the door.

Eric looked at the man who had saved him from the gallows and said just one word. "Why?"

Straton leaned against the door, and Eric noticed his gaze again drift toward the window, outside of which Margaret stood beneath the majestic oak. Looking at Eric once more, he said, "I had a very illuminating conversation with your sister today."

Eric's muscles instantly tensed. "Margaret knows nothing about any of this."

"Yes, I know. But now I understand why you did . . . what you did. You couldn't save her, so you saved others." He crossed his arms over his chest, and heat flared in his eyes. "She told me if she'd been offered the chance to escape from her marriage—the sort of freedom offered by the Bride Thief—she'd have embraced the opportunity. She'd have been spared those years of misery."

"And if you think that doesn't eat at me every day, you're sadly mistaken."

"And now that I know she suffered at his hands . . . that will eat at *me* every day." Straton's hands fisted at his sides, and his lips compressed into a flat line. "Until this morning, I thought that marriage to a nobleman was the best damn thing that could happen to a woman. And if that marriage was arranged, well, the woman's father was only doing what was best for her." A bitter laugh escaped him. "It wasn't best for Lady Darvin. Now I understand. Now I see that a woman should not be forced to wed against her will. Forced to spend her life with a man she loathes. A man who might abuse her. I couldn't see you hang for saving other women from such a fate. Indeed, I applaud your restraint for not murdering that bastard Darvin. I cannot say I would have shown similar self-control."

Adam drew a deep breath, then continued. "Interest in the Bride Thief will eventually wane after he's not heard from anymore. In a few months, I shall inform *The Times* that in view of the fact that no more kidnappings have been reported, I am forced to conclude that the Bride Thief has given up his illegal activities. At that time, I will also encourage the Bride Thief Posse to disband and reimburse the reward monies to the men who'd contributed the funds."

He indicated the mask still clenched in Eric's hand. "Burn that. And see to it that I never hear from the Bride Thief again. But if you decide to continue to help women through *legal* means, you may count on me to help in any way I can."

Eric tucked the wadded black silk in his pocket. "Consider the Bride Thief gone. I do plan to still help these women—through *legal* means—but I've not worked out any details. I'll let you know when I do." He drew a deep breath. In his mind's eye he saw his future, and Samantha's, spread out before him like a banquet feast.

"I don't know how to thank you . . ." Eric's voice trailed off. Actually, perhaps he *did* know how. "Tell me, Straton—do you care for my sister?"

A deep red flush crept up Straton's face. "Lady Darvin is a very fine lady—"

"I've no desire to dance around this with you. Give me an honest answer. Do you care for her?"

Straton's lips thinned. "Yes."

"Do you love her?"

Eric watched Straton's throat work, then the man jerked his head in a nod. "But you need not concern yourself that I'll act upon those feelings," he said in a tight voice. "I'm aware of my unsuitability for a lady such as your sister."

Eric crossed the room, stopping directly in front of Straton. "A lady such as my sister deserves a man who loves her. A man she loves in return. That is not what she had with her nobleman. Therefore, I'd say it's time she had a noble *man*." He slowly extended his hand. "You have my blessing."

Straton hesitated for several seconds, then clasped Eric's hand in a firm grip. "I never thought to . . . I wouldn't have imagined." A look of wonder came over his face. "She is everything I've always wanted."

An image of Samantha flashed in Eric's mind. "I know exactly what you mean."

Eric paused in the church doorway and watched Adam Straton approach Margaret. Satisfied that he'd secured his sister's happiness, he looked to find his own. And found her standing amidst her mother and sisters, who all chattered around her. Samantha, however, was looking at Adam Straton. As if she felt Eric's stare, her gaze flew to the church doorway and their eyes met.

She immediately disengaged herself from her family and walked toward him with those purposeful strides he loved. He waited for her, and when she arrived at the doorway, he pulled her inside and quickly explained what had happened.

When he finished, tears shimmered in her eyes. "He freed us."

"That he did, my love."

A tear traced a silver track down her cheek. "I nearly died when you went into the church with them. I thought they meant to arrest you."

"I must admit it was a rather bad moment for me as well." He cradled her face in his palms and brushed away her tear with his thumb. "The thought of losing you . . . before we'd had a chance to live as husband and wife . . . the hurt was indescribable."

"I desperately wanted to march into the church and apply my ear to the door, but Mama and my sisters would have followed me like a pack of hounds."

All the tension, all his fear for their future, evaporated like a puff of steam. Sliding his hands down her arms, he entwined their fingers, then leaned close to confide, "I must tell you that listening at doors is a very un-countesslike thing to do."

"Well, I did warn you I'd make a miserable countess."

"Not at all. You are marvelous. Miraculous." He smiled into her beautiful eyes. "So many 'm' words to describe you."

"And *you* are utterly magnificent." A bright blush stained her cheeks, and she heaved out a dreamy sigh. "And . . . manly."

A half-laugh, half-groan of desire vibrated in his throat. "Thank you. And now, I suggest we take our leave. Our ship sails at dusk."

Interest flared in her eyes. "Where are we going?"

"Italy. Rome, Florence, Venice, Naples . . . and every city in between. We shall explore the ruins of Pompeii, trek through the Colosseum, visit the Uffizi, view the works of Bernini and Michaelangelo, swim in the warm waters of the Adriatic . . ." He gently squeezed her hands. "Then we will come home to England and plan our next adventure."

Her smile dazzled and enchanted him. "That sounds . . . magical."

"Indeed it does. And you know, of course, that there is one more 'm' word to describe you."

"What is that?"

He raised their joined hands to his lips and pressed a fervent kiss onto her fingers. "Mine," he whispered. "At long last. Mine. Mine. *Mine*."

About the Author

Award-winning author Jacquie D'Alessandro grew up on Long Island and fell in love with romance at an early age. She dreamed of being swept away by a dashing rogue riding a spirited stallion. When her hero finally showed up, he was dressed in jeans and driving a Volkswagen, but she recognized him anyway. They married after they both graduated from Hofstra University, and are now living their happily-ever-afters in Atlanta, Georgia, along with their very bright and active son, who is a dashing rogue in the making. Jacquie is currently working on her next historical romance for Dell, and she would love to hear from readers. Visit her website at *www.JacquieD.com* or write to her at 875 Lawrenceville-Suwanee Road, Suite 310-PMB 131, Lawrenceville, GA 30043

Turn the page for a sneak
peek at the sequel to Jacquie D'Alessandro's
award-winning novel,
Whirlwind Wedding

Whirlwind Affair

Coming soon, wherever
Dell Books are sold.

Chapter 1

A shiver snaked down Alberta Brown's spine, and she gripped the *Seaward Lady's* wood railing. Hoping she appeared outwardly calm, she quickly scanned her surroundings.

Crewmen shouted to one another, laughing as they tossed thick ropes and adjusted sails in preparation for the ship's imminent arrival in London. Voices from the bustling English port drifted over the tangy sea-scented air, blending into an indistinguishable hum. Passengers stood in clusters around the ship's rail, chatting in excited tones, grinning, waving to people on the docks. Everyone appeared perfectly normal and eager at the prospect of stepping on dry land after nearly three months at sea on the voyage from America. No one's gaze appeared fixed upon her.

Still, she could not dismiss the eerie sensation of menace. The weight of someone's stare surrounded her like a shroud. Her heart thumped in slow, hard beats, and she forced herself to draw a deep, calming breath and return her attention to the nearby active port. *I am perfectly safe. No one is trying to hurt me.*

She prayed to God it was true.

Yet she couldn't banish the sick feeling it was not. She glanced downward, at the frothing water tossed upon the hull as the ship cut through the gentle waves, and her stomach turned over. Dear God, less than three hours ago she'd fallen into that indigo water. . . .

A shudder passed through her, and she squeezed her eyes shut. The shock of being shoved from behind, falling . . . falling, desperately clawing the air, frightened cries ripped from her throat, cut off when chilling water closed over her head. She would be forever grateful to the trio of barking dogs who'd alerted a quick-witted crewman to the accident. Yet, in spite of his fast thinking and her swimming ability, she'd nearly drowned.

The accident. Yes, that's what everyone was calling it. An improperly secured winch had swung around, catching her between the shoulders, propelling her over the side. Captain Whitstead had reprimanded the entire crew.

But was it really an accident? Or had someone purposely unfastened the winch and pushed it toward her?

Another chill edged through her, and she sternly told herself it was merely due to the fact that her hair remained damp under her bonnet. Yet she could not ignore the fact that her near-tragic tumble into the sea was not the first strange incident to befall her on this voyage. First had been the inexplicable disappearance of the silver ring David had made for her. Had she lost it—or had it been stolen? While the piece held no monetary value, she sorely missed the sentimental token, as it was a physical reminder of what she'd had . . . and what she'd lost.

Then there was that headlong flight down the stairs, which had thankfully not resulted in any broken bones, although the painful bruises marking her skin had taken weeks to fade. She'd felt a shove . . . Common sense told her it was merely an accidental jostling, yet she couldn't dismiss the feeling that she'd been pushed. And what of the mysterious stomach malady she'd suffered last week? No one else had been ill. Could someone have tampered with her food?

But why? Why would someone wish her harm? She'd asked herself that question dozens of times, yet could not arrive at a definite answer. She *wanted* to believe she was perfectly safe, but an inner voice warned her that the possibility she wasn't was all too real. Had some threatening menace from the past followed her to England?

She glanced around again, but noted nothing amiss. Her unease abated a bit and she gave herself a mental shake. The ship would be docked in less than an hour. She'd simply melt into the crowd and disappear into the anonymity offered by a large city. No one knew her here. No one knew. . . .

Her gaze lowered, riveting on her black mourning gown, the stark bombazine rippled by the brisk breeze. An image of her late husband's smiling face flashed through her mind, and she squeezed her eyes shut in a vain attempt to ward off the onslaught of pain that thoughts of David still brought, even now, three years after his sudden death. Dear God, would the ache squeezing her heart ever cease? Would she ever truly feel whole again?

Her fingers involuntarily drifted over the material of her gown, while in her mind's eye she pictured the small item hidden beneath the voluminous folds, sewn into the hem of her petticoat. To keep it safe. And always close to her. *This is the last leg of my journey, David. After I right this last wrong, I'll be free.*

"Alberta! There you are. The boys and I have been searching for you everywhere!"

Allie turned toward the familiar, imperious voice, grateful for the interruption of her disturbing thoughts. Baroness Gaddlestone approached Allie with a vigor that belied her plump figure and sixty-three years. Of course, part of the reason for the baroness's brisk pace was the three energetic Maltese dogs straining at the ends of their leads. "The boys," as the baroness referred to her furry brood, dragged their mistress along as if they were mighty oxen and she a produce-laden cart.

Pushing her worries firmly aside, Allie crouched down to receive the enthusiastic yip-filled greeting the small balls of fluff bestowed upon her.

"Edward, behave yourself," the baroness scolded as the smallest of the trio dampened Allie's face with joyful kisses. "Tedmund! Frederick! Cease at once!"

The boys blithely ignored their mistress, as was often the case when they were excited, but Allie enjoyed the noisy confusion that followed the dogs like a bouncing shadow. Indeed, she owed them a debt she could never repay. Their insistent barking had alerted the crewman when she'd fallen overboard. She therefore quite willingly overlooked their individual bad habits and focused on their undeniable charm. What did it matter that Edward was fond of marking as his own every bit of wood and rope within his reach? Of course, on a ship, this kept the small dog quite busy, and he fell into his doggie bed each night completely exhausted.

And how could she fault Frederick's predilection for nipping ankles when he'd all but dragged her rescuing crewman to the rail while his brothers barked themselves hoarse? Her gaze found Tedmund, who had wandered several yards away to engage in his favorite activity, this time with a discarded pile of rags. Oh dear. She had tried on numerous occasions to explain to Tedmund that it was not polite to try and make puppies with anything other than a female dog, and then only in private, but Tedmund remained unrepentant.

After discreetly removing Tedmund from the pile of

rags, Allie doled out equal parts of affection for all three dogs, then stood and gazed down at their prancing antics. "Sit," she commanded.

Three canine bottoms instantly settled on the deck.

"You simply *must* explain to me how you do that, my dear," the baroness said, her voice tinged with exasperation. "I've been unable to calm them since I told them we were arriving home this morning. You *know* how anxious they are to run in the park." She beamed a smile at her babies. "Don't worry, darlings. Mama promises to bring you for a nice, long walk this afternoon." The boys' tails swished across the deck like a trio of mops at the happy news.

Warmth stole through Allie. She genuinely liked the baroness, whose bright green eyes and rounded, yet somehow elfin features reminded Allie of a grandmotherly sprite. She was grateful to the woman for hiring her on as her traveling companion. Without the baroness, she wouldn't have been able to afford the passage to England. And there was no denying that the baroness's lively, talkative nature and her energetic pets had relieved some of the loneliness Allie had lived with for so long.

"You were looking for me, Lady Gaddlestone?"

"Indeed, my dear. I wanted a private moment to thank you for your excellent companionship on this voyage. My previous companion, who accompanied me *to* America, proved *most* unsatisfactory." She leaned closer to Allie and confided, "Several times I detected the odor of *brandy* on her breath. Most shocking. But worst of all, she had *no* patience with the boys. Edward, Tedmund, and Frederick could not abide her at all. Oh, that Mrs. Atkins was simply horrid, wasn't she boys?" The baroness wrinkled her nose and shivered, and the boys narrowed their black eyes and growled their agreement. Allie could almost hear them saying, "Yes, Mama, she was horrid, and if she ever dares come back we'll bite her ankles, chew her shoes, and piddle on her bedclothes . . . again."

"But *you*, my dear," the baroness continued, smiling warmly at Allie, "you are what I call a 'dog person.' Not everyone is, you know."

"I enjoyed your company as well, baroness." She looked down and winked at the trio of mischief makers. "You and the boys."

"Yes, well, I hope you enjoy your visit to my country." Her gaze flicked over Allie's black mourning gown. Sympathy softened the woman's features, and reaching out, she clasped Allie's hands. "Clearly you adored your David, but three years is long enough to mourn, my dear. I understand perfectly that it's difficult to move on. Heavens, I never thought I'd recover when Gaddlestone passed on. But time does heal those grieving wounds."

An arrow of pain shot through Allie, and she pressed her lips together to keep them from trembling. "Some wounds can never truly heal," she said quietly.

"I understand how you feel, my dear. But you're still young. Don't close your mind to the possibility of finding happiness again. The Season is just beginning. A mere word from your friend, the Duchess of Bradford, could offer you entrée into any soiree you wished to attend. 'Twould do you good to socialize a bit." The baroness gave her hands a final squeeze, then released them. "Come along, boys," she said. " 'Tis time for your morning snack before we disembark." To Allie she called, "I'm sure we'll see you on the pier, my dear," as the boys pulled her away.

Alone again, Allie reached into the deep pocket of her skirt, withdrawing the last letter she'd received from Elizabeth, now the Duchess of Bradford. The brief missive had arrived two weeks before Allie sailed to England.

Unfolding the thick vellum, she re-read the words, although she knew them by heart.

Dear Allie,

  *I cannot tell you how excited I am at the prospect
of your visit. I am so eager for you to meet my wonderful family, most especially my husband and darling son. Unfortunately I will not be able to meet you
in London as I'd planned—but for a very happy reason. At the same time your ship is scheduled to arrive, Austin and I shall be awaiting the imminent
birth of our second child! Indeed, by the time you arrive at Bradford Hall, I may already be a mother
again. Please do not worry that your visit will be in-
convenient. I recovered from James's birth with what
Austin calls alarming speed, and as you know, I am
most robust. And do not worry about your journey to
Bradford Hall. The estate is only several hours from
London, and I have already extracted a promise from
Austin's brother Robert that he will meet your ship
and escort you here. I've enclosed a sketch of Lord
Robert, and I shall give him one of you so that you
can easily find each other at the pier.*

  *I am counting the days until we see each other
again, Allie. I've missed you so!*

  Wishing you a safe journey, your friend,

Elizabeth

Allie pressed her lips together, staring at those last two
words that always brought an ache to her heart. Your friend.
*Yes, Elizabeth, you have always been my friend. If only I
had appreciated and understood that more. . . . I bless your
forgiving nature.*
Drawing a deep breath, she slowly slid the letter behind

the second sheet of vellum and stared at the sketch of Elizabeth's brother-in-law. Elizabeth's considerable talent with charcoals had only grown over the years, and the image all but leaped from the page.

It would be easy to pick this man out of a crowd. She perused his features and her stomach knotted. His expression reminded her of David in so many ways . . . his crooked smile, his laughing eyes, the boyish charm so evident in his expression. Except Lord Robert Jamison was even more handsome than David, something she would not have thought possible.

But it did not matter what he looked like. He sparked no interest in her other than the fact that she wanted him to get her away from the docks and the menace she'd felt as quickly as possible. Still, guilt pricked her at the thought of his wasted trip to fetch her.

How would he react when she told him she had no intention of traveling to Bradford Hall with him?

Robert Jamison stood on the pier, watching the *Seaward Lady*'s crew secure the majestic vessel to the berth. Dragging a deep breath into his lungs, a smile eased across his face. Damn, but he loved the docks. Loved the sight of crewmembers working in perfect unison hoisting sails and securing ropes. Loved the cacophony from the vendors hawking everything from meat pies to bolts of colorful silk. He even loved the harsh medley of smells that combined with the pungent sea-scented air to create a scent that could be found nowhere else in England.

An image of a grinning face flashed in his mind's eye. . . . Nate had loved to visit the docks, and more often than not, he'd dragged Robert along with him. *Come on, Robbie,* Nate would urge with a devilish grin, *I've heard tell of a new gaming hell near the warehouses.* And so

Robert would go. Isn't that what friends were for? Outrageous fun and venturing into dangerous places together? And keeping each other safe?

Briefly squeezing his eyes shut, he ruthlessly beat back his last memory of Nate, locking the pain away in the deepest recess of his soul, then returned his attention to the ship.

He scanned the faces of the passengers waiting to disembark, but saw no one resembling the smiling young woman in the sketch Elizabeth had given him. Of course, it was difficult to distinguish faces at this distance. Like everyone else meeting passengers, he waited at a safe distance away from the swinging winches unloading the travelers' trunks and the ship's cargo.

Slipping the sketch from his waistcoat pocket, he gazed upon the face that had piqued his interest and remained in his mind since the first time he'd seen it. It was one of the most attractive faces he'd ever seen—lovely not simply because of the pleasing features but due to the joy that flowed from her smile. The warmth and laughter shining in her eyes. And the sense of mischief and fun that seemed to radiate right off the vellum. He would have no trouble recognizing this woman in any size crowd. Indeed, his pulse quickened at the very thought of seeing this lovely creature in person. As he knew Elizabeth had hoped.

Tucking the sketch back in his pocket, he recalled the comment Elizabeth had made just before he'd departed Bradford Hall yesterday. *Perhaps you'll like my friend,* she'd suggested—a phrase he'd heard from the female members of his family more times than he could count. Ever since he had casually mentioned last year that he'd like to settle down and start a family, his sister, sisters-in-law, *and* his mother, were only too eager to toss eligible females his way. At first he hadn't objected to their efforts since his own search for a wife wasn't yielding any results, and he couldn't deny that he'd met an amazing number of charming ladies, some of whom he'd liked quite well, and several with whom he'd discreetly shared far more than a waltz.

However, as time wore on and he hadn't chosen a bride, the introductions had grown awkward, and his family—most especially Caroline—had grown impatient with him. "What on earth is wrong with you?" his sister now demanded every time he didn't fall madly in love with the latest woman she'd brought his way. "She's beautiful, charming, amenable, docile, wealthy, and for reasons I can't explain, she *adores* you. What the devil are you looking for?"

He didn't know, but he did know he hadn't yet found "the one." The one who made him feel that "certain something"—that elusive spark he saw every time Austin and Elizabeth exchanged a glance. Every time Caroline and her husband Miles were in the same room. Each time his brother William smiled at his wife Claudine. He'd seen it everyday growing up, between his parents until the day his father died. He couldn't name it, couldn't explain it.

But by damn, he wanted it.

Wanted the happiness and completeness his siblings enjoyed. Wanted to bounce his own child upon his knee. Wanted a wife to share his life with and to make love to every night.

Now all he had to do was find her.

But that was proving bloody well difficult. Damn it all, it seemed he'd met every unmarried woman in the entire country. Still, perhaps his luck was about to change. Elizabeth thought he might like the lovely Mrs. Brown. In fact, he recalled her exact words—*I have a feeling you'll find the happiness you seek in London*—and Elizabeth's "feelings" had an uncanny way of coming true. Had she been referring to Mrs. Brown? Or had she in some way meant the heaviness that lay upon his heart? He'd never discussed Nate's death with her, but she did have that unnerving way of knowing things. . . .

When he'd asked her to translate her cryptic comment, she'd merely graced him with one of those indecipherable female smiles that claim *I know something you don't know.* Well, he would know—whatever it was—soon enough. The passengers were making their way off the ship.

He craned his neck, scanning each person's face as they approached. A pair of young men. Definitely not. A middle-aged gentleman, followed by a weary-looking couple each holding the hand of a small child. Robert smiled at the children and received gap-toothed grins in return. Returning his attention to the passengers, he clicked off mental "no's" as a clergyman, a portly gentleman, and a gaggle of chatting matrons passed by. Where was the woman? It seemed almost everyone had disembarked.

His gaze flicked over a woman swathed head to toe in mourning black, and another mental "no" quickly formed in his brain. Although Elizabeth had told him Mrs. Brown was a widow, her husband had died years ago. She'd no longer be in mourning clothes.

Still, there was something about the woman's face that brought his gaze back to her. Those wide-spaced eyes, and that intriguing dimple in the center of her chin . . . and the way she was looking at him, as if she recognized him.

Confusion assailed him, and he lifted a hand to shade his eyes from the sun. This couldn't be the right woman. Where was the bright smile? The radiating joy? The sense of laughter and mischief? Sadness, seriousness surrounded this woman like a dark cloud. He gazed beyond her, but the only passenger behind her was a plump matron struggling down the gangway with a trio of small, yapping white dogs.

He returned his attention to the woman in black. She

walked toward him swiftly, her eyes scanning his face. He caught a brief glimpse of an errant brown curl that escaped her black bonnet. Recognition slapped him, and although he realized she was indeed Mrs. Brown, his mind struggled to equate this woman with the sketch Elizabeth had given him. They were precisely alike . . . yet nothing alike at all.

"You must be Lord Robert Jamison," she said, stopping several feet away from him. "I recognize you from the sketch Elizabeth gave me."

I wish I could say the same. Sympathy for her washed over him. Clearly she'd adored her husband, as his death had tragically depleted her. Her eyes, the color of fine, aged brandy, appeared haunted and anxious in her pale face. How sad that mourning had taken such a toll on her. How unfair that a man she so clearly loved had been stolen from her, taking all her laughter and joy with him. She looked tiny and frightened in her stark clothing, as if her state of grieving had literally swallowed her whole. He shoved aside the disappointment and pity he hoped didn't show on his face, then offered her his most charming smile and a formal bow.

"I am indeed he. And you must be Mrs. Brown."

"Yes." Not even a ghost of a smile touched her lips. Indeed, her expression grew even more grave as her gaze darted about their surroundings. He watched her, feeling uncharacteristically short of words. He racked his brain for something to say, but she surprised him into further silence by stepping closer to him. So close, in fact, that the tips of her shoes touched his boots and her black skirt brushed his breeches. So close that her scent drifted over him, a tantalizing combination of sea air and—he inhaled deeply— some sort of flower. Before he could identify the delicate, elusive fragrance, she rested her gloved hand on his sleeve and rose up on her toes, leaning toward him.

Egad, she meant to kiss him! Was this how things were done in America? The only other American he'd ever met was Elizabeth, and he couldn't deny she possessed a forthright, friendly manner, although not quite *this* forthright. Still, he didn't want to hurt Mrs. Brown's feelings by rebuffing her very un-Britishlike greeting.

Lowering his head, he brushed his lips over her mouth. And everything in him stilled. For the space of several heartbeats, he couldn't move. Couldn't breathe. Couldn't do anything save stare down into her shocked eyes while two impossible words pounded through his brain.

At last.

A frown yanked his brows downward, and he stepped back from her as if she'd turned into a pillar of fire. At last? Bloody hell, he'd gone mad. The next stop for him was Bedlam.

Two bright crimson spots stained her cheeks. "What on earth are you doing?" she asked in a voice that trembled with unmistakable outrage.

Bloody hell, now he'd done it. Whatever she'd been about, clearly she hadn't intended for him to kiss her. And he wished to hell he hadn't. His mouth still tingled with the hint of her taste, and he barely resisted the almost overwhelming urge to lick his lips. Or lean down and lick hers.

Undeniably unsettled, his gaze roamed her face, taking in her becoming blush, the dark lashes surrounding her golden-brown eyes, the pert nose painted by a smattering of pale freckles, the dimple gracing her chin, and then her mouth . . . such a lovely, plump mouth. Moist, deliciously pink, the bottom lip lusciously full, and the top lip, impossibly, even fuller.

Good God, what sort of cad was he to entertain even the hint of a lustful thought toward her? The woman was in *mourning*. Not that he'd had a lustful thought. Certainly not. That inexplicable tingle he'd felt had merely been . . . surprise. Yes, that's all it was. She'd surprised him. And that jolt he'd felt? Nothing more than embarrassment. Yes, he'd simply made an ass of himself. Not the first time, and unfortunately, most likely not the last.

Relieved he'd settled everything back into the proper perspective, he took another step backward. "My apologies, madam. I meant no offense. In truth, I thought you'd meant to kiss *me*."

"And why would I possibly want to do *that*?"